Reviews of
Hotel Calcutta
by the same author

'Sheer power of storytelling'

THE TELEGRAPH

'A persuasive artist … invites a hungry, urgent reading'

ASIAN REVIEW OF BOOKS, Hong Kong

'An astounding work that interrogates the myriad surfaces of reality'

INDIAN LITERATURE, Sahitya Akademi

'A dazzling "wall of stories"'

THE SUNDAY GUARDIAN

'His themes reveal a deep fascination with human response to the extraordinary'

HELTER SKELTER

THE BUTTERFLY EFFECT

RAJAT CHAUDHURI

NIYOGI BOOKS

The writing of this novel and the associated travel was partially supported by a Charles Wallace Creative Writing Fellowship, University of Chichester, UK, a Hawthornden Castle Trust Fellowship, Scotland and a Korean Arts Council-InKo Writers' Residency at Toji, South Korea.

Published by
NIYOGI BOOKS
Block D, Building No. 77,
Okhla Industrial Area, Phase-I,
New Delhi-110 020, INDIA
Tel: 91-11-26816301, 26818960
Email: niyogibooks@gmail.com
Website: www.niyogibooksindia.com

English Text © Rajat Chaudhuri

Editor: Sucharita Ghosh
Layout: Nabanita Das
Cover Design: Misha Oberoi

ISBN: 978-93-86906-52-6
Publication: 2018

This is a work of fiction. All names, characters, organisations, businesses, places and events mentioned in this book are either the product of the author's imagination or are used fictitiously. Any resemblance to actual persons, living or dead, events or localities, is entirely coincidental.

All rights are reserved. No part of this publication may be reproduced or transmitted in any form or by any means, electronic or mechanical, including photocopying, recording or by any information storage and retrieval system without prior written permission and consent of the Publisher.

Printed at: Niyogi Offset Pvt. Ltd., New Delhi, India

To Anuradha, Aldous and Maeji-ri

I know that history is going to be dominated by an improbable event, I just don't know what that event will be.

— Nassim Nicholas Taleb, *The Black Swan*

Contents

Captain Old and the Living Dead of Darkland	7
P.I. Kar's Korean Adventure	55
White Cloud Mountain	95
Magic Seeds	127
Tony Fang's Lair	191
Magic Seeds	199
White Cloud Mountain	253
P.I. Kar's Korean Adventure	279
Captain Old and the Living Dead of Darkland	317
In lieu of a Glossary	370

Captain Old
and
the Living Dead
of
Darkland

1

Captain Old steered his electric scooter through the warren of alleys around State Shopping Paradise on his way to station A. Since the time private vehicles had been banned, he had to sneak along these routes though driving down the main street would have been a better idea at that hour.

Those who had lost all their use to their families lay on the dark pavements, groaning in pain as their bones rattled — the putrescence of their rotting flesh pervading the muggy heat of the night. It was a dreary music they made crying, whimpering, muttering or laughing out in delirium and Old thought he could have spared himself this orchestra of the wretched. In any case, the newly recruited traffic sergeants would all be drunk.

He wouldn't bother to pick up anyone from the train station this late but his guest had insisted. Besides, the message he had received had been intriguing. What were the chances of anyone reaching out to him from that far? It was so long ago. Wasn't it around the time of the Fukushima accident? Two and a half decades! His headlamp sprayed the darkness as he searched for the right exit from a roundabout.

There were no street lights here any more and the only illumination was from the solar amnesia boards that had survived. Some of these were displaying the alphabet lessons in

Bengali and English. Others scrolled news about a revolutionary step in the production of elephant fodder, initiated by the SUPREME GUIDE.

A hulking form blocked his way as he steered his scooter out of a lane and onto a crossroad with tram tracks. Old jammed on the brakes, bringing the two-wheeler to a screeching halt. A trumpet blared through the darkness of the streets, lined with abandoned houses whose owners had fled or died. A trio of giants loomed over him. The one in the middle, raising his trunk, let out another dark metallic blast.

He drew back from the elephabus, the wooden carriage with cushioned stools straddling the backs of the three animals, kept in place by frame and harness. The Municipal corporation had put into service many of these over the years. A hardy man from a desert tribe was snoring away loudly, somewhere inside. Like the beasts he drove around the city each day, picking up passengers, this man of the desert had proved to be strong.

Old backed away from the resting giants and turned into another lane. In a few minutes he was cruising down what was once called Armenian street, just a stone's throw from bridge 1, across which was the railway station. Centuries ago, the first Armenians had arrived in this city and there was still a handsome church nearby with a memorial to the Genocide. The Armenians had long left and there were no services held in the church any more, but the handsome white building with its tiered bell tower set amidst a wide stone-paved courtyard, still attracted passers-by. In the decades after the war, this lively street of commerce had fallen on hard times and was now a rough neighbourhood that no one ventured into, after dark.

As he drove along the street, he heard a whistle [trumpet] from the doorway of an abandoned house. Old slowed down to look, realising his mistake too late. A stone came whizzing through the night, hitting the back of his head, throwing him off the scooter. Just the other day, he had bartered away his helmet for food coupons. [desperate times, violence]

He was thrown headlong, hitting sideways against a bamboo post used as a frame for a makeshift shop. His scooter fell, skidded, crashing on a cement doorstep. Two skeletal figures sprang out of the shadow under a doorway and pounced upon him.

They stood over him now, pinning him down with their feet. He saw the glint of steel and kept staring at them blankly, too dazed to react. One of the men shone a flashlight on his face, blinding him for a second. He had to do something. But the odds were stacked too heavily against him tonight.

Using all the force he could muster Old swung his feet, hitting the man at the back of his knee and in the moment's advantage he sprung up, lunging at the knife arm of the other.

As the first attacker doubled in pain, trying to regain balance, the other moved a step back and aimed a kick at Old's solar plexus. Luckily he missed, hitting his ribcage instead but the blow was savage. Old groaned in pain, he felt he would choke. He shouldn't have put up any resistance and given them what they wanted. But it was too late now.

The other attacker had regained balance. He tore upon him like a storm, pressing the sharp point of a *kukri* on Old's throat. A trickle of blood slowly meandered down.

'*Sala, hum pe hath uthata hei!*'

'*Tu kaun hei be?*' hissed the other, surprised at meeting resistance. [Bengali language?]

Old could smell the sweaty body of the man holding the dagger. He noticed the bleary eyes — malnutrition.

'Don't hurt me, I am giving you what I have,' he said feebly.

The duo laughed a raucous laughter and one of them kicked him again. He lost his balance and was flung to the ground. The knife man straddled him, holding him down with the dagger while his accomplice went through his pockets taking the wallet and a bunch of food coupons. They cleaned him of everything, even the small change of Cleanland coins that he had saved.

'Shirt!' one of his assailants hissed and Old quickly undid his shirt buttons.

Having collected the loot and after a parting blow, they heaved up his scooter. They took a second to decide which way to go. The motor started with a cough and they drove off into the night.

Captain Old, bare-chested, kept lying on the street, waiting for his breathing to stabilise. His eyes were getting heavy. He had to get up for the train might arrive any time. He pulled himself up slowly, wincing as pain shot through his bones. But he could breathe normally now, which was a good sign.

He peered into the darkness, looking out for more wayside robbers, as he stumbled along the few hundred eardies to the main road which went across the river. Slowly he dragged himself across the bridge to the train station — bathed in the greenish-white glow of petromax lamps.

2

Commander Kak, SUPREME GUIDE of Darkland, reclined in all his majestic splendour at the centre of the park opposite the railway station. Every fold and wrinkle of the dictator's aging body, his calloused hands, the giant mole on his left ear and his ravaged face were reproduced in lifelike detail. Even the hospital cot from where he governed half a billion people, strung up with youngblood pouches, his elbow in a cast, was there, for all to look and marvel at the resolve of the leader to continue serving his countrymen against the greatest odds.

His alabaster statue, seated in that reclining semi-Fowler's position, had been meticulously carved by PWD sculptors and lit up by a string of hurricane lamps burning rationed kerosene. In every park and public building, in every home and office, his reclining form was present, framed or carved, seated in his metal cot. He was watching them from shelf and wall, a hint of a benevolent smile on his lips while his iron will shone through his hooded eyes. From a distance, he looked like a god. The reclining Vishnu resting on his serpent pedestal, floating about in the eternal ocean.

But the thumb of his right hand was missing, blown away by a Molotov cocktail attack by a group of guerrilla fighters who had been trying to sabotage his government. It happened just a few months back, when the armed groups had launched a wave of attacks on the Darkland Areas Authority by defacing statues, blowing up rail bridges and setting off improvised explosive devices in factories. This was why two fierce-looking desert tribesmen — the cream of the local protector force — were posted next to his statue, outside the station. The solar panels lighting up this area had been stolen time and again till the Municipal corporation had switched to hurricane lanterns preferring its warm glow to the chilling green of petromax.

As Captain Old approached the Romanesque station building, the wheezing of the sick lying on the pavements was eclipsed by groans coming from the cages lining the approach road. He increased his pace, avoiding the bloodshot eyes inside the grilled iron boxes, where tortured guerrilla leaders were put on display, as a warning to citizens. 'Why don't they carry poison pellets,' Old wondered as he crossed a narrow stretch with cages on both sides.

It was well past midnight and the gigantic terminal was lit up with chains of petromax. Their green fire threw oblong shadows across the entrance hall, where the battery-powered electronic timetables had survived showing arrival and departure times of trains, some of which had stopped running years ago because of a shortage of healthy engine drivers.

Old waded through the sea of sweaty bodies crowding the main concourse, for trains that may have not even started on their journeys or those that would never arrive. People still travelled. There would be rumours about food and work in the foothills of the Himalayas, or along the banks of remote mountain streams. Whenever these rumours spread, people boarded trains on the wings of hope.

'Which way to the citizen's platform?' he asked a uniformed ticket examiner sitting on a bench near the twisted ticket barriers.

The ticket checker took one look at him and, as if noticing a piece of shit, averted his eyes and said, 'No. 8. Don't go anywhere near the other platforms if you aren't planning to get shot. All reserved for party officials arriving for the function.'

Old didn't thank him and made his way to platform 8. It was packed. Shrivelled nonagenarians dozed on wheelchairs with splayed wheels, others, purblind, their faces ravaged by age, stood blank-eyed scratching themselves, their emaciated frames propped up by walking sticks. Often someone would give up the ghost and crash in a heap on the cement floor. There would be some befuddled looks in that direction, creaking of tired bones, a whisper of sympathy and then indifference crept back.

He knew organ traders roamed the stations at night, blood harvesting gangs lay in ambush in the darkest recesses and so he had to watch out. The black market for youngblood had also grown by leaps and bounds, operating right under the nose of the protectors. This made it particularly risky for anyone to bring their children out after dark.

There was a Wheeler bookstall which had been looted for the paper and it stood forlorn in a corner, dusty and forgotten. The Burma teak panels had long disappeared but the wooden frame boards had remained intact. 'Classics make the best fires,' a neighbour had told him back when hostilities had begun, 'in this matter too; our Soviet friends did better than the Yankees. You can cook a square meal on the fire-licked pages of a Bulgakov or a Zamyatin but even a full blaze of the *Leaves of Grass* won't boil your corn broth.'

He remembered his neighbour's words as he pulled himself up and sat on top of what used to be display cases for books. Pushing himself back, he leaned against the frame. He was still raw from the fight. He massaged his ribs gently, hoping nothing was broken.

The familiar smell of books still lingered here, as if locked in a time capsule. His eyes were drawn to something. Through a cracked panel of the abandoned bookstall he could see an illustrated cover. It had escaped the looters. He pushed his hand through the crack, fishing out an old *Amar Chitra Katha* comic.

It told the story of Angulimala, the highway murderer who renounced violence and converted to Buddhism after meeting the Sakyamuni. In the ghostly light of a lamp, set high up against the decaying brickwork, Captain Old began to leaf through the pages of the comic book.

Evil Angulimala had just spotted the Buddha and was planning to make mincemeat out of him, when the toot toot of a steam train could be heard in the distance. The decrepit mass of humanity stirred, gathered their sagging energies and plodded along to the edge of the platform. Behind them they left forgotten bags and walking sticks, empty IV pouches and puddles of poop which Old carefully avoided as a Canadian engine hauling twenty-six rusty coaches chugged into the station. And the world was engulfed by smoke belching from the chimney, which gurgled out of the skylights and the clerestory windows of the centuries old station building, escaping into the moonless night, like black thoughts bubbling out of the ears of a maniac. Who would have guessed that carbonophilic steam desire would be resurrected to patch together a banjaxed population?

There was chaos. The hordes lunged at the metal doors of the passing carriages which were secured to ward off bandits that waylaid trains and went on rampages, killing passengers, robbing them of whatever food or rags of clothing they possessed. The old and the infirm could hardly put up a fight against the *katta*-wielding raiders and were often stripped to nothing and so one would find groups of bony doddering men, without a stitch on their bodies, cowering in fear and crying from hunger, shuffling out of the bogies into the fire-lit stations like souls stepping into the afterworld.

Women hardly travelled and, if they did, they would count themselves lucky if they didn't get raped by the dacoits or molested by fellow travellers.

The iron monster clattered to a halt, the superheated steam hissed in the memory of Boulton and Watt and from the first door that opened a group of shiny-faced men and women trooped out, escorted by four machine gun-wielding tribesmen of the desert. The new arrivals had [orange cheeks, the colour of clementines, and iridescent blue eyes that glowed neon-like in the dark.] *healthy, bright contrast*

The glass windows of this air-conditioned coach were foggy from condensation. A big C was chalked on the side of the blue wagon to separate it from the twenty-two ordinary coaches. The shiny-faced [Cleanlanders] emerged from their designated coach, fell into a single line and swiftly marched towards the exit, their way cleared by the tribal guards, pointing machine guns at the waiting passengers. Old noted with relish that someone had scrawled the letters U N T S after the C on this particular coach.

'Not a step forward!' the guards shouted at the waiting passengers as they escorted the platoon of men and women with the neon-lit eyes.

Doors of the other coaches now flew open. People streamed out, pushing and jostling with those trying to board at the same time and fights broke out — verbal duels degenerating into fist fights and *lathi* blows. Skulls cracked, bones splintered and the wailing of the injured rose above the general bedlam that pervaded station A through the night.

Old stood shirtless beside the dead-end buffers, near the steam-spewing locomotive. The engine driver and his assistants eyed him suspiciously. Passengers pushed and shoved making their way out of the platform. They bumped and elbowed, gradually sweeping him along till he again found himself near the broken ticket barriers. The fights on the platforms continued and the screams of the injured gradually rose to a crescendo till the brickwork of the old station shivered — the voussoirs slipped from the decaying arches and the lanterns toppled from their alcove shelves, landing on unsuspecting passengers. Howls of pain multiplied in the ghostly light.

As he watched the hundreds pushing their way out, Old caught sight of a tall white man, slightly stooped, walking out of the platform. It was difficult to tell his age. He didn't look like any of the blue-eyed platoon of Cleanlanders who had just left the station.

He had lines around his eyes and road maps of wrinkles on his forehead. A battered violin case slung over his shoulder bobbed above the heads as he worked his way through the crush of arrivals. Pushed and shoved from all sides he somehow managed to approach the ticket barriers where Captain Old was standing and waving frantically to draw his attention. But in the treacherous light and drowned by the sea of travellers, he failed to notice him at first.

The foreigner passed through the damaged gates. Old followed, a little behind him, weaving his way through the crowds. He had to stop him before he walked out of the station building because it was dark outside. Just as he was passing below the archway, Old managed to grab his shirt tail.

A gentle tug. The tall man stopped, turned around to check what was holding him back. His grey eyes radiated warmth but his milk-white beard was unkempt, ragged from the journey. He was wearing a rumpled shirt over brown corduroys and on his head was a fishing cap which had been red many moons ago.

'Henry David? If I am not terribly mistaken?'

'That's my name, yes. I am sure you are the Captain?'

Old nodded, 'That's the name, Sir, or Old you can call me,' he chuckled, 'but even if you stick a gun to my head I won't be able to tell you why they call me that,' a little conscious of his missing shirt. They were being pushed as they spoke and, failing to shake hands or stand still, began to drift with the flow of arrivals.

'Happy to meet you,' Henry said, 'but what happened, did you hurt yourself?' He had noticed the bruises on his ribs and the missing shirt.

'Uh! I was tossed around a bit but nothing serious.'

Henry offered Old a spare shirt but he turned it down saying the night was hot and home was not so far.

The two emerged into the darkness outside the station lit up by the headlamps of elephabuses and the illuminated figure of the SUPREME GUIDE. A couple of ramshackle taxis that operated under the cover of night, were parked on the other side of the street, at the edge of the swollen river.

Old shepherded the foreigner towards the cabs but other passengers had run ahead. The few taxis disappeared before their eyes. It was impossible to find another so they joined the rush for an elephabus. As they headed for the bus stop, a thin man with alligator eyes came sneaking behind Henry and took off with his fishing cap.

Before Old could react, the snatcher had melted in the crowd.

'Sorry for this terrible welcome,' Old said, 'I hear you got something really important for us?'

'It's all here,' Henry tapped his violin case, as they fell in line to board the carriage pulled by the doughty old beasts, moodily swinging their trunks. Their ears flapping, their eyes calm as they waited to take the exhausted passengers home.

3

The red flag of Darkland Area Authority was fluttering moodily on top of the colonnaded neo-classical edifice that used to be a newspaper office, now converted to the Protector's headquarters. Privately owned media having been banned, the convenient location of this building on avenue 1 was found appropriate for housing those who were in charge of law and order over vast swathes of territory.

The platoon of blue-eyed Cleanlanders who were dropped outside the gates of this stately building, were waiting to be received by a party liaison officer who would take them to the guest house nearby. But he had been snoring away on his terrace, chilled by a steel cold breeze that had picked up from somewhere before daybreak. Meanwhile the new arrivals watched the sun rise.

A flaccid ball, pink like raw skin, poked its head above the deserted houses of avenue 3 which had once been named after a Soviet leader. Its limp rays twinkled on the glass crown of the People's Needle standing tall at the centre of Weed Park, stretching all the way to the river. The Cleanlanders watched with wonder in their neon eyes as the crown, blinked red, caught the sun, and *supreme guide established same day as 'years of light'*

gradually the tower floated out of thickest darkness, gleaming like a harpoon, quivering in the belly of a whale. [Today is the first day of the seventieth Year of Light (YL 70).] The SUPREME GUIDE turns seventy, and this city, which is now the capital of Darkland, was slowly stirring to life to welcome the new day.

[Bonesteel-11, commander of the platoon] that had arrived by train the night before, crossed the street to have a look around while the others waited. There was a statue of the SUPREME GUIDE in the middle of a traffic island opposite the headquarters. He went up for a closer look. He touched the youngblood tube feeding the likeness of the leader. There was a crackling sound and angry sparks flew at him as he withdrew his hand.

statues very protected

'Fuck. It's electrified!' he told [Krava-4, one of the female officers of the security platoon.] Krava-4 giggled, eyeing him as if he was ice cream. She kicked away an old jerrycan and went up and grabbed the blood tube with both hands. A white tongue of fire shot up her arms and her big blue eyes went wide with pleasure. She was moaning softly.

'Stop it!' Bonesteel-11 hissed, 'There are better ways to get off than that,' he whispered into her ears. She was wearing silver ear studs and her whisky-coloured hair was shorn, military style, highlighting the fine angles of her face.

The party liaison officer accompanied by a flunkey now appeared in an official car and, welcoming the new arrivals, led them to the People's Autonomous Guest House which had nicely done rooms and its own generator set.

'Get yourselves in shape for the familiarisation session in the afternoon,' the officer told them in the lobby before handing them the keys. They went off to their rooms, in single file, swinging their arms, humming war songs composed by music-teaching computers.

The [kravas and bonesteels] were special splices deployed by Cleanlanders at the beginning, a little before the hostilities broke out. They had a robust immune system, superhuman endurance powers as well as special skin cells engineered from the genes of volcanic archaeons that could withstand extreme temperatures. But like everything that had passed through the hands of men, they had errors and after a few years of service, the Cleanlanders decided to retire this genetically engineered fighting force.

There were stories of mass burials in Cleanland media, never substantiated. But the more business minded of those nations redeployed the faulty splices to Darkland, squeezing dirty profits out of the government of the SUPREME GUIDE.

Here, in Darkland, they called them 'dishbabies'. Perhaps because of the idea that they were beget in petri dishes and not in a human womb. Nonetheless, it was no less vicious a racial slur as nigger used to be long before the war and Incident R9117 of Yangtze basin, where kravas decimated a whole community of migrants, still fresh in everyone's mind.

Early afternoon. The smooth-skinned men and women, their eyes burning blue, marched out of the guest house built by a long dead Englishman and, taking a short detour around the mosque, trooped into the protector's office in a disciplined single file. Bonesteel-11 was just ahead of Krava-4 and he whispered something to her. The krava blushed.

A square hall, one hundred eardies by one hundred eardies, with thick steel doors and soundproof walls. The walls have been painted grey not so long ago. Near the high

Protector's office description:
ceiling are decorative mouldings depicting a row of lions. White light filters down from a cuboid of imported furon lamps. Emblazoned on each wall, is one of the four guiding principles for the Darkland authority —[FORTITUDE, FELLOWSHIP, FLOURISH, FUNDAMENTALS.] Above each word is a four-spoke wheel in relief, symbolising the four principles and around the rim of the wheel the words SELF RELIANCE is written four times. *every man for themselves*

In the middle of the hall is a gigantic ellipsoid table made of glass, which can seat a hundred people. The chairs, all mahogany, are slowly filling up with the white uniformed officers of the protector force. Some are old and have youngblood pouches hooked up with a contraption above their heads. On the street these metallic IV stands are known as 'udders' but they more resembled inverted tripods. *udders = suppar*

The bonesteels and kravas troop in and are shown their seats. Just as they are settling down the Chief Protector arrives with a party official. The Chief Protector, himself a high-ranking party member, is a thickset man with white hair and a drooping moustache. The udder supplying freshly filled blood is a brilliant crimson. He walks up to the head of the table where there are two vacant chairs. The party man takes the one to the left, the protector to his right. A hush descends.

Settling down in his chair, the chief asks the party official if he would like to deliver a welcome speech. He doesn't. So the protector grabs the mike and sucking a yellow memory pill, launches off in a raspy voice, 'Welcome friends from Cleanland, welcome comrades. Under the leadership of the SUPREME GUIDE, the Protector's office of Darkland Area Authority is glad to invite you to this familiarisation meeting on this auspicious day. Today under the guidance of our [BENEVOLENT LEADER] who knows all and sees all, we are celebrating the beginning of the seventieth Year of Light.

'You all know how the SUPREME GUIDE led us through the darkest nights before the start of hostilities while also leading us in victory against the aggressors, in what historians now call the [War of the Great Basins.] I understand that some of us sitting around this table today may have been on the other side but we are all joined today in a common cause.'

A uniformed protector sitting to his right whispered, 'Sir, there is hardly anyone from the other side here today. The dishbabies are of the ageless variety — all eternal teenagers.'

The Chief Protector heard it but didn't correct himself. He must have had his reasons. He looked around the table with his beady eyes. Everyone except the dishbabies had their notebooks and pens in hand, eager to take orders. He looked pleased and was going to continue but a hand went up from the far side of the table. It was Bonesteel-11. 'Sir, with your permission, could you tell us a bit about this war. We have heard about it but back home we have never been told the details.'

'Did you hear that comrades? And our guests are supposed to be from a free country. What travesty!' said the Chief Protector self importantly. 'Yes, of course. I know how information is censored in your part of the world. But we will keep our disagreements aside for now. Don't worry. At the other end of Weed Park, which is a little over 5000 eardies from this building, you will find our state-of-the-art People's Library where you can find answers to all your questions about the war. The library is open round the clock and is accessible to any foreigner who wishes to know the truth.'

There was a murmur of appreciation. No one batted an eyelid at the irony of the fact that no Darklander except the highest-ranking party officials and those with special security clearance had seen the library from inside.

'Eardies?' a krava whispered to another.

The other krava rolled her eyes. 'Were you sleeping at the pre-dep orientation classes? [The eardy is their unit of distance. Length of the SUPREME GUIDE's ear multiplied by two.']

The Chief Protector eyed his audience, smoothened a crease on his uniform and continued with an outline of the history of the last fifty years.

Krava-4 was getting distracted. She had avoided lectures at the nurture academy where they went before combat training. While it was compulsory to have the ice cream, which conditioned their minds, the lecture rooms didn't enforce attendance. So she would sneak out and sit under the shade of a tree in the park across the road from where they all lived. It would be lovely in summer with the emerald grass and the mellow sunlight caressing her bare feet. They were not allowed to handle books but she found one forgotten on a bench and had began to turn its pages. It was the story of a little girl who lived with a cruel stepmother who always abused and threatened her. So she finds solace in the company of a ghost who has been living in their house for a century.

It was a touching story though Krava-4 was never sure what a ghost actually is. She had heard that bloodbabies contain a soul — which is like water in a cup. And this soul can turn into a ghost when they die — which was like the cup breaking and the water evaporating away but still there, hiding in the clouds. She would have loved to turn into a ghost too, like the one in the story. But down at the academy they said kravas don't possess a soul, so a phantom existence was not possible. 'What the heck!' she cursed her creators softly. She observed the world around her through her sunglasses. Little children skipped and played in the summer sun while their mothers sat in the shade of trees watching. The only games she had learned to play was VR Warcraft and a holopro version of Urban Jungle. The children giggled and laughed. The bright yellow flowers swayed in the wind picking some of the infectious mirth. She licked her lips, surprised to find an odd salty taste there.

'Over the years we have put in place systems to deal with all the fallouts,' the protector was going ahead full steam, 'you will be briefed by the departments. All dwelling units have been taken over and redistributed so that every healthy citizen has a roof over his head. New housing is being built continuously by our volunteer forces for the thousands still streaming in from the villages. We have turned all useless property into hospices and care homes. Food distribution and rationing is in able hands and the Nutrition Committee of the government works round the clock. Thousands of packets of safeoil and truckloads of lab-ham are being distributed through our robust public distribution system. Tibetan wheat is back in our godowns as is Siberian corn. The supreme ideology of Four Spokes enunciated in the Black Book is being followed to the dot. Still we need more help from your people,' and here he eyed the guests, 'to tackle the problem of hunger and the quest for an antidote. For obvious reasons that even children know today, it's more your responsibility.'

[handwritten: what are memory pills' purpose?]

The new arrivals looked at each other with their bright blue eyes and nodded.

'Why don't you manufacture ice cream,' a bonesteel put forth.

'Ah! That is a good proposition,' the Chief Protector said, clearing his throat.

'Yummy and nutritious,' the party official commented.

'But it's risky. We don't know yet if we can do it here.' The chief turned to speak with an advisor, 'Find out whether the state can set up ice cream operations.'

'I am afraid we can't, Sir. It has been checked. Besides, the ice cream they are suggesting is not our good old mint chocolate chip. It's the dishbaby variety, a different flavour for a different job. It's the only food they need,' he spoke in a low voice.

The chief nodded without expression and continued to speak. As he does so the yellow memory pill begins to melt dribbling an ochre juice down his fingers. 'So as you see, problems remain but we are not doing too bad. However there is this new menace with the band of guerrillas trying to disturb the peace that prevails here. They have created pockets of influence among the migrants and other groups. We know who their leader is but he is a sneaky little bastard ...'

He continued elaborating about the recent attacks and the steps that had been initiated. 'You have to be vigilant at all times,' he said addressing the kravas and bonesteels, 'our intelligence officers will brief you about specific assignments but you must always deal with these guerrillas ruthlessly. Most of their weapons are primitive, some stolen. So you will have a definite advantage over them. And report directly to your commander who will report back to me ...' The familiarisation went on for a little more than an hour.

[handwritten: what is war about?]

[handwritten margin note: what is kravas + bonesteels' role?]

The Chief Protector finished the briefing, rubbed his moustache and prepared to leave. He had a word with the party official who listened without expression or comment. The adviser whispered something to his chief and he again took the mike, 'Thank you for being a part of our struggle. Now you will be guided to joint briefings where you will meet other Cleanlanders with specials skills. I am told a new generation of karmics have arrived, which is good news as long as they obey orders. Tonight, our party has a little entertainment lined up for you. I will see you again at the zoological gardens for the evening function, the highlight of which is the Anniversary Day Parade of the Extinct. The tiger will lead and Comrade Bokanovsky, who has arrived from our northern borders with his new show, will be your host.'

4

'Japanese girls, freshly picked,' a hoarse voice whispered from behind the curtains of darkness. They had climbed off the elephabus and walked for ten minutes along the canal that now flowed where there used to be a street named after a battlefield. Then they had taken a left turn into a narrow lane where they heard the voice.

'Japanese girls ...'

'Thanks, *burima*. I will just do with the cleanweed. Besides I have a guest,' Old whispered.

The wrinkled lady who had appeared like a ghost, peered at him from inside the abandoned electricity distribution box, cackled loudly, showing damaged yellow teeth. She had east Asian features but years of living in the disused brick sewers below the

[handwritten margin note top: "Weird + prostitutes/escorts being sold?"]

city had turned her skin the colour of glass. She studied Old's face. 'Why, what's the matter boy? Since the time I arrived in this city, you have always proved to be a red-blooded male. Do you have a problem with the Japanese? I promise they are fresh off the boat.'

'Uh!' Old turned back to make sure that his guest wasn't listening, though he hardly cared, 'I had a rough evening and don't feel like anything but a few long drags.'

'You are becoming heartless, son, that you are. I can see it in your glazed look. What would these poor girls eat if people like you don't give them business? I cannot make them chew on weed. And who knows …' the wrinkled lady shook her head in disapproval.

'I am sorry, burima, another time. Can you hurry it, please, I have been up all night.' He stashed the weed in his trouser pocket and asked her to put it on his account.

Her yellow eyes had gone out of focus. She was not there any more. 'But won't you come down and have a look at least? They still have those old-fashioned fairy outfits with bows on their heads; you might even want to get married to one,' she murmured absentmindedly.

'Too late, granny, maybe another time,' he grunted and stepped back from the distribution box, its aluminium paint, with the skull and cross bones, still shining after all these years. The lady slammed shut the doors from inside and dropped back into the brick sewer underneath. Old smelled the weed, realising too late that he had been ripped off again with the chemical soaked stuff.

When they finally arrived at his flat on street 5.7, it was almost dawn. A blister of greenish clouds had scattered from the south

[handwritten margin note right: "Streets are numbered, not named"] and the sky was oozing pink morning light. They walked the few steps to the red brick building with the crumbling staircase, their feet heavy from the weight of the night. There was a chunk of lab-ham in the fridge but because of intermittent power cuts, it had spoiled. Old had received two weeks' supply of the imported meat as prize for winning the neighbourhood street-sweeping competition, two months in a row.

He took out the chunk of lab-grown meat wrapped in cellophane and placed it on the counter top. Washing it thoroughly he cut some thin slices with a carving knife, putting the rest back into the freezer. Taking down the heavy skillet he deep fried the slices in chilli-flavoured safeoil but Henry wasn't going to have any of it.

Old knew that the student who lived next door had stocked vegetables bought at a premium from the smugglers, so taking a look up and down the corridor, he picked the lock and sneaked in. He grabbed a handful of potatoes and stuffing his pockets with chillies and onions, stepped back into his office.

His guest was in the back room sitting on a rocking chair. He was leafing through a book whose foxed pages were turning into dust in his hands. It was one of his books but Old couldn't read the title from where he stood. As his guest turned over each page, it dispersed into a red powder which settled slowly on his lap. He read fast and in little over an hour he had finished the volume of which nothing was left, save a tattered cover and a pile of dust on his trousers.

Captain Old went about preparing a broth in the corner kitchen. Chopping the onion he pressed a slice to his nose. Bliss! And despite the tears streaming down his eyes, the pungency of the freshly cut bulb brought back forgotten flavours of spicy gravy to his mind.

Though he often filched onions from his neighbour, he could rarely use it for cooking. He employed onion for a different and unavoidable purpose, notwithstanding the fact that it left him smelling like a soup kitchen.

His guest enjoyed the simple meal. He dunked pieces of mouldy bread in the broth to make it softer while Old chewed on the stringy meat, nipping absentmindedly at the last slices of bread he had stocked. He had bartered a few bottles of safeoil for bread at the local ration shop and would have to scavenge for more, now that his food coupons were gone. But right now there were questions that needed to be answered.

The message that had preceded the foreigner's arrival had been crisp and to the point. This man knew something. And he had wanted to discuss it with him, him of all people! What could this grizzled Englishman, with one foot in the grave, know that hadn't been figured out already? Old didn't buy the story of the lost antidote that was circulated from time to time like comic book science fiction. They will have to talk, soon as his guest was rested and ready.

After the meal, Henry took out his violin, and played a tune which evoked visions of trees shedding their leaves, their bare branches like iron skeletons probing the grey emptiness, of cars swerving off roads on dead tyres where they light up in one final effulgence of petroleum. The notes filled up the empty rooms, pouring out through the windows, and the wasted people in the street below stirred in their siesta, dreaming of lost loves and places where they had spent their days of laughter.

The Englishman played the music for an hour sending the neighbourhood into a restive slumber. Old did his breathing exercises.

His ribs ached. He breathed normally but the bruises were still tender. Luckily there was nothing broken and hopefully no internal damage, but a dull pain remained in his chest. He massaged his trunk a couple of times and did a number of stretches before popping a painkiller. But the medicine took its time. He lay down on his cot and closed his eyes for a while.

But he couldn't sleep. Soon as he had lain down, from far away, across the Ash Barricades, a high-pitched feminine voice began to sing:

> *Buy, buy, buy*
> *You are thin*
> *We are spry*
> *Buy, buy, buy!*

[annotation: Japanese women being sold?]

The music washed over the city travelling far into the villages of Darkland. Accompanied by a rhythm guitar and electronic drums, the song looped on and on in every mind long after speakers had fallen quiet.

Old got out of bed, bleary eyed from the lack of sleep. 'Don't you need some rest?' he asked the Englishman.

'I am okay,' Henry replied. He had been listening to the song from across the border, a sad twinkle in his eyes.

Later in the afternoon, he wanted to see the river. 'This is the river that gave birth to a civilisation. I want to see it with my own eyes.'

[handwritten: what is a soul ticket?]

'There is nothing much there,' Old said, pulling out a wrinkled shirt. It would be warm outside at this time of the day. He pinned on his [spare soul ticket] with the image of the SUPREME GUIDE. The other one he had lost to the snatchers last night.

They locked the flat and walked down to the [Square of the Martyrs with its rows of old care homes and hospitals.] Over the years, little barter and pawn shops had sprung up upon the pavements and the ancient department stores opened by the British were now doing a roaring business, selling automatic wheelchairs, licensed youngblood and chip-embedded smart chamber pots which analysed and kept stock of urine output with an option to share the data on Fossilbook — the old people's social network.

[handwritten margin note: elderly, not prioritized]

The Darkland Areas Authority had let this neighbourhood be used for catering to the needs of the elderly, shifting administrative offices to the east of the city where there was less water scarcity and a regular delivery of fresh food from Cleanland.

'It's very hot today, isn't it?' Henry said. They were walking towards the square, negotiating doddering men roaming aimlessly, their empty eyes bereft of the will to live.

'We will have rains later in the evening.'

Henry looked thoughtfully at the signboards of care homes along the street, 'You have to see what I brought with me. And perhaps then only we should talk.'

'Surely.'

'Your soul ticket, Sir?' a young woman with bright blue eyes had stopped them. She was wearing a protector's white uniform. An automatic weapon was slung on her shoulder.

Captain Old recognised the dishbaby immediately. He had seen her at the station, the night before. Must be from a new batch, he told himself, because he had never seen that bluish glow in their eyes.

Henry had stopped in his tracks. He looked at Krava-4 with a mix of amusement and distaste and was going to say something when Old cut in. 'He is a Cleanlander.'

Krava-4 turned to face Old. 'And you? Do you have authorisation to have intercourse with a Cleanlander?'

'What?' Old realised she meant social intercourse. She could create a lot of trouble for them if she wanted. He couldn't let the situation escalate, so he said, 'I am not with him. We just happened to be walking in the same direction. I was trying to help out a tourist.'

'Is that true?' she asked Henry.

He nodded grimly.

'Huh! A tourist? What kind of splice is that? Are you an improved version of the sonmis that malfunctioned? But you don't seem to be functioning too well, are you?'

It looked like Henry's eyes would pop off their sockets.

'I don't want to get into this but the Cleanlander here is a bloodbaby and not a splice. He is a tourist, he is here to check out our country.'

Krava-4 listened and nodded slowly. She seemed to understand and turned to face Henry. 'I hope this is true,' she studied their faces, 'now run and I don't want to see the two of you together again.'

They were nearing the river which had swelled over the decades taking with it the High Court building and the Town Hall. From the eastern edge of the Martyrs' Square, they could

[margin note: tourists are typically dishbabies/splices]

see rusty stateboats skimming across the surface of the river, powered by black market diesel.

'Of course. I am waiting to see what you got. Otherwise I wouldn't have responded to your message and taken the trouble to receive you at the station. But I don't buy that story of the lost antidote,' Old said, as they crossed a street and went down to the river bank.

There were many people sitting here. Old men and women, hordes of the jobless, confidence tricksters with eagle eyes, out-of-job actors dressed like Mongol invaders, and bartermen with their assorted stock of Cleanland puff pipes, mouldy long loaf, three-headed *hilsas*, Tibetan wheat and millet, stolen prosthetics, memory pills, and pilfered youngblood.

A crowd had gathered at the water's edge watching a juggler showing his tricks. The churches and the railway godowns had all been washed away and the black water that flowed ceaselessly towards the bay carried no memories of all that it had taken with it. Not even that of the city's founder which had vanished in the hungry currents.

Captain Old and the Englishman stood on the half-sunk pavement beside the neo-classical pile of Governor's Care Home and watched the young juggler from a distance. People crowded around him, thieves who had fallen in love with nurses, boatmen and freshface couples, their buttery skin glowing in the evening light. 'forbidden' love couples

He was just a boy. Fresh faced with limpid brown eyes. A tattered red jersey embroidered with a Manchester United logo over an outsized khaki short. With his two little hands he was [juggling five long bones] white as chalk. The bones flew through the air returning to his practised grip and the crowd cheered

'Hurrah!' throwing at the little boy pieces of mouldy bread and ration shop toffees.

The femurs and tibias flew in a circle, rising and falling through the amber light, the girders of the half-sunk bridge 3 gleamed like the silvery scales of an aquatic monster, trapped in the poison river while Henry began to tell Captain Old about his friend, the Indian geneticist Tanmoy Sen, and what happened that day when the end-of-the-world fog had wrapped itself around his small English town. He stopped midway. He was asking Old if he could tell him anything about an incident in Korea.

'The lost travellers — it was so long ago, people hardly remember these days,' Henry said.

They looked at each other, realising the irony of the comment. Old nodded vaguely and looked away. He was too engrossed watching the juggler.

5

While watching the boy a thought had occurred to Captain Old. Could those be the bones of the city's founder, a Christian who had fallen in love and married a Hindu princess? When the river burst through its banks, many graves on the riverside were washed away and it had been party time for bone merchants who would dive into the turbulent waters to rescue the skeletons of old Englishmen. But fishermen out on the water, lying in wait for the three-headed hilsa, said the dead Englishmen swam faster than the skeleton traders and were often rescued by ghost ships flying the White Ensign.

> soul ticket needed for citizens of town?

They lingered on the banks for a while, watching the young boy with the bones as the sun vanished behind the scrapyards on the other side. The mountains of glass and twisted metal were covered with years of dust, and old rear-view mirrors sticking out from the scrap heaps caught the last rays, reflecting it back at them, blooming like blood flowers on the ridge of a black hill.

They had returned the way they had arrived. On the way back, Old said he needed to report the stolen scooter and so they headed for the Chief Protector's headquarters on avenue 1.

'I hope you will be able to recover your scooter,' Henry said as they made their way to the office.

'Slim chance, but no harm to try. The chief knows me, so I am hoping he will at least facilitate the matter.'

They were stopped at the gates by machine gun-wielding bonesteels from the batch that had come in the night before. Old's soul ticket was scanned and they checked Henry's travel papers before letting them in.

A guard led them up a flight of stairs with banister rails to a wide corridor with rooms on one side. They were taken to a biggish office room with a semi-circular table and wooden chairs arranged in a crescent. The glass-topped table had the red flag of Darkland on a pedestal and a metal sculpture of the SUPREME GUIDE besides stacks of papers and a pen stand.

The guard left them there and disappeared. They waited for fifteen minutes but no one turned up. Old was getting restless. A door to the right leading into an anteroom was ajar. Old padded up softly and peeped inside. There were two people sitting inside. The Chief Protector was meeting a hard-faced man with pouches under his eyes and rotten teeth. They were talking in low voices.

Behind them on the wall a holopro was beaming a snuff movie featuring teenage girls.

Old's stomach churned and he stepped back. He knew the freshfaces in the movie were all Darklanders, kidnapped by one of the criminal gangs. These movies were sold at a premium in Cleanland, distributed by networks that operated with impunity by bribing law keepers.

Henry was tired and had dozed off when a loud thump on his back snatched him out of slumber. He sprang up from his seat, very annoyed. But he managed to preserve his demeanour when he found it was a uniformed officer.

The Chief Protector had sneaked in behind them through the other door. Old had also failed to notice him come in and took time to react.

'Who is this?' the protector thundered, 'Oh! Welcome, Captain Old. This one here, is he with you?'

Old was smarting with embarrassment. He looked at Henry apologetically, turned to face the chief and said, 'Yes. As you can see, Sir, you have upset him already.'

'Oh! Then I must tender an apology to this Cleanlander,' he said in a mocking insincere voice. 'Is he a real clean one or just a painted circusman?' he added in a cop voice.

'His travel papers have been checked by the guards,' Old said in a flat voice.

His blood was boiling but he didn't let it show. He imagined the Chief Protector dead. Cold on a slab of ice. In fact he pitied him, he told himself, and pity absorbed the rage that had piled up when the chief misbehaved with the Englishman. They were all going to die and this was such a

[calming thought. That the vile and the corrupt will pass away sooner than later.]

How soon was the CP going to go? Old wondered as he studied his wrinkled forearms, the folds of skin hanging from the elbows. A pouch of youngblood was still fixed behind his head in an udder from which the crimson fluid drained slowly into a blood vessel of his neck. youngblood, preserving youth?

The CP went round the table and settled in his chair. He kept sitting still, saying nothing, letting the silence unnerve the visitors. After a while he leaned back and extracting a yellow memory pill from a bottle began sucking it loudly. In a few minutes he again sat erect and fixing Old with a look said, 'So what brings you here, Captain? We haven't had the honour for a while. Were you there at the YL 70 celebration? Funny I didn't see you. Perhaps you needed an invitation?'

Old was immediately on his guard. He didn't want to get in trouble with the protector force. A single complaint about disrespect shown to the SUPREME GUIDE or the founding ideals of the Four Spokes of progress could land him a life of slave labour in a sapphire mine in the Himalayas. Old didn't like the idea of cutting stones on a burning rock face for the rest of his life. So he feigned contrition, 'It's my fault really. My scooter was snatched from me last night quite unceremoniously. I resisted but these people were armed,' he stood on his feet and pulled up his shirt to show the bruise marks on his ribs, 'the pain ... it's hard to walk with it.'

The protector drummed his table with his pudgy fingers and thought. He seemed to peer far into the distance though the only thing hanging on the facing wall was a gilded portrait of the SUPREME GUIDE in his solar-powered ambulance, which had glass on all sides.

'Are you sure it was not one of our Equitable Distribution squads who took the scooter by mistake?'

'Aren't they supposed to be in uniform, wearing their soul tickets?'

'Well,' Old noticed a glimmer in the Chief Protector's eyes, 'sometimes they do, if there are uniforms available. But I see you are still breaking the law, Captain Old,' he continued slowly, 'you know private transport was banned in YL 65.'

'Err, I had been granted permission for this scooter, you remember. It is so difficult to manage without some kind of transport.'

'Tch tch. But that is only if you are on lawkeeping assignment with written orders. So what state duty was keeping you busy, Captain, in the middle of the night near station A?'

Old was surprised. Surely someone had reported the mugging and theft. In any case it was the job of protectors to know. He decided not to push with his defence and tried another tack, 'I was going to receive this gentleman here. He is on a touring visit. I will be grateful if you can activate local contacts and help me get the scooter back. If there is anything going on right now at the department, where I could chip in with my expertise ...'

'Quid pro quo! You are an old-fashioned guy aren't you? No wonder they call you that. You are lucky, Captain, there is no file in your name and somehow no one has bothered to put one together. That's why you can get away with all this indiscipline.' He picked up the melting pill and began sucking again, loudly.

Old mumbled an apology.

'But I like your suggestion [Give and take,] sounds nice, I must admit. There is indeed a lot going on in this town and we can do something about it together. Now tell me, what make was your scooter?' the CP offered a lopsided smile.

Old looked relieved. He would be stranded without the vehicle. 'Honda Electric Star.' *future*

'Oh! Vintage machine! If I remember correctly, they had to stop production before the War of the Great Basins.'

Old nodded, flushed with nostalgia for his two-wheeler. 'Yes. I made a lot of modifications to keep it in service. Then I lost it for a few years when all the trouble erupted but miraculously it was returned to me. I have a knack of keeping machines running. The scooter has served me well, all these years.'

'Always say Light Years, Captain. That is if you want to keep out of the mines. Anyway, I will see what we can do. We will pass word via party liaison to the community wardens and youth brigades. Maybe they will have some inputs. If it hasn't been smuggled out of the city or scrapped, you will get it back. But otherwise also, I can get you a powerful machine, a brand new Leopard like the one being issued to our armed units. Manufactured in Siberia.'

'Yes, thank you. I still believe my old horse is around somewhere, waiting for a good price,' Old said.

'Submit a written complaint to the duty officer at the local protector station. Tell them about our conversation. Meanwhile I will have a talk with the Sports Minister. He is very resourceful in these matters,' the CP said while pulling out dead skin from his finger tips.

'Let me know, if I can be of any help,' Old said. His stomach was churning, perhaps because of the stale lab-ham he had for lunch.

not years, Light years instead

'Come to think of it, we can indeed use your services. It has been a while that you were called in and from what I remember, you have performed reasonably well. The force will surely reward you if you can pull it off this time. Considering the difficulties of the assignment, we can offer you a month's supply of food coupons for this one. And you will get that scooter.'

'That is very kind of you, Sir,' Old said, offering an ingratiating smile.

'So let's get down to the details. There is a lot going on actually,' his eyes turned glassy for a moment, 'can we trust your friend?' He was staring at Henry and then back at Old.

Old was not sure what to say and noticing it Henry offered to sit out. 'I will wait outside,' he said.

As soon as he was out of earshot, the protector continued, 'The Red Dawn has been regrouping, I am sure you know.'

[marginalia: guerrilla group]

Yes. He had heard about it from his own sources; besides nowadays he often came across guerrilla graffiti and warnings scribbled on the walls of public toilets in the area around Weed Park. Everywhere in town some of the captured anarchists, all quite young, were being held in cages and tortured to instil fear in people's minds.

'Maybe you working on your own would be better placed for what I have in mind,' the protector said.

'Tell me more,' Old said in a flat voice.

'Yes, of course. But let us have some tea first. I will send a cup for the Cleanlander sitting outside. Earl Grey?'

'I always preferred Sri Lankan.'

'Did you spend your life under a rock, Captain? Where in the world can you get that today?'

The tea arrived. They sipped it slowly as the protector told him why he needed his help. But in a few minutes a bell began to ring shrilly in the corridor outside. Then another joined it from the street. Then another. It was relayed again and again, the [ringing of bells, spreading across the city over loudspeakers.] And more and more bells were heard. From hospices and train stations, from schools and graveyards. A naked metallic ring, like a mechanical bicycle bell but much louder and it rang across streets and houses, pulsing through elephabus stations and crematoriums, relayed on and on by the maws of loudspeakers strung up all across the land, trying to rouse the living and the dead.

The officer hurriedly stood up and touched his forehead with his left palm. While doing this he <u>dislodged the harness and so the youngblood supply stopped</u>. But he didn't try to set it right and stood holding the pose as long as the bells kept ringing. Captain Old followed suit. The bells kept ringing. Half a minute, piercing every remaining eardrum.

A wheezy voice came over the public address system, crackling through the city, echoing across towns and villages, hundreds of thousands of kilometres across the land.

'Good evening worthy citizens of our Beloved Darkland. Pay attention for a while and thank the SUPREME GUIDE for drawing us <u>one step closer this day to the bountiful future of Light</u>. A future of self-reliance, freedom from want and wealth and the day will soon dawn when we will stand head to head with the oppressors who have pushed us into this predicament. Work hard and whenever in doubt <u>ask yourself what you have done for the state and not what the state has done for you</u>. As you go home tonight from your workplaces remember to sweep clean the road in front of your house and ensure that not a morsel of food in your home is wasted.

'Wicked powers have again been plotting to disrupt our peaceful lives and have inserted agents to sabotage our forward march. But our brave protectors have thwarted these devious designs. Still, you have to be alert.

'Report anything suspicious, any incident out of the ordinary that you notice. Your local community heads are always there to guide you. Work hard, work with diligence and don't lie down to rest till our common dream of a kingdom of Light is achieved. Remember the day is not far. We have come a long way and every day our factory workers, our soldiers at the Ash Barricades are doing their bit to propel us on towards the glory which rightfully belongs to our great nation ...

'Under the leadership of the SUPREME GUIDE, we have recently inked a deal with the Siberian authorities for the import of Leopard electric scooters in lieu of our hardy mountain goats, whose meat is fancied in those parts. As we speak, the first consignments of Leopard scooters are being unloaded here while five thousand mountain goats are bravely marching northwards to whet the appetites of our northern comrades. To ensure food security we have ...'.

The speech transformed into a litany of achievements finishing with a resolve to pull down the Ash Barricades that Cleanlanders had erected after the war to stop people from slipping into their territories looking for food and work.

Meanwhile everything grinded to a halt. People froze in the middle of the streets to hear at attention (for it was forbidden to move an inch when the announcements were made), left palm on their forehead, and were crushed by rogue taxi drivers. Surgeons stopped their operations midway, drivers and passengers stood up in the elephabuses while the majestic beasts roamed on unguided, trampling rickety pawn shops or heading straight for a dip in the river. Through the day, morning and evening, this ritual was repeated a number of times.

Once the loudspeakers had fallen quiet, the protector picked up his cup of cold tea, took a sip, spat it out and settled back on his chair. The briefing continued.

Old had heard some of it. Whispers of sabotage, the firebomb attacks earlier that year. The prisoners in the cages. He had read the official news tickers scrolling across the amnesia boards warning people not to shelter the criminals. But he hadn't paid much attention. He had been too busy keeping body and soul together. But what the CP was telling him now sounded serious.

'These are small groups trying to sow dissent among our citizens. Now they have assembled under the umbrella of the Red Dawn organisation which is plotting to overthrow the benevolent rule of our SUPREME GUIDE. We have executed a few leaders, more still are in prison but we haven't been able to break their resolve.

'We have accumulated good intelligence. We know that they are again organising and planning something big. We don't know what. But it is well beyond doubt that they will try to disturb the peace that prevails in our land. This week is crucial because of the YL 70 celebrations. They will attempt something spectacular while at the same time mobilise the masses. I wouldn't rule out an assassination bid. There was a similar conspiracy hatched by one of these groups a few months back. But we managed to infiltrate the organisation and take out the gunmen. This time we haven't been able to penetrate the core leadership.' The Chief Protector paused to see if Old had something to say.

'So what do you want me to do? I am sure you have two or three teams working on this?'

The protector looked him in the eye, a cold glassy look, holding it for a few seconds. 'You have to take out their leader. We will supply you with pinpoint intelligence about his movements. But otherwise you will be on your own. We know they are about to organise a meeting where their self-styled leader is expected. If matters go out of hand we will provide backup but it would be tricky. They will have a definite advantage over us because of the location.'

'Which is?'

'The underground.'

'The underground?'

'Yes, the abandoned metro system. We have definite information that their leaders will be holding a mass meeting there, one of these evenings. As you know, the abandoned stations and tunnels have turned into settlements for the affected people and the migrants who have no better place to go. This group has a strong support base among these wretched people. And that makes our job difficult. We can't have too much blood on our hands, it has to be a clean surgical operation. With what little I know about you, you would be invaluable for this job.'

'Are you planning to wipe out the whole leadership?'

'Just one man,' he paused to make sure Old had heard him clear, 'the man who wears a mask. They call him Comrade Ashish

Comrade Ashish but that's not his real name. We don't have recent photographs but you will know how to identify him. We will feed you with all the details. He is supposed to be there at the meeting.'

A black rain had begun to pour as they left the headquarters and were walking homeward. Old wouldn't budge till the rain had stopped, so they took shelter under the doorway of a care home as it rained over the city and beyond, drenching the tired land.

It rained like this every evening of summer and people took shelter under the porticos of houses and inside abandoned offices to protect themselves. For the evening rain, while it brought down temperatures, blistered the skin badly and no cream or salve could treat those reddish boils. They went away on their own after months, leaving ugly scars that were difficult to camouflage. The city steamed under the curtains of poison water, sweeping down from the slate black heavens. The heat of day escaping from tin roofs and metal elephabus sheds hissed as the steam evaporated. For an hour each evening, the city waited in stunned silence for the rain to stop. And soon afterwards the mikes hooked up across the Ash Barricades came to their cacophonous life:

> *Buy, buy, buy*
> *You are thin*
> *We are spry*
> *Buy, buy, buy!*

6

It was night again. A night hot as a chimney. Another night of green petromax glows and battery-operated emergency lights. A night punctuated like every other by the cacophonous orchestra of the diseased and the hungry left out on the streets to wither away. The bodies, with just a flicker of life, massed on pavements or abandoned in weed-infested parks, whimpering '*ma go, baba go*'. The mongrels of the city had grown red fangs and flesh eaters prowled the suburbs.

Captain Old had smoked the last of burima's weed before fixing a meal for the Englishman. He told his guest that he had a dinner invitation and had left after sharing the last drops of an Islay malt that the Cleanlander had secreted in his bag from the hungry customs officers at the border. The fire of Scotland had upped his spirits despite the bad news that filtered in ceaselessly.

He cut across the narrow lane beside his home, bypassing the street once named after a famous battlefield, and through the crumbling brick pile of a pre-war mansion reached avenue 1. The avenue here was just a potholed road with large stretches of earth on which poison weeds flourished. The flame trees on both flanks that had been planted repeatedly for shade had withered but their carcasses remained erect, waiting to be turned into firewood by the homeless. Art deco lamp posts set up by a government long ago had somehow survived the street battles and on these were fixed the LED boards with the alphabet lessons. These battery-operated amnesia boards had been funded from a Cleanland project to provide street lighting: S for SUPREME GUIDE, A for ATOM, B for BLOODBABY, C for CLEANLAND, F for FELLOWSHIP, FORTITUDE, FLOURISH, FUNDAMENTALS ... L for LOVE, W for WAR, Y for YOUNGBLOOD — the red LEDs glowed ominously in the dark. They doubled also as street lights though the dim glow of the diodes struggled to push back the darkness.

He went stealthily among the shadows of the dilapidated residences and care homes. A few elephabuses were ambling down the avenue, headed towards Weed Park terminus. Stoned maniacs lurked in the gullies with their illegal taxis that ran on smuggled oil. Uniformed traffic sergeants wielding rusty Kalashnikovs kept a watch from their plastic pedestals at street crossings. In the dark by lanes, blood harvesting gangs waited under the doorways of abandoned buildings.

But they didn't bother him at all. He was well prepared tonight. He crossed the tram tracks and walked northwards, towards the park with the damaged equine statue of a valiant monarch. His head was gone and from the stump of his neck a devil's trumpet had sprouted its poison flowers, the white blooms shining in the silvery moonlight. People on foot were heading towards station B to catch the night trains that would take them back to the towns and villages around the city. They all moved in groups so that they could help each other.

The lone sergeant signalled the traffic to a halt for the people to pass. A row of state cabs and a couple of elephabuses lurched to a halt, waiting for the people to cross. And now a man came down from the sidewalk with a wicker basket of fragrant *champa* blossoms intoning in a melancholic voice '*champa ache, champa, champa neben, champa.*' He went weaving through the crowds, stopping beside the elephabuses and hand-pulled rickshaws, requesting passenger and pedestrian to try his golden yellow blooms. It seemed no one was interested and the flower seller was about to retreat. But just then an old man in a rickshaw waved his hand and took from him a dozen pretty blooms, offering food coupons to the flower seller. The old man caressed the fragrant blossoms and handed them all to the old lady who was travelling with him. She held the flowers in her shaky fingers, smiled demurely and looked tenderly at the old man. The traffic began to roll.

He moved faster hoping that the hand-drawn map given to him was right. Beyond the shuttered entrance of what used to be the Central metro station there was another bunch of amnesia boards. A little ahead, some medicine shops, *Memory pills out of stock* permanently scrawled on their windows. Then a gerontologist's academy, working in candlelight. A narrow lane. He sneaked into the lane and after a few steps found the grilled manhole.

He lowered his heavy shoulder bag on the ground and looked back and forth to make sure there was no one around. Then grabbing the iron grill, pulled with all his might. It didn't budge. Cursing under his breath he tried again and one more time. But the cover stayed put, as if it was welded to the frame. After a few more failed attempts he gave up and began looking around for something that could be used as a lever. But he was losing precious time.

He walked up and down the lane looking for a lever when someone grabbed his shirt collar from behind. He was going to hit back when a familiar voice said, 'Boy, you will get killed one of these days, I am sure about that.'

It was the weed and girls lady from the sewers. 'Oh, burima, you gave me a shock. I am working, can we talk another time please?'

'Yes, yes. It's this work that will take you one day. I am again warning you. Get out of the muck and lead a clean life.'

Old chuckled, 'Okay, I will think about it, burima.'

'That's a good boy, here take this.' She handed him a length of wrought iron torn from a street railing. 'You need this I believe?'

'Oh thank you, thank you!'

'Sure, and remember the Japanese girls are still waiting.'

Only when she had disappeared down the alley did he remember the fake weed she had sold him the other day. Old wedged the iron rail between the grill and the frame and put all his weight on the lever. Slowly the cover rose. He bent down and heaved it aside. He was sweating and wiped his arms and face on his cruddy sweatshirt. One last look around and he slipped nimbly into the sewer hole. There were rusty metal rungs on the wall. Grabbing these with one hand and the strap of his shoulder bag with another, he quietly climbed down into the pit.

At the bottom his feet landed in sludgy water trickling through the waste pipe. Putrescent fumes clogged his nostrils. He tied a piece of cloth round his face and stepped ahead in the darkness.

Some of the old buildings were still connected to the sewage disposal system, while others had to do with septic tanks and human scavengers. The sewage from most households were collected and dried into briquettes, supplied as free fuel to the city. Only the rich and the powerful got the benefit of sewage connections while the rest had to contribute to the fuel supply.

The waste pipe turned smoothly to the right and his first thought was it might be going towards the river. But the map said otherwise. Could he trust the map? After progressing a few eardies through the darkness he felt for the trap door which would lead into a service chamber at the street level. The ventilation shaft of the metro passed through the chamber.

Scraping his hand against the wall of the sewer pipe he finally found the valve mechanism that opened the sealed trap door. But it was not necessary to use it. The door was ajar. Whoever had gone before him hadn't bothered to close the door. It didn't smell good, this whole business.

The air inside the service chamber was cleaner. A small brick structure built by British engineers, it had withstood the ravages of time. He briefly lit the flashlight to locate the ventilation shaft. It was just above his head gleaming in the darkness. Old took out his stiletto and ripped apart a panel from the vent shaft — big enough for him to crawl through. Then switching off his flashlight he heaved himself into it.

The VAC shaft was much narrower than the sewage line. He had to double over and made slow progress. Bats fluttered past him fanning his sweating face with their wings. He thought he heard them sing an old melancholic air he had heard in another world. The darkness hurt and the stench of rotting flesh, despite the cover on his nose, was overpowering.

Then he saw the eyes. Not one or two but at least a dozen red pairs burning through the darkness. The weight of the weapon concealed in his shoulder bag was reassuring but he was not sure what kind of adversary he was up against. Minutes passed in silence. The row of fiery eyes glowered at him from a distance. He stood still, but his feet were going numb.

Old tried to shift his weight quietly but his bag knocked against the vent wall. There was a metallic noise. A flurry of movement and like a storm they came for him. An army of hungry rats.

He kicked at the bloodthirsty beasts careful not to make too much noise — if the map was right he should be above the northern end of the platform by now. Some slunk back into the darkness, others sneaked past him while the brave ones jumped and began climbing up his legs. Old chopped at them with his bare hands while making a low growling noise hoping this would scare them away.

A large animal scurried up his trunk and sunk its teeth in his back. He grimaced in pain and tore off the creature from his flesh, bashing it on the floor. For several minutes he fought the beasts till finally he managed to shake them off. The few that remained scampered back into the darkness.

But he had made a lot of noise. As he resumed his slow progress through the air shaft, he patted himself to check for injuries. He had been bitten several times. His fingers were sticky with blood. There was something else he realised right then which, despite the risk, made him switch on the flashlight.

Any predictions?

P.I.
Kar's Korean
Adventure

1

A dusty edition of the Bengali daily *Anandabazar Patrika* was spread out over the secretary table covering every inch of space. A table calendar, a rusty hand-wound clock and several books, among which was *The Rise and Fall of the Roman Empire*, were stacked on an empty chair facing the table to make way for a couple of ceramic plates and tumblers, wooden spatulas, eye droppers and a hair brush with an oozy green paste dripping a pungent liquid. Detective Kar stirred the paste in one of those plates with the handle of an old paintbrush till it was of uniform consistency. Using a spatula he transferred an amount to the hairbrush and began carefully applying it along his receding hairline. He studied the effect in the mirror in front of him. His mouth twisted with displeasure.

The alopecia had begun to trouble him lately. He had always been proud of his raven black mane. When he was still working for the Party, the elderly comrades would look sidewise at his thick mop of hair, allegedly styled like a movie star, and warning him would say, 'Bourgeoisie habits will get you in trouble'. He didn't pay heed to their threats and then he had turned into a private eye, with his hair intact. But over the last few months it had begun to disappear. Almost imperceptibly in the beginning but faster more recently. He had tried various unguents advertised by quacks, experimented with hair fall creams and beleric myrobalan, visited an allopathic physician, switched over to homoeopathy for a while, yet his hairline seemed to be receding every day. Soon half of his head would be bare and he dreaded looking at himself in the mirror when that happened. Lately he had discovered Chinese medicine at one of the cubbyhole chambers off Tiretta bazaar, run by a bald-headed doctor who spoke little. For the last few days he had been trying his new treatment. He was not sure whether it was working. It better did for he had spent a good sum buying the green paste-like substance from this man. Meanwhile the doorbell had rung twice but he was too engrossed in the application of the remedy which came with the guarantee of total hair coverage with six months of use.

The calling bell rang shrilly for a third time and Kar looked up from the mirror, his face screwed, his small piercing eyes blood red from lack of sleep. 'Has this city run out of private eyes?' he muttered, looking in the direction of the only other man in the room who was immersed in a film magazine. He signalled him to open the door. Chaitanya, his assistant, rose from his seat. Taking a good look through the magic eye, he unbolted the door.

There was an elderly couple outside — hesitating, not sure whether they should step in. Chaitanya ushered them in and, leaving them stranded near the chairs opposite the secretary table, went back to his corner table. Kar made no point to clear the table with the oozy dark substance splattered all over the newspaper. He kept sitting, the spatula in his right hand, staring blankly at the visitors. After three sleepless nights tailing a dangerous character in the alleys of Calcutta, Kar was so tired he could drop dead. He had been thinking of slipping out for an early afternoon drink at the Chhota Bristol but this sudden stream of visitors and the necessity to apply the hair formulation twice a day had kept him in office. And somehow they all had come with the same problem.

The couple hesitated for a few moments before taking their seats. Kar wiped his hands with a dirty handkerchief and with an apathy mixed voice asked, 'So who went missing?'

The elderly gentleman turned to look at his wife. She was staring at the detective and was about to say something when Kar said — 'I am guessing; is it a missing person?'

The man now nodded and began to speak slowly, 'I am a retired army officer, this is my wife. Our daughter went abroad for holiday and hasn't come back.'

'Looks like the same set of people — was it Korea?' Kar asked while foraging in the ashtray for cigarette stubs. He found one and stuck it into his face. He struck a match, the half burnt stub glowed and the room filled up with the acrid smell of cheap tobacco.

'Daughter, did you say?'

The father nodded, 'She just passed out of university and ...'

'Boyfriend *er songe paliyechhe* — must have run away with a lover. Women just out of college have the tendency to fall for one jerk or another,' Kar said nonchalantly and stubbed out the cigarette while digging for another in the ash heap.

His assistant tried to follow the conversation for a while, lost interest and went out of the front door.

The visitor taken aback by the detective's rudeness said, 'We have filed a police complaint and they have been saying the same thing. But we don't think so. We know our daughter. She wouldn't do something that would hurt us.' The old man hesitated, 'I see you talk like the police. So what was the use of coming here?' He turned his head slowly to look at his wife.

Right then a very thin man in a chequered lungi and shirt appeared hobbling through the door which had been left open. He was coming straight into the office and, seeing him, Kar sent him off to get tea for the visitors.

The elderly couple had by then recovered from the initial shock and were staring at the plates and tumblers on the table. It took them a while to take it in before they told him what had happened. As it turned out, their story was almost the same as the one Kar had been listening to since morning. Their daughter Bidisha had gone on a trip to east Asia, arranged by a local travel agency, and had not returned. The dates matched, and it was the same agency named by each of the people who had come to him for help. Kar was wondering how they all ended up at his office as he heard the elderly gentleman tell his story. It must have been his success with that bizarre kidnapping case which was widely publicised.

'Bidisha had just finished her postgraduation and we had planned a family trip. But my wife fell and injured herself. Then she had an arthritis attack and we had to keep postponing the trip till last month when we told her she could go on her own if she was keen. My wife had objections but I felt my girl was old enough to take care of herself,' he said and tried to sit straight but hunched up soon. His face was lined with worries and he kept looking at the detective, searching for something that will give him an iota of hope, while he told his story.

'You should have heeded her advice,' Kar butted in. He was in a foul mood having been stopped midway while applying the hair growth formula. Besides he couldn't figure out how his two-man agency could investigate a case which seemed to have unfolded on an international scale. Yet he heard him out.

'So my daughter left at the beginning of July with a tour group organised by this travel agency.'

'Lamplighter Travels?'

'You know them already?' the man said and perhaps his secret expectation that detective Kar would find his daughter increased.

But knowing the name of the agency was no big deal. That same day two other persons had reported about someone they knew, going on a holiday trip abroad and not coming back. This could have meant several things but all these people were almost surely travelling in the same group: By tallying the dates and the travel schedule Kar became certain that the three complainants had relatives or friends who had travelled to Korea with this travel agency. Not only that, now it seemed they had travelled the same day and in the same group.

'News of accidents?' he asked the gentleman.

'Wouldn't the police know that? We have registered a complaint against the travel agency but I have a feeling the cops would not be able to crack it. Now that relatives of the other missing persons have come to you, I am hoping things would move faster. But please be discreet. You know, my daughter is young and we can do without any adverse publicity,' the army man said and the skin of his face began to turn pale as he sunk slowly into his private sorrow.

A dim incandescent bulb hung from the ceiling adding to the gloom of this old house on Crooked Lane. The windows of the room were shuttered and the acrid smoke from a burning cigarette stub assaulted everyone before making its way through the door and down the stairs.

Now the lungi-clad man appeared with an aluminium kettle, three small cups and Thin Arrowroot biscuits on a plate. Kar took a sip and asked in a cop voice, 'You say your daughter was supposed to return on the fourteenth of July. This is the fourth of August. What were you doing all this while?'

'First we waited, thinking they may have just postponed their return by a few days. But there was no phone call, no email. We couldn't get in touch with her, hard as we tried. We spoke to the travel agency but they said they were also unable to contact their tour manager. The only news we received was that they had arrived in Korea a couple of days ago, and then suddenly all communication had stopped.'

'Then what?'

'We consulted friends and family, got in touch with expats living in Korea. But everything drew a blank. Confusing reports. We heard they were last seen in Jeju. Others said they had gone trekking in the mountains in the eastern part of the country. We waited for a few more days and then went to the police.'

'But still, this is too long to wait. When did you go to the police?'

'End of July.'

'And your daughter was supposed to return in the middle of July, you said.'

The old man fumbled a bit and nodded. 'I should have come to you earlier. The police doesn't seem to care.'

'The local police can't do much. But they must have moved through the home and foreign departments. I can try to look for your daughter but this is going to be expensive.'

They kept quiet, listening carefully to what Kar had to say.

'I can't guarantee that the media won't come sniffing but I will be discreet. This is big news. Strange, it is still not in the papers. Maybe there is someone powerful stopping it from leaking,' Kar said and began to think quickly. Was the travel agency involved or someone connected to the travellers? As far as he knew South Korea didn't have high levels of crime. While organised crime does exist they wouldn't target tourists just like that.

After the couple had left, Kar finished applying the green paste — covering the bald patches and massaging the leftover in his hair. He made a note of the names of the three new clients. At the top of the list was Mr Singh whose brother had disappeared. Next, this woman Sujata. She was looking for her ex-husband, a bank manager — Ujaan Banerjee. What was her interest Kar hadn't been able to figure out. If they had divorced recently, what is this sudden need to seek him out again? He would have to find that out.

Finally this elderly couple had come to report their missing daughter, Bidisha. Beside each client's name he scribbled a few comments — sketchy thoughts and preliminary observations. Kar counted the money these new clients had paid and put the cash away in the locker. He put the cheques away in a drawer. So far, so good. Chaitanya was still not back. These days he had struck up a friendship with one of those pot addicts who hung around in Waterloo street nearby and was often stoned himself. Kar had warned him several times but his assistant had laughed it away.

2

Early evening. The day had been wasted. There was no real progress with the case and two weeks had skittered away while they did background checks of the missing persons. The lady who had reported her divorced husband was clean, there was nothing in the records. Kar had consulted his old buddy Abul who was a senior officer in the I.B. and they had not hit upon anything worth pursuing. 'Our agencies have been looking into this for some time now,' Abul had said, 'if I hear anything I will pass it on, but be careful how you move with this, bro. If anything goes wrong and our spooks come to know I have been sharing information with a P.I. they will fry my ass in a slow cooker.'

Kar and Chaitanya were sitting glum faced in the office staring at a package that had just been delivered by Rampyari who was a cobbler but ran errands for them. The package contained a simple disguise of a Sikh, complete with black turban and flowing beard which Rampyari had bought from the theatre district. But he had been away the whole day buying the disguise from Chitpore and now it was too late to put it to use.

'Do you think you can hang this stuff on your mug and pay a visit to Lamplighter before they close for the day?'

'I can try, but in this rush hour it is doubtful,' Chaitanya said.

'This was your idea. I don't see the need for a disguise for hitting that joint. You can pretend to be an interested client,' Kar said.

'Just in case I have to visit again. I thought it's best to pretend to be someone else, don't you think so?'

Kar didn't respond and began to leaf through old files piled on the table. For some reason they were not getting as many snooping and tailing cases as they used to get before. Suspicious spouses and paramours helped them pay the bills but nowadays that business seemed to be on a downswing. With sophisticated phone-tapping applications available online and the cheap micro cameras flooding the market, people must be managing on their own he thought and sighed. Soon some smartass will write an article in the newspaper — 'Hi-tech Hits the Gumshoe'.

Over and above this he had been spending a fortune trying to save his disappearing hair. 'How long can a decent guy go on like this,' he often told himself. The bills for his extracts, ointments and hair growth tablets were eating up a chunk of his earnings and he dreaded the day he wouldn't be able to afford it any more. He didn't trust wigs except when these were necessary for an assignment. 'I don't know how to face the world when it's all gone,' he would lament, before Chaitanya offering a mischievous grin would say, 'Still a long way to go.'

Chaitanya gummed on the fake beard and adjusted the turban in the bathroom mirror. He changed into a formal dress, put on a pair of contacts and hurried out of the office.

From Crooked Lane he went into Dacres and, negotiating the evening crowds, managed to hail a yellow cab near the mosque. When the cabbie dropped him a hundred metres or so from the Bhowanipore office of Lamplighter Travels it was well past eight.

He paid the fare and crossed the road that lead to Padmapukur and stood under the portico of an old building planning out his moves. He could see the travel agent's office from there. The office had a frosted glass door with an etched globe through which a faint blue light filtered out onto the street. A uniformed guard stood outside the entrance speaking on a mobile phone.

His polished leather holster shone in the street light, the metal butt of his gun attached to his belt with a chain. He didn't pay any attention to Chaitanya as he pushed through the door.

There was no one at the reception but the connecting door beside the receptionist's table was open so he walked in. He was in a largish hall with several counters and cubicles with flat panel monitors and stacks of files on the tables and lots of notices on soft boards but there was no one here too. On the walls were posters of European and Far East destinations, mostly pictures of sea beaches, bikini-clad women wearing sunhats, ornate architecture and cable car rides. On every poster the Lamplighter slogan 'Travel That Changes Lives' was printed in bold type alongside the company logo — an earthen lamp in the middle of a stone ring. The hall was silent and empty. At the other end of the hall he could see a cubicle with another glass door and, thinking this would be the manager's office, he went up and knocked.

There was no answer. So he pushed through the door and walked in to find a small cabin with a table, a few chairs and a cushioned armchair. The chairs were empty. The computer was switched on which meant the manager, wherever he had gone, would return. Then he heard the sound of running water through another door. Someone, most probably the manager, was in the loo.

The table was glass topped and quite tidy with a few files neatly arranged at one end, a Viennese snow globe and some models of airplanes with names of airline companies. Chaitanya quickly went around the table and opened the topmost file. Mostly memos of hotel bookings. In the next file were bills. In another, invitation letters from organisers of various travel and tourism fairs, news clips of advertisements, a few letters. He was not looking for anything specific but any information about the bookings for the far east tour circuit from where these people had disappeared would help.

Chaitanya could still hear the water running in the attached toilet and he knew he was safe as long as he could hear it. Making as little noise as possible he pulled open the top drawer of the table. Nothing. Some brochures of Lamplighter Travels and stationery. The second drawer was heavy but this was also packed with tariff charts of hotels, visiting card files and stationery. In the bottom drawer there was a single file marked 'East Asia — July' and he quickly pulled it out and began to turn the pages. All the names of the people who had gone to Korea on the east Asia trip, photocopies of passports, the travel itinerary, printouts of emails, everything was there. He took out a small pocket camera and was going to take photos of the documents when the guard suddenly walked in and shouted at him. The sound of running water in the toilet stopped.

The guard charged towards him. Chaitanya dropped the file on the table and was about to say something when the guard came up and grabbed him from behind. He held him in a side headlock that almost choked the air to his windpipe.

'What are you doing here?' the man growled.

Desperately trying to release the stranglehold by pulling at his wrist, Chaitanya hissed, 'You will get into big trouble if you don't let me go. The police will be here any moment.'

That shook the poor fellow and he somewhat loosened his hold. In that split-second advantage, Chaitanya moved back a step and tangled his right foot with that of his adversary and thrusting his hips back, threw him over his shoulder right in front of the toilet door from which the manager emerged and froze. Though the security guard was strong and well built he hadn't reckoned dealing with a triple dan judoka at end of day in the office of a Calcutta travel agency. The ethereal beauty of the perfectly executed *hane goshi* throw immobilised him completely, and he lay on the ground squirming, staring at this Sikh man who had burst in like a storm.

'Who are you?' shouted the manager, his hands still dripping wet as he dug into his trouser pocket to get his mobile phone.

'It will be foolish to call for help. I am a private investigator and if you don't want news about the missing tourists splashed across the headlines, then better cooperate with me,' Chaitanya said coldly as he kept a watch on the security guard still squirming near his feet.

The manager made a face which seemed to say that he had just heard his funeral announced but still had a store of courage handy, 'I don't believe you and am going to call the cops in any case.'

Chaitanya now flashed his ID and slightly lowering his voice to sound reasonable said, 'You know as I do that the news of Indian tourists vanishing in Korea won't be good for your business. We have already received a couple of complaints and I know the police are investigating. This is for your own good. We may even help you to hush this up if we find you are not into any shady business that is.'

'What do you want?'

'Information. Tell me everything you know, but before that ask this pet snake of yours to get out of here and not show his stupid mug till we are done,' and he kicked the guard on the side and the man rolled over groaning.

The manager signalled to the guard while Chaitanya removed the gun from his holster and kept it in his pocket. 'Armed guards, eh? Is this a travel agency or a jewellery store?'

'Err, we have a forex business and so ...' the manager said.

The guard left silently. The manager went to his seat and Chaitanya, keeping the gun on his lap, sat facing him across the table. The manager was a thinly built man who loved expensive clothes. Chaitanya placed him in his early thirties.

'We have been in this business for two generations,' he started by saying.

As he began to speak Chaitanya switched on the voice recorder in his pocket, just in case he missed out any details.

'What happened this time?' Chaitanya began in an icy nonchalant cop voice. As he asked this question Chaitanya noticed a momentary flicker of nervousness in the manager's eye.

'We had a tour group going to Cambodia, Vietnam, Japan and Korea but Japan had to be dropped at the last moment,' his voice was quivering with apprehension.

'How many were there in the group?'

'Thirteen, including our tour manager. But as I said the itinerary in Japan had to be cancelled because of the earthquake. So we doubled the time in Korea and offered them some free destinations.'

'And then you lost everybody? All of them vanished into thin air? What happened to your tour manager? Didn't he report back?'

'He sends emails on a day-to-day basis and sometimes we are in touch more than once a day. If there is any change in itinerary or a problem with the scheduling crops up, he will inform us and if necessary discuss how to solve it. But this time ...'

'What happened this time? How long has he been working here?'

He is with us from my father's time — that would be more than a decade. We hardly have had any problems with him but this time, all of a sudden, he stopped communicating. We couldn't get through to his number!'

'I need the full names and details of everyone in the tour group. As for your manager, you have to tell me more about him. Don't withhold information. We will do our best to find these people and work with the police. If you cooperate you will be all right and your business won't get a bad name,' Chaitanya said but he was not sure how he could keep his promise. It seemed that the police already knew but for some reason had kept quiet. Perhaps because this was a sensitive matter involving two countries.

The manager picked up the Far East file which was lying on the desk and handed it over to him. Chaitanya took photos of the relevant pages, 'Now your tour manager. What's his name? Where does he live?'

'Bikas Roy. He is forty-three, lives in Tollygunj.'

'Any problems in the past? Who are his friends?'

'He is quite a diligent worker. Comes from a good background, has been with the company for long. Lives with his wife, who works for a beauty parlour, and a college-going son. Bikas babu loves to travel and prefers going on these tours rather than sitting at office doing desk jobs. Don't know much about his friends except one. A writer, I forget his name. The two go on trips together and once he went away without asking for leave and returned a month later.'

'Where to?'

'He didn't tell us but we found out he had gone to the Himalayas ...'

'Okay, give me Bikas Roy's address.'

The manager took it down from the employee's file and handed him a chit of paper.

As Chaitanya was about to leave, the manager rose from his seat and said slowly, 'Please keep all this to yourself, Sir. We are in deep trouble and if the media gets a scent of this we are done for.'

'We will do our best, assuming you are in no way involved,' Chaitanya walked up to the smoked glass door and pushed it open. The hall outside with the computers and cubicles was dark.

'Sir, one last thing. If you don't mind, can your agency help us find the tour manager? I know he is under suspicion but he is an asset for the company. We need to know what happened. Perhaps there was an accident in a remote area. We are ready to bear the expenses if that protects our goodwill.'

Chaitanya handed him the agency card, 'Come to our office and we will sort this out. We don't come cheap and my boss likes to see the good guys win. So don't think you can get away with murder.'

He left. After he was gone, the manager looked around his office. At the files on the shelves and the posters on the walls. His gaze moved down to the empty space on the floor where the guard lay squirming a few minutes back. He looked up and kept staring at the pictures of faraway places for a while and then, burying his face in both hands, burst into tears.

3

It was late evening when Chaitanya returned to their first-floor office on Crooked Lane. He quickly briefed Kar about his interview with the manager of Lamplighter Travels and whatever had happened there. Hearing about the fight with the guard, Kar furrowed his eyebrows, 'I don't like violence, you know that?' Completely ignoring this Chaitanya continued with the debriefing. He gave him the camera with the copies of the documents he had made at the office and went to the back room.

Kar downloaded the photos on the aging PC and examined each document carefully. He was mumbling something while clicking from picture to picture.

Chaitanya took some time to remove his disguise and take a shower. When he entered the office Kar was already among his cups. A pint of rum and a half-filled glass was standing on the secretary table that faced the entrance to the office. He had lately taken to drinking Bull XXX which he said reminded him of his first case. He was scribbling notes and seemed to be engrossed in thoughts.

Because of a diabetes scare, Chaitanya had been keeping clear of the dark rum and had bought his bottle of Director's Special Black on his way back. He poured a little whisky in a small tumbler and drank it slowly as he told Kar about the events of the evening. This time with more detail.

Kar nodded absent-mindedly when Chaitanya said that the manager had expressed his wish to hire them to find out what had happened to their tour manager Bikas Roy.

'We will get hired and extract as much from them as we can. This case is getting big. Looks like I will have to travel to South Korea to get to the bottom of it.'

Chaitanya gave a toothy smile, sipped the grain whisky and said, 'Good for you, dada, you haven't had a holiday in years.'

Kar looked irritated and screwed his face. 'I don't see how this will be a holiday for me. As it appears this matter is more convoluted then I could have imagined. I told you that one of the missing people has returned. I got a report from Abul in the intelligence branch. They can't make head or tail of it and no clues have emerged. It seems the tourist who has returned has gone off her rocker,' he said mirthlessly.

'Insane?' Chaitanya wore a befuddled look.

'Yes, I might get to interview her soon. Think we have done enough for today and congratulations for getting the manager to sing. We will need all the information we can get before heading for Seoul. I say this rum doesn't taste so good today. Let's get out of this hole and grab a drink.'

Chaitanya quickly put his bottle away and went to the back room to wash his glass.

Just as they were heading out, the office phone began to ring shrilly. Kar took the call. He spoke for a few minutes while Chaitanya polished his shoes with Kiwi polish, oiled his thick hair and brushed it back carefully. Kar enviously eyed his assistant's lustrous hair while speaking on the phone.

'There is some news to chew upon,' he told him as they headed out. 'The woman who came back. She arrived in a flight from Bangkok and has been acting funny perhaps feigning amnesia. We have to pay her a visit, sooner the better.'

'We can go tomorrow,' Chaitanya said.

'Yes, even if the world falls apart, we shouldn't miss our drink. Who knows, whether we will be around for the next,' Kar said.

They trotted over to Chhota Bristol which was crowded at this time of the evening but luckily they found a seat at one of the marble-topped tables near the middle. It was an old downmarket boozer where you shared tables with regulars and one of Kar's favourite watering holes in that part of town. 'Out of seventeen pulse points that this city has, this one is easiest to check,' he loved to say. It was rum again for Kar, this time Old Monk, and the same whisky for Chaitanya.

Kar paid for the first round and ordered some cheese cubes and a plate of fish fries which was not too bad for the price. Chaitanya drizzled the fries with salt and sipped his whisky while Kar took thin slices of the Amul cheese and transferred them to his mouth, one at a time, relishing the flavour then washing it down with the dark rum that burned its way down his throat. Chaitanya took a bite of fish fry and asked, 'So what's the name again of the woman who returned?'

'Tara.'

'*Tara! Joy Tara!*' Chaitanya cried out, the drink having gone straight to his head. Customers at nearby tables looked up, murmured disapproval, before returning to their paper plates of roasted peanuts. Kar grimaced.

'As I was telling you, Tara, we don't know her surname yet, claims to have been travelling alone. But the travel agent's records say she had booked with Harvinder Singh — the guy whose brother had reported him missing. Looks like Harvinder's brother is in the dark about this woman. Otherwise he would have told us or maybe not.'

Chaitanya nodded thoughtfully. 'She must have told the investigation team what had happened to the others?'

'Nope. They can't get anything from her. She doesn't seem to be in her senses, though she has been talking a lot. All gibberish, I am told,' Kar hailed the waiter for another round and put the money in his hand.

The patrons got more drunk with each passing minute and a jockey sitting at the next table began to warn everyone about the dangers of betting on horses. 'This guy, he owned three Mercs man and now you see him, begging near the Indian museum,' he went over and over again. His friend, an elderly musician, tried to tone him down saying that the world was not interested to know about the pitfalls of gambling while another man at that table began to lament about the deteriorating quality of modern Bengali songs and how the music of yesteryears could make one cry. This last one began to hum a tune.

The waiters puffed and panted shuttling from bar to table and back. They cleared the tables listlessly, stacking one empty glass upon another till they seemed to be moving about with glass towers in their hands. The manager grew busy checking the freshness of the marigold garlands that had been offered to Goddess Kali on the wall behind the bar, while at another table near them a grandpa went on explaining to his shifty-eyed grandson the advantages of dark spirits over white — 'You won't fall asleep with your woman,' he kept repeating.

'Something funny came up when I was going through the old files. The photo of Singh that his brother gave us — somehow he looked familiar. So I checked old files. A few years ago this woman had come to our office requesting us to tail a Sikh guy. He is our man. You remember? The bar owner from Bhowanipore?'

'Ah yes, of course!'

'So this is the same Harvinder who has now disappeared with this group in Korea but somehow his partner — this woman, Tara — has been able to return. I can't guess how this could be connected to his personal life and why this whole bunch of people would vanish with him and Tara. We don't know whether he is still married to his wife or how this piece of information can help our investigations but we can't ignore anything. Also we have to dig into the tour manager's background. He looks more interesting to me,' Kar said, carefully transferring bite-sized cheese slices to his mouth.

Chaitanya gave one of his toothy smiles and adjusted his glasses.

'One last round and tomorrow we will meet this woman. Abul says he can arrange a meeting. The I.B. as well as the external agencies want to get to the bottom of this. But we won't mention anything to Harvinder's brother at this time. Let this ripen a bit, we can buy time with our clients.'

They left after two more rounds and went tottering through the gully beside Metro cinema which was still buzzing with hawkers selling shoes and cheap Chinese electronics.

As they came out on Chowringhee, Kar asked his assistant, 'Talking of Korea, can you tell me what other than Buddhism the Koreans should be grateful to us for?'

Chaitanya shrugged, 'Submarines maybe.'

'Nah. Melons.'

'What?'

'All of Korea adores melons. There is evidence to prove that the fruit is originally native to this country.'

They laughed. Chaitanya hopped into a share taxi packed with loud drunks fighting over seats while Kar lit a cigarette, turned right, and began walking towards Lenin street, drunk as a lord.

It was raining in torrents since early in the morning. Chaitanya had arrived at the office before the rush hour began. Kar was scouring the newspapers for news about the tourists and Rampyari had just cleared the teacups when the manager of Lamplighter Travels had paid them a visit. Kar had extracted a hefty advance from him and the promise to pay for his trip in case he had to visit Korea to get to the bottom of this matter.

The manager was still shaky from last night's ordeal. He eyed Chaitanya with apprehension, perhaps noting some resemblance with the turbaned intruder who had thrown his burly guard like a pack of sticks on the floor. The police had been calling him day and night and he had had already faced several rounds of interrogation.

'They are threatening to seal off my office any day if I don't cooperate. But believe me, I know nothing beyond what I have already told you, Sir. The client parties are getting aggressive. Can you please do something quickly.'

Kar had tried to reassure him. 'Don't hide anything from the cops and keep us updated from your end. I can't do anything about the police harassment but I will talk with higher ups. Meanwhile we will get on with the investigation.'

'Hope I can get something out of her,' Kar told Chaitanya before leaving office. He took a taxi to Kalighat where Tara was temporarily living with a friend. Abul had called to say that she had refused to meet the psychiatrist this morning.

'Don't get your hopes too high,' he advised Kar with a wide grin while introducing him to the police investigating officer in charge of the case and a lady officer accompanying him. The I.O. and his female colleague were in plain clothes.

They rung the bell and after a while a middle-aged lady emerged and, recognising the I.O., quietly ushered them into a sitting room. 'Please wait,' she said and went inside.

It was a small room with a threadbare sofa, a low table and a couple of chairs. A window looked out on the street with a row of one-storey houses which hadn't been painted in a long while. The rain outside was heavy and through the window Kar could see little children playing, floating paper boats in the flooded street.

In a while the woman returned and called them inside to another room with a painted steel almirah against the wall, a bed, a moulded plastic table and a canvas easy chair on which sat a woman in her early thirties.

She had a wheatish complexion and a softly modelled face with limpid brown eyes and she stared at them curiously without saying anything. Her long hair was open, almost touching the ground. They got the chairs from the next room and Kar and the others took their seats. She was wearing a grey loose garment with many folds that could be passed off for a monk's habit but was actually an ill-fitting night dress. She was dribbling at the mouth.

The lady officer introduced detective Kar and Abul, reassuring her that they wouldn't take long and were there to help. Tara kept staring at them with no acknowledgement, staring at them as if they were transparent, as she kept looking at the patterns of grime on the wall behind them.

Kar cleared his throat and began in a gentle tone, 'I am a private detective. I don't want to disturb you. But we need your help.'

No answer. Her friend came into the room and kept a pot of tea and some cups on the table and went away.

'He wants to know what happened to you in Korea,' the lady officer added helpfully.

Tara's eyes twitched and she broke into a smile that was quite bereft of meaning and was just pure mirth. Her lips seemed to move but she had difficulty forming the words, '*Annyeonghaseyo,*' she said softly.

Abul and the police officers exchanged glances.

'*Annyeonghaseyo,*' Kar greeted her back. 'I am a friend and want to help. Did you get lost in Korea?'

'We together,' she said and put her arms on the armrests and stared back with no expression. Kar studied her face for signs of stress. Her arms were resting lightly on the wooden armrests. There was no sign of tension in her hands.

'I am listening to you. I know all of you went together. How did you come back?' Kar tried a different tack this time and waited for an answer.

The answers came slowly and in spurts but the words were not always well formed and they had to strain to make sense of whatever little she was telling them.

'F ... Forest. Lost in the forest,' she said.

'And then?'

'Next storm coming o me shelter beside big rock.'

Kar nodded slowly without changing his expression.

'It was night o and voices in the forest take me to river. River is there. I sit by river till the storm die o night die with storm.'

They were all listening attentively.

'Then what happened?' Kar said in an assuring friendly tone.

'I wake up o begin to walk. I follow the river,' she went on.

'And then, how did you find your way to the campers who drove you to the city?'

They could see she was trying hard to remember and the effort showed on her face. Her eyebrows furrowed. She looked at them as if they knew the answer and could help.

'You walked all day and found the campers, didn't you?' Kar asked.

She slowly moved her head from side to side. 'Fire by the water,' she said suddenly and pressed her temples.

The police had been briefed by their Korean counterparts. Some hikers who had been out camping had found her one evening in a forested area near the coast. She was quite distraught and running a fever. They had driven her to a doctor in the nearby town and contacted a police station. Luckily she had an ID so the Koreans could get in touch with her friends in India. Afterwards the police had gone looking in the forest for the other tourists but returned empty handed.

Because she hardly spoke, no one could be certain how she ended up where she was found. The lost tourists could have been somewhere nearby or she could have just walked for many hours and reached the area where the hikers found her. She still had some money on her person so theoretically she could have taken a bus and travelled from one place to another. The police, while trying to locate the tourists, had mapped all possible routes she could have taken but till then had not chanced upon anything significant.

There was silence in the room.

'Who was your guide? How did you go to the forest?' Kar asked.

But she couldn't say anything.

'Do you remember Bikas Roy, the travel agency manager who was accompanying your group?'

She nodded slowly.

'Bikas Roy. He was your guide, wasn't he? Was he always with your group?'

She tried to say something but could not find the words.

'Please try to remember. We need to find your friends.'

Nothing.

'Where are the others? Are they in a forest? Is Bikas Roy with them?'

She moved her head from side to side. It seemed she didn't remember anything but the effort to recollect brought tears to her eyes.

'When did you go to Korea?' Kar asked this time.

When she couldn't reply Kar said, 'You went to Korea in July, beginning of July. Do you remember?'

'I didn't go to Korea. I was there o with many friends,' she said and mumbled something which they couldn't understand.

This was going to be difficult.

'Have you been to Seoul? Seoul — the capital of Korea. Did any new friend join you there?' Kar asked.

She smiled and moved her head from side to side to say no.

'Okay. You didn't go to Seoul. But can you tell me how many of you went into the forest and if someone new joined you there?' Kar asked.

She began to count with her fingers. Stopped midway and started again. No figure could be arrived at but from her counting it seemed there were at least five of them if not more.

'Okay, we will leave you now. If you want to tell us more, please ask your friend to get in touch with me,' Kar said and folded his hands in a parting namaskar. They had a few words with the friend who was waiting in the next room and then left the apartment.

Kar had wanted to ask her more questions, among other things about her relationship with Harvinder Singh, but he didn't find her in a state to press her any further. On their way out of the building Kar asked the investigating officer whether an appraisal of her condition has been done.

'Her health is being monitored and a psychiatrist is working with her but it is still early days. The shrink says there is some sort of runaway amnesia that he hasn't seen before but he wouldn't go beyond that. Tells us, he needs time to run tests. From the medical appraisal we know there is no trauma, no signs of any physical assault. As you have noticed, her language skills have deteriorated considerably,' the lady officer said.

'How long has this group been missing,' Kar asked as he lit a cigarette.

'A month, roughly.'

'Do you have the name of the place where the campers found her? Also the contact details of the investigating officer in Korea? I will need more than the usual help from you for this one,' Kar told Abul.

'Sure mate. So long as you are ready to share the honour with our agencies when this is cracked,' Abul said, looking up and down the waterlogged street for the duty car.

'The police there has been very cooperative but they couldn't come up with anything. Then there is protocol but our embassy is doing its best. Sitting here we can do very little other than look for clues in what she says,' the I.O. said.

'What about the travel agency? Are they clean? Anything wrong there?' Kar asked.

'The manager has been interrogated several times. We have gone through their files, interviewed some customers. Just another decent business — cooking their books and cheating the government of tax money. Nothing that smells rotten, really,' the I.O. cracked his lips in a grin.

'We have a complete list of all the places that this group were supposed to visit, don't we?'

'Yes and we passed on that information to our counterparts through our embassy. They have been checking everywhere. No solid clue has emerged. Unless the tour group deviated from their fixed itinerary or something had happened on the way,' the officer said.

'Which means the tour manager Bikas Roy could have been up to something,' Kar said.

'Perhaps. He is not above suspicion but he has also disappeared. It doesn't make sense.'

The rain was incessant and the entrance passage to the building was getting flooded. They plodded through the water to reach their cars. 'The driver will drop you at Esplanade,' Abul told Kar. They climbed into the car. The police officers left in a jeep.

As they made their way towards the Intelligence Bureau office, both of them fell quiet. When the car was dropping off Abul at the Lord Sinha road office Kar asked, 'Can you please see to it that our people there are ready to help me if I need any support. Also I will need the name and contacts of the Korean investigating officer who is handling this, the name of the place where they found her, a short report of the investigations they have done, and anything else you might have.'

'Can't promise you about *our people* but I will talk with someone. The Korean officer's details, a contact in South Korean immigration and all that, you will get. Right away I can give you the name of the area the campers found her. It's a forest stretch next to a coastal town near the East Sea. Gangneung is the name of the town and this forest has a difficult name but I have heard it so many times now, it got stuck here,' Abul said pointing to his head, 'D-a-e-g-w-a-l-l-y-e-o-n-g'.

'Oh! That's quite a mouthful, but I will work on it,' Kar said as he bade his friend goodbye.

'Let me know before you take off. You have to get something for me. I hear the red chilli powder there is good enough to tame a tigress,' Abul winked.

'I will remember that,' Kar said grinning.

4

The first thing that Kar did after arriving in Seoul was to get hammered. He had always believed that a good dose of alcohol at the beginning of a case gets his brain cells ticking right away. After checking in at the Utopia hotel arranged for him by the manager of Lamplighter Travels, he had showered, made some phone calls and opened the bottle of soju that he found in the minibar. His room had a king-size bed, huge mirrors on the ceiling and garish patterned wallpaper which made him wonder why he was there. When the soju was finished, he had shaved and applied the green hair loss prevention extract bought from the Chinese doctor in Calcutta. He wouldn't take risks with the quality of water in a foreign country and made it a point to use the formulation at least once a day to counter adverse effects of water and the change in diet. Later he went over to a convenience store to pick up a few more bottles of the rice spirit and a fat bulgogi burger from McDonald's. He had kept the green bottle on the nightstand, switched on the TV and was drinking from a paper cup. The marinated beef burger was tasty and from time to time he was popping generously salted fries into his mouth.

A K-pop band was belting out an energetic number and he ogled the lead singer. She had bronzed hair and was wearing a colourful top over skinny jeans and red shoes. Kar felt he had been wasting his life chasing weirdos, missing all the fun. He decided he would fire Chaitanya on his return to India and get someone like her to help him with his cases. With a woman around, he reasoned, cracking cases would be a cinch. Now only if his Chinese medicine man could fix his hair loss problem.

The bulgogi burger vanished in a few minutes and with it the packet of fries. He rung up room service for more grub. It was bulgogi again, some grilled mackerel, sticky brown rice, a bowl of seaweed soup and, of course, the crunchy tangy flavoured kimchi with seasoned vegetables sides. He dug in with his hands and polished off his plate, washing it all down with more soju.

He washed his hands and put the plates and bowls away. The paper cup was still on the nightstand. He poured some more soju and slid his legs under the duvet. There was news of a terror attack in Africa, and closer to where he was a factory on the border of the two Koreas had been reopened.

He emptied the cup slowly watching pretty Korean women and handsome young men singing to ecstatic crowds. Abul through his MEA contact had introduced him to an officer in the Indian Embassy in Seoul. This guy had promised to meet him when he arrived. He should have called him and arranged a meeting for the next day but he had decided to do some work on his own. It was not a very good idea to be operating in a foreign country without informing the official channels but it could also give him some flexibility.

Kar took a swig from the bottle and thought about his interview with Tara. There has to be some reason for the changes that have affected her. The difficulties with language and the runaway amnesia — were the others also suffering from a similar condition? Perhaps this had prevented them from making contact with anyone and seeking help. But then how could all these people bloody vanish from the radar.

The last update he had received before taking the plane said the tour group had visited all the places that was on their itinerary except Seorak mountains. This was to be their final stop but the tour manager had cancelled the bookings for this destination on the night before they were supposed to arrive.

This could mean several things. Bikas Roy could have been instructed to change the last stop in the itinerary. But the manager of Lamplighter Travels said they never do this except in extraordinary circumstances. Could it be, someone else influenced him?

The Korean girl band was going full steam as the crowds went berserk listening to the infectious beat. Kar's head swam as he tried to reason what could have propelled the tour manager to change the itinerary. Why didn't he inform his office and what happened to his goddamn mobile phone? There have been no reports of accidents so that could be ruled out.

He didn't know when he had fallen asleep. There was a loud knock on the door. He sprung up from bed. The hotel phone was blinking with missed call alerts. Through the peephole he could see a man with a chiselled jaw line and a tangle of hair. 'Who is it?' he asked.

'This is Kim,' said someone in a low cop voice.

Kar opened the door slightly keeping his weight against it and peeped into the corridor. 'Youngjin Kim, NIS,' the stranger hissed through the crack of the door.

'Oh come in. I thought we were meeting tomorrow.'

The officer was hesitating and suggested he wait outside and then they could go out and have a coffee somewhere.

'Don't bother. Just walk in. I have a kettle in my room,' and he hurried into the room to put on his trousers lying on the floor.

His quick eyes sliced through the semi-darkness of the hotel room as Kim walked in cautiously. Wearing a dark suit over a blue shirt, he looked somewhere in his early forties. Kar was going to make the coffee straightaway but Kim signalled him not to. They exchanged greetings while Kar got a can of Cass for himself from the minibar.

Abul's contacts had worked. He had been sceptical when he was told that an intelligence officer will meet him after he arrived. The embassy had facilitated this meeting with Kim from Angibu — the South Korean intelligence service — and he will have to thank them when this matter is wrapped up.

Kim spoke fluent English and he launched into the conversation with an apology. 'I am sorry, I didn't wait for your embassy guys to introduce us formally. This way we can save time. I knew you were arriving this afternoon so I just drove up from office to say hello. Hope you don't mind, detective.'

'Not at all. In fact I was thinking the same, you know how official channels slow down everything.'

Kim nodded, 'So you are here on behalf of the Indian travel company, is that right?' He didn't shift his gaze as he watched Kar pour the beer.

Kar had been expecting this question. 'Yes, actually both the travel company and relatives of the tourists. They seem to believe a P.I. from home would have an advantage and could work more closely with the local police,' he plastered a stupid smile on his face.

'I see,' Kim nodded slowly, while not removing his eyes from Kar, 'so how do you plan to help us? Any leads from the woman who returned to India. We couldn't get much out of her.'

Kar didn't like the tone of the questions but he couldn't react. He might need help from this man. 'Zilch. I interviewed her before coming to Korea but she is incoherent and she seems to be suffering from amnesia. The shrinks are working on her.' He told him whatever he had been able to gather from Tara. Kim nodded gravely and seemed to sink into deep thought.

'So I was wondering where to start,' Kar said tentatively after a while.

'Both the police and our agency are on the job. Your embassy has provided some background information. But being on your own and having met the relatives of the missing people, you may have some flexibility. What we just came to know is that the

Indian travel agency made some unusual arrangements for this tour.' Officer Kim was a quiet sort who spoke in bursts and then again retreated into silence.

'Like?'

'They didn't use the services of their regular counterpart here. Usually they have someone from a Korean travel agency accompany them on the tour. Did not happen this time.'

Kar poured some more beer and listened intently as Kim spoke.

'The police has been able to obtain CCTV footage from a Lotte superstore and a few other places visited by the group. There is always a woman with them, she has Korean features but you can never be sure. I have her photo,' he dug into his jacket pocket and fished out his phone.

A young woman's photo flashed on the screen. Kar studied the image. It looked like a security camera grab from the entrance to a superstore. There were shoppers in the background and enlarging the image he could recognise a few faces from the tour group.

He focussed on the Korean woman in the group. She had a small round face with wispy bangs of hair on her forehead. In another image she was smiling. The group was coming out of a restaurant. Next to her was the banker from Calcutta and Bikas Roy — the tour manager.

'Who is she? Any clues?' Kar asked.

'Not yet. The police are sending around the picture and I am in touch with some people in the North. Nothing has come up yet but we will get to her very soon. There is no record of her name in the hotel registers which is a problem. We have checked with the travel trade, no one recognises her. We can't fathom why the tour group will suddenly ask a Korean woman, who is not from a travel company, to accompany them.'

'Perhaps a guide, who speaks English?' Kar suggested.

'Could be, but her photograph is not on any list of registered guides. In this country it has become a fashion among the young to visit the plastic surgeon. They work on the eyelids, perk up the nose and do all sorts of pinching, polishing and stitching to look more *attractive*. This makes ID-ing a person a tricky affair. But we will get her finally, if she is in this country.'

'That doesn't sound so hopeful,' Kar said and immediately regretted having said it.

Kim raised an eyebrow. He lowered his voice by a notch so that Kar had to lean forward to hear him. 'We have one of the best uniformed police forces in the world. At this moment our field officers and all the technology at our command are scouring the country to locate your people. We are checking the vehicle number identification systems and highway security camera data. Till the time we find them, it is not clear why the tour manager cancelled the regular guide and opted for a stranger. Unless ...'

'Unless what?'

Kim went very quiet again and thought for several seconds. The faint sound of Seoul traffic filtered into the room like smoke through a crack in the door. And inside the room the two went on pondering over the question of the mysterious woman and her motives.

'It's late, let me make some coffee,' Kar said.

'Don't bother, I can survive without it tonight.' He looked up at Kar and noticed his tired drunken eyes, 'I think you need rest. Let us talk tomorrow.'

Kar wouldn't have any of it. He poured the last of the can in his glass, 'You were saying something about the regular guide being cancelled?'

'I met the police team this evening. They are leaning on a theory. They suspect that the Indian tour manager was up to some funny business with this woman in the picture or maybe someone in the group had hitched up with her. Anything in the background checks of these people that could reinforce such a theory?'

Kar couldn't think clearly with all the alcohol gushing through his veins. 'That's quite absurd,' he said, 'you just can't invite a woman you meet on the road to join you, while touring with a group of strangers. Could you? But still I can't give a clean chit to the tour manager. From what we have heard about him, he is the unpredictable sort. As I get to know more, I feel he could have been up to something.' He told Kim what he had learned about Bikas Roy from the manager of Lamplighter Travels.

Kim listened carefully. 'Please check with the travel agency in India if they know this woman somehow. She could be an independent guide and perhaps they have worked with her in the past. We don't have her name but show them her photo. We have shared it with your embassy but haven't heard back from them yet.'

'Sure,' Kar copied the photo to his phone and emailed it to Chaitanya with a note. He looked out through the window. The Seoul night was throbbing quietly, like the cold heart of a giant. Monster LCD panels flashed images of models selling cars while headlights wove idiosyncratic patterns on miles of twisting asphalt. Down Hibiscus street where his hotel was, late night bars stared one-eyed, gawking at the billboards as they waited for the tribes of darkness to appear at their doors. Through the glazed glass hotel window, the electric night was an ocean of light washing over the high rises, a city of desire that had claimed dominion over the night. Looking out reminded him also of the K-pop girls with their smooth faces and coloured hair, belting out their power-packed lines.

Perhaps it was the beer and soju hitting his tired brain. Kim was saying something but his words didn't carry to him any more. He checked his watch surreptitiously.

Kim had taken out a piece of paper from his wallet and was jotting down something mumbling to himself. Kar went up to the minibar and got a bottle of water.

'We are working on every lead. The police have searched garage lots, closed workshops, abandoned warehouses but nothing has turned up yet. We have scoured the routes out of the forest where one of the tourists was found by a trekking group. We have interviewed bus drivers. As the days go by my only apprehension is they might just have been taken to another country.'

'What do you mean?'

'It's very unlikely for them to kidnap a bunch of Indian tourists. It would be too unwieldy an operation. They would usually target us or the Japanese. But who knows. Did you check the English language skills of every person in the group?'

'What for? Do you want them to sit for a test when they reappear?' Kar said with a hint of derision. He was feeling drained and hoping Kim would call it a day.

Kim ignored the sarcasm and continued, 'In the past, agents of the North would kidnap someone who can teach them

English or Japanese. But they would prefer native speakers of the language.'

'Ah! I see. That doesn't sound nice. I will dig that one out. Just in case we are dealing with a whole tour group of English tutors.'

'Please do that,' Kim said, putting away the paper in his pocket. He looked up at the clock on the writing table. 'Ah! It's past midnight. I should get going.'

About time, Kar mumbled.

'Good night and see you at midday?' Kar said quickly, rising to walk him to the door, hoping he would not change his mind.

'Just in case every lead turns up a blank we can try the shaman.'

'A shaman!' Kar said feigning surprise. 'Why, have we given up already? What about the police and your people in the North. No help from them, eh?'

'In the police headquarters, there is a team of three officers working on this case backed up by the police force spread out across the country. As you can see our agency is also on the job, otherwise I wouldn't be sitting here with you in *this* hotel at midnight. We would know pretty quickly if they were kidnapped and taken away to the North. Now you are here. My hunch is we will have some information we can work on very soon.'

There was something not right about Utopia hotel, he could make that out from Kim's comment and he suspected the same. But he chose to ignore it. 'I hope so too,' Kar said sleepily.

'Unless someone has lured them away to a hidden valley. That would make matters difficult. We won't be able to rescue them by any ordinary means.'

'What do you mean by a hidden valley? Don't you have helicopters? Hasn't this country been mapped?'

Kim drew in his breath sharply but didn't stop speaking.

'There are secret valleys in mountains around the world protected by the Masters. These are places where they say the righteous will be sheltered in times of great strife. Who knows if they have ended up in one of those unmapped rabbit holes.'

'Holes, really. Isn't this taking it too far? So these are subterranean shelters from nuclear missiles, are they?'

'Uh no. These are valleys with natural shelters deep in the mountains. They are not on any map.'

'Not even on a Google map?'

'Nah.'

'Looks like we have our work cut out. The Masters, will they be armed? What kind of backup should I have if I sneak into any of these retreats for the *righteous*? How many of your men do you think would be needed to storm one of these bastions and get our folk out safely? And why on earth would they be held there at all?'

Kim looked at him strangely without smiling. 'There is a cafe a few steps down the main road, to your left. I will meet you there tomorrow midday. Perhaps I should introduce you to the police officers working on the case before you do something drastic. We won't be able to help you if you break the law.'

Kim stepped silently out of the room. Kar locked the door after him. He was too tired for fairy tales tonight.

White
Cloud
Mountain

1

Some secrets are well kept, others, they once said, are to be discovered in the East. Many years ago, this is how it had begun for Ujaan. Recently single after a painful separation, he was travelling to forget. Travelling east. The flight was half full and the drinks trolley had passed down the aisle for one last time. Wide awake on the night flight to Korea, after a touristy scamper across east Asia, he had been thinking how it had all ended. The lights of the cabin had been turned off and only a few reading lamps glowed ahead like the luminous eyes of aliens taking a free trip across the ocean of night. As he pretended to sleep, he watched from the corner of his eye, the man on the other side of the aisle feeling up the woman next to him under the cover of the red airline blankets.

He had met the two at the Calcutta airport, right at the beginning of their journey in India, just as he had met Mr Roy, the tour manager from the travel agency, and the others. They were a small group of twelve. He had come alone and waited for the travellers to join him in the main concourse.

It had been a smooth take off from Calcutta. Just behind his seat were Mr and Mrs Bose, an elderly couple travelling with their son. Amar Bose, who had taken a window seat, was flying for the first time. While his son, worried about his frail health and a ventricular murmur, insisted that he not look out the window when the flight took off or landed, Bose ignored the advice and seemed to enjoy when the aircraft soared towards the sky. 'This is no big deal, it's just like kite flying!' he said gleefully. 'What were you worrying about all this while?' he gently chided his son.

The son didn't answer while the plane had climbed above the clouds, leaving the bejewelled city behind them, pushing forward through the darkness.

'How far have we gone?' Mr Bose chimed in after a while as the cabin lights came on. 'Have we crossed Kamalgazi? Can you see our party office through that window?' he asked his son. 'It's too dark on this side.'

The son eyed his father from across the seat and shook his head despondently, 'Much further than that, we should be in Bangladeshi airspace in sometime,' to which the elderly gentleman just nodded his head unimpressed.

In the aisle seat in front of Ujaan was the tour manager of Lamplighter Travels, Bikas Roy. Everyone called him Bikas babu. An affable gentleman of mild manners and a balding pate with gentle brown eyes, Bikas babu was an old hand in the travel trade who took every care of the tourists right from the airport to ensure that they had a hassle-free holiday.

There were three young men in the tour group who had gone to the same college, and when one of them had asked Bikas babu if they would be able to watch a K-pop show, he said, 'I will arrange for the tickets and drop you at the venue if that will help.' His words were laced with honey and he knew how to keep the tourists happy.

The three friends discussed the proposal among themselves then, undecided, concentrated their attention on the only woman solo traveller in their group. They whispered among each other, one saying to the other that Bikas babu could have given one of them the seat next to her. Ujaan could not see them clearly now in the darkness of the cabin. An elderly gentleman was also travelling with them and he was snoring peacefully.

Ujaan went up to the lavatory and washed his face, carefully combing his hair with the plastic comb he carried in his pocket. He had grown a stubble which accentuated his jutting chin imparting a misleading air of confidence to his persona. He checked his belt bag one more time before exiting the lavatory to make sure he had his passport and money in order.

It had been a messy separation. He and Sujata had rowed endlessly over Rick's custody for the last few years and sometimes, in that period, he would be assailed by thoughts that made him a stranger to himself. Rick was only ten and now staying with his mother. What was his capacity for cruelty and was it just a function of the imagination? Things had gone worse over the months but even then there had been patches of normalcy when it seemed they were back in those days they had met. But illusions didn't last and after it was all over, they had left the rented house at Saket and he had moved back to Calcutta. The bank which he worked for in Delhi could find a position for him in his home town and that helped. Meanwhile Sujata had rented a new accommodation where she moved in with their son, Rick.

There was nothing happening in the city right then so he thought it would be a good idea to set out for a trip. He had saved quite a bit and travel seemed to be just what the doctor ordered.

It was six or seven in the evening, when the tickets had popped into his email box. He had been sitting in the living room of his Gariahat flat staring blankly at the television. The latest Shah Rukh Khan starrer was being screened but he had turned off the sound. He had got up late that day and asked the maid not to come and had fallen asleep again.

Now on the flight, thoughts of the separation crowded back into his mind as he tried to adjust himself in the rationed comfort of economy class. The elderly Mr Saha was snoring loudly and a baby was bawling away somewhere at the back, keeping half the plane in a restive slumber.

He had wanted to travel east and the travel agent had suggested Cambodia, Vietnam, Korea and Japan. They were beginning the third leg of the trip, heading for Korea and after that they would board the ferry from Busan to cross over to Osaka. But while in Phnom Penh the news of the tsunami and the nuclear plant disaster had splashed the headlines. The travel agent had to pull Japan out of the itinerary offering more time in Korea instead. Now they would have two weeks there.

The man across the aisle was Singh, the owner of a chain of singing bars with a reputation for sleaze. Ujaan didn't remember the woman's name though Bikas babu had introduced everyone in the group. Was it Aditi? Perhaps she was Tara? His memory was not going to get better and the last few years of nervous roller coaster had taken its toll.

Tara or whatever her name was had asked him if he would mind exchanging seats with her. She had arrived at the airport on her own but it looked like she knew Singh from before.

This exchanging of seats was a funny business. Once Ujaan had been on a return flight from Johannesburg which was half empty and the passengers had exchanged and readjusted their seating positions in such a manner that the distribution of weight on the plane had got affected. The pilot felt it was unsafe to take off and all passengers had to return to their designated seats.

He regularly faced this when travelling on trains where big families always requested the lone traveller to sacrifice his seat and shift to another so that they can stay together. Sometimes this went to a point of irritation and he often refused these requests but he could not say no to this woman with dark silken tresses forming little curlicues near her waist and a dazzling set of teeth, so white that the reflection could turn you blind.

As the plane ploughed through turbulence, Ujaan thought about the last few days with the tourists. Then further back — the memories he had left behind and whatever he would have to do to pick up the bits of his life and bind these together again. He rarely got to see his son, now studying in class five in a convent school. After they had separated, Sujata had stayed back in Delhi where she worked for a development NGO. The memories were all scattered now, falling off like withering leaves.

He knew little about Korea except that there had been a fratricidal war that never quite ended and the suffering on both sides. Then there came the economic upsurge of the South, the miracle of the Han and *Hallyu* — the Korean Wave — while the North had all but closed up to the world. Like many others, he was much taken with the great technology companies of that country that washed like a deluge through the consumer markets of the world.

So he was happy to find this travel agency offering an east Asia tour which included Korea. He looked forward to a quiet few days of travelling. Perhaps his mind would be washed clean. He stared down the aisle. The airhostess looked hot in her red uniform but she didn't bring him a second drink. All else was going fine with the flight. The soporific hum of the jet engines had put bar owner Singh to sleep, a satiated smile on his lips.

Then everything was quiet for a few hours as hundreds of gallons of fuel propelled them across the eastern skies.

Bikas babu got up early, washed himself and was taking a stroll down the aisle to make sure that everyone in his group was fine. 'Another four hours before we arrive in pretty Seoul,' he told Ujaan, seeing that he was awake. Ujaan smiled and nodded.

He tended his flock well, their tour manager. After making sure that everyone was comfortable he went back to his seat and pushed up the window flap. A calm watery sun peeped at them from over the horizon. Soon it would be morning all over the East. Another day — another experiment with living. How could they know which experiment would succeed and which was doomed to fail? It was too early to look beyond what was in plain sight. Life can only be understood backwards; but it must be lived forwards. What the wise man had said is true for everything that happened and all that remained to unfold. Ujaan noticed Bikas babu's eyes glint as it caught the rays of the morning sun. He remembered the catchline of Lamplighter Travels. It was printed on their stationery in a curvy stylised font: *Travel That Changes Lives*. Surely it meant something, Ujaan thought, as he tried unsuccessfully to extricate his backpack, jammed under the seat in front.

2

The jet trail made the sign of an arrow above the South China Sea, as the metal bird banked low over a carpet of feathery clouds that spread as far east as Okinawa where lived the immortals and west right up to the Chinese coastline. Ujaan had a window seat and next to him was a pretty Hong Kong girl in a white top and black hot pants, grabbing a smart phone with a banana green cover. Every few minutes she would lean over towards the window and take pictures of the clouds.

The Hong Kong woman had long legs with pearly white skin and Ujaan secretly watched her all the way to Incheon. He couldn't sleep on flights and his mind was now behaving like a racing car with a maniac at the wheels. He rehearsed opening lines and planned how to approach the woman who was travelling with their group. He watched the Hong Kong woman surreptitiously, through the corner of his eye, he inhaled the perfume that she was wearing, he asked her meaningless questions about customs forms drawing responses in Mandarin, while always trying to put away the thoughts of the past.

The smallish apartment in Saket which they had bought. It was just a few weeks before he left that they had received a good offer and sold it finally. Before that it had been raging hell. The court appearances, the selling off of whatever they had collected, the gatherings of family life and then the gradual wiping out of good memories, the unravelling of a nest twig by thin twig. In the end they hadn't forgiven each other and burned one another with all the hate that breeds on the dark side of love. He would rarely be able to meet his child. Rick was too little to understand what was going on between his parents but gradually he became a quiet boy, talking little, playing even less, and sitting quietly in his room, his school books strewn around him, most of the time.

The little flat would still be lying empty he guessed. It would be dark in there, behind the shuttered windows. The uncanny silence of the empty apartment penetrated through the hum of the aircraft. He was sitting in a vacuum. Then everything began to replay in his head — the muffled sobs, the shrill exchange of words and the banging of doors. There was a dog howling somewhere, responding to their arguments one night. It had disturbed their sleep and they had fought over it again.

Ujaan checked and rechecked the disembarkation card to make sure he hadn't misspelled his name or written a wrong address. He had three different addresses in three official documents which all pointed to the same house but had subtle distinctions in spelling, position of commas, order of information among other things. This was due partly to the diligence of government officials in different departments who had different ideas about how the parts of an address should be organised and also because the authorities took pleasure in cutting up areas, redistributing postal codes, defining and redefining administrative divisions according to their whims and plots.

He kept worrying secretly as to what might happen if he was stopped at immigration or by the customs or by some unknown authority that was waiting for him behind a counter.

Bikas babu came strolling down the aisle. 'Fill in everything alphabet by alphabet from your passport,' he went on repeating to each of them. Someone didn't have a pen and he immediately gave him one. Then Sujata who was travelling alone said she couldn't find her headset and he rushed to offer her his. More people needed pens and he could somehow provide one to each till finally other passengers not from their group began asking if he had a pen or could help them fill in their disembarkation cards and arrival forms. Finally he checked their forms and returned to his seat smiling. But his confident demeanour was no assurance for Ujaan who replayed all his worries in his mind.

The aircraft made a smooth touchdown. Just when the doors had been opened and people had begun to queue out, Ujaan felt he needed to take a digestive pill because the pasta on the flight had tasted funny and may have been stale. He unzipped each compartment of his cabin bag looking desperately for the medicine pouch but failed to locate it. He relinquished his position in the exit queue and went and sat down on his seat. He put his bag on his lap and began to go through each compartment diligently, but to no avail. He pulled out items of clothing, mobile phone chargers, reading glasses, a morning pouch, but the medicines didn't reveal their position. Finally, remembering that he had forgotten to pack his medicines, Ujaan sighed and got up. He hurried down the aisle which was empty now. The last of the passengers had left the aircraft and the cleaning staff was moving in and they eyed him suspiciously. His hands had begun to sweat. He couldn't breathe normally.

He grabbed the straps of his backpack with both hands and walked awkwardly following passengers from different flights that had landed but could not recognise anyone from his own. Where were the others of the tour group? Where was the bloody tour manager?

His mobile phone won't be working so it was useless to call anyone. He tried to follow the arrival and baggage claim signs but these were too numerous and the directions they showed were all confusing. Some pointed to the ceiling which usually meant straight ahead but following these he ran into a bank of elevators which did not seem to go in the same direction. He stepped onto a moving walkway that was trundling along towards a concourse with security check signs and designer boutiques with a lone man with an umbrella standing at one of the windows. Stepping off the walkator he hurried on along one of the passages that was wide and empty till he ran into more signs and directions. Here the arrival sign looked like splayed fingers, pointing in directions where he could see restrooms and lifts for the disabled.

As the airport began to clear he felt more nervous. His stomach churned and he was feeling sick. Now he realised that there was no one around and he was walking straight towards an elevator that was going down to what looked like a railway platform. There were about ten passengers waiting here with their luggage but the platform was abnormally quiet. He stepped off the elevator and right at that moment he panicked.

How did he turn up at a railway station? He must have made a terrible mistake and missed the immigration counters and the custom clearance. Where was his check-in baggage? If he is stopped now, he will surely be put behind bars with North Korean agents and body snatchers. As scary thoughts began flooding his mind, a train clattered into the platform. The passengers rushed towards the doors and boarded. He stood still, undecided. A burly guard was standing in one corner and eyeing him suspiciously. There was no time to think.

As the train slipped out of the platform Ujaan turned back, heading towards the elevator. He went quickly. But the elevator was coming down. He stepped onto it and began to run up against it and, missing a step, fell, rolled over and was thrown onto the platform.

The guard came running while shouting in his wireless set. Security personnel rushed in from everywhere and surrounded him, ordering him to remain on the floor.

One of them patted him down to make sure that he was not armed. Then someone asked him to turn slowly and try and get up. He could though he had injured his shoulder in the fall. Thankfully there were no bones broken.

It took an hour and half for him to explain everything and finally when he was shown his way through immigration and customs and walked out of the airport it was late in the afternoon.

There was a bus stop right outside the arrivals hall and luckily he knew the name of the hotel and could get a ticket for the next bus. The bus journey was smooth and uneventful. This somewhat quietened his nerves. There was a dull pain in his shoulder from the fall but otherwise he was still in good shape. The rumbling of his stomach had died down and he didn't have to panic about the medicines he had left back at home.

It was a weekend and the streets were throbbing with energy though it was hot and humid outside. The bus crossed the bridge over the Han and cruised smoothly over a couple of flyovers before dropping him off at the gates of Hotel East.

Stepping out of the bus he collected his luggage and because he wanted to smoke badly he walked over to the nearest cigarette kiosk and bought a packet of Marlboros. There was a smoking area right next to the hotel and keeping his luggage at his feet he sat down on a bench and took a few deep drags.

The women in their shorts and soft cotton tops were doing the sensuous runway walk and he wondered if the whole country was preparing for a fashion show. He smoked two cigarettes in a row while he watched and was going to light a third when he realised someone was standing a few feet away, staring at him.

'Where had you been,' Bikas babu asked curtly unable to hide his irritation.

'That is a question I should be asking you,' he said and stood up on his feet. He massaged his shoulder.

'We have been looking high and low for you and was just about to inform the police when I find you here, smoking. I am sorry, but why didn't you take the car with us? We have responsibilities ...'

'You are the tour agent, you should know how to handle any eventuality,' Ujaan said, 'but in any case, you never waited for me. I lost my way in the airport.' He was in no mood to divulge more. He was too peeved with the fact that the tour manager hadn't waited for him.

'Okay, give me your luggage,' Roy said in a reconciliatory tone, 'I am sorry but you were not coming out and so we thought you had left ahead of us. Now give me your bags please.'

'I will manage on my own.'

'I apologise for not waiting, entirely my fault.'

They walked the few steps to Hotel East and he went up to his room on the twelfth floor. An average-sized affair with a small bed and coffee-coloured walls. He spent a long time watching the buses curving through the traffic lanes and the brightly painted cars zipping along a wide street. And then the sun went down over the high rises and the LCD panels blinked on. Giant billboards, hotel signs and more signage, a flood of desire mapping out the night. He felt lonely. What was he doing with this group of strangers in this far away country?

At night he had dinner in his room while the others had theirs at the downstairs restaurant. He was still in a foul mood from the airport mishap and didn't want to see their faces. The anguish of separation from his son Rick gnawed at him but he refused to acknowledge it and so it transformed into irritableness and distrust, which he directed at the people around. He now suspected that his co-travellers had conspired to leave the airport early and Bikas babu was really not to blame, though the tour manager had accepted it was his fault.

Staring out through the window, he absent-mindedly chewed the *dak galbi* and though the grilled chicken was rich with flavours he couldn't appreciate it. In the distance Samsung signs flickered on high rises and LCD screens flashed advertisements to anybody who would look. Further down the road, Sejong the Great, having endured the punishing sun through the day, stood relieved on his pedestal, watching over the city of signs. The king commanded a busy intersection with banks of traffic lights, speeding cars with late night revellers, and the few pedestrians cruising along the pavements, like sleepwalkers, hypnotised by the night.

Ujaan was feeling restless. His mind was hyperactive from the excitement of arrival. But it was past midnight now. He should get some sleep. There was soju and beer in the minibar but he didn't feel like a drink. He dialled the front desk absent-mindedly but kept down the receiver without speaking a word.

He went up to the window and peered down at the street. A taxi was parked in front of the hotel but there was no one on the pavement outside. He stood there watching the empty street for a while longer. Then he put on a sober shirt, a pair of dark trousers and, carefully tying his shoelaces, stepped out of the room. The corridor was empty. He really didn't want to meet anyone from the tour group at this hour.

At the lobby level he looked around to locate the exit. It was next to the reception. The night clerk was busy on the phone and didn't look at him as he sneaked past. The ring of the elevator bell was still echoing down the wood-panelled hall as he pushed through the glass doors and went out into the street.

The taxi that was parked outside a little while ago had disappeared. The street was empty. Ujaan began to walk in the other direction away from the crossing. He walked for a few minutes. Some blocks down a department store was still open and he thought he would go in but decided against it. He didn't need to buy anything.

A row of office buildings with people still working in the upper floors under harsh lights. A couple of fashion stores, shutters down. Beyond the fashion shops was a high-fenced compound with a sentry box. He could see the eyes of the guard shining through a slit in the box painted olive green. He thought he would turn back but looking ahead saw a brightly lit building on the other side. He crossed over to the other side of the street.

The sign in English said it was a dessert cafe. He wouldn't mind an ice cream so he pushed through the door and walked up to the counter. There was one man behind the counter with a display window featuring shaved ice desserts. The man was rubbing his eyes, he looked sleepy.

'A chocolate chip ice cream please.'

They didn't have the ice cream but the man at the counter suggested he try their *bingsu*. Ujaan ordered a yogurt flavour and looked around the cafe. Two young men were sitting at a table near the other exit. He wanted to be all by himself, so he looked around for a nook where he could be on his own, unwatched. It was not a big cafe. A man with enormous cup-like earlobes was sitting near the counter having coffee. He was glancing at him from time to time.

The cup-eared man made him uncomfortable. Then he noticed the staircase at the back. There must be a sitting area upstairs, he told himself. He went up the stairs and found the upper level was empty. There were about ten tables here, a few against the windows. He went and sat at the far corner beside a window with paper cherry blossoms. From here he could watch the street but other than a few speeding cars there was no traffic outside.

Something was lying on his table. A happy face with dark round eyes. It was the size of his palm. He picked it up and turned it around. It looked like a child's toy. Someone must have forgotten it. What was he to do now? He was wondering whether he should leave it with the counter boy when the eyes began to glow red. As if it was aware of his presence. The face began to vibrate on the table.

Ujaan picked up the vibrating face and hurried down the stairs.

The man at the counter was busy wiping plates. Ujaan went up to him and kept the happy face on the counter. The man took it and handed him a plate of creamy white ice flakes topped with sliced mangos. He took the plate and went up the stairs, careful not to drop it.

He went and sat at his corner table and dipped into the milky shaved ice. The bingsu was cold and delicious. He popped a slice of mango into his mouth. It melted releasing its lemony sweetness. Tucking in a few more spoons of milky flakes, he looked up. Someone was standing there, right next to his table.

Her hair was cut into bangs covering her forehead. A small oval face with fine bow-shaped lips and a pert nose, she was dressed in black. Black short skirt, black top and a cropped rust-coloured jacket open at the front. The woman was of medium height with a full rounded body and gorgeous legs. She was glaring at him.

'You are eating my bingsu,' she said.

'What?'

'I said, you are having my mango bingsu and you have taken my seat.' She looked very angry as she swept away her bangs, fixing him with a look.

'But ...'

'This is so rude. How could you?'

'I ... actually I didn't know ...'

'Of course, I left my token on the table.'

'But I ordered and paid,' he said, still not understanding what was wrong.

'You should be ashamed!' she was screaming now, suddenly flying into a temper.

'Now,' he cleared his voice, 'you are plainly misbehaving. I have paid for my order and if you don't believe it, then go and ask at the counter downstairs.'

'Where is my token? I left it here on the table. You took it and grabbed my order. How stupid!'

Ujaan was going to say something but the woman rushed away angrily stomping her feet. She went down the steps fuming. He could hear more heated conversation from downstairs but didn't move from his seat. He was sweating from shame and humiliation.

After the voices had died down he rose from his chair and went down the stairs slowly. There was no one in the cafe now and the counter boy had his back turned towards him. The man with the cup-like ears had disappeared leaving his coffee on the table.

He quietly slipped out through the door, his face red with embarrassment. His head throbbed wildly as he retraced his steps back to his hotel, down the empty road where the stoplights were burning up the leftovers of the night.

3

It was crystal clear the next morning. The happy face had fooled Ujaan. He hadn't collected his token from the counter and instead taken hers. How stupid. But that woman had been rude. He would wring her neck if they ever met again.

The day's schedule had gone haywire with their Korean guide reporting sick. Bikas babu had apologised profusely, promising to make it up with extra destinations. So it was a do-it-yourself first day in the city with time spent at museums and visits to every supermarket that they could find. Harvinder had picked up a shelf full of baseball caps made in China —

gifts for his bartenders back home. He planned to make it part of their uniform. Some of the tourists bought paper lamps, others, expensive electronics. They were exhausted from their shopping and at day's end took a relaxing walk along the river to work up the appetite. Dinner was steaming seafood hotpot in a traditional restaurant following which they had returned to the hotel, retiring to their rooms by early evening.

Ujaan took a long and lazy soak in the tub and opened the bottle of mushroom wine he had picked up at a Lotte store. Pouring a little in a glass, he held it up against the light. Weak yellow. It reminded him of tonics prescribed to the elderly to bolster up their constitution. But it didn't taste bad and after two glasses he felt like having more.

One more. At some point in the evening, he realised that the bottle was empty. He checked the desk clock. Twenty minutes to midnight. The pine mushroom buzz was exhilarating and he felt like listening to music. Anything would do right now but when he got out of bed he felt like venturing out.

The street was empty like the night before. A light breeze caressed his face as he started to walk towards the crossing, swinging his arms. He went past the crossroads, and then along a diversion wall where heavy earth-moving equipment were parked, and then right up to the subway station. There was a cafe right next to it. With no definite plan he pushed through the door.

It was a bigger place than the one he had gone to the night before but at this hour it was almost empty. Only two or three tables were occupied. Last night the mango bingsu had been divine but he hadn't touched it again after that bitch had misbehaved. He studied the display boxes wondering if the same flavour would be available.

They had the mango flavour and the picture looked similar to the one at the other place. Juicy slices of mango on a bowl of flaky milk flakes. He sat near the counter and, careful not to repeat his mistake, collected his token. He got the bingsu without any mishap. So far so good.

Ujaan popped in a few slices of juicy mango before digging into the bingsu.

Heaven! Whoever created this dessert was a genius, he told himself, enjoying every spoonful.

'Hey!'

He didn't hear it at first.

'Sir!' A little louder this time.

A woman was sitting across from him in the next row of tables. He hadn't noticed her come in. It was the rude woman from last night! She looked calm and was watching him with her dark shiny eyes. There was no hint of aggression in that look.

'Yes?' he said curtly.

'I see you have collected my order again,' she whispered.

'Bullshit! If this is a joke, I am not impressed and I don't speak with impolite people. I have enough good friends.'

She hesitated before speaking again. 'Then why are you eating alone every night?'

'None of your business,' he said and to cut off the conversation spooned up a mango slice.

'I wanted to say sorry for last night. I realised later that you must have made a mistake. This is a crazy country and it is not possible for a foreigner to make sense of everything.'

He looked up at her and wondered what he should say. 'It's all right. We don't use smiley tokens for ordering food back home,' he said.

'Thank you. That's a weight off my chest.'

'I didn't expect to meet you tonight. I avoided that other place, just in case ...'

She smiled gently. 'See, how hard it is to get rid of bitches,' her teeth were pearly white, like a toothpaste advertisement.

'I can see that.'

'I promise not to bother you again. But I should have told you my name. I am Jiyoo Park. Guess you are new to this country?'

'Splendid detective work. Yes I am. My name is Ujaan.'

'Let me know if I can be of any help. To compensate for my terrible behaviour at least,' she said.

'I see. But I don't know you, do you live nearby?'

'Not very far from here.'

Ujaan thought he would get a coffee. He had finished his bingsu and was feeling quite full. He did not mind the conversation with the woman. But he had already forgotten her name. Maybe it was the mushroom wine playing tricks with his memory. He rose from the table but she was already at the counter before him.

'What will you have, Mr Ujaan. Please let me get it for you.'

He couldn't say no. She ordered two americanos and they went back to her table surprised, finding each other face to face, waiting for coffee.

'Uh ... What was your name again?' he asked.

'Jiyoo. Are your travelling alone? Let me know if you need assistance while you are here.' There was a calm determination in the way she spoke.

'Jiyoo. Does it mean something?'

'It can mean several things,' there was a change in her demeanour. She looked down at the table as she spoke.

'Ms Jiyoo. Why do you want to help me and besides that why do you think I would need assistance of any sort?'

He couldn't figure out if she was just a woman of the night trying to snare a tourist.

She was slightly taken aback by his questions, then composing herself said, 'I work nearby and sometimes come to this cafe for a late night snack. I find tourists are often friendly ...'

'And you help whoever you find here?' he spoke before she could complete, the mushroom wine pushing him ahead.

Their order was ready and she went up to collect it leaving her green bag on the chair. He looked at the bag and then at her, standing at the counter. Her silken hair was bouncing as she spoke with the man handing her the coffee.

She had a piece of cheese and garlic toast left on her plate but she did not touch it. They sipped the coffee in silence. The cafe was completely empty now.

'I don't sleep well, so I work long hours and talk with those who are like me.'

'That's okay. I too haven't slept much these last few months.'

'Me, I didn't sleep a wink for some years. Now it's getting better,' she said taking another sip.

'You must be joking!'

'I lost count ...'

'But you don't look tired!'

'Then there must be someone protecting me.' Then bringing her voice down to a low whisper she said, 'Since I started planning my escape,' she put down her cup softly, 'my mind had refused to shut down.'

He shifted in his seat. He was not expecting this.

'I don't know why I am telling you this. But you are a foreigner. I feel I can trust you. I left my country a couple of years ago. I am from the North.' She looked around to make sure the man at the counter was not listening.

He wanted to know more but she would not talk about it. 'Another time, if we meet again,' she said.

'Don't you think it's time to go home?' Ujaan asked her after a while. He had finished his coffee and was worrying it was getting late.

They left the cafe together and it turned out they were headed in the same direction.

'You needn't walk me home,' she said.

'Are these streets safe for women?' he asked.

'Absolutely and I know how to take care of myself,' she said.

'Taekwondo?'

They both laughed. He noticed how the light danced in her eyes.

The night had spread itself thick over the city as they left the dessert cafe. He again asked her questions about her escape but she would only say it had been a long and difficult journey to Seoul, 'But I always believed I would make it.'

'So where do you work now, Miss Jiyoo?' Ujaan wanted to know as they made their way back to his hotel.

'Just Jiyoo is fine, Sir. I work at a PC bang, which is an internet room and video parlour rolled into one. People come to play games and surf the net, we are open day and night.'

'Oh I see. You can drop the "Sir" and call me Ujaan. Perhaps that's the reason why you lost sleep — they never close shop!'

'We work shifts. It's not like that,' then she looked back, as if to make sure she had come the right away.

'Are you okay?' he asked.

'Yes, yes. I just thought we took a wrong turn.' She eyed him strangely. 'Tell me, do you know this country well enough?'

'No, this is my first time here, but we are in a group and have someone from the travel agency to take care of us.'

'May I ask his name?'

'Uh? He is the tour manager — Bikas Roy,' he said absent-mindedly. She was wearing a flowery perfume and he caught a whiff of it as they walked side by side.

They were still strangers to each other, well almost, but the night brought them closer. The night with its secrets made them walk close beside each other, brushing each other's hands unmindfully, like friends would do sometimes. And this night, wherever it had come from, also reminded him of the life he had left behind, their empty apartment gathering the dust of each nameless day.

'I can help your group with the tour programme if you take me along with you,' she said after a while.

He remembered something. Their local tour guide hadn't turned up and they had been running around the city like headless chickens.

'We had a problem with the local tour guide who was supposed to join us today. But I believe our tour manager must have arranged an alternative,' he said.

'I know very special places and I speak the language. And if you are sleepless, we can find a cafe and talk like tonight,' she looked at him. The night lights were watching her too. They had arrived outside his hotel.

It sounded exciting. Was he dreaming and would wake up to find her gone? Could he really influence Bikas babu to take her on? What's the harm to try?

'Okay, I will talk with him tomorrow. We have a couple of days in Seoul.'

'Excellent! I must leave now and you try to sleep,' she said.

Won't you stay a little while longer? Won't you let me steal your bingsu again? he wanted to say.

'Here is my number. If it works out give me a call in the morning.'

'I am not sure if our tour company will take on a freelancer but I will ask them.'

She gave him an impish look, 'I will enjoy doing it as long as you don't steal my bingsu order again.'

4

At the centre of the darkness there was another deeper dark. It was like the outside and the inside. The outside darkness mutable, ever-changing. The colour of smoke gushing out of a factory chimney, slowly transforming, shape-shifting, streaming, twisting, dissolving into a distant arc of blue. At its sinuous edges the smoke was thin enough and the blue light faint enough for one to melt into the other in a charged sensuous game that seemed to go on forever — this fornication of light and dark. The other darkness was closer to Ujaan, enveloping even choking him and he tossed in bed to see if there was a light nearby. He could smell the air freshener that they used to spray in their Delhi flat, a cloying synthetic reality released from an aerosol can. The darkness was so overpowering it hurt and he shut his eyes tight. Blue, green and red phosphenes swayed against a curtain of black and he watched their dance for a while.

There was a faint tinkling sound. Metal on metal. He opened his eyes again and now the darkness around him was gauze-like and he could see a woman sitting on the sofa, eating noodle soup out of a bowl. Now and then the metal chopsticks made a small tinkling noise against the bone china.

She looked up and saw him staring.

'Did you sleep well?' she asked.

'Uh, when did I fall asleep? How come you are in my room?'

'Why last night after we returned from our city tour,' she said but didn't answer his last question. She was looking vivacious in a royal blue chequered mini skirt teemed with a white long sleeved top with the slogan Little Monster painted across it in black. Her hair was shining in the faint morning light filtering through the window.

He rubbed his eyes and slowly sat up on the bed. It was five in the morning by his watch but how come she was in his room? He remembered she had left around midnight and then he had fallen asleep.

'I had been waiting for you to wake up. Meanwhile I thought I would have some noodle soup and kimchi to start my day. This is such an expensive hotel, I could as well do with some basic stuff.'

'Won't you feel hungry with so little to eat?' he asked her after a while.

'It is enough for me, I can't eat more than this in the morning,' she said and smiled. 'You were very kind to tell Mr Roy to take me on as your guide. I enjoyed going out with your group yesterday and my leave application from work has been approved without much haggling.'

'That's so nice,' he said.

She went up to the side table to put away the bowl. 'You look tired. Did you sleep well? I know yesterday's city tour had been hectic. When I first arrived in Seoul, I was quite overwhelmed.'

He shook his head. 'I am fine, just a little drowsy.' Then he remembered there was something still unexplained. 'But how did you get into my room?'

'I never left!' she smiled. 'You had fallen asleep after we returned and I thought maybe I should go home now. But I didn't feel like leaving, so I sat here through the night looking at you sleep.'

Really? He thought she was making it up. She might have got a duplicate key or taken his. It didn't bother him. He was watching her as she spoke. 'We will travel together,' she said. 'We will trek in the White Cloud mountain and we will go to the sea. You will be happy in the mountains. Now the weather is pleasant there.'

He went and stood in front of her. She looked up as he lightly touched her forearms. Their eyes met. She was watching him, a hovering unsure gaze. Where will this journey lead the two of them? He bunched her loose fitting long sleeves and caressed her slender arms. The silk gave way to the roughness of damaged skin. He stopped. Looking down he noticed the long pink scar marks on both her forearms. He looked back at her, deep into her eyes, and was going to say something but he checked himself. 'How do you know, I will be happy?' he asked her instead.

She didn't resist his gentle probing touch but pulled the sleeves of her shirt back. 'I have read your mind and know what is good for you,' she smiled, 'now get ready. Mr Bikas wants me to meet him at the lobby in half an hour. I have to get going.'

He sat down beside her, her hands warm in his, their fingers locked. She turned to look into his eyes with that curious unwavering gaze as he increased the pressure of his grip. He pulled her a little closer and hugged her. She leaned into him and he could feel her heart beating against his.

'We are getting late,' she said after a while.

'Will you tell me who hurt you?' Ujaan asked tenderly, caressing her arms.

'It was something nasty that happened to me. I will tell you another time.'

Ujaan removed his hands and leaned back on the sofa. She rose slowly and walked up to the dresser. Picking up her bag, Jiyoo brushed her hair and touched her lips with a blood red lipstick before slipping out of the room.

He waited for the door to close behind her and went into the shower. He soaped and scrubbed and let the steaming water run down his body for long before coming out of the shower stall. Then he towelled himself dry, shaved with extra care and put on clean underwear, a pair of white cotton trousers and a T-shirt over which he pulled on a light jacket.

He opened a can of juice for he did not feel like meeting the others over breakfast downstairs. He will pick up a sandwich at the bus station. What about Jiyoo? She had walked in unannounced and made her way into private spaces whenever she wished. Had he led her on? He didn't think so, it seemed so natural. He remembered how she said *elevato* without the r and could not help smiling. His heart warmed with sudden joy. He looked at himself, smiling in the mirror.

It was time to move. He took his backpack, locked the door, went into the corridor and right up to the bank of elevators and then remembering he had left his passport in the room went back again to get it. When he was finally downstairs all the others were waiting for him in the lobby. Jiyoo was also there and she made a face at him when no one was looking.

It was a sunny day in Seoul with the mercury touching thirty but the streets were full. They first visited Deoksugung palace which was near their hotel and watched the change of guard, everyone clicking away at their cameras. Ujaan took some pictures but did not know who he will share those with. It would be months before he would meet his son — Rick was with his mother in Delhi and the next meeting would not be before winter.

He ambled along with the group dropping in and out of taxis, seeing the sights, meandering through crowds of protestors till they all felt hungry and exhausted from the heat. They had sticky rice and steaming seafood straight out of a hotpot for lunch and then took a leisurely walk along the Cheonggyecheon stream. Jiyoo would stop now and then and assemble the group to tell them a bit about this place or that, how the stream had been covered up by a highway and how the government took pains to have the highway removed and the stream restored.

Most of their group went into a Lotte supermarket while Jiyoo influenced Harvinder and his partner Tara to try the sweet bingsu. So Ujaan joined them. She stole a look at him over her plate, mischievous, as if suppressing an urge to laugh out loud and he blushed remembering his first night's blunder at the cafe.

Harvinder, a flashy and exuberant man, did all the talking while Tara hardly spoke. Singh wanted to see Gangnam because he had heard that popular song and so it was decided that they will have dinner there after visiting the Seoul Tower. Bikas babu meanwhile herded back the others and Ujaan could see the tour manager looking very relaxed perhaps because Jiyoo had proved to be an expert guide.

Spooning in the sweet ice dessert, they chatted about the island of Jeju which was next on their itinerary. They would take a flight from Seoul and stay for two days before returning to cover other attractions of the country: a temple visit, trips to Busan and Incheon, and finally a leisurely last few days in the White Cloud mountain.

The sun had set as their group made their way to Seoul Tower, up on a hill in the centre of the city. They rode a cable car and then went up to the observation deck. The city looked like a system of sinuous nerves lit up with chemical power, the slow fusing of atoms, the excitation of electrons shooting out white heat and light, the arterial roads glowing with overload of information, the branching streets dimmer but bright still. They were staring into the innards of a giant information processing supercomputer, the silicon chip of the super processor running at many gigaflops, magnified before their eyes.

There were many tourists at the observation deck. Some of them took pictures while others watched silently, intimidated by the might of this cybernetic marvel that went on accomplishing millions of tasks without fail. Each of them imagined their separateness, their distinct memories, loves and cares but the machine which they had just a glimpse of had absorbed them all into one intelligent being. All inextricably linked. Waiting for someone to start a fire. A single line of malicious code — one single spark.

They were quiet as they went down. Down to the terrace where lovers fix love locks to a fence and throw the keys away believing this would make their bond unbreakable. Harvinder produced a tiny combination lock from his pocket and he and Tara hung it on the fence and he closed the lock spinning the numbered dials. Then he realised there was no key to throw away.

Jiyoo had a lock of her own. She went up to the fence alone. A pink heart-shaped lock. She opened it carefully and hung it on the fence. She stood silently for a moment looking at her lock on the fence. Then she closed the lock, pulled out the key and threw it away.

Ujaan watched her all the while and as she walked back to join their group their eyes met. Then he averted his gaze and tried to peer into the distance beyond the luminous nerve networks of the city.

Magic
Seeds

1

But when did it really begin? Perhaps on that March day, decades ago, when the daisies were powdering the emerald meadows of Sussex, where Tanmoy Sen had arrived, a disillusioned man. It was a lovely season indeed. The nodding bluebells had lit up the woodlands and daffodils were poking their heads out to listen to blackbirds, singing in the hedge.

But it grew hot over the weeks and soon, even under the shade, it was not pleasant any more. The radio said that the hours of sunshine were the longest in recorded history while not forgetting to point out how temperatures had risen. Nobody really bothered. As for Sen, he was happy to have escaped.

He never planned to return and indeed he wouldn't. The morons back at his old institute had danced through the night at the news and screwed the brains out of the voluptuous Esplanade girls who sold their ware in the posh hotels of Chowringhee, where his office was. Right at the end, where it abruptly spread its tentacles, one progressing further south towards the temple of the goddess, another moodily swinging east to the garbage hills now converted to hotels and cathouses, and the last one traipsing west, where the river was, the old river that begat a civilisation and was sullied by it.

He still had a few friends there, so he came to know how they partied through the night at the news of his departure, and partied through the day at the five star hotel that came up on a dung heap east of town. It was organised by the director under the cover of a seminar. The director and chief geneticist — Dr Chaturvedi — with his trail of journal publications, citations and tomes swinging from his rump like a caudal appendage. When it was nearing daybreak, Chaturvedi and his coterie of scientists had made a bonfire of the copies of Tanmoy's latest paper on direct gene transfer to plant cells and in the roaring flames of his scholarly pursuits they had mulled their Burgundy and gently poured the red juice of France down their parched gullets.

Not that he wasn't warned. The signs were all there, right from the beginning when he had returned to Calcutta, after completing his post doc in a British university followed by a decade of teaching in England and the States. He had joined the Institute of Genetic Engineering and Medicine in his home town. Known as GEM among peers it was regarded one of the best in all of Asia.

Direct gene transfer was his area of expertise and he had done solid work with tobacco and maize as well as publishing more than thirty peer-reviewed papers with the best in his line, which meant people like Havelock at the Israeli Centre for Genomics, Datta at the Swiss centre, Turnbull of GeneLab UK, and Bykofsky in the States, who was once described rather frivolously as the Dalai Lama of epigenetics.

Over and above this he was getting invited to seminars all around the wide world. From South Korea to Sweden and everywhere in between. He knew he was secretly envied at the institute and efforts were often made by the enemy camp to stymie the progress of his projects using dishonourable means. But no one took the clandestine fight out into the open. His credentials were impeccable and he had a solid body of work to back it up. Dr Chaturvedi, however, was a different sort of beast altogether.

Armed with a management degree, obtained after his PhD from a North American university, he had started off with teaching in the States but had gravitated back to the Calcutta institute and strapped himself to the Chair of Director, warding off all kinds of competition with his business school skills and political connections.

Despite his stature as a leading academic, Tanmoy Sen was an approachable and genial man. Full of humility, he was someone who had taken success in his stride. He was temperamental sometimes and had his little quirks but his peers and indeed his friends, like the Englishman who arrived at the railway station decades later, would vouch for him and say, 'This is a genuine guy.'

He had a kind face and fleshy lips which seemed always on the verge of a smile. But it was perhaps his penetrating eyes and smart answers that he gave in class that drew the attention of teachers at boarding school, where he had gone at a tender age. 'This is an uncommon kid,' they used to tell each other in the staff room, and the history teacher, who was a polymath, would say, 'Mark my words, one day he will be sought after the world over.'

His teachers agreed and they bent the rules to give him special attention. The biology teacher in class eight, who was quite taken by this bright kid, made a secret understanding with the school management to provide him an intelligence enhancing supplementary diet consisting of almonds and fresh milk which the young Tanmoy partook of, in the confines of the kitchen larder, away from the prying eyes of his classmates.

But despite all the attention that his teachers and hostel wardens showered upon him, Tanmoy was a brooding and melancholic child in his schooldays. He had lost both his parents in an accident and was growing up under the care of an uncle. The uncle was not too happy with his charge and at the first opportunity had shunted him off to boarding school. The death of both parents and the burden of negotiating school life away from home and amongst a strange world of bullies, buddies and doting teachers had an unsettling effect on the young child. While he remained at the top of his class, year after year, he tried to run away twice. But every time he was discovered and returned to the confines of the hostel.

Professor Tanmoy Sen spoke softly, haltingly, measuring his words, often touching the frame of his egg-shaped glasses which turned a smoky brown in the sun. He sported a salt-and-pepper beard when the work was slow but unlike the romantic he would trim and comb his greying fuzz with care.

He had already spent a year and a half at the institute in Calcutta and was looking forward to some news about money for his projects when he bumped into Chaturvedi one day. The director was coming out of the toilet. Tanmoy had been in high spirits, having just received supporting evidence for the results of an experiment and was planning to have a celebratory drink, when the director stopped him in his tracks and fixing him with a stare and a wicked smile said, 'Congratulations, Sen!'

Tanmoy beamed and thanked him, imagining he was pleased too about the positive feedback about his experiment results, when the director let a wisp of a grey-black cloud colour his face, but with his eyes still smiling said, 'We have exciting work coming our way and I want you to take charge of it. You know,' he lowered his voice conspiratorially, 'there's no one here who can handle this.'

'I will do my best,' Tanmoy said, a little warily, and asked, 'so the ministerial task force has agreed to open their purse strings wider for the gene transfer projects?' Gene transfer was his main area of research and he had been trying to secure funds to advance it further. While he had been writing proposals to mobilise private funding, mostly for research into disease, which is what interested the corporations, his focus had always been on gene transfer.

Chaturvedi was a short, bald-headed man with shiny steel-rimmed reading glasses that dangled in a black noose around his neck and his thick oversized jaws camouflaged his expressions well. His eyes lit up for an instant hearing Tanmoy's question and then changed colour abruptly, looking like dead fish eyes. He hung his hands on both sides, then slowly moving his head from side to side said, 'I fought tooth and nail. But the additional budget for gene transfer was not granted.' He made a resigned expression that also said 'I have done all I could, but this is beyond my powers' and kept staring at Tanmoy trying to anticipate his reaction.

If Tanmoy didn't get to know the real story, he would have trusted him for a few more days. So impeccable was his deceit.

But luckily Karen was there. After hearing the devastating news he had excused himself and headed straight back to his office. Chaturvedi had seen it on his face and had tried damage control. 'Substantial funding has been cleared for the other project which I was asking you to take charge of,' he said quickly. Without stopping to hear what it was all about Tanmoy had thanked him curtly and excused himself.

He switched off all the lights of his office room, threw a towel on the PC and put the telephone off its hook. Through the slatted window to his left, yellow sunbeams picked up the powdery insect shit floating in the air. There was a dictionary of biology lying on the floor and putting it under his head he lay down on the couch. But sleep eluded him.

How could the government do this when food security was a top priority for the country? The work he was doing had interfaces with advanced crop research going on in major institutions around the world. It didn't make sense.

There was shuffling of feet outside and then a knock at the door.

He didn't budge. They knocked louder. He remained steadfast in his resolve to keep quiet. Whoever was outside seemed undecided whether they should knock again. A minute passed. He could hear nervous breathing from outside the door. Then, whoever it was, decided to quit. He heard receding footsteps.

After a while his mobile phone began to sing its sodden tune. He had forgotten to power it off and had to take the call. It was Karen.

'Have you gone home already?'

He considered the question. Could she be calling from the director's office and would hand over the phone to him if he said no? Chaturvedi knew he would take her call and so might have pressed her to find out if he had left. So he kept quiet when Karen said, 'You can tell me, there is no one here.'

'I have a terrible headache.'

'Oh! Where are you?'

He wondered if he should tell her the truth. She had been nice to him all along and would share her problems. He had defended her once, when one of Chaturvedi's henchmen at the institute, a cell biologist called Pandhe, had made a report against her for not following up on a job. It hadn't been her fault.

Sometimes they would meet after office at a cafe and then he would drop her home. They interacted at a professional level and once he had invited her over for a home-cooked dinner. But that was about that. They hardly discussed their personal lives which in case of Tanmoy was not very different from the life of work. He had spent all these years in laboratories and classrooms around the world and had till then remained single.

GEM was a partner in a number of networked research projects with laboratories around the globe and Karen had been loaned to them from the Israeli Centre for Genomics. He had facilitated her move to this institute, having been acquainted with her work. A molecular biologist with brilliant background, Karen was one of the brightest scientists that he had come across.

'I have locked myself up in my office and plotting murder,' he told her over the phone.

'Hey! What kind of joke is that? Are you okay?'

'Just heard some delicious news from the horse's mouth,' he replied in an even tone.

'What about? Do you want to share it with me?' she said tentatively. The tone of her voice told him she knew something was seriously amiss.

'I am not in a mood to speak with anyone.'

'Come on. We can have something to eat at one of the Tibetan joints. The boss is leaving early. He is flying to Berlin tomorrow. Maybe you will feel better once we are out on the street.'

He considered her proposition. She had always been friendly. Though she worked closely with the director, he knew she would not betray a confidante or harm him for her own professional advancement.

She lived in a rented flat near Gol Park not far from where he lived. There was a leafy avenue on the way and he would park at a distance and they would take a walk under the trees.

'Where do you want to meet? I am in a foul mood so don't blame me later.'

'Taste of Tibet? In half an hour?'

'Wait, not there. Can you come to the planetarium, please?'

'The planetarium?'

'Yes, right outside the ticket booth?'

'Are we going for the show?'

'Yes.'

'Isn't that slightly unusual?'

'I want to tell you something and can't think of a better place than this.'

'If you say so,' there was a soft sigh at the other end of the line, then she hung up.

They went to the planetarium where there was a special show on Halley's comet running for the week. It was already dark inside when they entered the dome and it was difficult to settle down in the stargazing seats.

'Wouldn't it be a good idea if the pews at churches were tilted at an angle so that the devout could look heavenwards without fear of muscle cramp?' he had written in his diary that night after briefly noting the meeting with the director and what he thought about him: 'Bloody spliced monkey!'

Halley was the hero of the evening. They started off with Mark Twain who was born the same year in the early part of the nineteenth century that the comet had appeared. Karen's arm was lightly touching his and in the darkness it sent mild currents through his elbow which travelled up his shoulders and petered out somewhere near the heart. The projector threw a bright image of the comet gliding across the starry heavens, its diaphanous tail a milky white brushstroke across the night.

'The American author Mark Twain was born exactly two weeks after the comet's appearance in 1835. He obviously noted that fact and put it down in his autobiography saying ...'

The commentary was unimpressive and the commentator had a hopeless voice. It was as if someone had forcibly put a refrigerated condom on his cock and was forcing him to fuck while he was trying without success to shoot his load and get over with it. 'If I was wearing slip-ons I would have thrown one at him,' Tanmoy nudged Karen and whispered.

'How can we talk here?' she whispered back. 'You were going to say something.'

'Yes. The task force didn't grant the additional funding for my project. So from the new financial year I will be helping at the canteen.'

'Oh! That's terrible! Did you speak with the boss about it?'

'The first recorded sighting of this periodic visitor was in 240 BC by the Chinese and this is mentioned in the *Records of the Grand Historian*. It must have looked much brighter then, with no electricity and light pollution dimming our skies,' the hopeless voice went on.

'Yes, he delivered the news this afternoon, and he was blushing with glee,' Tanmoy said.

'But your project was top priority for the institute, wasn't it?'

'Yesterday's news I suppose. Something must have happened in between for the government to change its mind.'

The comet was skidding across the planetarium dome and the red dot of the commentator's laser pointer sprinted after it while he struggled on hopelessly from the Chinese to the Babylonian tablets and on to further sightings, inching closer to modern times.

'But you got good results from the vector independent gene delivery experiments. I read your paper,' she whispered loudly with rising curiosity. Some stargazers immediately behind them made noises expressing annoyance.

'I am completely flummoxed,' he told her, trying to speak as softly as possible.

Some members of the audience were clearly irritated having been distracted from their comet. They asked them to shut up or get out and let them have their stars in peace.

But Karen didn't seem to care. 'Oh my God! Now I realise what's been going on. A few days ago the boss was preparing the quarterly reports for the task force and as you know he makes me correct and clean his shit. I found it strange that the results from your protoplast incubation experiments were mentioned cursorily. I had asked him casually ...'

'And then?'

But it was no more possible to carry on the conversation. Two people behind them had risen from their seats and were loudly protesting. 'Will you two stop talking?'

The commentator's voice wavered and he forgot where he was, mixed up the names of the space probes launched to study the comet at close quarters and so the Giotto probe became the Apollo mission. Then he realised his mistake and apologised.

'He said that there will be a separate report and he will personally champion the project. I guess he did just the opposite. I am sure he knows all the task force members!' She said those last few words so loudly that the whole audience could hear her.

'Bastard!'

There was a moment of pure silence. The commentary had stopped. Everyone behind them had risen from their seats. Voices began hollering at them. Very angry voices. They were determined to throw them out so they rose to leave. Karen quickly stepped out into the aisle and he followed her. If he could get his hands on Chaturvedi now, he would have strangled him on the spot. They hurried down the aisle.

The audience began to calm down as soon as they saw them heading for the exit. Perhaps on cue to the calming of tempers the man with the frozen penis began his shaky delivery like a nineteenth-century Studebaker juddering to life, 'Our earth is a little ping-pong ball in a great forest of galaxies, nebulae, stars and supernova which we call the universe. It all started with the Big Ben!'

Karen cursed in Hebrew as the heavy doors swung shut behind them but the stargazers were already too engrossed to care.

2

It was in London when they had first met. They had seen each other before at Novingdon, but no one had really introduced them. It was a weekday evening of a long gone February when the unusual rains had lashed the city seven nights in a row. They had both taken shelter under the awnings of The Blue Boar which was some way from the station. But both had a train to catch and it was getting late.

'Haven't we met before?' Tanmoy had asked, recognising the other man in the glimmer of light filtering through the glass panels of the pub. He spoke softly, almost inaudibly.

Henry David was busy saving his violin from the downpour and taking a look at him with his grey eyes had replied in his grainy voice, 'Uh-yes. Back in Novingdon town, isn't it?' He had stepped closer to him under the doorway, away from the rain — cider on his breath, his beard glistening with raindrops.

The rain was bone-chilling cold. The windows of The Blue Boar had frosted over with the heat inside and pressing his face against the glass, Tanmoy could hear boisterous laughter and see the ruddy-faced publican moving from table to table. Then he had turned to face the street and there was Henry right in front of him, a hulking giant of a man, his black parka dripping acid rain as he snapped shut his umbrella, sending a flurry of ice cold droplets into his face.

The last three days had been a blur of work, classes and meetings at the central London offices of Sante Inc, the global agricultural biotech major which was funding their work. He had met old colleagues who had come down from the States. They were all part of the network of institutions working on advanced crops. Though the meetings had ended inconclusively, he was confident that Sante, which has been pumping millions into this research, will commit more funds for their UK lab.

'Rough weather, mate,' Henry had said while peering through the window of the pub checking out the scene inside.

'Are you planning to get back to Novingdon tonight?' he had asked.

'Yes, indeed.'

'I hope we won't miss the train. How far to the station from here?'

'I am lost as you are.'

'Perhaps we should go inside and ask?' Tanmoy had suggested.

'Keep away from the crowds,' he had looked at him strangely and said.

Tanmoy didn't know how to respond, taken aback by this unsolicited advice. He had grinned and looked away in the direction from where a bus was coming. But the bus stop was a little further down and it was impossible to go out in the pelting rain.

There was a tug on his sleeve. 'If you would listen to me, Sir, go back to where you came from.'

Tanmoy wondered if this was a racist comment, but before he could arrive at a decision Henry said, 'I have seen you in our little town down south. Go back there. London is not the place for you.'

'What the fuck do you mean?' he was going to shoot back, peeved by his comment, when the stranger smiled disarmingly and said, 'Look over there.'

He looked. The rain was falling in sheets now blurring out the street lights and the chilling wind was eating into his flesh. Up the street were a row of dismal houses with black chimneypots and when he looked up there was no light at any of the windows but one. A two-storey house with gabled roof and a mock Tudor facade that looked older than the others and at one of the upper floor windows there was a light.

'Look up,' he said pointing there. 'That is one of my patients and he ditched me today.'

'Your patient?' Tanmoy said tentatively while hoping the rain would stop soon.

'I am a medicine man. I treat rare disorders with music,' and he patted his violin case.

'Uh-huh.'

'I came all the way to examine him, but he didn't show himself.'

'Treating rare disorders with music. That's interesting but why do you think he didn't meet you? Didn't he make an appointment?' Then he wondered why this almost stranger was telling him all this and made a questioning face.

'He is one of the more unusual patients. I have been treating him for years but after today I will have to think.'

Tanmoy was restless because he was getting delayed by the rain and there were very few trains in the late hours. Yet he was intrigued by this gentleman with the violin. 'Why do you say "unusual"?' he asked.

'That's a long story but very briefly it is about his silence. He had been to the war and since he returned he has forgotten how to speak.'

'I am sorry to hear this. Was he wounded?'

'Only when I play this,' and Henry lovingly patted his violin case, 'he will begin to talk but when I am gone he will again retreat into silence. It is not that he has lost the power of speech but something shuts him up completely when he tries to speak with others. I have tried recordings but it doesn't work.'

'And what do you play?'

'Some of our old songs, folk and things like that.'

'So what does he have to say, when you play the music?'

'He always talks about this battle, where he was wounded.'

'Which would that be?'

'The battle of Chipyong-ni. It is called the Gettysburg of the Korean War. Have you heard about it?'

Tanmoy shook his head.

'He is American. They were fighting under the command of Paul L. Freeman alongside the French. They were encircled at Chipyong-ni by the Chinese who had a huge numerical advantage but these brave soldiers put up a solid defence for two days till support arrived and the enemy retreated. Both sides suffered heavy losses but the Chinese lost thousands of fighting men.'

'And he tells you the story of this battle?'

'Yes, in vivid and excruciating detail. Listening to him you could visualise the scenes, the horror of the war. Under the glow of flares dropped from the C-47 Skytrains the Chinese and the United Nations forces fought hand-to-hand battles through the night. UN and Chinese soldiers died in the same dugouts locked in death embrace. My patient was a machine-gunner. He was burned badly in mortar fire.'

'Must have been a traumatic experience.'

'The Chinese, he says, used bugles and whistles to communicate and sounded hand-cranked sirens when they attacked. That disoriented the enemy. But the French soon learned that trick!'

'So what do you think he is doing there now, sitting by the window?'

'I bet he is watching. Watching the street. Which is what he does most of the time. As if he is waiting for someone. But when I turned up today, he just pretended to be not there.

'I arrived early this afternoon as I had told him I would,' Henry continued, 'but when I rang the bell there was nobody answering. I rang it several times but still everything was quiet. I rang and knocked and hollered for the best part of an hour, Sir, crowing like a madman over the sound of this devilish rain, and then an old lady, who lives there, opens the door. And what does she tell me? Listen to this, Sir, she says no one by that name lives here. Now tell me, what am I to do? I tell her I have been visiting him for decades and describe how he looks, but to no avail. She thinks I am a lunatic and bangs the door shut on my face. Ill manners have nothing to do with age, I tell you, Sir. So I went into a pub up the street and had a few drinks, hoping to sit out the rain. But see how it gets heavier by the minute. Then I walked back just to see if this man was really hiding and there he was at the window. Now what does a simple man make of it, you tell me? Good that I at least found you here. We are taking the same train aren't we?'

'I will take the Southampton train calling at Novingdon.'

'That's my train and I will get down a few stops later for a connection. Now the question is how to get to the station.'

They waited for the rain to let but it went from bad to worse. After a while Tanmoy said, 'You think your patient is up there in his flat right now but for some reason he didn't want to meet you?'

'Do you doubt it?'

'Not really, but why should he ...'

'Good question! He sits there by the window and watches the street. That's what he has been doing for years. But he made a grave mistake by refusing to meet me today. That he did,' and his face was suddenly ashen and dark half moons appeared below his eyes.

'What shall we do now?' Tanmoy said.

They braved the pouring rain and went to the tube stop, which was quite some distance, but when they arrived they learnt that there was a strike on all lines and no services were running.

The rain had not let and the evening was getting old. It came in torrents, ploughing the street, driven by a mad wind that beat mercilessly against their faces, gnawing off the flesh from their bones. If they couldn't get a taxi in a few minutes it would be difficult to reach the station in time for the last train.

But the weather didn't seem to affect Henry. They were standing under the shelter of a bus stop but by the time the next bus was due their train would have left. Henry kept muttering to himself, cursing his patient under his breath, while the storm went on howling above their heads.

'If we don't get a taxi now we can't catch the train,' Tanmoy said.

Henry's face seemed to light up at the comment and he caressed his chin, 'Then we have to put up somewhere for the night.'

Tanmoy hated this turn of events but there was hardly anything they could do. 'If it comes to that I would like to be somewhere close to the station, so that I can catch the morning train.'

'Brilliant,' Henry replied and in his excitement knocked off his umbrella and went diving into the sheet rain to fetch it. The rain grew heavier still but there was no cab or any sort of transport in sight. So they began to walk through the storm, sheltered by his umbrella. Several blocks later they arrived at a major crossing where they found a taxi rank.

'The Gribble Inn, please,' he told the cabbie.

'Is it near the station?' Tanmoy asked.

'Close by,' he said but even the cabbie hadn't heard about this place and so Henry took charge. He directed him further north and east, through a block of office buildings that were all closed at that hour and past empty parks getting washed by the downpour, snaking through a maze of streets and lanes till in about fifteen minutes they arrived at the gates of an old dilapidated-looking building with the inn sign falling off its frame.

'I thought we were putting up somewhere close to the station,' Tanmoy said.

'This is the best bargain and not too far really,' Henry said.

The night porter opened the door. The pub had closed and they were led straight to a single room at the back. Tanmoy was dripping wet, their boots squelched mud and his companion let out such an earth-shaking sneeze that The Gribble shuddered on its foundations and sleeping guests groaned in their tiny beds.

The only room available was cold, for the heating had broken, and so they sat in the empty smoking lounge, chatting till it was dawn.

This was how they had met for the first time. Tanmoy Sen had arrived in England only the year before:

'The work is exciting,' he had noted in his Moleskine diary, 'it takes most of my time and some more. But at this point there are too many assumptions that we are making. I cannot say if we are on the right path until we have crossed a number of hurdles and tested several options.'

This was the bargain that genius struck with fate and it was always an equal wager. Perhaps if he had met Henry David earlier, things would have turned out a little different?

Tanmoy would have Henry in his thoughts often. Most of all he remembered this encounter at The Gribble and earlier outside that pub. He had noted in detail that first meeting with Henry right down to every turn that their conversation had taken. Henry had put his feet up and talked about his patient who would scarcely speak and when he did, it was about the battle of Chipyong-ni.

The violinist was smoking a briar. The acrid smell of tobacco had filled the lounge room right up to its crumbling ceiling and with each drag the fire of his pipe glowed even brighter, like the beating heart of an animal wide awake in the abyss of night.

3

When Tanmoy had put in his papers at GEM and changed his mobile number, Karen had not been at office. Later she would send him an email which had a twinge of hurt in it. 'At least you could have taken me into confidence before leaving like that,' she had written. It weighed him down for a few days, her email, but soon he was drawn back into the routines of work.

The British laboratory where he now worked had poached the best brains in the world that kept them at the frontiers of genetics research. He was doing cutting-edge work with crops as part of a global network of laboratories, working on improved paddy varieties that would be a source of vitamins while withstanding extreme weather conditions which had become more frequent as the years went by.

There was freedom here too, he could do his thing. And he was teaching students at the university which had its own satisfaction — the adrenaline rush of speaking to a class of bright young minds. Learning from them and sharing his experience. But what he most enjoyed about his work at the university, of which GeneLab UK was a part, was their readiness to lead the SuperRice project which would have a direct impact on health and food security in unpredictable times.

He had settled in well in the pretty little town of Novingdon with the Roman market cross and a very handsome cathedral with a bell tower that could be seen from France. Not really but the townfolk made up that story and indeed it was quite an imposing structure.

He was sitting at The Red Lion, one of the old pubs of Novingdon, that afternoon. He was waiting for Eugene, a scientist colleague at the university, who was working on a gene mapping project. His Korean name was Ryu Yujin but he preferred to spell it the other way.

It was the end of a week and Tanmoy had put on his cream white pair of chinos and a printed shirt with sunflowers on a navy background which complemented the smoky brown of his glasses. He had a fancy for loud colours and bold prints and his students would always comment on his style though he was not really fashion conscious. He picked up what he liked and was quite ignorant about materials or cuts.

Tanmoy had stepped out for a drink like he did every weekend. And it was always at this high-street pub, The Red Lion. Later, if he felt like it, he would take a taxi which would drop him off at the Secret Knowledge which was a waterside night club a few miles out of town.

Out from his laboratory, past the animal house, an alley snaked and met the main road which climbed a low hill before joining up with the street leading to the town square with its market cross, weathered but intact. To the right, as one entered the street, you could see the Roman wall with daffodils blooming at this time of the year and the bright grass green on its ramparts. Further up, past the Chinese takeaway and a couple of tea and coffee places, the street became festive with quaintly named cafes and ale houses, their chairs out in the sun and young buskers strumming away on their guitars, singing sentimental melodies to the tourists and pensioners walking their poodles. Here if you lingered you would catch the scent of fresh baguettes mingling with Issey Miyake notes that the well-heeled town dwellers wore, until you walked right up to the cathedral, with its Chagall window and a granite facade, looking quite like a grim-faced ancestor.

Though it was a Saturday the crowd was still thin at the Lion which was good for he could stand next to the bar and chat with the green-eyed barmaid — Nicole. Nicole was friendly with the patrons, bantering and laughing at the wisecracks of the elderly clientele who patronised this ale house. She had cascades of honey blonde hair going down to her waist and a well-rounded body that filled in her white polo neck and charcoal black trousers.

Like every time Tanmoy ordered his pint of Landlord bitter and a packet of salted peanuts which he believed must have been genetically modified, because the nuts were big as horse testicles. There were two other customers at the bar — a pink-faced old timer with a twinkle in his eyes and a grave-looking spectacled gent with a walrus moustache, sitting on the padded bar stools discussing horses while getting properly drunk.

'Will you play "Piano Man"?' Tanmoy suggested and Nicole cued in the track.

'You like this song?' she asked him.

'Shouldn't I?' he said, his fleshy lips curving into a smile, and this conversation with minor variations would be repeated every time he made the request.

'Guess, you should,' she would reply and look at him, holding the gaze just for an extra second, before returning to the ale pumps. That extra second or two, once every weekend or sometimes twice on a single day, if he was lucky that is, shuffled some of the stuff inside him, knocking down a few walls, so that the layout of the city changed completely and new maps needed to be drawn. It was easy to get swept away and he had no encumbrance, except for his work, but he couldn't tell the same about her. He had never seen her boyfriend but resisted asking her about him. That would spoil the fun.

'Are you at the gene lab?' she had asked him the first day he had popped in and he was quite surprised that she already knew. Of course it was Eugene who had told her but it hadn't occurred to him then. Eugene was a regular at the Lion and he was quite friendly with the waitress.

He now pushed in through the doorway, a tall and thin man wearing ill-fitting clothes, his big bony arms dangling by his side. He tied his hair in a ponytail and the wrinkles on his forehead, over a slightly weather-beaten face, made the Korean look much older than him, but they were almost the same age. There was a saintly detachment about the way he carried himself, his slow walk — the calmness of his eyes. A silver cross hung from his neck which popped out between his shirt buttons whenever he leaned forward to speak and the scientist immediately pushed it back. His eyes shone, when he would be discussing work, and Tanmoy was reminded once again what an asset he was for their department.

They greeted each other while Eugene waited for Nicole to notice him. 'Your friend has been waiting, you are late!' Nicole came up to them and chided Eugene and, without waiting to hear his order, brought a double gin and tonic.

Tanmoy had finished his pint and got himself another. 'Seems it might rain,' Eugene said looking out through the window as more patrons arrived and the pub got noisy.

'Are you waiting for someone or can I join you?' Eugene asked.

'Not really. I am on my own,' he took a fleeting look at Nicole who was away at the other end of the bar taking orders.

'Let us go and sit near the fireplace if you don't mind,' Eugene suggested. Tanmoy was hungry and so they ordered cod and chips and walked up to one of the low tables.

The Korean scientist finished his double gin while Tanmoy dug into his fish and chips. They talked about the new students at the university, about their teaching and the staid life of the little town, where the only exciting news in the last six months was about a knife assault at the church side parking lot. After a while Tanmoy asked, 'How has your work been?'

'We have analysed and interpreted the results from the genome sequencing done by our consortium and are publishing some of it in *Nature Genetics*. So there should be excitement ahead. What about you? I only seem to hear good things about your project?'

'Good luck to you,' Tanmoy said, 'my baby refuses to walk. We prop him up sometimes and give him a little push but he doesn't go beyond a few tentative steps. Sometimes I feel I have too much on my plate. It is one thing to make the paddy tolerant to drought and frost but quite another to transform it into a storeroom for specific vitamin like compounds. Yet I believe it should be possible, only the right donor genes and the appropriate transfer methods have to be found. Like everyone else, I am banking more on direct gene transfer and no viruses, at least not immediately, but finding the best donor genes for such a heavily engineered crop is a different ball game altogether. We have been looking high and low in gene libraries, raiding our collective knowledge, but progress has been slow. There is still nothing to write home about.'

'I know you will make it,' Eugene said and sipped his drink. From where they were sitting, they could see Nicole pouring cloudy ciders for a boisterous group of men with tattoos on their arms.

Tanmoy slathered a nice chunk of cod with tartar sauce and devoured it hungrily. He wanted to pick Eugene's brain and discuss the problems in detail, especially about the new gene editing technique, but Sante had an iron grip over information sharing and he was not allowed to go into specifics of the project outside their research group.

He went off to the loo to relieve himself. Before coming out he washed his face in the mirror and was amused to see how much his pupils had dilated from the alcohol. He should shift to light beer he thought as he came out of the washroom. And just then he noticed Nicole staring at Eugene. The same lingering look, only this time it lasted longer. Eugene held the gaze. Was she just flirting with customers and keeping her landlord happy or was something going on between the two? Perhaps he was reading too much into it. He decided he had had enough to drink and gulped down the last of the ale left in his glass.

4

The same stream of life that runs through my veins night and day runs through the world and dances in rhythmic measures. It is the same life that shoots in joy through the dust of the earth in numberless blades of grass and breaks into tumultuous waves of leaves and flowers.
—Rabindranath Tagore

It was around this time that Tanmoy had that first encounter with the violinist, Henry David. Because only one room had been available at the inn they had planned to sleep in turns. But before that they had been sitting in the lounge. Henry had been smoking a briar and the pungent smell of the tobacco had filled the room as they waited for their dinner. The innkeeper had promised to get them baked haddock but it took ages to appear.

Tanmoy had had a long day of meetings at Sante's London offices and was dozing off. He tricked his tired grey cells with raunchy thoughts to keep himself awake. The only woman who came to his mind was Nicole but somehow he couldn't drive his thoughts in the proper direction. He could recall that she wore bold men's perfumes which clothed her with the scent of forests but that was how far he could go.

It was no use. His eyelids were again getting heavy. He shifted to a leather armchair from the sofa and sat up straight. The rain was pelting the roof of the old inn and the wind howled down the chimneys, whistling through cracks and rattling the doors on their rusty hinges.

They had asked the porter to put out the lounge lights while they waited. It was quiet in there. In his hypnagogic state Tanmoy could see double helical DNA strands slithering along like snakes, coming right through the window. The strands were luminescent with bright colours pulsing through them and the groups of genes joined the strands like lighted bridges across oceans of darkness. The radiant DNA strands like expressways twisting through the night, twining lives and ancestries together. The bridges swung as the raging wind roared down the chimney flue and the battle between death and life raged on. There, in the smoky lounge of The Gribble Inn, he heard, watched and marvelled at the possibility of life defying death, of human intelligence bridging great chasms of darkness. 'Those iridescent bridges were swinging over the sea of death. It was a vision of hope,' Tanmoy told his diary later.

'I guess the haddock is still swimming in the North Sea,' Henry said after a while. 'Why don't you go and get some rest? I see you are very tired.'

Tanmoy in his half sleep went on watching the illuminated DNA strands slithering in through the window, getting joined up by the gene bridges until suddenly there was a burst of dazzling light. He looked up. Henry had pulled the master switch and all the lights had come on together.

'It's no good thinking of work when it's time to sleep,' Henry said.

The old fox, he is playing guessing games, Tanmoy thought, slightly irritated. Of course I would be thinking of work, what else could keep me awake? 'How do you know it is work that keeps me awake?' he said.

'Just a guess, Sir,' Henry said guardedly, 'maybe you are hungry?'

Sure he was. Because of the back-to-back meetings he only had time for a soup lunch and was planning to catch a quick train back to Novingdon and have dinner at home but was delayed by the rains. Then this violinist had turned up and began to talk about his patient.

The night porter finally appeared with their dinner and two plates. Henry divided up the fish and they polished it off in the blink of an eye. They looked at each other not sure what to say.

'I guess they have closed the kitchen for the night?' Tanmoy spelt out what they both already knew. He was still hungry but too tired to do anything about it.

'That's what the porter told us. And at this hour there won't be any food joint open in this neighbourhood. But, wait, I may have something, Hope it hasn't spoiled,' he went looking in his backpack.

Half a bottle of wine and an enormous sandwich that would last a small army through a minor war. He placed both on the table.

Goodness gracious! That drink is spiked and will knock me out for sure and no one will ever come to know how I met my end, flashed through Tanmoy's mind. Though he had seen Henry at the university and he had told him that he was a music teacher there, Tanmoy didn't trust him yet. This bearded pirate must be in cahoots with organ traders and his kidneys will go to the service of some ailing Russian oligarch looking for an organ donor in London, he told himself. But he was too tired to stave off the apparent friendly gestures of the stranger.

'Have a look, perhaps you can swallow this stuff. Not a king's dinner I am afraid but this will do us plebeians good,' Henry said after studying the bottle carefully and handing it over to Tanmoy. He took the bottle from him and read the label — *Saint-Estèphe Grand Cru*. This chap had style, unless the wine was fake, which seemed more like it.

Henry tore the sandwich into two with his bare hands and handed one half to Tanmoy. Tanmoy uncorked the bottle and poured two drinks. Henry placed his share of the sandwich on a piece of tissue and they clinked glasses.

The wine was rich which made him think that whatever poison had gone into it was camouflaged well. He didn't have a god so he recalled the face of his class eight biology teacher and hoped he would not have felt too sad at seeing his most promising pupil leaving the field in such an unceremonious manner. He mustered up the courage and took another quaff of wine and bit into the sandwich. It tasted horrible.

'Watercress, I am afraid,' Henry said apologetically.

Tanmoy dug into the slightly soggy bread, the face of his biology teacher fixed in his mind. It was always better going out on a full stomach than getting kicked out hungry and thirsty, he told himself. The wine began to work its magic.

'Are you a therapist like me?' Henry asked, washing down the sandwich with a generous sip from his glass.

'Ah! That's a bit far out but my work has a definite impact upon health. I am a geneticist.' Did he use a slow-acting poison? He was still suspicious and was quite uncomfortable being cooped in with this stranger. They were on their second glass now but still nothing had happened. He hadn't rolled off the chair dead and Henry David was sitting ramrod erect. Must have taken an antidote, Tanmoy decided, but how come *he* was still alive?

'That's interesting! Tinkering with nature?'

He didn't want to get into a discussion about his current work. There were protocols of secrecy. GeneLab UK though housed in the university was largely funded by Sante and they were inflexible about information sharing. So much so that this sometimes slowed down the pace of their work or led them through circuitous routes. He had to be careful.

'I am too tired to discuss my work but it will do a lot of good for millions, someday soon,' he said.

'But tinkering is dangerous, nonetheless,' the stranger said while masticating the enormous sandwich.

Tanmoy was beginning to get offended but something drove him to carry on this conversation. 'There is danger in everything, in all forms of striving. We cannot sit back in a cave and warm our hands in the fire. Cave dwellers fashioned tools to hunt better. Wrongly designed bridges do come crashing, space shuttles melt in the upper atmosphere vaporising astronauts, but that's no reason not to try.'

'We play too many games with the order of things. Nature is not to be mocked, see what I mean?'

'I am a scientist,' Tanmoy said, touching the frame of his glasses, mildly irritated by this solicitousness, 'and we are just trying to better understand this order of things as you put it and get it working for greater good.'

Henry's glass had been empty for a while. In the light of the lounge room Tanmoy could feel the warmth of his grey eyes. He didn't look like an organ trader any more but he was beginning to get on his nerves. His wrinkled face and blotched skin was of a man who spent quite a bit of his life outdoors. The beard cut in a square had unruly tendrils creeping out like little children peeping through a hedge looking for friends. Now that he had removed his fishing cap, for the first time, Tanmoy saw his hair matted and hanging loose around his shoulders. Though he had noble features, his hands were sinewy and muscular which showed that he was a man habituated to hard labour.

Henry filled their glasses again and said, 'Greater and lesser, larger or smaller may not mean anything at all, Sir. I am a layman who doesn't understand the workings of your science but I feel we need to strike a balance. We are not the only species on this planet. Nature has rusted because of our lack of care and the violence we inflict upon her. Don't you hear how sea levels have been rising and then it rains in winter so much that we fear this country will be washed away?'

'My work would keep millions of undernourished people healthy even during extreme weather conditions. They will get basic nutrition. If that goes against the natural order then so be it,' Tanmoy said. He had finished his piece of sandwich and was cleaning his dirty fingers on the printed tissue which had the image of a steamship drawn across it.

'Disease is also a gift. A gift which we could do without. It is the sap of life flowing through nature leaking or spilling out because of our disjointed living. You can't go very far, Sir, tackling it with your hard-nosed science. There will always be repercussions, things will go wrong. See how critical antibiotics have been failing. The only way to engage with suffering is to align our physical and mental beings with the stream of life flowing through this universe. To be in rhythm with that flow.'

'I see,' Tanmoy decided this man was completely nuts, 'our humanity, doesn't allow us to see fellow humans in pain or suffering. And if a gift hurts, better get rid of it. Also I believe evolution is a splendid mechanism to keep us in check. It will control actions that would imperil our survival.'

Henry yawned covering his mouth, got up from the sofa and said, 'Pardon my language, Sir, but did evolution prevent us from developing the atom fucking bomb or stop us from using it?' He lit his pipe again and began to pace up and down the passage between the tables.

'Yet science has made great strides in the treatment of disease and that means less of suffering. Everything has its positives and negatives,' Tanmoy said.

'The old masters knew all the secrets of the body which we have forgotten now. Go to the ancient lands, go to Siberia, to the

Himalayas, there you will still find healers of the ancient tradition. The shamans, the lamas, the lung-gom-pa, they can cure anything, even make one live hundreds of years but without tinkering with the natural order. They were here in this country too but they didn't write down the ancient teaching. So it's all lost.' It seemed Henry was going into some sort of trance. He spoke very softly and Tanmoy had to strain to hear him. Was he tripping on some drug, he wondered, for Henry's voice had suddenly changed, as if he was speaking from the depths of the earth.

'It is said that when King Conchobar was injured in the head and dying it was the holy healers who saved his life. There were no antibiotics then, no pain killers, no gene tinkering. Their medicine was all the gift of the earth.'

'Perhaps. Good luck to them,' Tanmoy said. He rose to get to the room and sleep for a while. Let him enjoy his trip in the empty lounge, he thought, mildly irritated. But just as he was about to push through the door he heard the birds chirping on a tree in the backyard.

'Shit!' He hadn't been able to sleep and it was morning already.

The wine was down to the last drop. The stranger had a little left in his glass while his was empty.

Henry switched off the light. The sun hadn't risen yet but a soft blush had spread across the English sky, pushing night to the far edges of the jagged skyline of whimsical high rises. Birds were twittering on a rowan tree next door. The storm had died but a fine rain was still falling on the empty flooded streets. A sycamore in a corner of the backyard was swaying its branches gently, leaves glistening in the spitting rain. Looked like it would be a wet day.

5

This grand show is eternal. It is always sunrise somewhere; the dew is never all dried at once; a shower is forever falling; vapour is ever rising. Eternal sunrise, eternal sunset, eternal dawn and gloaming, on sea and continents and islands, each in its turn, as the round earth rolls.

—John Muir

Winter came and went. The first winter seemed harsh perhaps because Tanmoy had not experienced it for a long time. He had got used to the muggy days of Calcutta. He worked at the laboratory, took classes, met students and then retired to his house spending the freezing evenings nursing a malt with an unpronounceable name. A mad wind blew through those nights and in the first year it snowed a lot. The bare branches of the elms that stood outside his window looked like thin men shivering from hunger.

   He remembered watching the snow falling on the banks of the Esk years ago, when he had first arrived in this country to teach. It was laying a smooth carpet on Roslyn glen and beyond in Edinburgh where he had lectured on supercrops at the university, earlier that week. Later he had driven up to Greenock to visit the birthplace of James Watt. The cairn of Watt at the local cemetery, built from stones gifted from around the world, had stones from various gradients of the Indian railways. He was quite moved to see those Indian stones in the memorial of the inventor. Tanmoy had always vouched for this man. No matter how the world had changed and what has happened since, this was the invention that transformed millions of lives. Nothing would ever be the same again. He could relate with the scale of Watt's imagination.

Spring arrived late that year, daffodils bloomed and the wood pigeon got down to its business. The days grew brighter and a hot summer followed. The heat was such that train schedules went awry and twice Tanmoy was stranded in the Midlands because of suspended services. Meanwhile people applied sunblock on their pigs to protect them from the punishing sun. And it was just the beginning of a row of sweltering summers till in about five years the weather changed again.

'The ignorant are insensible to the pleasures of science, and have no notions of the attachments which this may produce.' He read the book again and again. *The Life of James Watt* by Muirhead, the book had become his only companion, wherever he went. There were numerous quotes from this volume in his diaries.

James Watt had come up in their conversation one day. They were now midway through the SuperRice project. In six years Tanmoy's research group had almost perfected the gene insertion techniques that will be used to splice donor genes into paddy. The work for identifying bacterial species and other donors whose genes could be spliced into rice to get the desired traits was just beginning. Still it was a long way to go. Over those years Tanmoy had become better acquainted with Henry. He somehow liked the company of the bearded musician. The university had a flourishing music department and because Henry could mesmerise an audience with his violin or the harp the department had offered him this part-time appointment. They would often meet over a drink and though they seldom agreed and often argued about the big questions, their bonhomie had survived.

Henry lived in a camping ground eighty miles from Novingdon and one day he had asked Tanmoy to come and be his guest. This was a few years after their first encounter at the London inn on that rain-soaked night.

It took more than two-and-half hours with a change of trains to reach the little town of Aberbourne. Henry was there at the station wearing a roomy summer jacket and floppy black trousers, his fishing cap pulled low over his eyes. His luxuriant beard with the tendrils of hair still peeping out blended in well with the setting of this small railway station, the little town with a pub by the tracks, the blazing mustard fields in the distance and a brook meandering lazily along.

From the town to the campsite was three miles and as buses were few and far between they walked. Tanmoy had forgotten to bring his raincoat and knowing the English weather was worrying that it might rain anytime while Henry, whistling and humming, marched along. 'Sorry I should have arranged for bikes,' he declared after a while, 'but I had been away last night and came straight to the station.'

'It's okay, how far are we from there?' he had asked in his soft, halting voice which Henry didn't hear as he kept marching gaily. In about an hour's time they arrived in a village with old flintstone walled houses, a church and a pub. He was thirsty and exhausted from the long walk so they went inside.

'We don't want to get late,' Henry remarked. Tanmoy ordered a pint of bitter and pork scratchings while Henry went for Frobisher's orange juice.

There was no one at the pub except for the portly publican, himself filling their glasses. Henry engaged him in small talk about politics and how the country was being handed out on a platter to corporates. The publican seemed to agree. 'Now they will drill for oil in Shetland and if they could they would bloody well sell the North Sea,' he said.

'Half of it is sold already, and there are no Iain Nobles around any more,' Henry joined in with a sigh. He related the anecdote of the Scottish banker who had founded a college of Gaelic culture and language. 'The story goes that once Noble was driving through the highlands and he gave a lift to a young Israeli hiker. As they passed through beautiful Scottish countryside, Noble, with some pride, pointed out to the young hiker mountains and lakes and forests, saying this loch belongs to Laird so and so and that glen there you see, it is owned by such and such family and that ben yonder, it is the property of the Duke of X and so on. After a while the young hiker turned around and said — "It's all very pretty but how can a forest, a lake or a mountain belong to anyone? In my country it's unthinkable!" And those words had a profound impact on the banker. In a short time Iain Noble would give up banking and establish that college of Gaelic culture and language.'

'No, no man half as conscientious as him. The world has changed, you see. A new set of people have arrived. Think about good old pubs. No one goes to pubs these days. Young people, they fancy the bars,' the publican said.

'If they have the money,' Henry said.

'Otherwise it's Wetherspoon.'

'You bet. I see pubs vanishing from England in the next ten years and then maybe a few of them will be maintained as museums. Dear old John Barleycorn, may his soul find peace in India,' he quipped and looked at Tanmoy.

'Huh,' Tanmoy smirked, 'we detest the old and the infirm. Whatever shows signs of aging is pulled down and has to give way for new development, high rises, shopping malls. Why just a few years ago there was this major court battle surrounding one of the oldest Raj era hotels in my home town, Calcutta. It had come into the crosshairs of land sharks. The media here picked it up too. That hotel was saved by a miracle but that's a different story.'

'Why don't you tell us about it. This is what we are fighting against and we would like to learn from others. Mindless development, exploiting nature to the hilt in the name of a better future, often driven by the hubris of science,' Henry said.

'I think you should not drag science into everything. It is our fault if we are ready to sell our souls. What does science have to do with it? Well anyway that particular hotel — the Hotel Calcutta — was owned by an Englishman. It was saved by the grace of a monk.'

Henry sat up straight with interest. 'Ah! Just like an Indian story. I wish I could visit that country soon.'

'Yes, indeed, you must. I too miss my city sometimes. But in any case this monk did something and the hotel is still there. But such monks appear once in a blue moon and they come with no warranty,' he spoke haltingly, stopping mid sentence to take a sip.

The conversation continued. 'Any more drinks for you gentlemen? I know Mr David, he is not one to touch a drop when the sun is above the horizon, but what about you, Sir?'

He would have half a pint. Tanmoy passed on his glass. The publican filled it up and disappeared through a door behind the bar.

'But to return to my point, science has got nothing to do with it. It is men who decide how to use our understanding of the laws of nature,' Tanmoy said.

'A little learning is a dangerous thing,' Henry mumbled while putting on his jacket. 'We have to get going. Still more than a mile and it might rain.'

Tanmoy finished his drink. It was still sunny outside with a gentle breeze blowing.

The road from Elmsby, which was the name of the village, went past some houses and a graveyard and soon they were again in the gently undulating countryside with sheep grazing in picture postcard meadows while the air had the briny smell of the sea. A little way ahead they branched into a bridle path that went through farmsteads and pasture land with cattle, and because of their sheer numbers or perhaps because they moved so little, it looked as if they were all clay animals laid out in the sun to dry.

Beyond the farmsteads, another rolling meadow — greenly incandescent, dotted with daisies, sprayed over the earth with all the wanton joy of a child. Birds were feeding on berries so they stepped softly.

'Science has been throwing stones at the darkness for long and it has become good with practice. But stones can be thrown only this way or that. You can't participate in the great work that is within us and all around us just by aiming stones and listening for the sound; that way you knock the world out of kilter,' Henry said after a while.

Though he could not make sense of what the music teacher meant, with the gentle breeze blowing in their faces, and the unspoilt charm of the country around them, his words still seemed to convey something at a deeper level. Tanmoy kept quiet.

'And often these stones miss the target. One aimed with good intention ricochets and hits us. Leave aside those aimed with mischief in mind and the games power plays with science,' Henry said in his rich grainy voice.

There were squirrels flitting about on the branches of a tree whose leaves had turned red and gold. A halo enveloped the canopy and looking at it he felt drawn towards it. The flaming canopy was slowly taking hold of his mind, hypnotising him and drawing him to its depths, following the tracks of the mischievous squirrels.

Thoughts wormed their way into his ecstasy — the risks that he had learned to ignore. Risks which are hard to anticipate and so not to be taken seriously. Even if some tests were done, no one could be completely sure how the human body would react in the long run to the transgenic rice they were creating. These thoughts occurred to him briefly, then they quickly disappeared. In the balance, wasn't SuperRice going to feed the hungry millions affected by drought or untimely frost besides providing nutrients?

He had become completely engrossed staring at the tree, while these thoughts sailed through his mind, when he noticed that it had begun to rain. Henry had stopped a little way ahead and was signalling him to take shelter under an ancient oak. He stepped up under the old tree. The giant oak protected them from the rain as they watched the country all around transform.

It rained in torrents blurring out the landscape, painting the country with brushstrokes of watery light. They stood still, breathing softly till the rain and the light had transformed them into little moist patches on the green and grey canvas of land and sky. Later when the clouds dispersed and the light was clear and warm, the world seemed to have woken up refreshed from a slumber, fresh and rejuvenated — blue-eyed like a newborn. He looked up and saw a skein of geese flying inland, weaving patterns against the blue sky.

What was happening to him, he wondered, as they made their way along the last stretch. He had been watching sceneries with this green apostle. He had been daydreaming. The charm of the countryside had been growing upon him, taking hold over him like a fever.

The rich russet hues of the autumnal bracken seen a few days ago had also moved him like this. He had noted it in his diary that night and something similar the next day. It was obvious that his mind was wavering but still the anticipation of a major breakthrough kept him on track with the SuperRice project. 'Was the music teacher a new age guru of some kind,' he had written in his slanted handwriting. 'Am I losing my senses or has the violinist cast a spell?'

Henry went padding across the rolling fields and he was being towed along, drawn invisibly to follow in his footsteps. He could now see a copse in the distance. To the left the land spread out all the way to the east where the railway tracks were a thin shimmering line near the horizon blending into the pale blue of the sky, while right ahead, the sky was immense and that was where the sea was though they couldn't see or hear it from where they were. The brook seen from the railway station appeared from the west, flowing right across the bridle path and they went over a small bridge straight into the copse of oaks and elms that sheltered a sloping meadow ringed by wildflowers and sprays of yellow daisies.

'We have arrived,' Henry said, skirting the meadow and pointing ahead, where there was a trailer van parked in a clearing of the woods.

'I thought you said you lived in a camping site,' Tanmoy said.

'Yes you can see the other campers, they have spread out eastwards along the brook. Here we give each other some space, you see,' he laughed heartily.

It was past midday and though Tanmoy had plans to return the same evening, Henry dissuaded him saying there was room enough in his trailer for two. 'No worries, Sen, I have quit smoking in the last few months so you won't have to breathe poison like that time at The Gribble.'

They walked through the stand of oaks to another clearing where there were two more trailers with smoke curling out from the chimney of one and a young woman sitting on the steps of another reading a book. Henry greeted her as they passed.

The sound of water gurgling on rocks could be heard in the distance. The brook had taken a turn, keeping the trees to one side, and had flowed further south to meet the sea.

They sat against smooth stones on the bank and ate bacon sarnies and a hunk of cheese which Tanmoy had packed for the day. Henry had picked blackberries and offered him some before feeding the minnows, dancing merrily in the clear stream.

'So what do you do here?' Tanmoy asked finally.

'The weather is fine now, so I am out in the woods. Otherwise I park the trailer in a camping site just outside town. It's easier to go to work from there. I have a small house in Aberbourne where I must invite you one day. But this space is special. See these trees, they are quietly listening to us speak. They absorb our presence, the vibrations that go out from us, and tell them who we are. You can hear the trees too. This place, old folks down here call it Greg's Oaks. No one knows for sure who Greg was really. Perhaps a farmer from a nearby village, a shepherd maybe. The trees would know. It's good that so many of these ancient oaks are here, watching over us, like ancestors.'

In those idyllic surroundings, whatever he said seemed to make sense and even if he peppered it with a bit of balderdash, Tanmoy didn't mind. He had grown fond of the music teacher and had even shared details of his work as they sparred endlessly about right and wrong, risks and rewards. He shouldn't have but he trusted the violinist. 'So you can talk with the trees?' he said grinning widely.

'You can too. It takes time but the world of animals and plants communicate with us if we are prepared to hear. The earth is alive and whatever grows out of it, walks over it or flies its skies are its sense organs. The earth speaks through them. When the winter is harsh she goes to sleep, birds migrate, snowflakes drizzle the sleeping valleys, the trees go bare, then again as the sun returns with spring there is colour and gaiety all around. Lustrous new leaves, the scent of bluebells in the forests, sunny days, birdsong. Life follows death as the seasons grow old making way for the new, in nature as it does in our lives. Being one and the same we remember and respect that.'

'That's good but wasn't the world created for humans? That's why we were given a powerful brain, to be masters of creation.'

'I think stewards would be a better word. And yet we act foolishly,' Henry said.

Just then, a young boy jumped down from the branch of a tree with an automatic weapon in his hand and before they could realise what was happening he headed straight for Henry, held the gun to his head and pulled the trigger. The shot made a piercing sound and the gun lit up a bright orange. Henry rolled off the rock he was sitting on.

A woman came running, consternation written large on her face. The boy's mother. They had seen her earlier, reading a book. She grabbed the boy by his wrist and scolding him, snatched away the toy gun.

Henry got up from the ground and, smiling, said, 'Let him play, Marie. But give him a better toy if you can.'

'It's his elder brother bringing all this junk home, god knows from where. I am sorry! Hope you are not hurt?'

'Not at all,' Henry said. 'By the way I have a guest tonight so I am not going up to join you for dinner. We will eat here.'

The woman apologised, and bidding them goodbye walked back towards the trees, still holding the boy by one arm and keeping the gun out of his reach. She was wearing flared jeans and a black and white sailor top just like her son, and the sight of them slowly disappearing between the trees was pleasant and reassuring. It seemed to say that everything was as they should be.

But the little soldier had distracted them with his ambush so they got up and took a walk around Greg's Oaks. Henry pointed out other trees, the slender birches, the beeches with their canopies of yellow and gold, the shady planes, the maple with its leaves turning red, and copper beeches with their crown of russet leaves, and it was as if he was introducing members of his family.

They circled the meadow and came and stood right in the middle where it was still warm. The oaks stood around the little meadow, leaving a path at the far end which was covered by a carpet of orange and gold leaves. In Russia they called it the gold autumn, the music teacher had told him earlier.

As a wind began to blow, the trees seemed to play with each other, bouncing the wind off their canopies, passing it on to those on the other side, and listening quietly they could hear the great oaks breathe and whisper and the younger trees break out in titters. The wind grew stronger as they walked towards the trailer, bringing a shower of leaves sprinkling down from the branches which lit up by the slanting beams of sunlight looked like diamonds raining from the sky.

The day slipped away chatting and walking through the woods or watching the minnows in the brook swimming to a rhythm, with their trenchant pauses and spurts of movement, driven by some animal electricity. As the sun began to sink over the western horizon they walked back to the trailer and cooked a meal of mashed potato and roasted mushrooms which they ate with slices of ham and bread, sitting on the steps.

The little boy with the gun had reminded Tanmoy of Henry's London patient who had gone to the war and would not speak unless he heard his violin. 'How is your soldier doing? Does he still refuse to speak?' he had asked.

'After that night I thought I would never attend him again but the landlady apologised and so I had to relent.'

'And he still does not speak without you playing the violin?'

'Well, over the years he has been talking more. Which is an improvement, no doubt. But not without the music. And it's always about that battle. Last time I saw him he was telling me about the heroism of the French Battalion, which fought alongside the U.S. Army's 23rd Infantry Regiment, under the command of a much decorated lieutenant colonel. Ralph Monclar, a *nom de guerre*, who walked with a cane and wore glasses. "Monclar was a visionary among soldiers but he had the eyes of a romantic." And he tells me about the fifteen-year-old Korean boy who joined Monclar to defend his country. He says the Chinese soldiers, who were mostly peasants, would sing on their way to the battlefield and how they died in heaps on the barbed perimeter wire in the village of Chipyong.'

'Does he still suffer from trauma after all these years?' Tanmoy asked.

'Sometimes, when he is talking about the bayonet fights and the bodies cut into pieces by machine gun fire, he goes quiet for a while. I can see him travelling far away, his eyes tell me he is not there with me any more.'

'It must be taxing for you too, for who likes to hear stories of bloodshed?'

'I don't, even if they are laced with tales of heroism.'

'But the world has to go on,' Tanmoy said.

Henry didn't answer. He poured a cider for the two of them and they drank it slowly, watching evening spread across the land. After it was completely dark, he took out his violin, playing soulful notes of a song that echoed across the meadow all night.

The night wind was refreshing so they sat out for a while more. Tanmoy had been thinking about his work and had got slightly distracted. His glass was empty but he didn't make an attempt to fill it up immediately. 'I must have mentioned to you many times before, how James Watt has had an influence upon me. Now leave aside the great inventors, even if you think of an innovator like Watt, hasn't he made a difference to the lives of millions?'

'While further polluting the planet and digging out all the carbonised trees from under the earth?' Henry's eyes gleamed in amusement.

Still Tanmoy was not going to accept it. Perhaps it was because he had felt strong emotions while visiting Watt's workshop preserved at the museum, or the biography of the inventor which he always carried had had an influence. He had been impressed by the diligence of this man who was not only the father of the steam engine, which he made much more efficient, but also the holder of patents for letter copiers, furnaces and other things and there were so many more which he did not patent at all. Was it all tomfoolery? Then why, standing in the carefully preserved workshop of the Scotsman, did he have this uncanny feeling of the presence of a great mind. Hovering among his old workbenches.

'I am sure you know that James Watt was a potter too and experimented with ceramics?' Tanmoy said pouring some more scrumpy into his glass.

'He could have been anything but he committed grave mistakes. The steam engine drove the industrial age and that was the beginning of pea soupers, ugly cities, new diseases and a lack of harmony with nature. Well, you can give him this much that his age was different and most people didn't think ahead of the possible effects on the environment. But that is blindness, a ruinous innocence. He is like that child with the gun only this time the gun is for real. Come on, you are not allowed to behave like a child! And pardon me for saying this, even your work, tinkering with the codes of creation, it could backfire, you know. I apologise if I have offended you. We are friends. I want to learn from you too.'

Henry had got quite carried away. Maybe he had too much to drink or it was just that he had to say it straight and he considered the scientist to be level-headed.

'Tell me how my work is more dangerous than say, building nuclear reactors which is helping to light up millions of homes and driving economies.'

'Caged monsters, both. You can only imagine what will come to pass if the monster escapes.'

But Tanmoy believed that once safety tests were conducted, the benefits outweighed the risks. He didn't want to argue any more. So he took a long sip and, letting the cider pleasantly pucker his mouth, swallowed it slowly and said, somewhat frivolously, 'So you are scared of monsters, Henry?'

'I will tell you what the Celt had told Alexander when the king asked him what it was that his people feared the most? The Celt had replied that they feared nothing, *so long as the sky does not fall or the sea burst its limits.*'

6

The day looked bright. More so because Nicole was with him. That was the bright side of things. But who was this man wearing a flat cap following them right from the time they had taken the train to London, Tanmoy wondered. He hadn't alerted Nicole, didn't want to scare her. That would mess up his plan. Well, the plan was simple. He had been working on it right from the time he had begun to visit their local — The Red Lion — in the little town of Novingdon.

The theatre of Novingdon had been a little tame all this while. No high comedy, no nerve-wracking excitement, nowhere a spot of heartbreak. Tragedy was dead, the circus had moved to another town and here he was stuck with good old Eugene and the researchers, the molecular biologists and plant physiologists, chained to their microscopes and PCR machines, trying to save the world.

No, he was not bored with the project nor had he given up but he needed diversion, some excitement, and the emptiness of the little town had left him thirsty for company. Henry was a diversion no doubt but his company was calm seas all the way, not a smidgen of excitement on the farthest horizon. The violinist, though he was a friend, gave him depression sometimes, with his save-the-earth lectures.

Nicole was the only possibility of escape from the dreary doldrums that his life had become. But she was always behind the bar at The Red Lion and conversations were limited to things like the unpredictable flow of customers at the bar or the fireworks on Guy Fawkes night. She would banter with him a little, as she did with other patrons, while slow pouring the Guinness. If the bar was crowded, the Guinness provided an extra minute of conversation over bitters and so he ordered it. If it was a slow day, he would listen to her talking about this new place she went with her friends or about this famous poet who would drop in sometimes and present her beautiful cards with quotations from his books. He would tell her about this blind bartender he knew in India who would never pour short and who knew when one of the regulars needed his next drink. Her green eyes remained with him for the rest of the week, he memorised her curves, plotting them in his mind from complex algebraic equations. But that wasn't taking him anywhere.

So he had been bold. He had asked her out. She had refused politely. Then a year had gone by and another. He had changed pubs and soon he had set up a bar at home and didn't visit a pub so often. Then more years had passed and he had forgotten her till one day he had bumped into her at Tesco. And the old attraction came flooding back with fury.

What was the best course now? She was hovering in front of the wine racks. He suggested an Argentinean Malbec. Thanks to good old Henry, he understood wines a lot better these days. She had mellowed and looked more full. Her eyes were still fiery in their brightness. She looked unconvinced. 'We haven't seen you for ages?' she had said in a matter-of-fact voice while examining the label. He had mumbled something about work.

Indeed the work had been very demanding the last few years as they approached the final splicing experiments to see what characters were expressed in the new transgenic rice varieties. The splicing work had begun, he had incorporated newer methods, and the glasshouses were already full with the first experimental crops of transgenic rice. Almost a decade of hard work by his team and the network spread out in universities all over the world was moving towards fruition. In between, new plant physiologists had joined his team, a brilliant molecular biologist had left but was soon replaced by another, advancements made by others had enriched their work. But still it was his baby. He knew his contribution to the SuperRice project would never be forgotten. He had become more and more confident as major hurdles in gene transfer were crossed. Tanmoy had been indeed busy.

She pretended not to hear his excuse about work and asked if he would be visiting their pub. 'I sure will,' he had said.

And in fact he had been back to The Red Lion and had fallen into his old habit of a weekend pint. She still looked lovely and a huskiness had come to her voice as she had matured into a very attractive woman. Does she have children? He had asked her and she had laughed out loudly at his question. 'I am not married, if that is what you want to know!' she had said patting his shoulder playfully. A few more weeks. He had bit his tongue and asked her when she had a day off.

This was that weekend. She had some work in London, a few errands to run and Tanmoy suggested they have dinner together and it was convenient for her too. They could take the short train ride back to Novingdon together. Though she never went out like this even if she knew the customer well, she made an exception this time. The scientist looked like a nice guy. Besides she had those errands to run.

They hopped off the train at Victoria. Everything was running with clockwork precision except for this bloke in a flat cap turning up at the station and keeping an eye on them throughout the journey. He had a small chiselled face with a one-day stubble and very dark eyes. Didn't look like a nice guy.

It was midday already and the Piccadilly service from Green Park was bad. Some trains had been cancelled and the platforms were overflowing. They managed to fight their way into an eastbound train that packed them in like sardines. Chewed and mashed up, they were spit out at Covent Garden where there were long queues at the exit lift. Someone in that crowd was farting. The man in the flat cap was there too. He had followed them while they changed tubes and had come right up to Covent Garden where Tanmoy had nothing to do but watch the crowds. The lift disgorged them like processed meat from a slaughterhouse conveyor belt. Nicole said she would return exactly in two hours.

Tanmoy had put on his favourite brick red linen shirt, pairing it with his off white trousers, a little loose at the waist. He didn't care much about these things nor about the fact that the zipper of his fleece jacket had got stuck midway and he could neither pull it up or down. He took a stroll up Long Acre right up to Leicester Square which was buzzing with tourists and weekend crowds, some coming from Chinatown, others waiting for buses or taking selfies with the Hippodrome behind them. A young Englishwoman and a nervous-looking Indian man came hurrying from the direction of Piccadilly Circus, stopped in front of the casino, discussed if it might rain and then the man saw her off at the tube station with a wave of his hand. Somehow the sight of these two people walking up together — the man nervous, the woman friendly but with ten other things going on in her mind, then the woman leaving and the man lighting a cigarette, outside the casino, distracted him for a while. He was almost melancholic, which he hated. He thought he would call Nicole immediately but then realised he was not carrying his phone book with her number and he didn't use a mobile phone.

He ambled on. At the next intersection a particularly crestfallen gentleman was emerging from a steak house that was widely acknowledged to be a rip off. Meanwhile the man in the flat cap on the other side of the street had lit a cigarette. He hadn't realised that Tanmoy could see his reflection on the glass storefront. How could he get rid of this piranha?

Nicole was waiting when he returned to Covent Garden — her face flushed. She looked restless.

'Something bothering you?' he asked.

'No, I thought I had muddled up the time we were supposed to meet with something else.'

'I am late,' he apologised.

'Actually not. I told you it would take about two hours but it didn't. So where do we go now?'

'Let's take a stroll along the river and then hang around in a pub till it's time for dinner,' he left it there hoping that one thing will lead to another.

The grey river with the gulls swooping down for bread crumbs was a big bore but the bridges looked exciting. The mammoth steel arches leaping from pier to pier, the hulking joists, the granite deck hugging the banks, were all from an age when heavy industry was the fount of power, when people like Watts and Boulton were laying the groundwork for the age of steam. The Scottish mechanical engineer had always been an inspiration for Tanmoy and this day he showed Nicole the inscription on Watts' statue at Westminster Abbey:

Not to perpetuate a name
Which must endure while the peaceful arts flourish

But to shew
That mankind have learnt to honour those
Who best deserve their gratitude ...

And so it went. He sat for a while at the foot of the Watts monument while she smoked a cigarette. A forest of cranes were working on the other bank, a spindly chrome and glass structure was jabbing a finger at the sky, another was being pulled down. Lovers sat on the grass near the memorial for the abolition of slavery. He walked in step with Nicole along the old river. The man in the flat cap didn't give up.

When they arrived at the pub, he had disappeared. Tanmoy had suggested this gin palace. 'Perhaps the last one standing' he had read somewhere. London creaking at its joints but still sharp eyed — like an aging cricket star.

The Princess Louise defied the most fertile of imaginations. It was a maze of passages and secret chambers with gorgeous mahogany partitions, gilded mirrors gleaming on its walls, decorative tiles in the corridors, stained glass windows and plush leather seating. At its heart was a horseshoe bar serving seven partitioned sections originally meant for people from different social backgrounds. That was how they preferred to drink in those times. There were frosted glass snob screens in the wooden partitions and each section was lit up with crystal chandeliers and table lamps that shone on the ornate tiles, reflecting golden light back on the faces of the patrons, turning paupers into princes.

In the shadowy snugs of the centuries-old gin palace, grey-haired men with rubicund faces, who had lived two hundred years and more, read the *Evening Standard* sitting at mahogany tables from the time of Victoria. Mirrors were everywhere, etched and gilded, their glass surely from Belgium while the mosaic floors had a distinct Byzantine flavour.

They went into the front right room pushing through a door set with etched glass panels and straight up to the bar where a young man with shaved head and nose ring was taking orders. He asked for a bitter while Nicole settled for a deep red Abruzzo that came in a bottle, polished black like the stranger's eyes. She sipped the wine sitting cross-legged on one of the upholstered benches against the wall. Tanmoy sunk into a plush armchair. They talked shop for a while, he filling in about his years of absence from The Red Lion while she told him a little about her plan to pursue an art course in London and travel to South America.

'How has your work at the laboratory been?' she looked straight at him over the rim of her wine glass, her fingers curled lightly around its thick stem. She had painted her nails a rich red, and was wearing a crimson lipstick that complemented the smoky green of her eyes.

'From the time I took charge, some seven or eight years ago, we have made good progress. We crossed several hurdles, now we are in the crucial phase. The real fun has begun when I am designing and creating, when I see my ideas stand up and walk on two legs.'

She looked exciting in a maroon top over a little black skirt and diamond stripe black tights but Tanmoy was careful not to get into the specifics of SuperRice, even if everything about the evening got him drunk.

He took a sip from his glass and set the paper bag he was carrying on the table, 'I brought something for you,' he said softly.

She looked surprised, 'But it's not my birthday!'

'Have a look,' and he handed her the bag.

She looked strangely at him before opening it. Inside was a glass jar wrapped in muslin.

'Unwrap slowly.'

She unwrapped the jar and gasped. The glass jar had begun to glow in her hands. A pair of glow butterflies went fluttering about inside the jar and a green incandescence spread around the table, flickering like candles in the wind.

'They are the colour of your eyes,' he said quietly.

'Are they real?' she asked, still looking very surprised, intently watching the butterflies.

'Absolutely. Genetically modified butterflies from my lab. I gave them glow-worm genes. It's such a joy to see your ideas come to life,' he lightly tapped the glass jar and the butterflies pirouetted around each other as if under his command.

'I can't take this,' she said, wavering between surprise and bewilderment.

'You have to — specially created for you,' he made that up. 'You need not keep them locked up in the jar. They can fly about in your bedroom if you wish.'

'I am really touched,' she said giving a furtive glance in the direction of the bar, then looking down at the table, 'let's leave this place.'

'Why. There's still a lot of time and I have hardly touched my drink.'

But she was restless and he couldn't make out what had changed the weather. That's when Tanmoy noticed the dark-eyed stranger sitting in another section of the bar, staring, watching them in a mirror on the wall. The bastard had seen him give her the butterflies and hadn't been able to wipe off the astonishment on his face. He had taken out his phone and was speaking to someone. Had she noticed him too?

The horseshoe bar counter served seven radiating sections, three on each side and one facing the street. Six of these partitioned rooms opened into either of the twin corridors that ran parallel to each other along the left and right walls of the ground floor while the street-facing room had double doors opening into both the corridors. These twin passages were sumptuously decorated with alternating mirrors and tiles, a patterned ceiling in gold and a frieze with bas reliefs of swags and urns.

At the front of the building, the corridors had separate access to the street while one could also step in directly into the street facing drinking space without entering the corridors at all. This street-facing section had double doors with etched glass panels, one to the left the other to the right. So the Louise had four doors opening onto the street, two for the twin passages, and two double doors leading into the street-side section.

 If you sat facing the bar counter in the street-side section, there were three sections radiating from the right wing of the horseshoe bar and three more from the left. It was pure and exquisite symmetry. Three rooms on each side, one corridor each, one door to each corridor, a double door on each side of the street-facing section. Three and three and one is seven, and one and one is two and two and two makes four.

From the corner of his eye Tanmoy could see the man in the flat cap nursing a pint, occasionally looking up to make sure they were still there. He had kept his phone before him perhaps waiting for a call. He was sitting in the middle left hand side snug facing the bar and watching them in the mirror which was to Tanmoy's left.

They were sitting face to face, their table parallel to the bar in the front right hand snug and just by turning their heads a little, both of them could see him easily.

'Aren't we going somewhere else?' Nicole asked, a sense of urgency creeping into her voice. She had kept the jar with the butterflies on the chair beside her.

'Are you all right?'

'I am feeling suffocated with all these mirrors and lights,' she said and looked around and he noticed for a fraction of a second she took in the stranger.

'Okay let's go to the front bar. It looks bigger.'

She reluctantly accompanied him and they came out into the right corridor with their drinks and again entered through the double door into the street-side bar.

They sat at one of the low tables at the centre of the room, facing each other. There was no one in there. He whispered something mischievous and as she cocked her head to listen, the light from the window bounced off her honey blonde hair. The dazzling light blinded him for a moment and he saw colours dancing in front of his eyes. The table being small, her legs touched his, firing up his neurons, the currents travelling right up his spine and into his recently shampooed hair which crackled and sparked.

The light from the street washed over the bar counter and looking up he had suddenly realised that the man in the flat cap was not sitting where he had thought he was. In fact it was his image reflected twice in the mirrored walls of the compartments that had fooled him. He was actually right there in the compartment they had just left. They had, all this time, been watching his reflection. The mirrors on the walls of each bar played tricks. So he was right there and must have been eavesdropping! Had Nicole also realised this or had she not spotted the stranger following them through the day? Perhaps he was just imagining things.

The thousand reflections of the stranger in the etched Belgian glass mirrors made his head reel. Each image reflected itself back and once again and a few more times, on and on, endlessly, *ad infinitum*. Three and three and one is seven, and one and one is two and two and two makes four and anything divided by zero becomes infinite. An endless game of repetition, through centuries, over eons — the code of life getting replicated. The double helix DNA strands slithering through space-time, bridging infinite distances, throwing off detritus, getting smarter and better at the game of life, getting smarter and better, while throwing out the detritus, as it snaked through space-time, through curtains of arithmetic dust. He felt pressure on his bladder and excusing himself hopped out through the street-side door. 'Take care of the butterflies,' he called out to her and went into the street before turning back into the pub through the left passage.

About three-and-half-feet wide, the passage had a timbered dado set with diamond-shaped tiles. Above this were gilded mirrors alternating with brightly coloured decorative square tiles — three tiles and three mirrors followed by a painting then three more mirrors with tiles in between, the pattern repeated over and over again. The other wall was made up of mahogany screens and etched glass panels separating the different bars and snugs. Halfway down the passage hung a bowl chandelier, brightening up the gold patterned ceiling and lighting up the Byzantine floor tiles. The mahogany screens to the right were interrupted by three doors with frosted glass panels and etched borders.

Tanmoy pushed open each door hoping it would lead to the washroom only to find customers. The first room was occupied by four Russian gangsters sitting in a fug of cigarette smoke, playing whist and cursing loudly while downing shots of vodka, in another a French legionnaire was practising his harp while a glass of wine lay unattended at his table. The legionnaire had a cane leaning against his bench. In the last room, two hooded figures in cowls were staring coldly at the door, an empty glass standing at the centre of the table between them.

He went back to the street and entered through the right hand corridor entrance and checked each door on the left hand side to find empty snugs with yellow lights burning, men in grey suits arguing loudly about the economy and a cowboy having a spritzer all by himself. The stranger in the flat cap was nowhere to be seen nor had the washroom revealed its position. His bladder was going to burst.

He hurried out to the street and walked back into the left passage. Going slowly this time, he stopped at the door to each of the snugs, making sure it was not the entrance to the loo. Once more while checking the third door, leading to the snug with the hooded figures, he spotted a shelf on the wall to his left. On it was a cherub lamp, porcelain pill boxes and an oak-cased mantle clock which said it was midnight. Just where the shelf ended was a hairline crack in the wall which he hadn't noticed before. It was a door! He pushed and it creaked open.

Why do the Brits hide their loos?

Beyond the door was the landing of a carpeted iron staircase that went down into the basement. The passage from the right hand entrance joined the landing here through another door. The washroom was down those stairs. He sprinted down the steps.

A carved mahogany door set with a glass painted panel led to the men's room which had three marble urinals and two WCs. The tiles on the floor and the walls of the washroom were even more gorgeous than those out in the passage. The marble urinals were embossed in gold with heritage emblems.

The stench of urine was overpowering. He covered his nose. The door to one of the WCs was closed and because it was fitted high he could see the shoes of a man inside.

It was hard to breathe in the nauseating fumes. 'Centuries of imperial piss,' flashed through his mind as he rushed to the first urinal and unzipped his fly. A door creaked open behind him.

Someone tapped him lightly on his shoulder. 'What are you doing with my woman?' an icy voice spoke into his ear.

With his fly still open he swung around and saw the flat cap first. It was him. He must have been inside the WC for he could just catch a glimpse of the open door to the cubicle when the stranger raised his hand holding the butterfly jar. Thinking he was going to smash the jar on his head, Tanmoy panicked and, trying to dodge the attacker, lost his balance on the slippery floor. He fell headlong and his glasses smashed to pieces. He had knocked his head hard and was squirming in pain. The stranger in the flat cap hovered over him for a few moments, undecided, then padded away quickly. As his brain was turning into jelly he could see the butterflies, fluttering about in the heritage loo, circling over him, flitting from one urinal to the next, their firefly genes pumping green luminance into the smothering darkness pushing in from all sides.

A pleasant fragrance — wafted into the restroom. Flowers? It was powerful enough to drive the ammonia smell of piss away. The flowery scent was inside his head or wherever his consciousness was hovering about, for he couldn't tell if his body was still with him or left behind on the toilet floor. He thought he heard the click of pencil heels.

The tingling sensation of cold water being splashed on raw skin. His senses were returning. He opened his eyes slowly. He could see the WC doors and, at the edges of his vision, the washroom ceiling. He was lying on his side. Trying hard to focus.

A young woman with a round face and intense eyes was bending down, splashing him with water. Her jet black hair was cut into bangs, covering her forehead.

His shirt was getting wet but he did not have the strength to stop her. The scent of flowers — more distinct. 'Who are you?' he muttered through the throbbing pain.

'I thought I have lost you. Wake up, I am a friend,' she said.

She extended her hand, 'Can you get up or should I call for help?'

'No, no, I think I can manage on my own,' he said, worried what other trouble a group of people might bring.

'Is he still here?' he asked.

'Who? There is no one here, get up slowly. Here, let me help you,' she held his arm gently.

His head swam as he tried to sit up but failed. Then he retched violently and lay still for some more minutes. A muscle cramp was beginning to form down near his toes and he resisted it with whatever willpower he could muster.

Finally, with some help from her he could manage to pull himself up. Holding the wall for support, he advanced a few steps. His legs were shivering. 'Thank you,' he said leaning against the washbasin. There was a nasty swelling on his head where he had taken the knock and part of his face was turning blue. He wetted a bunch of tissue and patted his head with water. He washed his face and asked her to wait outside the door while he used the loo.

'I don't know your name,' he said with some difficulty. In the low light of the corridor, he noticed she was carrying a thick peacock blue coat on her arm and was holding something that looked like a measuring tape but could also be a length of garrotting wire.

'There. Lean against the wall if you are feeling dizzy,' she said.

He was still dizzy, his head was throbbing with pain but he managed to drag himself up the stairs to the corridor. They made slow progress, as he stopped every other second to steady himself.

Right till the end of the corridor. He leaned against the door which led into the street-facing bar, pushing it open just a crack. He peered inside. It was packed with unknown people. Nicole had vanished. She was no more there. There were other people sitting at their table. He stepped back into the passage in black despair.

She was holding the front door for him.

'You didn't tell me your name and why you are helping me?' he said as they stepped out of the gin joint into the light of evening.

'You can call me Jia.'

Tony Fang's
Lair

1

The man who came out of the tube station and was marching briskly through the throngs of Covent Garden was wearing a baseball cap and sunglasses not because it was bright outside. In fact it was a grey October day in London.

The trees had begun to go bare and throughout the day the sun had shone intermittently, like a searchlight, trying hard to penetrate the fog that hung over the city. His grey trousers were wrinkled and a down jacket open at the front flapped against his chest as he went weaving his way through tourists, watching a magician forcing a three-foot-long stiletto down his gullet.

Tight circles of the curious had formed around the living statues off Long Acre, a man pretending to be a sailor, beer mug in hand, sitting on thin air, one leg crossed over the other, his suit burnished gold, just like his face was and, a little further up, a hulking Roman centurion complete with helmet and battle dress all sprayed a shiny silver.

The children stared, amazed at the man sitting in an invisible chair, swinging their hands under his buttocks to check if he had a hidden support of some kind. The man in the black jacket ignoring the tourists went on steadily, weaving through the throngs. He passed the cafes still crowded with revellers, not paying any attention to the man in a bowler hat playing 'Yesterday' on a street piano, past the jewellery and bric-a-brac stalls, beyond the tobacconist's grilled showcase and the Polish apple seller, into a little lane that snaked its way between old houses.

He walked slowly down the meandering lane for some distance then cut back into a side street. Following which he came to an intersection and crossing over to the other side, slipped into a cobbled walkway with Chinese restaurants with brightly painted facades. It was past midday and because of the gloomy weather there were not many people here except for some tourists peering at the framed menus posted outside.

He went past a Chinese supermarket which was not busy at this time of the day, past little shops with neon-lit signs advertising 'mobile phones unlocked here' and gaily painted Chinese pharmacies into a narrow alley with a closed souvenir shop with graffiti on its shutters. He had walked all this way instead of getting out at the nearest tube station as a matter of caution.

At the entrance to the alley a pretty Korean girl was selling pork and seaweed buns from a street-side kiosk and he looked the other way to avoid her gaze. Some way down the alley and invisible from the street was a smallish eatery. A rough-looking character in jeans, sneakers and a dirty fall jacket was smoking outside the entrance, keeping a watch on the street.

He stopped outside the restaurant and exchanged a quick glance with the man in the fall jacket, then pretending to tie his shoelace made sure he was not being followed. He ducked to his right and pushed through the brightly painted doorway. Smells of fried meats and sauces were wafting into the air as he entered the tiny restaurant with red lanterns hanging from the ceiling and white tablecloths on its low tables.

There were not many people inside. Two men in suits having lunch and an elderly woman trying to feed a naughty little kid who turned away his face every time she gave him a spoonful of sticky rice. Near the back was an elevated area with microphones and drums and the blow-up of a musician who would be performing live that night.

The man wearing the baseball cap looked around trying to adjust his eyes with the low light of the eatery. Then he went past the tables and into one of the private cabins at the back with red silk curtains printed with fire-breathing dragons.

There was someone sitting at an empty table. He had small dark eyes and a blunt nose and his skin was white as a corpse. He was chewing gum and did not get up to greet the other man. The man wearing the baseball cap took a seat opposite him and rubbed his hands nervously. He didn't take off his jacket.

A short man in a grey suit and sunken cheeks entered the cabin and whispered something to the man who had been sitting there and went away.

A waiter appeared.

'What will you have?' the man with corpse-white skin asked.

'Chicken feet and Tsingtao for me.'

'A cider for me please,' the man wearing the baseball cap said in a nervous voice.

They sat in silence. The waiter brought their orders while the man went on chewing his gum. He pushed the beer to one side and went for the chicken feet. He spat out the gum on the floor, under the table.

'Why did you want to meet me in person and not follow the usual arrangement?' the man asked. His voice was cold, uninflected. 'I am a respected citizen of this country. All my business — legit. Do you want to put Tony Fang in trouble?' He had a controlled menace in his words.

'I have brought something important. It should go to the right place. You know ...'

'We have not received anything from you that is of real interest to those folks. It has been years,' Tony Fang said.

The man in the baseball cap had an uneasy expression on his face, fumbling for words, 'This took so long because the work was difficult. They were groping in the dark and many mistakes were made on the way,' he spluttered out.

'Cut the excuses and let me see what you got there,' he said sipping his beer. Then putting both arms on the table he began drumming with his fingers. There was no expression, no muscle movement on his face.

The other man dug his hands into his sling bag looking for something. He hadn't touched the cider yet.

'These people, they want results. No time for anything else. I have other businesses. You give something they can use and I tell them this is what I got. If they say OK, we want to have a look at it, I pass it on. I don't care whether it is circuits for missile guidance or bush meat. If they say it's crap, then it's bad for me. Because I wasted my time. And you know what it means for you.'

'I understand but in this line of work, things don't happen in a day.'

'What have you got?'

'Paddy. This one, I am told, can beat a drought and provide extra nutrition.'

Tony Fang nodded. His mobile phone rang and he pressed it to his ears listening quietly without speaking a word. For a minute. Then he disconnected the call and shot a cold look at the visitor.

'You sure this works?'

'It does. These are the first batches. From what information I have, I can tell you that these have been lab tested for drought resistance and as a vitamin source. But it will take more time to complete all tests.'

'Don't bother. These people who want it can do the testing themselves,' and he poured the remaining beer in his glass.

'I think so too. I've heard they are going to design one that will even tolerate frost!' baseball cap said with some enthusiasm.

'Cut the scenes and show me the dope.'

The visitor pulled out a shiny metal tube about six inches long and a small wooden box of the kind used for storing tea. He kept both on the table. 'Everything including the sample is in there.'

'You better be right this time,' Tony Fang said taking both the tube and the box.

The other man swallowed, 'As I told you, this is yet to clear field tests and safety trials but has shown much promise in the lab.'

'I hope they will agree with what you are telling me.'

'There is nothing quite like it anywhere in the world today.'

'Smart one you are, aren't you? I am sure you know what it means to fall foul of these people?' he said icily.

The other man could feel sweat break out on his forehead but he couldn't move his hands and try to wipe it away. He nodded slowly.

Tony Fang rose to leave. The short man with sunken cheeks appeared and helped him put on his trench coat. He transferred the tea box and the metal tube into his coat pocket and put on his dark shades. The man in the baseball cap stood up on his feet. Before leaving the cabin, Tony Fang turned to look at him and said, 'Wait for five minutes before you leave and never come back here again. And you better give these people what they want and everyone will be happy.'

Magic
Seeds

7

'This potent commander of the elements — this abridger of time and space — this magician, whose cloudy machinery has produced a change on the world, the effects of which, extraordinary as they are, are, perhaps, only now beginning to be felt.' Words written in praise of Watt by Walter Scott, impressed him the most. Magician indeed, how succinctly and beautifully Scott had summarised the genius of the great inventor, Tanmoy had noted in his diary. He had underlined Scott's words in the biography.

Jia, the woman who found him lying on the floor in the washroom of the pub, had been kind to him. She got him admitted to a hospital. His injury was such that the doctor wanted to keep him under observation for a night. She had come in right the next morning. 'He can go home,' the doctor had said. He was discharged and she drove him all the way to Novingdon in a car she had hired.

These were those final years of the project when Tanmoy had been doing the crucial splicing work, selecting and inserting genes from alien species into paddy. Meanwhile Jia, who came out of nowhere like an angel, settled in quietly, making herself almost invisible in his house. She needed a place to stay and he had obliged.

Her room opened into the garden and she used that door to get in and out of the house, careful not to disturb the professor. She had written to the South Korean embassy for her papers and twice went to London for appointments. 'It will take some time,' she told him, 'but they are getting me provisional documents soon.'

'What did you tell them about coming to this country?'

'Oh that's a long story, but essentially I said, I lost my things. I hope your work is good,' she would smile and say.

His head injury healed fast but left an odd mark, yes it indeed looked like a butterfly stuck to a lepidopterist's board. Also he could not think straight for long any more and if he tried hard, his head would fill up with coloured butterfly wings doing a dizzying dance. 'Sometimes they are Red Admiral butterflies with their bright orange on black wings flapping about wantonly in my frontal lobe, or else there were swallowtails flitting from cerebellum to hippocampus or even a clutch of glowing spliced hesperiadae blushing playfully between my ears' he told his Moleskine diary. His memory began to be eaten slowly by these winged beauties and soon the butterflies began to play games with his reasoning. But it happened gradually and at such a deep level that no one really noticed.

Eugene had inquired about the medicated dressing when he had arrived at the department the week after the incident at The Princess Louise. 'Holy smoke! What happened?'

'Black Saturday!' he had said ominously. 'Can you believe it, I got mugged!'

'Oh no! Where?'

'Near Oxford Circus this weekend. I was walking back to a friend's place close to the tube station. It was a bit late. This guy came asking for cigarettes; he grabbed me from behind and asked for my wallet.'

'Oh! Did you see a doctor? I hope the bruises are not too bad,' his voice was quivering with concern. But Tanmoy still could not tell him about his date with Nicole.

'Luckily it's not. The doctor says it will heal soon, no internal haemorrhage. I didn't have any money on me, that's why this happened. He knocked me senseless and made off with my backpack.'

'Lost anything valuable?'

'Stuff I bought that day but nothing expensive, really. But I lost my prescription glasses in the scuffle and had to get a new pair made,' Tanmoy said and then tried to change the subject.

He asked him about his work, knowing very well that this would draw him away from his immediate concern. The diversion was necessary because he didn't want to share the circumstances that led to his head injury. And he kept the world of frolicking butterflies in his head, his secret masters, hidden from everyone. Only the diary knew.

Right then, there were more serious matters to attend. And foremost among these was Jia, who had appeared, unannounced.

That day after she had suddenly appeared in the restroom of The Princess Louise, he had wanted to know her name and how she chanced upon him in the men's washroom.

'How did you find me?'

'I don't know. I suddenly realised I had left the fashion store where I worked and was standing in a restroom. What a mishap and it happened in the blink of an eye. Then I found you lying on the floor,' she said while trying to hail a passing cab.

'My goodness! A fashion store sharing the loo with a gin palace.' Tanmoy made an incredulous face.

'Mue. It's not here. It's a store in Gangnam-gu in Seoul, South Korea.' She had helped him into the taxi.

Perhaps she was making it up to lighten the mood, he thought, and it worked on him. 'Huh? Did you see a woman with green eyes passing by, on your way here?' he had said leaning against the back of the seat, pressing both hands against his forehead to relieve the pain.

'Green? No, never. Green is not my favourite colour. Does it hurt?'

'Do you remember seeing a man with a stubble, wearing a flat cap at The Princess Louise?' he had asked her later.

'I didn't see anyone,' and she had revved up the engine of the convertible in which they had driven back to Novingdon.

He liked her story about the Korean fashion store and how she had been teleported to the restroom of the gin palace. The story remained with him as she had narrated it and that was perhaps why, he had agreed when she asked for his help to find a place to stay in Novingdon. His house had a guest room and she was welcome to stay; meanwhile he would try to get her part-time work at the university.

'Sir, I need two jars of kimchi and a few kilos of *gochujang*,' she told him a week after settling down in the guest room. Her papers hadn't come in yet so she avoided going out unless absolutely essential. Tanmoy would run all the errands.

Where in heaven's sake will I find kimchi in Novingdon? he wondered. The Romans didn't bring kimchi with them and nor had the Anglo Saxons heard about it when they pushed up their boats on Kentish beaches.

'Try the Chinese supermarkets in Gerard street, if not then Seoul Plaza in the New Malden Koreatown should have everything. I am told that the bingsu in Koreatown is as good as home. But please don't forget the gochujang, I can't survive without it.'

In the span of a few weeks he had grown quite fond of her. She would keep to herself most of the time, leafing through fashion magazines, cutting out pictures from their pages and sticking them in a scrapbook with notes and drawings. He would see her only at breakfast. He returned late from the laboratory and she would have already gone to sleep when he sat down for dinner.

Weekends were slightly different, the only time they had longer conversations. One such weekend, she had told him about the fashion house in Seoul, where she had been working, when this mishap had occurred. She had been fitting out an overweight American lady, a diplomat's wife, who wanted a custom-made *hanbok*. She had just taken the lady's fur-trimmed peacock blue coat and was straightening out the measuring tape when it happened. He felt amused learning those details and listened to her with a twinkle in his eyes. Tanmoy had a soft spot for imaginative people.

'That accidental teleportation was a mishap, I wasn't prepared for it,' she had said, her eyes smiling at him as she spoke, and he almost wondered if she just might be right.

Another day, Tanmoy found her in the kitchen, preparing a fiery gochujang paste to go with Korean-style grilled beef ribs and thought that if he hadn't sold his soul to genetics and had instead given his heart to a dark-eyed woman, then he would have a daughter like her. She had almost saved his life.

He was not going to The Red Lion any more. He believed Nicole had walked away on him when he had gone to the loo and did not come back. So be it. He didn't care. But he would soon find out that she had left The Red Lion too and nobody could say where she had gone.

One day he was feeling lethargic while marking students' papers at the department. Leaving it midway, he had returned home without visiting the lab at all. And it was the same the next day too, he wasn't feeling like doing anything. Was he getting the flu, he wondered. Fatigue had taken hold of his body and his mind buzzed with hundred thoughts which didn't go anywhere. On the third day, as he was walking in through the gates of his house, he saw her reading a book sitting in a garden chair. Her silken hair was shining under the warm rays of the afternoon sun. She saw him come in and followed him a little while later into the house.

He was in the kitchen heating up a bland fish curry made from trout that he had prepared the day before. She offered to help. 'Let me fix you something tasty. I have glass noodles and chicken and I promise to make it much better than what you get in the canteen.'

He didn't object and went to his bedroom to lie down for a while. After sometime, she brought the steaming bowls of chicken noodles to the dining table and they ate together, washing it down with cups of barley tea.

'Thanks. It was delicious,' he had said.

He was planning to retire to his room after lunch and rest for a few hours but she kept asking if he was unwell and needed to see a doctor. No he was fine, he said, just feeling a little out of sorts.

'You might feel better once you are back at the lab. I think it's just the weather.'

He didn't have an answer to that, feeling a little guilty himself for not attending to his duties. Was it the ghost of Henry hovering at the back of his mind, giving him wrong ideas? Though they argued often and never seemed to agree, the music teacher's ideas would worm their way insidiously into his thoughts, wavering his faith.

'From whatever little I have heard, I feel your work is important. Wouldn't it have an impact on millions of lives?' He couldn't resist her mild suggestions and returned to the lab.

Whenever he was distracted, she would notice it and remind him that his work could change lives. She just wouldn't allow him to sit at home. He found her solicitousness slightly annoying at first, the fact that she should be so bothered, but when he returned to his lab, gradually getting engrossed with the splicing work, he thanked her silently for pushing him back.

Meanwhile, with his recommendation, Jia had obtained temporary employment at the administrative office of the university. She was helping with student records, IT support and sometimes standing in at the front desk of the reception. She visited London a couple of times to speed up the work at the embassy and had soon received provisional documents though her passport would take some more time. She returned with things for the house. A pop-up toaster one week, to replace the old that turned out carbonised toasts.

Tanmoy told her about Henry one day and how, years ago, they had met accidentally and had to spend a night at a London inn. He told her a bit about Greg's Oaks and the countryside, asking if she would like to visit. 'He is a good friend.'

'Why not?' She had flashed her brilliant smile, 'You make him sound very interesting. Can we go this Sunday?'

'Not yet. I am running a backlog of administrative duties at the department. Maybe the week after that?'

Tanmoy bumped into Henry the very next day. The music teacher was carting in some stuff to his department office when he met him in the corridor. They exchanged greetings. Did he have a little time, Tanmoy had asked.

'Yes, of course. Give me five minutes to put this stuff in the office and I will be right back.'

So they had gone for a coffee at the Costa cafe beside the reception which was empty because the session had just got over and the students had left. He told Henry about Jia, saying that he had let out a room to a young professional, a relation of an ex-colleague, and that she was temporarily employed with the university. Also he needed to store a few boxes of papers and things with Henry because he was short of space at home, having let out the guest room. The music teacher didn't have a problem.

'The guest sharing my house, Miss Park, she wants to visit Elmsby,' he slipped it in casually, not sure how Henry would react.

'My pleasure. Come next weekend,' Henry sounded welcoming.

'I told her about Greg's Oaks.'

'The powers that hold water and earth together have willed that our paths should cross,' he said, putting his coffee cup down midway into a sip. 'Bring her next week.'

Tanmoy felt relieved that he had agreed. His visits to Greg's Oaks were like holidays. He felt rejuvenated. On returning to Novingdon he would drift slowly back to his pet project, to his classes and teaching. To his meetings with Sante – the corporate bosses fuelling his SuperRice dream. 'Thank you, we will try to catch the six fifteen from Novingdon, next Saturday, if that is okay with you.'

'Get down at Shoreham-by-Sea and I will be there to collect you. Remember those sturdy shoes,' Henry said, munching his cheese tomato sandwich slowly, studying his friend's face, while the scientist, slightly conscious, for no particular reason, emptied his cup of espresso in a hurry.

'Will see you next week then,' Tanmoy said, suddenly in a hurry to leave. Something in the conversation had made him uncomfortable though he could not put his finger to it.

'Fair journey to you both,' Henry had wished.

It was easy to convince Henry about the little fib of an ex-colleague who had recommended her as a lodger in his house. She thanked him for cooking it up before getting busy with her fashion magazines. She had a whole bunch of them, their pages flagged with stick-ons. There were always sketchbooks and loose sheaves of paper strewn about her room with coloured sketches of dresses and notes in the margins, written in Hangul.

8

It was a cold and misty morning. On the high street, the Tesco delivery van was unloading supplies and men in fluorescent jackets went about clearing the litter bins and doing all other kinds of work that keeps a city running. As they were walking by the Tesco Express, they saw two officers emerging from the police precinct on the other side of the street. The officers took a look across the street for a second and then got into a parked staff car riding away towards the asylum at the other end of the street.

The green and white Coastway train was already at the platform when they arrived. They rushed through the ticket barriers and hopped into the nearest coach. Tanmoy kept his backpack on his lap and cramped himself into the narrow Southern Railway seats while she looked out of the window watching the Sussex countryside glide by.

The train cut through charming country with rolling meadows and far away views of castles, standing like sentries teleported from the past. Inside the coach people were hooked to their tablets and smart phones or were mostly keeping quiet. Sometimes he could hear a man talking loudly on his phone in Bengali. Obviously he was talking with his wife or girlfriend who was in Bangladesh, and they were discussing intimate stuff with the man oblivious of the fact that there could be others in the train who knew his language. Tanmoy closed his eyes to shut him out but as soon as he did that the butterflies swarmed back, in thick curtains of colour.

Henry was waiting next to the ticket barriers. He shook hands with them and smiling broadly led them out to the car park.

The Toyota Yaris he was driving sped through empty streets of the little town with the briny smell of the sea in its air and took the highway. 'I hear Korea is very pretty?' Henry said looking sideways at her while driving. Tanmoy had taken the back seat.

'Your country is beautiful too,' she said, looking straight ahead.

'Thank you,' he looked sideways at her for a moment and continued, 'and you have been a peaceful people for most of your history while we have been plundering around, poking our nose in every business. Business and commerce is what has guided our interests.'

She looked undecided for a moment, 'Indeed. Wasn't this country invaded time and again, centuries ago — the Angles, the Vikings, the Romans and so on?'

Henry nodded thoughtfully.

'The European powers established colonies and did large transfers of wealth yet some of them left a few things behind, like the railways. It was built for their own good but we are grateful that they did build it,' Tanmoy joined in.

'Well but just think of the rapaciousness of the early explorers, the iron fist of the colonisers. Explorers you see are lauded for discovering the world but who were they really if not the advance guard of proselytisers and colonising powers? The instinct to explore, venture forth, discover new worlds, hides something murky under its glamorous cover. Greed will finish us off pretty soon, if we don't make amends. The ancient civilisations of the East still have much to offer in restoring a balance. I call them the inward-looking civilisations. They are intuitive, while ours are the extroverted kind, we are bred on reason and the scientific temperament that begets hauteur and hubris.' Henry was getting into the mood and Tanmoy looked at Jia through the mirror to make sure she wasn't getting bored already. But her face didn't reflect anything.

'What about Japanese expansionism? It's an *eastern* civilisation as you put it. I mean every nation has skeletons in its cupboards, we can't make sweeping generalisations,' Tanmoy said.

'Yes many of them do but down here we are talking of mass ossuaries and not a cupboard or two. Still this Japanese car is good. I will give them that though it's hard to forget the atrocities of the war. It belongs to a friend who runs campaigns for environment protection and he says it is a very clean and energy-efficient car.'

'There are all kinds of energies in every nation,' Jia said quietly as Henry took a turn and the flat green country opened up on both sides. There was hardly any traffic out there and all along, the hedgerows were decorated by little white blossoms of Queen Anne's lace and other wild flowers. Leaving the expressway, they drove through sunken streets, shaded by giant trees and past old villages and medieval churches before arriving at Aberbourne where Henry and Tanmoy always enjoyed a pint before walking on to Greg's Oaks.

This time they drove through, right to the edge of town, and Henry parked the car next to an old house painted white with drooping wisteria blossoms on its walls. He dropped the key into a letter box. 'We will meet this friend shortly,' he explained. 'We will walk from here, the sceneries are pretty.'

It was an hour's walk through rolling fields and stands of silver birch, elms and ash till they reached the little meadow circled by the giant oaks. Because they had approached by a different route they passed the trailer where the young boy with the toy gun lived with his mama before arriving at Henry's trailer. There were two more trailers parked nearby.

They saw a couple sitting on the grass, talking, the woman knitting a sweater. A little further three kids were playing with remote-controlled cars which got stuck in the soft earth, their motors screaming.

Henry unlocked the door of his trailer and got some deck chairs. They sat eating sandwiches and cider till it began to get warm and they had to shift under the shade of the trees. Presently a young man and his wife came up and joined them. 'This is Alex. He was kind to lend us his car today,' Henry introduced his friend and his wife Georgina. They were campaigners for the environment. As soon as he heard this, Tanmoy, who had brought his James Watt biography and was planning to read it, hid his book, surreptitiously, sliding it slowly under himself till he was comfortably sitting on it.

They talked long and argued energetically about the need for conserving energy and countering consumer culture with Henry and his friends on one side and Tanmoy defending things he didn't always believe in. Meanwhile James Watt steamed under the weight of his buttocks.

The discussion moved to Tanmoy's work and he told them briefly that he was working on genetically improved crops. He didn't reckon that he was lighting a short fuse.

Soon as they heard this, Alex and Georgina looked at each other and then cast a questioning glance at Henry. And Alex stood up, finished his bottle of cider, put a foot on his chair, rested his elbow on the backrest and began in a declamatory fashion, 'These are exactly the kind of things we are up against,' he said looking straight at Tanmoy, searing him with his righteousness and then back at Henry, 'I didn't have any idea that you keep such interesting company, Mr David?'

Henry was shocked to hear Alex address him by his second name. But Alex would not stop — he had been drinking from long before they had arrived. He went on like an encyclopaedia about the dangers posed by genetically modified food and how countries have sold out to corporations. He went on firing example after example at a stunned Tanmoy who just looked at Jia from time to time and then back at Henry while the poor Scottish mechanical engineer sweated under him. Perhaps if he was around, a thought that occurred right then to Tanmoy, the old Scotsman would have taught a thing or two to this green imbecile who assumed he knew everything about science and welfare and was the sole steward of human well being.

'Enough, Mr Alex,' everyone looked at Jia as she spoke. She had been sipping from a flask of whisky and the look she directed at the campaigner was full of contempt. 'Who do you think you are talking to?' she began in an icy voice. 'This gentleman has made innovations in his field which right at this moment are saving lives of people, do you know that?' Tanmoy was once more pleased and surprised to find that she was aware about his contributions to the field. She stopped, measuring her words carefully, 'His work has the potential to benefit millions around the world. It's easy to speak of saving the planet sitting and enjoying the good life of a highly advanced capitalist economy, but do you know how millions live in abject hunger and poverty? Have you seen men roasting rats or chewing up dragonflies to escape starvation?'

Henry's sympathies were clearly with Alex and he felt determined at this point to protect him from this sudden onslaught. But he was a mild-mannered man. He patted his luxuriant beard and said thoughtfully, 'I am sorry to say this, Tanmoy, but what if there is a mistake. Are we adopting enough precautions, going forward?'

Tanmoy wasn't ready to jump in. Jia took another sip, smiled mysteriously, 'If people like you were given to run the world, then half the planet would have perished. There would be no medicine, no transport and no electricity. You wouldn't be sitting in the warm shadow of a tree knowing very well that if you fall sick or need to go somewhere quickly then a vehicle will come to your aid. And you will be quietly saying thanks to Rudolf Diesel while assailing him in public. Have you ever heard of hungry children looking for undigested morsels of food in cow dung?'

Like all hot air balloons with the power of speech, Alex was blown to bits by this spirited counter-attack and lost all his arguments, some of which were good indeed.

'What about alternatives, can't we look for alternatives that are not as risky or dangerous?' Henry said meekly, almost defensively, as if he was ashamed to put forward this argument. Alex meanwhile had quietly taken his seat, his lower jaw had fallen open and Georgina was trying to move her chair in the line of fire between her husband and Jia.

Tanmoy cleared his throat and spoke slowly, 'Ah! I know what all of you are talking about but scientific advancement is predicated upon risk taking. To progress and innovate we need to step into the dark, into areas where no one has ventured before, otherwise we stagnate. We cannot do much without risking a little but nowadays we have enough understanding and we do take necessary precautions.'

How could he tell them that this was only partly true, how could he ever explain, that even then, as he spoke, they were making lovely loops in his brain, flitting from medulla to mesozoa, singing and screaming and dancing and wiping away bit by bit all of his reason, replacing it with their own magical thoughts, till he was just an automaton controlled by their whims and wishes.

It had grown over the years, their empire inside his mind, but he couldn't get rid of them really and he enjoyed their sweet symphonies playing on inside his head while making a breakfast of his wits. How could he tell anyone that they have become more powerful and more numerous every day, colonies of red, green, blue, orange, tigers and tornadoes printed on their wings, and they were now almost in charge of what he did, as he laboured away at his laboratory.

Jia glanced at Tanmoy, then sweeping away her jet black bangs, turned sharply to face Alex who was now half hidden by his wife. 'You know,' she said, 'by spreading all this negativity you are doing a great disservice. A lot of advanced research gets held up because of people like you trying to influence government policy. Ethics and environmental vigilantism and excreta — they are just plugging up the free flow of reason that can do immense good to humanity. You know, you should indeed be locked up. In this country you get too many liberties.'

'You bloody Mongol!' Georgina sprung up from her seat and lunged at her like a wild animal, determined to throw her off her chair. In the blink of an eye Jia threw the flask at her and jumped smartly out of her seat. It happened so fast that everyone was stunned. Trying to save herself from the flask of malt coming at her, Georgina ducked right and her feet got entangled with the legs of a chair throwing her straight at Tanmoy. Tanmoy's chair toppled and the two fell in a heap over each other, just as *The Life of James Watt* flew out from under the seat and landed smack in the centre of the action.

Henry rose to check the damage. Alex quietly picked up the book and had opened the first page to read the title when they heard the sound of a car approaching.

The squad car drove right up to the trees and three policemen, guns drawn, began to close in on them. 'Raise your hands and don't move.' Tanmoy and Georgina were brushing the grass off their dresses, cursing each other silently, checking if anything was broken, when the police ordered them all to raise their hands. 'Move back from the chairs,' an officer barked.

One of the officers checked a picture. 'Yes, it's him,' he said and went up to Alex, 'Greengob Alex?'

'Alex Greengob, yes that's my name. What is this officer?'

'Sorry, Sir, we have a search warrant. Now will you kindly cooperate and hand over that book please and your jacket and then maybe take us to your trailer?'

No one uttered a word as the officer went turning the pages of the book and then went through the pockets of Alex's fleece jacket. He brought out a large packet of weed.

'Okay we are arresting you for possession. I am sure you know your rights? You can make a phone call to your lawyer once we reach the station.' One of the policemen led him away to the car, while another went to search his trailer.

The others stared silently at the unfolding scene. 'Err, can we have that book. It belongs to this gentleman here?' It was Jia.

Tanmoy swallowed. What a stupid girl! Now they will ask to see her passport and he will be dragged into a royal mess.

'Ah! Do you know this man we took into custody just now, Ms ...?' the officer's eyes narrowed.

'My name is Jia Park. I don't know him. We just met. But the book belongs to this professor.'

'I am sorry, in that case you have to collect it from the court. We are seizing it and will need to send it for forensic analysis.

Can I have a look at your passport please, Ms Park?' the officer said in a matter-of-fact voice, 'And you too professor …?'

Tanmoy's hands froze inside his jacket pocket as he pulled out his university ID. 'Good,' the officer matched the photograph with Tanmoy and returned it immediately.

'And you?'

Jia looked furtively at Tanmoy, and a flicker of an expression passed over her face which he could not decipher. She looked at the officer and went up to the chair to fetch her backpack. She opened the zipper and pulled out a dark green passport in a protective cover. The officer went through the pages, checked her photo and then returned it to her. 'South Korea,' he smiled, 'sorry for this trouble, Ms Park. These camping grounds have become a den of vice so we have to pay visits,' then looking at Henry, 'you have to clear this area soon. As I told you all many times, the new highway that will pass through Elmsby will bring down the travel time to London by twenty-three minutes. It will make your lives much easier.'

The other campers had by now assembled and were watching from a distance. They were shocked to see what had just happened and were whispering that the police might have planted the weed on Alex to put more pressure on them to clear out from the area. Tanmoy looked surprised. Indeed he was. He was wondering when she had collected her passport and why she had never told him about it.

9

A thick fog had devoured the English town from early afternoon that day. It spirited away houses, it dissolved the high street into a dismal aquarelle by a master of gloom. It sucked meaning from whatever was sentient as it spread its furry tentacles around the land. In its grey embrace, trees turned into smoky monsters lurking along lonely stretches, ready to waylay the unsuspecting and the innocent, men and women lost their colour and turned into frail creatures who roamed around the streets and avenues like dark characters of tragedies written centuries ago. In London too, the fog played havoc, banking low along the Thames, swathing itself around brick houses and pubs and bringing the traffic to a crawl. Foghorns boomed through this greyness, shaking the old city on its foundations and on the top floor of his Georgian house, Henry's patient still sat speechless, thinking about a long forgotten battle.

Through the sealed windows of his laboratory, Tanmoy Sen saw the world drowning in soup, heavy as tears. He had never experienced such a fog in the ten or more years that he had been working at GeneLab. Nicole had disappeared from Novingdon many months ago but he hardly cherished her memory. For some days, the emerald fire of her eyes disturbed his sleep but this soon dissolved into the phosphorescence of the butterflies he had gifted her. 'The winged beauties never leave me alone' he scribbled in his Moleskine pocketbook, before dozing off in his office. Over the last two years, he had taken to working late into the night. Then he had begun to stay back while Jia slept in his house in that room full of fashion magazines.

Early in the morning he would take a nap in his office where he had a sleeper sofa installed. But he didn't sleep much. The butterflies chased him through day and through night and he had to pay attention, for they were the commanders of his reason and masters of his instincts. They would never leave him alone. And so it went over the final years of creating new splices with a variety of alien species genes to bring out the desired traits in the experimental paddy crop. He didn't allow anyone to take charge of this crucial final step of the project and worked alone, slogging into the late hours when the laboratory was deserted and he was watched over by none.

There were questions raised at one point, by a Sante officer. They required a periodic security audit of GeneLab but it was agreed that Tanmoy's style of keeping the crucial final steps under his close control in fact enhanced security. It is said that the light of madness shines in the eyes of the insane but no one, not even Henry, noticed anything amiss except perhaps his slurred speech which they put down to fatigue. 'Take a break sometimes, Prof. Sen,' they advised him but Tanmoy was too far gone to care.

Meanwhile the butterflies appeared and disappeared at their whim, directing his thoughts as they willed. 'The intricate designs on their wings keep me in a blissful trance — fractal geometry, the dizzying symmetry of absolutes. The Cyclops and the Dusky Diadems, the Satyrs and Blue Glassy Tigers, the Duke of Burgundy and the Dingy Skippers flapping and flying from lobe to lobe, from cerebellum to amygdala. Day and night, like a chorus of magic birds they descend upon me, erupting into fountains of colour, weaving intricate designs inside the web of my thoughts. They are the masters of my reason, the guardians of my emotions.' His diary entries became more florid.

The glasshouses were bursting with the crop of a number of varieties of experimental rice. By the time this was harvested he would have another batch ready for sowing. It was a lot of work and despite the greenhouse crew and some students to help him, his days and nights mingled with each other till he lost track of time.

Tanmoy hadn't ever come around to ask Jia how she could produce her passport when the police asked for it that day at Greg's Oaks. She had been busy with her university job while he had remained in the laboratory for longer hours. SuperRice was inseparable from his life now and the lab assistants became his only family. As long as Jia paid the token rent and didn't invite any trouble, he was happy to have her live in the same house.

It was three in the morning when something disturbed his slumber. His small office beside the pre-amp room with all the expensive equipment was at one end of the laboratory and he thought it might be an equipment malfunctioning. After checking the new bacteria cultures prepared by one of the PhD students, he had gone into his office for an hour's rest at about two in the morning. He planned to be up at dawn, have a coffee and return to the work. This had been his routine for months now.

The office was dark. He put on his glasses and switched on the table lamp. Through the porthole of the door he noticed a light shining outside the laboratory. Had he forgotten to turn it off? Surely no one had come in at that hour.

He pushed back his chair, went round the table towards the door. He put on the white lab coat and blue gloves and on his way out switched on the electric kettle. Opening the door he walked the few steps to the laboratory. He swiped the key card, there was a click and he pushed the glass door open.

Everything looked okay except for that light burning outside. He remembered hearing a sound. Like the whirr of a motor.

He went up to the ultra-low temperature chest freezer to check if the compressor had malfunctioned but the reading on its display was all right. Minus seventy-nine degrees centigrade. Back to take a look at the liquid nitrogen and carbon dioxide supply tanks. They stood in their place, undisturbed. Inside the pre-amp room, the Allegra centrifuge and PCR machines were switched off, no sign of a short circuit or electrical disturbance anywhere. He went out and checked the expensive microarray scanner, the standby power module near the door was working quietly, a green LED shining on the front panel. He was a little groggy and hovered for a while at the head of the rows of work benches and cabinets. Then he began to walk slowly down each row. The gene guns were in their proper place and no microscope was broken. On the long wooden racks, the white bottles of reagents, test tubes, salts, the titration funnels, everything was in its place. There was nothing leaking, no solution spilling over, no device behaving whimsically. Nothing here.

An improbable thought occurred to him. He went racing back to the closet in the anteroom where he kept the newly harvested varieties of SuperRice. Different species of genetically improved paddy seeds, grown in the first batch in their glasshouses. He swiped through the steel door, entered the anteroom and punched in the code for the locker. The lock clicked and he pulled the door open. He opened the safe used to store critically important research products. The vacuum-packed tubes with the seeds were gone.

Had he taken them out for labelling and left them in his office cabinet? Quite unlikely. He pushed through the door and stepped out of the laboratory. He hurried across the file room and dashed into his office. He was panting as he switched on the light. A few journals on his table, which he had planned to read. He went through the drawers just in case he had unmindfully kept them there. Empty. Next the cabinet. It was empty too but for a couple of brown envelopes, rolodex cards and an old conference folder. Nothing. Somebody had sneaked into the laboratory in the dead of night and made off with the fruits of a decade of research.

Whoever it was may still be around. He thought he would raise an alarm. But he had to check the laptop first. This was where he kept records of the experiments and only two people had access to the login password. He and an official from Sante.

He rushed back to the pre-amp room, went around the bank of instruments to the stack of metal drawers where he kept the laptop. The drawer which he kept locked had been forced open, the computer was gone.

How could they enter the anteroom and open the safe containing the new seeds? Only the administration had access to the codes and duplicate swipe cards. An insider? Then a nasty thought occurred to him and he stood there dumbfounded, as if shaken up by a nightmare.

He dragged himself back to his office, switched off the light and dropped into his chair. He dialled the number from the office phone. There was no ring on the other side. The phone was dead.

A cold chill took hold of him as he sat there paralysed, his heart thumping madly. He began to sweat. His knuckles were chalk white as he made a fist — the veins of his forearm bulging angrily. He swung his fist hitting his jaw hard. Then again. And again. Harder every time with vehemence. Right and left. Hitting himself madly. Mercilessly repeating the blows. He fell from the chair and hit his head but he kept hitting himself till his face was all bloody and his fists sore.

10

What has he been doing all this time? A pall seemed to be lifting from over his mind as he lay there on the floor of his office. Numbed by pain. A weak tree uprooted by a deadly squall. The mist was lifting slowly. Could they have gone far? With tremendous effort he rose from the floor and reached for his desk phone. He dialled the number again. This time also the call did not connect. Breathing hard, Tanmoy Sen again collapsed on his chair.

There were lights shining inside his head but something else was happening to him now. His mind was suddenly very quiet. An odd silence had crept back slowly. But for the shooting pain there was no other distraction. The dizzying dance of the butterflies had suddenly stopped.

A series of doorways was opening up, one after the other. Each door swinging silently on it hinges. Letting in light. And the light streamed through to the depths, a little brighter every time as one after another they opened the gates. Letting it shine through.

He stood on the threshold. The realisation dawning upon him slowly: He had messed up his dream. After years of toil and the hard work of so many, he had let his fancy rule and completely sabotaged the final steps of a long and arduous project. The spells had been cast and the quirky genes were already lying in ambush in the chromosomes of his magic seeds.

He had been random, even whimsical. From alert geneticist he had turned into a punchbowl mixer. Now with the computer gone no one would know what sorcery was buried in the souls of those seeds that he had developed over the last two years. Till they unleashed their occult powers. No one would find out, till they sow the seeds and taste the rice or break into his passwords. Either way, it might be too late.

Henry came to his mind. His friend had been right. It's dangerous to play games with the fruits of the earth. But he wouldn't have reckoned the way things had gone wrong. He remembered the Group CEO of Sante, Sturmhofer. The CEO wanted SuperRice to be engineered in such a way that it would be good for only one season. The farmers shouldn't be able to save and reuse the seeds because this would mean lost business. But he had largely ignored these guidelines and created batches that could be used again and again. It hardly mattered any more.

Memories of their last meeting came crowding back. The CEO was a man of substantial girth with a roly-poly face, like one of Sante's spliced tomatoes that had bombed on the market. He accompanied by their Technology Head and a Japanese colleague had flown in from the States and come rushing to Novingdon when they had reported their first success with a rice that could synthesise vitamin precursors. They had meetings with him at the department. It was still a long way to SuperRice which would also tolerate extreme weather but the visitors had been very upbeat. One of them had reviewed all access rules to the laboratory. They had questions but in the end they had looked pleased.

Meetings done and after a lunch of juicy roasts at the staff canteen, the visitors had taken a peck at the medieval cathedral of Novingdon followed by a whirl through a local art gallery which had a substantial collection of Stanley Spencer's images of disease and hospitals imbued with strong religious motifs and symbolism. On the way back to their BMWs parked near the graveyard, Sturmhofer had remarked, 'I like that guy's paintings over there, what was his name again?'

'Stanley Spencer,' someone had said.

'I guess we could do with a few of those inside the elevators at the headquarters, couldn't we?' he looked around and his colleagues nodded in assent.

'Good,' he had remarked, getting into his car. 'Keep at it, professor. The world is looking up to you.

'By the way,' he had said, rolling down the window, 'we foresee some opposition from earth lovers when our baby begins to walk. We will take care of those greens all right. We will have our environment safety officer come over and straighten things out. The earth lovers will love us all.'

He had bade them goodbye and the cavalcade of limousines had zoomed past the graveyard and rolled slowly up the road towards London. Because the route went uphill, they could see them for a long time, three tiny specks of black, in a row, a metal centipede crawling over the earth, gradually disappearing into the sea of traffic headed northwards.

Tanmoy, alone in the deserted lab, wondered how Sturmhofer would react if he was here tonight and was to know that his pet project was in shambles because the chief geneticist had failed miserably. On all counts. But he wasn't. He was thousands of miles away and he wouldn't get to know anything for a few more hours.

Too late. He stood up with difficulty and tried to steady himself. He had brought ignominy to his department. Pain shot through his head and he felt dizzy. His right hand was going numb. He wouldn't raise an alarm. More memories came flooding back as he stumbled towards the laboratory.

He went quietly, stepping along the rows of work benches and cabinets. Stick-on notes scribbled by his students were on the rack shelves — equations, formulae, figures, volumes, words, numbers. They reminded him of the annual exhibition at his boarding school where at the Biology department his projects always won the first prize. He would put up little notes on coloured paper, explaining his experiments.

The clipboard with the temperature readings was hanging on one side of the giant chest freezer. The lab assistants meticulously recorded the internal temperatures comparing it to the display readings. Hour upon hour. -79°, -78°, -80° ... He activated the auto lock mechanism and pulled up the heavy steel door. A burst of freezing smoke engulfed him with the faraway love of frozen worlds. He went into the swirling vapours, pulling down the metal door over him. Going slowly down. Deep down into the cold forevers of smoke and ice.

11

The military aircraft that flew back Jia and Eugene was an old Soviet Antonov, hardly fit to fly. It had taken off under the cover of darkness from a secret landing strip of an east European nation and bumping through air pockets had flown an easterly route making two stops, one in the desolate Kazakh steppes to paint the undercarriage and another for refuelling in the midst of Siberian waste buried under tons of snow. Besides the two of them and a pair of stony-jawed intelligence officers who constantly scratched their heads, the aircraft was carrying back a polished Bechstein grand piano, a couple of surface-to-air Igla missile launchers and mountains of Swiss cheese. It had landed in the little military airfield outside Pyongyang just when the hills were rising up from an ocean of mist.

A jeep was waiting for them. They were first driven to a Research Department for External Intelligence facility in Pyongyang where after a round of debriefings they were put in the back of a covered truck with a thick-necked Bowibu officer. The black truck drove along straight roads flanked by cornfields before entering the mountains. For hours it went bouncing over damaged roads, past numerous checkpoints with green uniformed military guards, finally arriving at the gates of a prison camp facility in the shadow of a hill about two hours drive out of the city.

Eugene and Jia exchanged glances as the truck rolled into the massive prison facility which looked like a phantom town preparing for a carnival. Sitting in facing black benches they peered through the flaps to find hundreds of pale shivering skeletons, their heads down, as if in deep contemplation, watching a small floating platform at the centre of a blue mountain lake inside the prison compound. Some of them were on the platform setting up chairs and sweeping the floor while others swam back and forth with microphones, water bottles and flower arrangements to decorate the stage.

A large number of inmates stood in neat rows on the banks of the lake waiting. A little way to their left were rows upon rows of chairs slowly filling up with uniformed men from various security departments and the military establishment. As Jia and Eugene got off the truck they could see a pithead in the distance with coal trolleys being pushed back and forth and the low group of dismal buildings where the imprisoned miners lived.

A woman, about her age, was standing at the edge of the water, at a distance from the main group of prisoners. A glassy-eyed bag of bones, her skin pale from malnutrition. But when she saw Jia getting off the truck, her dead eyes lit up. She was trying to tell her something, but there was hardly any time. Jia recognised her immediately. She walked up to her and trying to avoid any show of emotion, took her hands in hers and asked, 'Where have they taken papa and omma?'

'I haven't seen them for weeks,' the woman whispered, 'where were you, all this while?'

But there was no time for Jia to answer. The Bowibu officer was looking for her. She disengaged her hands but passed on a few tubes of paddy to the emaciated woman. Perhaps she could find some use for the seeds and in any case no one would miss a few samples. Luckily the Bowibu officer was some distance away and didn't notice. Everyone was waiting for the show to begin.

Eugene and the Bowibu officer were standing near the entrance of the low squat building to the left of the prison gates. She sneaked in quietly and stood behind them.

'Welcome back, Jia-shi! Can you play the accordion?' an elderly man in a suit came out of the building and asked her. He had narrow eyes and he massaged his hands as he spoke.

'Yes, I learned it when I was a child,' she said.

'We have a little event happening shortly. Play a soaring tune, you know what I mean. One that will lift spirits and will impart an aura of grandeur to the occasion.'

She blinked from fatigue of the long journey and nodded slowly. 'Yes, Sir,' she said.

'Sorry I didn't introduce myself. I am Hyon Mansik from the State Security Department. We will have time for introductions later. Now let's get going with the programme. Professor, can you dance?'

Eugene stared at him blankly.

'I am sure you can, come with me. We don't have time.' They walked back to the edge of the lake.

There were people on the floating platform now and an old-fashioned boat with a lone oarsman was moored to the bank, waiting for them. An accordion had already been kept on the boat and like the platform, the boat was decorated with little white flowers. The three of them boarded and were rowed up to the platform.

'You start when I give the signal,' Mansik said while jumping up to the floating platform. A two star general of the North Korean army stood there flanked by two armed guards. At the table a stony-faced judge sat turning pages of a fat dossier.

She strapped on the accordion as the boat moved away from the platform. The sun had already begun to disappear behind the row of hills and suddenly it was chilly on the water. Mansik gave a short scathing speech following which he read out charges against the general. The judge listened, an unwavering look directed at the audience. The general who had been kept standing all along, now began to recite a long confession. Slowly, with stresses and intonation and it sounded almost like poetry. Tears were welling up in his eyes as he finished with an appeal for mercy. All eyes were on the judge.

The judge said something which was not audible because he didn't have a mike. The guards now pointed their rifles at the military man as he slowly removed his insignia. Then he took off his belt. Mansik screamed, 'Music!'

Jia who was sitting athwart on the flower boat, began with some improvisations building up to a rousing tune that floated across the water stirring the prisoners and the uniforms. They shifted their weight and moved their feet, undecided if it was okay to dance. They looked up at the floating stage and back to the edge of the lake where four Russian ZPU-4 anti-aircraft guns had been lined up, aimed and waiting.

The boat moved in circles around the blue lake, the music became joyous, lifting spirits as Eugene threw his legs and arms around trying to mimic steps he had once learned. The general, stripped of his stars, stood half naked, shivering on the platform.

Mansik signalled another boat to ferry him and the judge. The guards left their guns on the second boat and dived into the water, swimming away from the platform just as the ZPU-4s roared in concert like a rousing brass crescendo in the final movement of a symphony. The audience clapped, kept clapping, tears of joy streaming down their eyes, as the platform with the general lit up a brilliant red under a low evening sky, just as the final bars from the accordion were floating in from the edges of the indigo blue water. The lake boiled and blistered. The hills danced in the red fire like old men bobbing their heads.

A guard escorted the two of them into the low squat building. A small room with a few chairs and a table. She and Eugene took their seats and waited. No one came in. Fatigue had been creeping over her and she had fallen asleep with her head on the table.

She was woken by the thump of boots on concrete. She was thirsty but there was no water in the room and they had locked the door from outside. Eugene had also vanished. She had dozed off again and was dreaming about the house in Novingdon and briefly about the Indian professor. She saw an ambulance driving madly down the high street and the wail of its siren filled up her head and she woke up with a start.

Hyon Mansik was standing beside the table, watching her. His jacket was gone and the sleeves of his shirt were folded up exposing thick hairy forearms. Beside him were two middle-aged men, one of them in uniform. The other person was in a grey suit and when he took a seat, she could see he was wearing a CZ semi-automatic in a shoulder holster.

She didn't hide anything from them because she had hardly anything to hide. She had done as they had told her because she cared for her family and believed she would be able to free them some day. But why this interview when they had already been debriefed and had delivered what had been asked for? She had handed over the tubes of spliced paddy to the RDEI at Pyongyang and Eugene had given them the laptop and some more samples.

'Once more, welcome back, Park! I must congratulate you for the wonderful music. Like a true daughter of the soil, you have excelled in the accordion. The audience was eating out of your hand. Now let me introduce you to these gentlemen,

Colonel Kang, Military Security, and this is officer Song from the RDEI,' Mansik began. The two officers gave her glassy looks. As the interrogation progressed, they took notes, consulted her biography. Later they joined in with questions, watching her closely all the time.

'We want to hear everything. Sooner this round of debriefing gets over and you have told us everything truthfully, we will see to it that you can return to your duties. Tell us your name, where were you born and about your parents and family. It should be like an autobiography, you know what I mean. But before you begin, will you please hand over any more samples of rice that you may have in your possession. You and the scientist have already handed over a few tubes and a laptop. I understand you have some samples on you,' Mansik said and pulled the metal chair closer to her.

Jia: I have handed over everything to the RDEI, Sir.

Mansik: Okay. Then let us begin.

Jia: My name is Park Jia. I will be thirty-one this November. I was born in Pyongyang. My father is a civil engineer and my mother trained as a teacher. I have a twin sister Park Jiyoo. [At the mention of her name Mansik's eyes narrowed even further and the two other interrogators looked at each other.] My grandfather went to the war where he was killed, fighting the UN forces in the Battle of Chipyong-ni. Our family had a good *songbun* which allowed us comfortable accommodation in a residential apartment in the capital and other privileges. After completing our graduation followed by military training, my sister and I pursued higher studies at the university. Meanwhile my mother taught in a school.

Mansik: Tell us more about your sister. Did you meet her today, after you arrived?

Jia: Both of us studied at Kim Chaek University of Technology with the hope that once we had completed the course, we will find good jobs in a state institution. Because we were the same age and took the same courses, most of our friends were common. We were both actively involved in the Socialist Youth League and did our duties for the Fatherland with pride and honesty. But then it all began to unravel before our eyes. Today just after arriving here I met my sister briefly. I asked her about father and mother but she said she didn't know where they could be.

Mansik: I will find out what happened to them but tell me, did your sister tell you that she was planning an escape?

Jia: What? No! I could only ask her about our parents. I thought she looked too feeble to be able to run away. When did this happen?

Mansik: We should not get into irrelevant issues now. The guards will capture her very soon and bring her back. I will see to it that you meet her. But now let's return to the past. There was an official named Cho Jungho at the school where your mother taught. When did you first hear his name?

Jia: I overheard his name when mother mentioned him to father one night.

Mansik: What did she have to say about this Cho?

Jia: She didn't tell us anything till it became unmanageable. What we gathered from her conversations with father — he was a vile character. He had something for mother and had been after her since the time she joined this job. She resisted his advances but she was scared because everyone said Cho had good party connections. We could hear mother telling papa about this man every night.

Mansik: How did your father react to all this?

Jia: Father would assure her that everything would be fine and he will talk with someone high up to help mother find another job. But Cho became more aggressive. This continued for months and we couldn't do anything to help her. While mother did her best to ward off his advances, Cho became insufferable. He threatened to get father arrested if she didn't give in to his advances.

Mansik: What happened after that? Your father got involved in the pilferage of building material and selling it with the help of a criminal network. Stealing of state property is a very serious offence.

Jia: My father never did anything of that sort. He was an honest man. Our family believes in the Juche ideology and follows its principles. We are law-abiding citizens looking up to our Leaders. Like every citizen we had images of the GREAT LEADER and the DEAR LEADER in our homes, we wore our lapel badges with pride. We attended self-criticism sessions, we worked hard. This story about father was a fabrication of Jungho, who with the help of his connections got my father arrested on trumped up charges.

Mansik: I believe your father was arrested soon after and there was indeed quite a bit of evidence about his involvement in this illegal business.

Jia: I will never believe this. It was all set up by Cho Jungho and those who were helping him. Later, after they took father away, I heard that Cho had an uncle who was very powerful. From the day father was arrested, we were looked upon with suspicion and all three of us were shadowed wherever we went. Anyone who visited us was questioned and because of this, friends and relatives began to keep a distance. We lost our good songbun in spite of being a family of patriots, despite the fact that my grandfather fought valiantly for our country during the war.

Mansik: Who told you about Cho's connections? Was it a woman called Jung Jimin?

Jia looked at him with tired empty eyes. Should she sacrifice a friend? If she didn't, she may not be able to get her family out of this muck. The normal rules of ethics did not apply here any more.

Mansik: She was here till a few months back so we can cross-check what she told us with what you know. It's for the purpose of perfect record keeping and the security of our people.

Colonel Kang pulled out a file with a neatly stacked set of typed sheets. He turned over a few pages. With his red pencil he made a small note at the corner of the first page as she began to speak.

Jia: Yes, she did. Jimin was a girl I knew from my childhood. They lived in an upscale neighbourhood but had relatives who lived in our apartment block. She was a quiet sort of girl and I hardly knew anything about her. I still don't, except she comes from a very influential family and we had taken accordion lessons together. I was quite surprised when she recognised me one day on the metro. This was just a few weeks after father's arrest. I was pleasantly surprised to see her after all these years. She was a plain girl but now she was in designer clothes and her vanity bag would have cost my father's whole year's wages.

Mansik: You went to a noodle restaurant with Jimin next. Tell us about this meeting. Who else was present?

Jia: Just the two of us. The place was crowded so we couldn't talk much. This was a few days after our chance meeting on the metro. I was surprised to learn that she already knew what had happened to father and gave me assurances. Jimin was friendly and warm. I told her that we were not sure if we are safe in this country any more. She didn't say much that evening but asked me to meet her another day.

When I discussed this with my sister that night, she got scared and said I was being stupid, seeking help from strangers. I told her that I knew this woman when she was a girl. My sister was not convinced but still without telling her I went and met Jimin the next week.

Mansik: What happened at that meeting?

Jia: It didn't sound too difficult, what Jimin suggested. She said she knew a broker in the South who had helped many people get out of this country and settle there. She said she will make all arrangements and though we would have to spend a fortune it will be not too much to pay for freedom. She was quite convincing and when I came back and told my sister, she didn't put up much resistance. In any case our lives had become a nightmare after father's arrest. It was difficult to convince mother though.

Mansik: What about your father? He was still in prison.

Jia: Yes. Mother refused to leave him behind. I told her that once we were safely out of the country and settled in the South we can take Jimin's help to get him out of prison. But trying anything while we were still here would be risky for all of us. So mother gave in finally. Jimin had said that even if our father came out of prison camp, which was quite unlikely, this country would never be safe for us. We had lost our good songbun and would be under suspicion throughout our lives. Jimin assured me that she would seek help to get father released but this would take time. I was not so sure because I knew once they found out we had defected, they will never let him go, in fact, they could pressurise us to return. But still we convinced mother somehow and she agreed to come with us.

Mansik: Then you tried to get out of this country but were discovered on the way? How were you found out? Don't leave out any details. Tell us about the people who helped you.

Jia: With a bare minimum of belongings and some money sewed into our stockings, we set off for the train station. There was someone waiting for us there. Besides the three of us there was a man and a woman who were also trying to leave. The guide, how old was he, perhaps in his forties. He said his name was Jinho. He was a man of few words, only speaking to us when he had to give instructions. He gave us our travel permits which must have been obtained by bribing some police officer. By this time travel restrictions were not as strict as before and it was comparatively easy for us to go from one place to another, unless of course one was heading to Pyongyang.

The trains travelled across the country, stopping for hours because of power cuts. It took us two changes of trains and more than three days to reach Musan via Chongjin. Winter had already set in and our progress had been slow. Mother fell sick on the way with a raging fever and we had to stop while the others moved on ahead of us.

We arrived at the Chinese border. The Tumen was frozen and it was a dangerous crossing with guards on both sides looking out for defectors. But Jinho knew what was to be done and he bribed the guards on this side and we safely crossed into Chinese territory.

After trekking for miles through a wooded hillside we were to stop for the night at an agricultural farm which was a kind of safe house. But the Chinese police stopped us on our way. They arrested all six of our group including the Chinese guide who was taking us to the safe house. Jinho had seen us across the border and gone back, so they could not get him. The Chinese police pushed us back handing us over to the Bowibu.

The Bowibu interrogated us for days. We were starved, beaten with batons and kicked mercilessly and finally put on a truck that travelled for days bringing us back to this prison camp where father was being held. We were in bad shape when we arrived, none of us had slept for days, and whatever money we had, had been taken away.

Mansik: I see. I have to give you that you are brave. Brave but foolish. So all of you were brought here including the others in your group. What happened thereafter? Tell us about your meetings with Lee Byunghun who was in charge of this camp at that point. Didn't he suggest that you get trained for this assignment in England? You don't need to hide anything because Lee is not in charge any more, he is helping out in a coal mine, on the other side of the country.

Jia: I first met officer Lee Byunghun during our military training. There were other officers too but he was the one we saw most of the time. He was a man of pleasant disposition and he didn't push us too hard. I thought he was a kind man. If I was sick, he would allow me to rest and watch the other students shooting guns at cutouts of American soldiers in camouflage jackets. When it got too cold outside, he would often let us train indoors. He was very good in technical matters and we loved to attend his classes about weaponry and ammunition. When father was arrested I tried to contact Byunghun but learnt that he had been transferred.

Still I managed to pass on a message. Byunghun gave some assurances but nothing happened. Months passed and we were getting more and more worried about father. This was when my friend Jimin came along suggesting we leave the country.

But the biggest surprise for me was waiting here at this prison camp, after we were captured by the Chinese and handed over to the Bowibu. Lee Byunghun had moved from the army to the State Security Department and was now posted in this prison. He immediately recognised us. He had changed a lot in the years since I last saw him at arms training. The soft demeanour had vanished, replaced by a harshness that came as a shock to me, 'Aha! Who do we have here?' he said during the initial processing before we were led to the prison quarters. 'We are going to have a family reunion it seems,' he said grinning as one of the staff took down names and other details. His snake-like eyes flashed in the grey light of the morning as he went down the file of men and women cowering before him in fear. For me it was the end of all hope.

Mansik: So you say Lee didn't help you in the least? But he made an offer to you while you were being held here? Tell us about that meeting.

Jia: It was in the middle of winter that we were brought here. We were fenced in and worked day and night till our bones broke or the soul just left the body. We were hungry and tired. The broth of corn and cabbage leaves that was served was hardly enough for our overworked bodies. And they didn't spare mother either. She had to work endless hours at the textile factory, sewing uniforms for soldiers. We hardly saw father, who was sent down into the coal mine with other prisoners. Every day the number who came out from the pit was less than those who went in.

Every day there were beatings. From our cramped quarters we could hear the cries of the tortured shrill in the chilly night of the mountain. The guards at the camp were ruthless and outdid each other in their brutality to impress the officers. We heard dreadful stories. A man who had stolen food from the kitchen was badly beaten, blindfolded and tied to a chestnut tree and shot. Next day we saw the corpse of another prisoner, who had argued with a guard. His head had been smashed, flies were buzzing over the body and maggots streaming out of the mouth and swarming over a blood-caked face. Brain matter had poured out of his cracked skull and, like molten cheese, splattered the grass. Now I know how the human brain looks like.

You have asked me not to skip on details so I am telling you everything. Each day was a struggle against despair and I suffered silently seeing the rest of my family in this plight. Still I hoped that someone would find out and tell them that this was all a big mistake, our family had really not meant to leave this country and that father's imprisonment was a conspiracy. I would do anything to get them some relief, anything really. And by a quirk of chance, right at this time, Lee Byunghun made me this offer.

One night, a few weeks after we were brought here, just as we were returning from the garment manufacturing unit, where we sewed uniforms for our soldiers, we were stopped by two armed guards. They asked my sister and mother to go and ordered me to follow them. I was expecting the worst. It was a long walk from the factory to the prison office and moreover this was in the middle of winter. My tattered pullover was no protection against the biting cold. I felt my fingers go numb.

The prison office, I guess it was this same building, was lit up with powerful lights. The guards led me in and I was asked to wait in a small room with no windows. After an hour of waiting, officer Lee walked in.

'I have some news for you,' he said, his thick-set jaws giving no indication of the kind of news he was going to reveal.

I nodded without saying anything and that flared up his temper. 'You don't care, do you?'

I was still shivering and didn't know how to respond.

'You are all in it together. Your family has betrayed the people. Your father has been stealing public property for years and you know it very well. If you tell us the truth about your father then I might be able to protect you, otherwise ...' and he suddenly flashed a wicked grin that sent a chill through my spine.

'I have always known that he is an honest man,' I said softly. It was a desperate situation. For once I even thought of sacrificing father to win freedom for the three of us.

'You are lying,' he shouted glowering at me.

I did not know how to convince him. He kept silent for a while and then a phone began to ring somewhere inside and he went out of the room.

When he returned after almost an hour, he looked more composed. There were two others with him, whose names I can't recollect. One was from party liaison, the other was foreign intelligence.

Lee's anger had vanished from his face. The three of them took their seats. They studied me quietly for a while and Lee began in a friendly tone, 'We will make you an offer. I know you went to one of our best universities and can fluently speak English and Chinese. Now you can use those skills to help our Fatherland. We will send you for training. I believe you already have many of the skills so you can train quickly and take on the assignment. You will be told about it later. But remember, we will be keeping a close watch on you. If you try anything funny you won't see any of your family again. As for your father, I cannot guarantee anything. What will happen to him is no more in my control.'

I had trusted him once but he had failed in his promise. But now I had no choice. If I did what he was suggesting, there was a chance that the three of us would be released. I was to be sent for special training to a military facility near the capital. I wouldn't have to train for the whole thirty-month stretch but just for a few months. After that I would have to go overseas.

'I will do it,' I said.

'I knew you would. You were always a smart girl,' he said. 'You will be taken to the training facility tonight. A truck is going out shortly, they will drop you there. I am sending word, there will be someone to meet you.'

'Can I tell my sister and mother that I am going away?' I asked not with much hope that permission will be granted.

'Okay. Remember, not a word about where you are going and why. Just tell them you will be away for a while. The guards will accompany you,' he said.

Mansik: So you trained at the academy, were given your papers and sent overseas, to that English town?

Jia: Once my training was over Lee met me again. At that meeting I was briefed by the RDEI about the exact nature of my assignment. I would have to enter the UK with a South Korean passport. My cover would be of a fashion designer attached to a fictitious Seoul fashion store. I was visiting UK to research fashion trends for a new line of clothing. My job was to get friendly with the scientist in charge of a critical project at GeneLab UK. They were developing new kinds of genetically modified rice strains, rich in vitamin-like compounds, which could resist extreme temperatures as well. They said these super seeds could withstand the effects of changes in climate and unpredictable weather. If I could get the procedures and samples back to my country then my mother and sister will be released. And this paddy, he said, will save hundreds of millions of our citizens from starvation. I was also asked to keep a watch on a Korean scientist who was working for us. For some reason, he had lost the trust of the department. I think I believed what he said and if it could save the lives of starving people, why not. I could imagine the risks but my family mattered to me more than anything else.

Song: What happened after you arrived in the UK?

Jia: Our embassy put me up in a house in New Malden for a few days. There Comrade Ryu Eugene came to meet me. He was working at GeneLab on another project. He briefed me about the research being done there and about the Indian professor Tanmoy Sen who was coordinating the SuperRice experiments. I had to win his confidence and get as much information out of him as possible. Comrade Eugene visited me twice during those first few days, before I met the Indian professor.

Song: Did you get any indication that Ryu Yujin might have been withholding information from you and may be working for others? Anything at all?

Jia: Never. He was cooperative and briefed me well about the professor's habits. I came to know from him about his daily routines and his soft spot for a barmaid — Nicole Sykes. It helped us coordinate our first meeting with the professor in a way that helped me win his confidence.

Kang: We have reason to believe that our scientist, Comrade Yujin, had been sabotaging our interests. I will tell you how we know. We received a sample of spliced paddy some years ago that poisoned our soldiers. They didn't die but some of them went colour blind. And because they were on field duty they committed grave mistakes, hurting us badly. We are still counting our losses in terms of accidents and damaged equipment. You are aware that part of your duties in the UK was to watch over him and report back to us if you noticed anything suspicious. But you sent us nothing significant about him. You have mentioned in this morning's debriefing that you used to share your kimchi and gochujang with him, when you met outside. But how did this help? He was smarter than you and managed to sabotage us. You couldn't dig out anything about the people he met or the places he visited. Tell me how Yujin being a scientist sent us that sample of spliced paddy which harmed our soldiers?

Jia: I am sorry, I really know nothing about that sample. This must have happened before I arrived in Novingdon, which was about two years ago. I can't vouch for anyone but he seemed to me a dedicated worker. He helped me with information about the laboratory and the systems and procedures there. But thanks to the professor — Dr Sen, if he hadn't unwittingly arranged the administrative job, we wouldn't have got access to the secure area with the computer and the samples. The professor was really nice that way. I did my own background work on him and found his papers cited hundreds of times in scholarly documents. Also, this might be irrelevant but Professor Sen was very taken by James Watt, he almost worshipped the Scottish mechanical engineer.

Mansik: James Watt? That steam fellow? What about him, comrade?

Jia: I would not know but he was always reading his biography, like a prayer book, it was for him.

Mansik: That doesn't sound right. You should have followed that lead.

Jia: I am sorry. I leafed through it a few times and it read like an ordinary biography to me.

Mansik: No coded language or anything?

Jia: No.

Mansik: Okay, now for some basic questions before we move on to other things. Tell me the height of the Juche tower.

Jia: One hundred seventy metres, Sir.

Mansik: Where did the March 1st Uprising start?

Jia: Pyongyang, Sir.

Mansik: Good. Do you know anyone called Katya Sintsova?

Jia: She is a Russian girl in a short story. She comes from a solid communist background but she makes many mistakes in life and is cheated by her American lover who is actually a descendant of a Russian landlord and not American at all. Katya suffers a lot through the book ending up as a prostitute in Munich. The North Korean narrator of the story ...

Mansik: Okay. I see you have a taste for storybooks too. But why are you covering for your comrade the scientist? Maybe I should tell you that he had not been all that sure about you. In fact he told us today that you had acted unprofessionally by getting into a relationship with the Indian professor. Can you deny that?

Jia: I am terribly surprised to hear this. I would have done anything that would have helped us get the spliced seeds and eventually to see my family released. But Professor Sen was never into me, if you know what I mean. He had a crush on this green-eyed barmaid but then she disappeared from Novingdon quite suddenly. We never saw her again. As for me, I was thankful to the professor — he arranged this job for me at the administrative office and was quite kind to let out a room to me. Because of this, it was easy to infiltrate the university system. Beyond that there was nothing between us.

Mansik: Okay, let us move on. Later we will get the scientist to sit with you and see if he still holds on to what he said earlier. Right now he is not in good shape. Would you like to walk down to the basement with us and say hello?

Jia: I guess that's an order?

They led her downstairs into the basement, lit by fluorescent lamps in steel holders. The basement was a warren of small cells, most of these empty. It was very cold here and a strong smell of detergent and antiseptic pervaded the area. She could hear groans and muffled sobs from behind the locked doors. From her training she could guess what this underground facility was used for but she wouldn't allow herself to get scared because if one of her defences were broken, she would end up a nervous wreck or dead. She believed she had done nothing wrong and helped her country and so they should keep their end of the promise.

They took her to the farthest end of the cavernous establishment. There was a steel door set in the brickwork with a grilled opening near the top.

'Look inside,' Mansik said.

She did as advised.

The cell was bare concrete, just big enough for two men. A yellow light embedded in the ceiling glowed dully inside. She saw two men clamped to metal rods on the wall opposite to the door. Their hands and feet were clamped together. Their faces were masks of concentrated pain and the only sounds in that cell were the low moans escaping from the mouth of one of the prisoners. The other man was either dead or had lost consciousness. It was not difficult for her to recognise the tall stringy scientist. She had been trained to bear torture but the sight of Eugene's battered face in that dim-lit prison cell scared her. She drew in her breath silently and wondered what the poor scientist could have done to incur the wrath of his interrogators.

Then they were back again at the interrogation room. Mansik offered her a bowl of seaweed soup and a plate of rice with a fried egg. She was hungry and tried to eat but her body revolted. She remembered Eugene in the cell. With effort she controlled the nausea that was pushing up inside her like a beast. The questioning resumed shortly.

Song: We are almost done with you, Comrade Park. Once we are through, you will be taken to your room where you can rest for a few hours. Take as much rest as you can because we will need to question the two of you together. I am afraid, this will take a while. Now let's talk about this snakehead who goes by the name Tony Fang; did he help you all the way or was he playing for the highest bidder?

Jia: I wouldn't know that. I never met Tony Fang in person, but he did help us that day when I first made contact with the professor at a pub in central London. He set it up in such a way that I could win the professor's confidence and then accompany him back to Novingdon. The only problem was that Professor Sen was too nervous and there was a small accident. Nothing serious. He hurt himself that day which was not so bad because it was easier for me to help him and win his confidence.

Mansik: Who is this man Henry David? That name sounds familiar. Was he a capitalist agent?

Jia: An agent? I didn't notice anything suspicious about him, comrade, though he did try quite a few times to dissuade the professor from carrying on with his gene splicing experiments. I did my best to frustrate those attempts and I was successful because the professor continued with the project and we got the samples.

Song: How did Katya Sintsova lose her leg?

Jia: In a car accident, Sir.

Song: Now about the seeds and the laptop. Are you sure you got the right samples? Anything you missed or forgot to hand over to us?

Jia: Eugene kept a tab on the progress of work at the professor's laboratory. Also my position in the administrative section helped and we knew exactly what we have to take with us and where to find these. There have been no mistakes. Eugene and I knew the professor's schedule, the time he comes in and leaves and when exactly he retires for a few hours in his office at the lab. I had obtained the key codes to the safe and Tony Fang supplied forcing equipment so we could collect everything quickly and the same night we made our way out of Novingdon. Tony Fang had sent a man with a car. As for the samples, I have handed over everything that I was carrying with me.

She said this calmly looking him straight in the eye. Song nodded thoughtfully. Mansik had drawn curtains over his eyes. There was a knock at the door. Kang went up and opened it.

A guard was standing outside.

Mansik saw him and went up to the door. The guard whispered something. Kang and Mansik looked at each other. They conferred in low tones outside the door and returned to the room. The guard closed the door and left.

'A prisoner has just reported that you passed on a small package to your sister, Park Jiyoo, before you were brought in here.' Mansik said the words in a cold even tone.

She could see the blood rise in his face. There was a long silence as the officers watched her. Jia kept staring vacantly at the wall behind them. Her heart began to thump wildly. There was no way out of this perhaps but still she knew she had done the right thing. Mansik was leaning close to her and she could smell the stale sweat on his shirt.

He brought his face closer and she could see the veins of his temples bulging as blood rushed through them. 'Do you have anything to say?'

If her sister had really managed to escape, as they said, she still had a chance to push through with the denial. Maybe she could get away with it. 'I don't know why they said that. I have not given anything to my sister.'

'It will be better for you to come clean, comrade, because I don't want to see you in that cell down below with the scientist.' There was a sudden menace in his voice.

'I have not passed on anything to my sister,' she said once again calmly.

'Too bad, then,' Mansik said and rose abruptly from the chair. Her head burst with pain as Mansik's booted leg swung and hit her, throwing her to the floor. The metal stool she was sitting on rolled away on the concrete. Song rose from his chair and handcuffed her as she writhed in pain on the cold concrete.

They marched out of the room without another word. She could hear the door clanging shut through the walls of pain pressing in from all sides. As their steps receded down the corridor, someone switched off the light. Jia Park shivered. The room was suddenly cold and the shadows hiding in the corners leaped out, throwing themselves upon her, wrapping around her, layer over layer of black, burying deep the speck of light of her fearless heart.

White
Cloud
Mountain

5

Jiyoo had suggested it to the tour manager. They had returned from the beaches of Jeju and then spent a couple of days in Chuncheon and after that travelled to East sea beaches before returning to Seoul. The original plan was to head for the Seorak mountains, spend some days there and do a couple of easy treks. The group was looking forward to some relaxed days among the lush green valleys.

At dinner that night Jiyoo said the White Cloud mountains would be even better if they are looking for solitude and undisturbed time. 'Parts of it are still untouched by the tourist trade,' she explained. They could walk the many trails and spend time in the lap of nature. No one had any objection and so new bookings were made. 'I know a good place up in the White Cloud mountains where we can all stay. It's a new destination, never advertised, so you will have a very special and authentic experience. And the weather will be pleasant at this time.' She convinced them easily and she had already won over their tour manager.

The tinkle of metal chopsticks on glass drew him out of his early morning dreams. They had had a few glasses of wine up in his room, chatted till late and then he had fallen asleep. Ujaan rubbed his eyes. He was feeling a little groggy. The travel for the last few days had been hectic and he could have done with a few more hours of sleep. He was mildly irritated but her presence in the room soothed his ragged senses. For the last few days of travel they had been sharing rooms secretly. She would wait at the coffee shop and slip in after everyone of their group had turned in and they would chat till late. Later, when he fell asleep, Jiyoo would grab a pillow and curl up on the couch.

His gentle snoring sent her off to sleep quite soon but she would have thick dreams and had to get up in the middle of the night to wash her face. Though she felt much better these days, the past came back to haunt her sometimes. Yet she was happy to be in his room, with him asleep, while she waited alone in the darkness for the first light.

Ujaan sat up in bed leaning against the pillow. She had showered and put on fresh clothes — a green suede jacket over a white top and black tights. Her face was glowing in the light that streamed in through the lace curtains washing the room with the freshness of a new day.

She finished the bowl of noodle soup and kimchi and kept her chopsticks down.

'Good morning,' she said, 'we have to start in an hour. I thought I must wake you up somehow.'

'Uh, okay.' He crawled out of bed lazily. She looked up at him as he lightly touched her hair. She sat still. He moved his hands down, massaging her shoulders. Then he took her hands pressing her palms with his fingers. Her eyes gleamed in the soft light and she turned up her head and kept looking at him with an unwavering gaze. What she was trying to say with her silence was in her eyes but he could not read it yet.

He moved his fingers lightly over the pink scar marks. They looked violet in the fuzzy light of dawn. 'You have to get ready, or we will be late,' she said folding her arms, leaning back on the couch.

Ujaan stepped back. He went to the dresser looking for his scissors. He needed to trim his beard. 'Wait for me,' he said before walking into the bathroom.

When he came out of the shower she was gone. He dressed quickly, threw his things into his bag and found she had left something for him on the table.

A packet of chestnuts. She knew he was going to skip breakfast like every day and so made this habit of leaving some snacks for him. Some days it would be chestnuts, at other times bananas or apples. He would put the apples away in his bag and forget these completely till they began to rot and then he would throw them away. But he loved bananas and would eat them quickly washing them down with a glass of aloe vera juice before joining the others.

He was hungry today so he finished all the chestnuts and was about to leave when he saw the note stuck to the door lock.

I have left our bus tickets in front of the mirror. We will sit together. I have put the others in the front of the bus.

He smiled and folded the note carefully before putting it away in his backpack.

As always he was late and the others of the group had checked out and were waiting for him on the street where they were trying to get taxis to go to the bus stand. The three friends who were travelling together gave him funny looks as he walked in nonchalantly. They were whispering among themselves. Jiyoo, who was busy hailing taxis, didn't notice it but he knew they were talking about her for they must have found out by now that she spends the nights in his room.

Harvinder Singh was looking fresh in a spotless white T-shirt and jeans and he had stopped a passerby and was asking him to take pictures, his hand high up above his head making a victory sign. He was beaming widely while his partner, Tara, the lady with flowing black hair was waiting for him to finish. The elderly Mr Saha was busy studying a travel brochure while the other woman Bidisha was talking animatedly with Mrs Bose about the grilled pork dish they had for dinner last night and how this was considered to be one of the tastiest in the world. Mr Bose looked a little distracted. He had ordered fish for dinner because he said the galbi was just *kancha mangsho* which is Bengali for raw meat, but when his fish had arrived it was absolutely raw in a strongly flavoured sauce. He had given up after a few brave efforts to chew the raw fish and thrown up back in his room, cursing his son for not warning him about the food. The others in the group had loved the grilled pork, wrapping the meat with lettuce leaves and dipping it in the bean and red pepper paste as Jiyoo had shown them how it was supposed to be enjoyed. The chopsticks came in the way but nonetheless they had enjoyed the dinner.

The bus from Seoul Express bus terminal went slowly as it negotiated city traffic picking up speed on hitting the highway. The seats were wide and comfortable and the tour group settled in along with the other passengers who soon got busy with their tablet phones. Bikas babu and his group were sitting two rows behind the driver while Ujaan and Jiyoo were next to each other further down the aisle.

Ujaan had taken the window. For the first hour they were all lulled into a silence, watching the road but soon Singh began cracking jokes and the three friends began a noisy conversation. Sometimes one of them would turn around and try to chat up Bidisha, but she was too engrossed in a book and so she mostly answered monosyllabically. She was sitting with the Boses; Mrs Bose was now and then asking her about her career plans and how her mother was managing with the rheumatoid arthritis. Mr Saha was still reading the travel brochure while Roy was checking some bills.

The bus was full. Ujaan watched the road silently while Jiyoo was looking ahead, a flickering light playing in her eyes. The manager had told her that this final leg of the trip should be unhurried and peaceful, providing a soothing experience that will remain with the travellers. 'This is how we organise the last few days of every tour,' he had explained, 'after the hectic back and forth from one sight to the next, we give them a few quiet days at the end, in the lap of nature. They should be able to tap this well of peace whenever the affairs of life get too much for them.'

'You won't be disappointed,' she had said.

They cruised on at a good speed along the expressway and Ujaan began to feel sleepy watching the traffic which was mostly cars and buses and a few trucks. When he began to doze, Jiyoo pressed the palm of his hand. He opened his eyes and looked at her. Half smiling she offered him another packet of chestnuts. The LCD screen behind the driver's cabin flashed advertisements and he could hear Harvinder talking loudly to his partner whose voice didn't carry to him.

The memories of the empty flat in Delhi with the windowsills gathering dust and the stillness inside didn't haunt him as much as they did even a few day ago. He remembered Sujata only fleetingly and it was more of ordinary things rather than their fights that came to his mind nowadays. Sujata going out to the dry-cleaner's shop with the laundry bag, Sujata discovering a new bakery and telling him about it, Sujata sitting alone in the hall watching music television in the dead of night while Rick slept. These were no more haunting images. They just flashed for a moment on the screen and disappeared without leaving an impression, like the advertisements on the LCD panel inside the express bus in which they were now travelling.

The bus rolled into the small city of Wonju in less than two hours. The area near the bus terminal was bustling with weekend crowds, young women in hot pants and tops, smartly turned out men with fashionable haircuts and always some soldiers who didn't seem to belong to this country. He had seen them all over Korea, American soldiers going about their way, catching a bus, waiting in queues or chatting over smoked meats and soju in downtown restaurants.

At Wonju they did a quick McDonald's lunch and hopped onto two SUVs that were waiting for them. The cars drove south through business and residential streets, passing barber shops, churches and Chinese restaurants before hitting the highway near the Yonsei university. They passed the sprawling university campus and drove on southwards before taking a left turn near the small settlement of Maeji-ri with a church and a Buddhist temple, which was almost at the base of the mountains. For half an hour or more they drove up along winding mountain roads lined by pine and fir trees, patches of land growing cabbages, rice paddies, across gushing streams roaring through stony gorges and for miles they saw no one. The road began to narrow after a while and the two drivers slowed down, driving cautiously to avoid scraping against trees.

The mountain had now closed in. All around them were rows of green hills, wooded valleys, deep gorges and waterfalls gushing away. Till now they had seen road signs warning the motorist of switchbacks but for a while now they had been driving along an unmarked stretch. The electricity poles had also disappeared.

'Are you sure about the route we are taking?' Bikas babu asked after a while.

Jiyoo, who was sitting next to the man at the wheel, assured him that she was. Driving on along the narrow unmetalled road for some more time the two cars came to a halt near the foot of a waterfall. The sound of water was the only thing they could hear when the car engines died and they got down.

'Are we at the right place?' Bikas babu whispered to Jiyoo making sure no one heard him.

'Yes' she said. 'You can leave the luggage in the cars, those will be brought to your rooms.' They did as they were told.

Jiyoo signalled to the drivers to drive away. 'We have to walk a little but we are almost there. The last stretch of the road is a bit tricky so it is better that we walk,' she assured them. Everyone was quiet and followed her as she walked a few steps ahead, skirted a massive boulder and went behind it. There was a dirt track climbing up the hill with the forest pressing in from both sides.

Ujaan fell in step with her at the head of the group while the others followed in ones and twos. The track was wide enough for two people to walk side by side but it was not too steep. Ujaan was worrying about spoiling his patent leather shoes but his sneakers were packed away in the luggage.

The trail was strewn with stones with bigger moss-covered rocks flanking the path but gradually the undergrowth moved in and covered the trail. On both sides were forests of pine and birch with their slender branches blocking the path but they could yet make their way through these. As they moved further up, the trees had wider trunks and their canopies almost cut off the sunlight.

They moved through the semi darkness, the call of crickets and the sound of their boots on the leafy undergrowth animating the silence. Sometimes a twig snapped under a boot. Here the trees looked older and they were tall enough to touch the sky. Sunbeams flashed through the green roof of the forest but they hardly touched the floor, swinging between the leaves and branches like lighted sabres.

Jiyoo and Ujaan had moved ahead and could not hear the others now. The scrunch of dry twigs under their boots could be heard no longer. The crickets were quiet. Then Ujaan saw the tiger.

It was perched on a giant rock straight ahead, glaring at them with fiery eyes. He froze. Jiyoo saw him too but did not panic. She pressed his hand and signalled him to keep quiet. 'Don't move,' she whispered.

The tiger stood still on his perch glaring at them. Ujaan felt a tightness in his chest as his legs began to shiver uncontrollably. The big cat opened his mouth wide and gnashed his teeth in a fierce gesture. Ujaan could hear his heart thumping against his chest in the dead silence of the tall trees.

Jiyoo didn't move, her gaze riveted on the eyes of the beast. She raised her hands slowly. Right up to her chest making an inverted steeple, then moving her palms up, slowly, then slowly down, then up again — a few times — while fixing the animal with her unblinking gaze. The tiger's whiskers quivered. He seemed to smile and lowering his head vanished silently in the forest.

They resumed their walk but he was too surprised to ask questions.

'What was that, Jiyoo?' he asked a little later.

'Never mind. It's my master's pet. He won't harm us.'

'Uh? Your master? What do you mean?' Ujaan said as they crossed a little stream gurgling over polished stones.

'Don't worry. You will meet him too,' she said cryptically.

'Where are the others?' Ujaan asked, realising that they must have fallen far behind.

'They are right behind us, let's keep going. We are almost there.'

They walked on. The trail went downhill, weaving gently through rows of sturdy pines. Jiyoo broke a branch using it to push back the dangling branches of trees. The forest was still very quiet.

Suddenly they heard a flutter above their heads and looked up to see a giant bird. It was riding down a sunbeam, its wings beating as it landed a few feet from them. An enormous three-legged crow, its black beak shone in the sunbeam which had cleaved the darkness of the forest.

She signalled Ujaan to stop. Looking straight at the giant bird she made the same gesture with her hands she had done before. Nothing happened. She murmured something inaudibly and kept repeating the gestures. The crow skipped back landing on a small rock. It turned its head from one side to another then took to the air with a flutter of giant wings. The small trees swayed in the draught as it soared higher still and in a minute it was gone. The canopy of the forest closed in again and all was quiet as before.

They exchanged glances. Jiyoo's face revealed nothing but he noticed drops of sweat on the nape of her neck. He did not know what to ask her. She signalled to him to push ahead and so he went, following the walking trail, grabbing the straps of his backpack.

They had been hearing the sound of water all along and now could see the stream ahead. It cut right across the path. They began to approach it but a hoarse noise stopped them in their tracks. It was the sound of bellows pumping air through tortured tubes or it could have been the rasping breath of one who was about to die. Then they saw him.

There was a makeshift wooden bridge over the stream and right in the middle of the bridge sat a man in a grey robe glaring at them. It was hard to say how old he was and his eyes flamed so bright that it was impossible to look at them without hurting your eyes. He was sitting cross-legged, breathing loudly through his mouth. His chest rose and fell as he inhaled and exhaled. As they approached the bridge they were buffeted by strong winds. The air that escaped from his lungs blew so strong and hard that they could barely move a step ahead. They had been caught in a sudden storm.

Jiyoo took Ujaan's hand and pushed along through that gale. But it was next to impossible. Before they could understand what was happening the man hurled a handful of dust at them and a fire leaped up from the ground right in front of them. It crackled and rose higher in a matter of seconds. The heat singed their skin and they had to step back quickly.

'Stop it please! Let us in! I bring friends,' Jiyoo screamed at the top of her voice, sheltering themselves behind a gingko tree at the edge of the water. The flames died as quickly as they had sprung up from the grassy bank leaving no marks of cinder on the ground. Their eyes were smarting from the heat and smoke but when they looked again the man on the bridge was gone. There was no one on the other side, the fields were empty.

They crossed the little bridge making sure it had not been damaged by the fire. When they were on the other side, Ujaan looked at Jiyoo, 'Will you tell me what is happening here?'

'Never mind. Just special effects,' she began to walk faster.

'What do you mean? Where are the others? How will they come here with that bloody tiger patrolling the track?'

'Don't worry, the gates have been opened. No one will bother them.'

It was still dark under the trees though it was early afternoon. They kept walking for a few more minutes through forests of pine, juniper and other evergreens. After a while they could see farmland through gaps in the trees. They were entering a little valley with rice fields and vegetable patches and a row of log cabins in the shade of a hill.

The trees thinned out and now they were padding through a field of cosmos growing wild, rice paddies and vegetable patches along the stream — chattering over smooth white stones. As they weaved their way through the pink and purple blossoms swaying their heads in a light breeze, the music of mountain water in their ears, they heard other voices.

Harvinder Singh and Tara had caught up with them, the others were just a little way behind. Singh was panting a little but he was cheerful as ever. The three friends had fallen quiet, staring wide-eyed, looking around them, sniffing the fresh air of the mountain.

'This looks straight out of a fairy tale,' Bidisha told the younger Bose as they clicked pictures.

Saha seemed to know the name of every tree. 'This one is a maple,' he told Bikas babu, 'it will turn fiery red in autumn.'

'But who is that joker in the fancy dress throwing Molotov cocktails at us?' Ujaan whispered to Jiyoo as they approached the log cabins.

'Ssh, he is my Master.'

'Your Master? You never told me about a master. What kind of master is this now, throwing grenades at guests?'

'He is a master of the Short Path, the Keun Sunim,' Jiyoo said as she went after a butterfly flitting around the orange hedges. A smile spread across her face and he watched her, happy like never before. Her mirth was infectious and soon all of them, including the elderly gentleman, were snared by an overflowing joy, skipping and cooing like kids who had discovered a chocolate castle deep inside a forest.

6

A grey mist had swathed around the hills of White Cloud mountain and from a distance they looked like green men smoking. The vapour cloaked the crest, riding the soft undulations like horsehair hats worn by men of high office in the time of the Joseon kings. It was early afternoon and the sun was already watery, sailing above the brow of the western hills, a spur of which pushed right up to the edges of the stream, flowing quietly today.

Further north, about ten kilometres, beyond a forest of pines, the stream joined the river. There was no road leading up here and the trail that snaked through the forest often vanished under brushwood or got blocked by large boulders that the *sanshin*, the local mountain god, sent crashing down the slopes to show his wrath.

The terrain with the thick forest to the north acted like a natural barrier shutting out strong northern winds and curious hikers from probing this deep into the mountains. Steep rock walls surrounded the other three sides of the valley.

As the sun began to dip behind the western wall of the mountain, the mists in the valley below thickened till the little line of wood houses, the vegetable patches, the recently harvested paddy fields, terraced into the edges of the hills and along the stream, now barren with drying stalks of hay, the cosmos growing wild on the waterside, and the dogs all disappeared in the swirling vapours. There was still a tongue of brilliant red in the western sky but otherwise the little settlement seemed to have pulled down a curtain, hiding itself away from the world.

The three friends were huddled near a waterwheel each taking a turn to try and turn it. But the heavy wooden wheel which was fed by the forest stream refused to budge. One of them grappled with a spoke trying to free it from vines that the water had brought from the mountains but he gave up midway. Moving aside slowly he eased himself on the grass, supporting his weight with his hands behind his back. He looked exhausted.

His friends meanwhile checked if stones had jammed the free movement of the bearings and having found nothing grabbed the spokes with their hands and threw their weight on the wheel but it just shivered a little, made creaking protests and remained motionless. They gave up pretty soon and settled down on the grassy verge to rest.

'What the fuck has got into that thing,' one of them said, leaning against a rock.

'Ask the Big Monk,' another yawned. He looked up at the low sky trying to focus on a skein of geese headed east. The light is not good enough he thought or perhaps he was just too tired. But why? He had hardly done anything much the whole day.

In the morning the three of them and Singh had gone for their constitutional into the pine forest crossing the stream across the makeshift wooden bridge. They usually went deep into the forest right up to the point where the stream met the river but this day they were not up to it. 'Let's turn back,' Singh had said panting, 'I am feeling a little out of sorts,' and so they had turned back. None of them were feeling like walking that far.

Singh, the boisterous Sikh who owned singing bars back in his country, had become very quiet from the day Tara had disappeared. When was that? Nobody remembered the exact day and while talking among themselves sipping their *boricha* they would say, 'The skies were high and blue that morning, as if autumn had already arrived.'

The sun did rise here, the magpie took off from the branch of the maple tree and the cicadas sang endlessly stitching together day and night. But there were no clocks and no calendars to tell what day it was. They had their watches but once they arrived here the watches began to play tricks or perhaps it was their minds, disregarding instruments that tried to impose meaning on what was essentially infinite.

'What is the time?' one of them from the tour group asked at dinner one night. This was in the week after they had arrived. The old settlers looked at each other and then bent down their heads and concentrated on the steaming seaweed soup in the wooden bowls before them.

'Keun Sunim keeps track of time o he will tell us when we need to know,' an old Korean said after a while. So they stopped thinking about it slowly and, gradually, it slipped away from their minds too.

The little dynamo powered by the stream was only good for lighting up the kitchen and dining area and soon their phones were dead and as the days went by they left the phones in their bags and didn't miss them any more.

Sometimes from up in the eastern hills they could hear the reverberating sound of the cloud gong or the beating of an old wooden *beopgo* that went dumm, dumm, dumm-mmm, du-dummm. The deep bass of the wooden drum filtered through the evergreens, its pitch changing with the wind and it seemed that the visible and invisible universe was rapt, listening to the beat. The settlers looked up at the forest, listening and watching, as, over the days, the skies began to turn dark with monsoon clouds.

They saw Ujaan cycling down the path that twisted through the farmlands bordered by vegetable patches. He was coming from the direction of the pine forests. Where had he gone at this time of the day? One of the three friends wondered but soon lost interest in finding out.

The trio of young Indians had been working with the Koreans in the fields. Nobody had asked them but they had joined in all the same. The work was laborious no doubt but they enjoyed it as it filled up their days.

Meanwhile Bidisha and Mrs Bose helped in the kitchen, peeling and shredding burdock roots, slicing potatoes or cleaning the little fish that they caught from the stream. Sometimes they improvised with the cooking. The sticky rice was different from what they ate at home but they rustled up a delicious kedgeree with rice, eggs, beans, potato and fried fish which everyone enjoyed.

The settlers worked hard to grow their own food as it was difficult to get anything from outside. The paddy harvest had been good this year and the branches of the apple and pear trees were bending over with fruit. The cabbage had grown well too and everyone looked happy as the new leaves sprouted, glistening in the morning sun. Soon the Koreans who lived in the retreat would get down to harvesting the cabbage and preparing the kimchi, the fiery gochujang, the bean pastes and soy for the *onggi* jars. Rows upon rows of the earthenware jars were stocked near the main kitchen and whenever one passed by its doors, the scent of food would draw them in.

Ujaan was now within earshot. They waved at him. He stopped and waved back.

'Have you seen Mr Saha today? He was not there for lunch.'

'Yes, Bidisha said he was not feeling well o was resting,' Ujaan said.

'I know, this wet weather is chewing up his joints. His arthritis has worsened,' one of them said, 'he had been complaining about it.'

'He is not quite the teenager any more,' another added, why these endless rains have been hard on me too, he told himself. Ever since the rains had begun or perhaps even before that, when he could not say, he had been overtaken by fatigue.

Besides working in the fields the Koreans went to the sawmills which turned out floorboards for the dwelling units. Some from their group accompanied the Koreans into the forests to collect wood for the firebox that kept the huts warm. No one grumbled or complained but as the days went by, an overpowering fatigue seemed to be taking hold of the settlers.

A small group of Korean women, who lived at the edge of the settlement, right next to the stream, were working with the mulberry twigs. Steaming the twigs from the young trees, scraping off the bark, then boiling it in an iron pot with a white powder. They worked silently, smashing the dried bark and washing again before mixing it with water and gum prepared from hibiscus roots. The difficult task of straining of the fibre through bamboo screens followed before the final drying in the sun. It was slow laborious work and that day the little group of women seemed not up to it. Two young women who were scraping off the bark from the twigs gave up after a while and went to sit in the shade of a tree. Sweat was streaming down their foreheads and their faces looked drawn, their eyes weary.

The strong mulberry paper was used for their doors and window screens, for making little plates, baskets, lanterns and small items of furniture. When the typhoons turned inland, there was always some damage to the settlement so they needed to have replacements ready. Some of the elderly Koreans, many of them from the North, loved to wear clothing and shoes made from this strong *hanji* which they smilingly said would last a thousand years.

Ujaan was picking up the hanji making technique from the Korean women so he spent a large part of his day at the paper unit. Now as he parked his bicycle one of the three asked slyly, 'Where is your friend?'

He didn't know where Jiyoo could be. In fact he had gone looking for her in the pine forest hoping he would find her there and they would have some time to themselves. He had crossed the bridge over the stream and gone deeper inside but after cycling for half an hour he had turned back, sad and exhausted.

The forest was too big for him and alone there he had an eerie feeling. Someone was whispering his name from behind the trees. He got a little scared. Then as he was rushing back on the bicycle he had seen the eyes. The forest had grown eyes, an eye on each tree, small, intense and those were her eyes, each of them or the eyes of someone she resembled.

His hands were trembling when he had reached the clearing. While cycling back he had remembered the day they had followed the trail and reached this hidden valley across the bridge over the river. How long had it taken them to reach the settlement, he could not remember. Did they arrive through the forest or down the hill? Did they pitch tents in the woods on the way here? Isn't it time to return yet? The days after their arrival were a blur. One was fusing with another like thought bubbles against the gleaming face of an endless present.

'Perhaps she is with the children,' he told them. There were little children living with their parents in the settlement and Jiyoo taught them to read and write. But he was not sure. Sometimes she would disappear and Ujaan felt very lonely when she was gone. The eyes in the forest flashed through his mind and he felt a tingle in his spine.

'Is it? I thought she hadn't come down from the mountains yet,' one of the three tourists said.

'What do you mean?' Ujaan said.

The other man kept silent for a while before beginning to speak. 'It was the evening of the storm ...' his two friends leaned forward to listen. He went on speaking but Ujaan couldn't hear him clearly so he came closer to the group pushing his bicycle along and resting it against a tree.

'I was near those orange hedges there,' he said pointing to where the path branched off, one climbing up the wooded hillside. 'We had been digging the water channel for the field that day o I was completely knackered. So I thought I will go up o sit on that ledge by the hillside and watch the gathering storm. I was walking up that track,' he said pointing up the hill.

None of them had been up there because the forest was thick and after a few metres the track was hardly visible. Now with the incessant rains of the last few days, the forest had closed in, the undergrowth had become thicker every day, completely cutting off the twisting path up the slope. Moreover the Koreans said there could be leopards up there if not a tiger.

'So I was thrashing through the thick undergrowth, pushing my way up o it was beginning to get dark as the clouds piled up in the sky. The ledge as you can see is just a little way up there.

My idea was to reach it quickly, before it got dark. But the light went too fast o I could hardly see anything up ahead. I was also out of breath.

'The call of the cicada was the only sound you could hear, pulsating through the undergrowth but then I heard something. I stopped in my tracks. I thought it must be some wild animal o instinctively I moved behind one of the trees. I crouched and held my breath. The cicada also fell quiet as if it knew something was about to happen.

'I heard a rustling sound o then soft steps on the bed of rain-soaked leaves. It was coming up my way. If it was an animal it would surely have got my scent so I began to say my prayers. Shivering with fear, I was betting between a tiger o a leopard when I saw her.'

Everyone was listening. Ujaan had remained standing. He was not sure where this was going.

'Who?'

'His friend, Miss Park,' he pointed towards Ujaan and all of them looked up at him. Ujaan had begun to feel uncomfortable but he couldn't get away now. Besides, what exactly was this man saying?

'She suddenly appeared a few metres down the path. There was still some light o I could see her quite clearly from where I was hiding behind the tree. I didn't know what I should do. I thought about coming out o asking her where she was headed, but then ...'

'She saw you?'

'No. It was odd. She was walking quite fast, as if the wind was carrying her along. O she was looking straight ahead. It was bewildering. She was looking high up, her gaze fixed at the canopy of trees. It was an inward look. As if she was sleeping with her eyes open.'

'Jeez!'

'Still I was going to ask her if it was safe to go further uphill because it was getting dark fast but she was gone in a flash. The forest closed in after her and the insect orchestra resumed its performance,' he turned to look at Ujaan, 'I haven't seen her since then.'

'Sure you had not seen a ghost?' one of them asked.

Ignoring the question, 'Perhaps she told you something?' he asked Ujaan again.

What could he tell them? He knew very little. And what he did, he had begun to forget. Perhaps it was the incessant rains that fell every evening and all through the night that was rusting his brains. He rarely saw her at daytime except during lunch. In the evenings sometimes she would slip into his cabin and they would sit on the floor talking till the moon peeped through the window. Sometime early in the morning she would leave but he would be fast asleep by then.

He now remembered catching a glimpse of her on his way back from the hanji workshop but that may have been two or three days ago. Keeping track of the days was getting extremely difficult.

He had heard her mention that her Master, the Big Monk, lived up in the hills but had never been there himself. Those who had ventured that far said it was an arduous climb. He had been dissuaded by Jiyoo. She told him there was only the monk living in a small house beside a temple. But then what business took her into the forest late in the evening?

The Big Monk — Keun Sunim, the Koreans called him. He lived up on the ridge but was rarely seen in the valley. But he did come down the day Tara had disappeared. Ujaan remembered what had happened and so did the others. Yet they could never agree about the details.

They usually had an early dinner in the log house next to the kitchen after which some of them would retire to their rooms to sleep or meditate. Others sat in the wooden pavilion by the stream, hearing the sound of water chattering on the stones. They would sit quietly there, Koreans, Indians and some others who had come from far.

That evening there was a fire further down the road where the stream curved and entered the forest. A group had lit a bonfire by the water and the aroma of grilled meat came floating up to the camp with the sound of water. They could hear snatches of conversation and muffled laughter and a little later one of the women began to sing a folk tune ... Tara had been with that group.

Ujaan had been sitting alone near the gingko tree which looked like its canopy had been swept up from below by the wind. The monk had appeared and sat beside him. He had bowed and they kept sitting quietly. The monk was staring at the water but there were worry lines on his forehead. Something had been bugging him. 'There would be more rain this year,' the monk had told Ujaan. He had never asked how he knew. There was no TV, no internet or other communication system there.

A little later one of the women from the group down by the stream had come and asked if they had seen the Indian woman with long hair and dreamy brown eyes. 'No, we thought she was with you,' they had said.

'She had been roaming around, keeping mostly to herself, while we sat around the fire. A little while ago I had seen her sitting on one of those burial mounds at the edge of the forest. I remember how her long hair was billowing in the wind,' one of the women from the group had said.

They had heard stories of those who had died in pain and the mention of the burial mounds made them uneasy. But those sleeping under the earth were their near ones, not wicked spirits or fox demons who would waylay pedestrians at night.

'Did she go inside the forest?' the monk had asked.

Then the men had gone out into the forest with their hanji lanterns and a group went looking through the camp but Tara was not to be found. That was the last time Ujaan had seen the Keun Sunim. Where was he now? Perhaps up in those hills. Wasn't it strange that the only time he remembered seeing the monk was the night that Tara disappeared. He couldn't understand how these events could be connected.

But Jiyoo was different. She was Korean and she knew this place. She would know her way around. She would return.

But these three were still waiting for him to respond. What could he tell them? Should he tell them the obvious? That he thought she might have gone to see the monk up there in the hills. No, he wouldn't, for he himself didn't quite believe it. How would she make her way through the forest in the dark. He would just tell them that she might be unwell and keeping to herself. But what this man had seen up in the woods didn't fit with that.

He will just keep quiet. That's what he will do and he was about to make his intentions clear by turning away from them when, from the other side of the stream, a familiar voice hailed them. 'Gentlemen, can you please come over here. Someone needs help!' It was Bikas babu.

They all turned. 'What?'

'Mr Saha has hurt himself. He fell down in the toilet. I can't find the doctor who lives here. We have to take him to the Keun Sunim.'

They all looked up at the hills and then at Bikas babu, the tour manager, who was the reason why they were here in the first place. Perhaps for a second they had remembered who he was but the thoughts of home were already washed clean from their minds.

It was getting dark when they set out with Saha on a makeshift stretcher. The elderly man stared at them, his lifeless eyes like dead corals in the glimmer of the hanji lanterns. A Korean man led the way.

It would be a long night for the group of six men and the injured man on the stretcher. Perhaps it would take them days to reach where the monk lived? Will this groaning old man survive? Nobody quite remembered the exact route up to the temple.

The group that had set out through the darkness were all young, Ujaan, the Korean, Bikas babu and the three Indian men. But very soon they would be out of breath and would have to halt for rest. It was as if the forest had sapped their energy. And still there was this arduous climb ahead which they did not know took how many hours. But nobody thought about these things yet. The people of the valley kept to themselves and just helped each other. The happy and the content never asked questions.

P.I.
Kar's Korean
Adventure

5

The waves of questioning left him dizzy. The naked lamp hanging from the ceiling of the small windowless room turned him blind. Metal chairs were scraped on the floor as a new set of interrogators arrived. The sound hurt his ears. One of them took notes, another tapped his pen a thousand times on the table. He felt disoriented when the suited man suddenly stopped the tapping. The silence was like a slap on his face.

'When did you join the communist party?'
'Who is your leader?'
'Why did you come to this country?'
'Who sent you here?'
'What do you know about the lost tourists?'

It went on and on, repeated through the day and late into the evening. Often they were threatening — 'No one knows you are in our custody, so answer truthfully,' hissed an agent, leaning forward so close that Kar could smell the kimchi on his breath.

He told them that there has been a mistake and wanted to see officer Kim.

'There are hundreds of Kims in the NIS,' their hard faces would crack into a grin as they looked at each other. Then they left him for an hour alone in that empty interrogation room with the heavy metal door, the table and three chairs, one of which always remained empty.

'Which year did you go to North Korea?'

How did they find out, he wondered. It was so long ago. Kar told them about joining the communist party at home when he was in college. He had been involved in student politics and quickly rose through the ranks.

'I worked for the party for a number of years, earning a small wage, but this was years ago. I became a mid-ranking official in the party. That was when the party selected some young leaders to be sent as part of an official delegation to North Korea for the World Student Youth Festival.'

'How many from your country?' one of them asked as the other scribbled furiously in his notebook.

'Thirty delegates from my country. Thousands from other nations.'

The younger agent studied him coldly as the other asked, 'Were any of these people part of the tourist group? Perhaps their children?'

Kar thought for a while. If he told them the truth they would never let him go. There was now no way to contact Kim or the embassy. He had to fight this out alone but his strength was sagging from the barrage of questions. How could he tell them about the disillusionment that turned him into a private eye, that he had had no truck with the communists for years. Yet some of his comrades from those days remained among his most trusted allies. They were his final port of call in a crisis, they were the cards he kept close to his chest as he navigated the alleys of crime and corruption in the dangerous back lanes of his city.

'Two of them from the group of lost tourists were party members. They are much senior to me,' Kar said slowly, measuring his words.

The interrogator didn't change his expression but Kar's trained eyes could notice the tightening jaw muscles.

'What are their names?'

'Amar Bose and his wife Priya Bose,' he said slowly. He was getting drawn into trouble which was not his doing. What did these spooks want from him? Where has that bloody Kim disappeared? He reckoned it must be evening by then but he didn't want to ask them the time. That would harden their resolve to break his defences though he himself was not sure what there was to defend at that point.

'This is all a big mistake,' he told them for the nth time, 'I want to speak to my embassy,' he repeated again and again. 'Where is officer Kim? I am a private investigator appointed by near ones of the lost tourists.'

It all seemed to fall on deaf ears.

'Describe the area in Pyongyang where you were staying?'

'Huh?'

'Who all did you meet?'

'That was a decade ago!'

'What ceremonies did you attend?'

He remembered glimpses of the official functions, then a stroll along the banks of the Taedong, blue under a clear sky. The drooping willows on its banks. From the top of the Juche tower, Pyongyang on that spring morning with its wide river and distant hills, its parks and monuments had looked pretty. But in his mind, the city had acquired an aura of greatness, as the capital of a nation founded on communist principles. He had stood transfixed, watching the distant hills from the top, watching the city, heart thumping with the madness of first love. He remembered the imposing tower block where they were put up with comrades from many nationalities, the clanging of the trolleybuses on the street and the eye-catching Kimilsungia flower arrangements at the official ceremony.

'Tell us what you did while you were in Pyongyang. Don't leave out any details,' the man with silvery hair barked, snatching him out of his recollections. The officer looked him straight in the eye as he repeated the question Kar had been asked through the day. The other interrogator, an officer with a narrow forehead, tapped his pen impatiently as he waited for his response.

Early in the morning, Kar had woken up with a dull headache. Kim had called to say their meeting with the investigation team at the cafe was being rescheduled to the next day. He had had a filling western-style breakfast of bacon, omelette and sausage and then taken a stroll.

The multicolour cone near Cheonggyecheon stream was gleaming in morning light and the streets were filling up with tourists. He meant to visit all the places in Seoul that the tour group had visited as it might throw up something, perhaps a clue. But his brain was still one lazy pile of shit and his feet felt heavy.

Reluctantly he had taken the subway and climbed up the hill to the base of Namsan Tower. A hot coffee and then he was gazing at the city through the glass walls next to which Jiyoo had fixed her little lock as Ujaan had watched her, his heart breaking to pieces.

He had an appointment at the embassy which went smoothly following which he had taken a taxi. It had begun to drizzle when the taxi dropped him at the gates of Changdeokgung palace. Roaming around the king's secret garden with a bunch of tourists, sporting a spring forest of coloured umbrellas, he got lost in his own thoughts. What could he find here that would lead him to the lost tourists, he wondered while watching the ripples of water in a lotus pond.

The palace tired him out. He had had too much to drink the night before. He soon abandoned the group and retraced his steps to the gates. The clouds had banked low, almost touching the high rises and fat drops of rain had begun to fall. Kar pulled on the hood of his jacket and hurried down the pavement. The street outside suddenly looked deserted, empty except for fast-moving cars. He tried to hail a taxi. One of them slowed but then refused to take him.

They didn't even ask his name when they closed in upon him from behind. There were two of them in black ties and grey suits. He was standing at the edge of the pavement. 'NIS,' one of them had said, 'you have to come with us.'

Kar had not protested as they drove him to the squat-box-like headquarters sitting like an old TV set on the street. He had tried to recall Kim's full name but the name eluded him. His headache kept coming back and then the barrage of questions had begun.

'Give us the names of the student leaders you have met on this trip.'

'I just arrived yesterday!'

'Do you know this woman?'

They showed him a photograph. Kar squinted to see her face better under the yellow light. She looked like the Korean woman whose photo Kim had shown him last night.

The previous interrogators hadn't shown him this photo. He nodded, 'I saw her photo last night,' and he briefly told them about his meeting with Kim.

But they didn't seem to hear him. 'She had defected from the other Korea and now she has gone missing. We know for sure she was with the tourists.'

He could sense a change in their tone of questioning now. He asked them the woman's name but was met with blank stares. They were asking him inane questions now and the man with the narrow forehead had pocketed his notebook. The aggressive body language had changed and his interrogators were pretending to talk to an equal. 'Are kidnappings common in your part of the world?' one of them asked and he told them about petty gangs kidnapping for ransom. The various uses for the ransom. One of them got a call on his phone and left the room. The silvery haired officer followed. Suddenly he was all alone and exhausted. No one came in any more.

He couldn't guess how late it was in the night when the heavy door opened again. Slowly. As if the person outside was hesitating, having second thoughts before walking in. It was officer Kim.

Kim apologised profusely promising to explain everything. He drove Kar back to his hotel and offered to buy him dinner but he refused. 'I had to leave the city as this new lead about the woman emerged. We have been able to ID her. But that's not much. She is a defector and that complicates everything. I can confide in you, but never quote me on this — it is not all good news for those who come here from the North. Hell, it's not a bed of roses for anyone! But at least they have freedom and no fear. Those who can't cope, drop below the radar. They become reclusive. Some just disappear. But a defector who vanishes is a suspect because the enemy is wicked. Despite our stringent checks they have time and again infiltrated spies in the garb of defectors. We are worried this might have implications for your case. I will introduce you to the investigation team. Have a good night's sleep, tomorrow might be a busy day.'

Kar had raw beef *bibimbap* and two stiff drinks in a backstreet restaurant thronged by working-class people before taking the elevator to his strangely decorated room at Utopia hotel. He thought he had switched off the TV but still he could see their faces. They were now sitting in chairs circling his bed.

Circle after concentric circle, the dark suited men, some with black ties, a hard glitter in their eyes. Thick necked, big rough hands like metal spades, some with teacup ears and each one of them held a bunch of violet Kimilsungia blooms between his fingers. They sniffed the flowers from time to time and then they looked up at him. Not all together but one at a time. And slowly, letting the words form without hurry, fixing him with their stare they all asked him one by one — 'When did you join the party?'

6

Kar had slept badly. He had eaten nothing during the long hours of interrogation at the NIS headquarters and the raw beef at dinner hadn't gone down well. His stomach was aching when he awoke. He didn't feel like getting out of bed but the phone had been ringing off the hook.

It was Kim at the other end of the line. They had planned a lunch meeting with the investigation team but now Kim was saying that the police was too busy with the case and could only meet him late in the evening. Meanwhile, if Kim heard something new, he promised to fill him in with the details. Kar made some sounds meant to convey that he was okay with the new schedule but kept quiet when Kim apologised again for the harassment he had to face the previous day.

His insides rumbled and the dull ache was getting worse by the minute. He felt bloated. Tongues of fire were licking his chest. He lay down again rolling from side to side on the spring bed but the aches grew worse still. His intestinal gases were bubbling through the undigested food, the borborygmi filling up the hotel room like the protestations of a hurricane trapped in a mountain pass. He cursed loudly and scrambled again for the latrine.

The ceiling with its giant love mirror revolved slowly as he lay on the hotel bed watching himself with tired eyes. Long ago when he was with the party his mentor had instructed him about the efficacy of *triphala* powder in curing stomach ailments. His mentor, a comrade of the old school, had demonstrated how to prepare the infusion. But there was another herb he had mentioned whose name eluded him.

It was hopeless. He knew he was going to die in this far away country, killed by a stomach bug, probably a biological weapon engineered by powers across the border. He was seized with panic and rushed to the door and was going to step out in the corridor when he saw the headless man. He was walking calmly towards him from the other end of the dimly lit passage. He was smartly dressed and was holding his head in his hand. Kar stepped back quickly and bolted the door. He heard voices outside but didn't dare to investigate its source.

The belly ache was becoming unbearable. It felt like a knife being slowly twisted in his gut. What irony, he who had once believed in selfless dedication and sacrifice to the socialist cause, had dedicated his best years to party work, was now being eliminated by a weapon devised by comrades from the edge of the continent. He rubbed his eyes sadly as the aches crowded back, growing with renewed belligerence. He rummaged through his bag but for a few strips of Crocin, there was no other medicine there.

It was dark inside his room. Daylight had faded but the terrace of a hotel block across the road was a bar of molten gold floating among the heavens. A ship for heavenly creatures. He had rice and chicken soup in his room and took a short nap. Now he was feeling better.

He lay on the bed thinking about the developments of the last two days. Kim's ideas sounded almost out of a fairy tale but the defector angle. What could he make of it? If the tour guide was indeed a defector from the North, what could she have to do with the disappearance of the travellers? Did they fall into a trap laid by northern agents? He had heard northern operatives being injected in the south in mini submarines and by other means but how would they manage a whole raving bunch of tourists? Kim hadn't told him much about the other defectors disappearing and he made it a point to find out more, when they met. There were a few possibilities — defectors were targets of assassination attempts by the North's agents, they were spies planted as defectors, they were kidnapped and brought back to the North or they just returned disillusioned. Could it be so that this bunch of innocent vacationers were caught in this crossfire between two nations?

There were no more calls from Kim or the embassy. He washed his face, took out his laptop and tried to connect with the hotel Wi-Fi. The service was down so he had to call the hotel desk. They apologised for the problem and told him there was a PC Bang, five minutes' walk from the hotel. If he could come down to the desk, they would give him a map with directions. He needed to do some research about the area where Tara was found by the campers, besides he had to send emails to Chaitanya and Abul.

He wrote a note for Kim saying he will be back in an hour, just in case he called the hotel. Then he took out a scissor from his bag and reluctantly snipped a strand of his hair which he carefully pasted across the zipper of his bag. He put the bag back into the wardrobe. Throwing on a fleece jacket, he left the room.

Two rough-looking men were inside the elevator when it reached his floor. Kar put his head down and stepped into a corner as the mirrored elevator box shot down to the lobby. After his brush with the NIS he had to keep a low profile. Time was running against him. Perhaps these are house detectives he told himself, as the doors of the elevator slid back and the duo stepped out.

Kar went to the reception, collected the map and left the note for Kim. When he walked out on the pavement, it had become very dark and cars and buses had switched on their headlamps. A wind had also picked up and it looked like it would storm soon.

Kar stepped back into the hotel and borrowed an umbrella. He checked the street map and began walking down Hibiscus street. He had hardly gone a few steps when a gust of wind slapped hard on his face almost blowing his umbrella away. Buffeted by strong winds, he began to walk faster as silvery knives of rain slashed sideways on his face.

Soon it was raining hard. The evening traffic crawled for miles as sheets of rain reduced visibility to a few metres. The stop lights blinked desperately through the torrents and in the midst of all this Sejong the Great stood defiantly braving a typhoon that had made landfall near Incheon. Thrice in a single month.

He had missed the weather report. His jacket was okay but his trousers were getting soaked all through. His shoes were not made for this kind of weather.

As he strode down the street pummelled by ice cold raindrops, he didn't fail to notice the gingko trees, their fan-shaped leaves had been turning crimson with the fall. It was tempting. If he could sneak up and clip a few young branches, he would have enough stock of leaves to last him a few months. The Chinese doctor back home charged heavily for the gingko extract and he suspected it was adulterated with less potent stuff. He was not going to miss this opportunity to pack in a few months of hair fall prevention supply now that he was in Seoul. But this would have to wait.

His face was freezing in the chilling winds. He walked for a few more blocks, all along thinking when to collect the leaves and how to secret his stock through airport customs on his way back home. Just before he entered the internet cafe he noticed the duo he had seen in the hotel elevator. They were stepping inside a convenience store a few buildings away.

The PC Bang was on the ground floor of a shopping arcade. A large hall divided into sections for smokers and non smokers, loud at this time of the evening with a mix of young and old.

Kar purchased a card from the woman at the reception and went and sat at a terminal. The internet cafe was throbbing with energy. The hall was divided into sections and there were coin-operated machines near the entrance dispensing Coke, green tea and a host of soft drinks. Though the cafe was slightly rundown, the computers all looked new. Teenagers were glued to the terminals playing Blade & Soul, Lineage and other MMO games, some were chatting with friends. Older people pored over their emails.

Kar crossed the hall and turned left into the smokers' section which was partitioned away with glass doors. There were tea stains on the shiny red tables but the leather chairs looked comfortable. The bright circular lamps, the blue and gold coloured tables, the dark brown leather chairs, the billowing chatter of the young and the occasional thump of Coke cans landing in the dispenser of the coin-operated machines gave this place the character of a halfway house between a railway station waiting room and a coffee shop.

Everything on his screen was written in Korean so he asked for help. The woman at the reception showed him how to select the language. He logged in with his card and typed gmail.

There was a message from Abul. The subject line was direct. 'Tara is dead.'

Kar took a moment to let it sink in before reading on. 'She passed away in her sleep. The doctors are trying to ascertain the cause. For the last two days she had been suffering from a wheezing cough. She was finding it difficult to breathe. They put her on life support but they could not save her.' Nothing about her psychological appraisal or the amnesia.

He couldn't believe it. He had interviewed her few days before he arrived here and she had looked fit. She had been incoherent during the interview but she hadn't shown any signs of fatigue. He will have to inform Kim when they meet later in the evening but before that he needed to find out more from Abul.

He began to write an email. Who was with her when she died? What does the friend, she was staying with, have to say? Was the psychiatric evaluation completed? Then an email to Chaitanya asking him to go through the old file on Harvinder Singh which their agency had handled. He also instructed him to visit the office of Lamplighter Travels and look for something. He spelt out what he wanted clearly and asked his assistant to be careful. Not to take risks. Finally he opened a document file and noted down a few points for the client reports. Then he logged out of gmail, leaned back in his chair and lit up.

The ventilation in the smoking section of the PC Bang was struggling to cope with the cigarette fumes. A pall of smoke floated in the middle of the room, hanging from the ceiling like ectoplasm, undecided which way to escape. There were twenty terminals in here, all occupied. The clients, mostly local, except for an American soldier playing patience. The gamers were firing up Starcraft and chatting while taking swigs of imported beer from silvery cans.

Kar took a few more drags and stubbed out his cigarette. He could hear the storm howling outside whenever someone pushed through the glass doors. The streets were emptying out fast. Inside, the smoke and games and the beer-fuelled conversation continued.

Kar focussed back on the screen. He needed to look at a few maps of the area where Tara was found and buy a bus ticket for the journey. He was fiddling with the mouse buttons when a white screen with a text box popped up with the message — 'You are connected to a stranger. Say Hello.'

What? He hadn't pressed any keys. But then he noticed he had somehow got connected to Omegle, a random video chat site. He was going to close the new window when a small video screen popped up with a woman in a deep blue-and-white hanbok. He could see she was typing.

The woman was sitting on an old fashioned chair, the kind you would find in English pubs, and behind her was a garden table laden with food. There were two glass jars of orange juice, heaps of melons, yellow persimmon, figs, a heap of apples and clementines. Pork ribs and portions of meat were piled on large plates and a row of smaller plates of seasoned vegetables and kimchi were lined on one side. The video woman had the head of a fox.

'Who are you?' Kar typed. His gaze was fixed on the screen as she responded.

'*Annyeonghaseyo*,' the woman typed the letters slowly. 'I am the stranger.'

'Hello, but how did you connect with me?' Kar asked. He looked around. No one was watching him. An old man next to him was typing away vigorously, he had lines on his forehead. A young woman with a plain hairstyle was at the next terminal. Why did she look familiar? Kar wondered then realised it must be a mistake.

'Now that you are in Seoul, I thought I must talk with you,' the woman wrote.

'With me?'

'Aren't you the detective?'

The LEDs ringed around the webcam were shining like blue stones on fire. Kar made an unconscious effort to cover his face. He tried not to look surprised.

'Where did you get that from?' He typed it slowly while his mind raced, searching for explanations. Other than the embassy, only the security agencies knew about his visit.

'I will find out soon,' the fox-woman typed. 'Can you use the headphone please?'

Kar was intrigued but tried to keep a straight face. He could disconnect and walk away or he could wait and see where this was going. He put on the headphones and spoke into the mike, 'Is this a game?'

'Nope. I am completely serious. Please can you tell me, Sir, if you are the investigator.' She had a soft and pleasant voice.

'I have been investigating all my life,' Kar said ponderously. A vague statement, he will keep it like that till he can wrench out some information from whoever this was at the other end. He hoped the other customers wouldn't notice.

'Then I know who you are,' the woman said.

'Why should I believe you?' Kar said and studied the room where she was sitting. Behind the table was a bright yellow wall with a green double window fixed with a big red lock. The wall reminded him of a kid's playroom.

'Please don't misunderstand me. Come with me, I will show you something.' The red fox eyes gleamed and he could feel her penetrating gaze through the screen.

She pulled her chair back and stood up. The embroidery work on her blue *chima* skirt caught his eye. She turned slowly, went around the food table and walked towards the wall which was the colour of ripe melons. Now he could see a double door, green like the window with an identical lock fixed to it. She pulled out a bunch of golden keys. The keys jangled in her hands as she put a key into the lock. The door opened with a screech and now she was in another room.

A red room with a red paper lamp hanging from the ceiling. Three slightly weathered plain wooden chairs pushed against the wall, all occupied. In the middle chair sat Chaitanya, staring blankly.

On each side sat a burly stranger with Korean features wearing white baggy pants and loose white shirts. Looking at the back of their hands Kar decided they were farmers. Chaitanya was wearing a checked half sleeve shirt and slightly worn trousers.

The woman began to talk rapidly in Korean with the two men while Chaitanya kept staring blankly ahead as if he was oblivious of what was going on around him.

She turned to speak with Kar. 'See your friend is with us. Do you need any other proof.'

Kar knew he was in a tight spot. If he walked away from the terminal he wouldn't be able to find out anything from this woman. Obviously she knew something. He tried to talk with Chaitanya through the microphone but he didn't seem to hear him.

'No use, he doesn't have headphones. But you need not worry. He will be fine.'

Blood rushed to his head as he spat out the words, 'Stop playing games, whoever you are! Why are you keeping him prisoner with these two jokers?' He pulled out his mobile and dialled the office number. It would be afternoon at home, so Chaitanya should be there. But he couldn't connect. Neither could he connect to the temporary mobile he had given him before he left. He leaned back on his chair and sighed. 'Okay what do you want from us? Who are these people in the room?'

Kar noticed that the room had vanished from the screen and the woman was again sitting on the pub chair he had seen earlier. His head reeled.

'You are looking for the lost travellers, aren't you?'

'Yes but first I want to be sure my friend is safe.'

'He will not come to any harm,' the ruby eyes glistened from the fox-head, 'you can call him once you leave the cafe.'

Kar was lost for words. Should he call Kim? He didn't have a local connection, the call will be terribly expensive. What will he tell him? That he was being tricked by a vixen. Never. He will play on for some more time.

'Okay. So where are they? Do you know that you can get into serious shit if this is a practical joke? The security agencies of this country and mine will be hot on your trail and they will get you one day.'

'Please don't bother about me. I can help you reach the travellers. Some of them have fallen ill.' There was a ring of genuine concern in her voice.

'Ill?' He remembered something and asked, 'Who?'

'A few of them. And much more has happened than I could ever be able to explain to you.'

'What is happening? Are they all right?'

'They are managing right now but I don't know beyond that. You come with me and see for yourself. Maybe you can help.'

'How? Where do I find you?'

The fox eyes lit up again as she spoke. 'Listen to me carefully. You can thank me later. Go out and look across the road. There is a Shinsegae store to your right. A red Tucson is parked on the adjacent street.' She gave him the registration number.

'But I need to be sure my friend is okay before I come with you. I will make a call first,' Kar said.

'You will have enough time for that. You have seen he is fine, now don't delay this any further. If you come with me you can see the travellers tonight. Perhaps you can help them, but don't try to spirit them away if they don't want to come with you.'

Kar cursed under his breath, 'But who are you and why are you pretending to be kind while holding my countrymen prisoner. Where are they now? What do you want from us?'

'I want nothing but your help. You will see for yourself when we arrive. Perhaps you would be able to help us out.'

'Okay, I will come with you,' Kar said and rose to leave. There was a plop on the screen and the video window closed. He looked around. Everyone was engrossed with their terminals. The American soldier was still absorbed in his card game while a noisy group of youngsters fought giants on computer screens.

The street was deserted and except for fast cars shooting through the rain, there was no one in sight. He checked the stop light and quickly crossed over to the other side. The Shinsegae hypermart was still open but there were no customers outside. He went around the shopping mall to the narrow street. The gleaming red Tucson was third in a line of cars. It had scratch guards on its doors. He sneaked in from behind and knocked on the window, on the passenger side.

It was too dark to see who was sitting inside. The window was rolled down just a little. 'How do you do?' a voice from inside asked.

'Good question, after being led out in the rain by a fox,' Kar said while trying to shield himself from the gusts of wind beating against his umbrella.

'Jump in,' the voice from inside said. She sounded like the vixen alright but he couldn't see her clearly through the tinted glass.

'You want us to start off now? But I haven't informed the hotel.'

'No problem, Sir. Your luggage is in the boot. You can see for yourself. I have checked you out of the hotel.'

'What!' Kar was going to burst out but resisted the impulse. He was getting drenched despite the umbrella as the wind hard-slapped the rain against the car. The trees on the avenue were flailing their branches in the wild wind. He quickly ducked into the front seat and turned to look at the driver.

She was wearing a long sleeve T-shirt over black denims and rain boots, the blue-white hanbok nowhere in sight. Instead of the fox, it was a young woman at the wheels. She had a small oval face and her dark hair was cut in bangs. Her shining eyes were fixed on the road. She turned the key in the ignition. In the low light of the dashboard he realised she was an attractive woman.

'Who are you?' Kar barked at her at the same time unmindfully brushing his thinning hair. 'I am not going anywhere unless I get some answers.'

She didn't seem to hear what he had said but then her eyes narrowed seeing the gleaming steel of the Makarov levelled at her. 'Change in rules. From now, I will be giving orders around here,' Kar said coldly cutting the engine and snatching out the key from the ignition. He checked the back seat again to make sure there was no one there. 'Now get slowly out of the car and come around. No more games, darling. We are switching seats and I need a good navigator.'

She quietly stepped out into the rain and came around to the passenger side. A faint flowery perfume floated across from her. They fastened seat belts.

Kar turned the key and the Tucson's engine came to life with a low growl. Keeping the gun to his right he eased the car out from the parking line and hit the main road. Walls of rain tumbled down from the sky. She barely spoke, except to give directions as Seoul dropped back behind them into the night.

7

It wasn't an ordinary storm. The murderous rain slowed them down. The traffic was crawling as people were returning home for Chuseok — the autumn harvest festival. Next day was the big feast.

Kar was thinking fast as he manoeuvred the car through miles of rain-swept streets. He hadn't informed Kim about this sudden change in plans. He had a hunch that he should do this alone. If there was trouble he will call for help. Perhaps this was a foolish decision he told himself but he trusted his instincts. The woman hadn't given him any trouble yet and was doing as he had advised.

Driving in an easterly direction out of Seoul they had crossed the Han, twisting away across the city, through the endless acres of Gyeonggi-do, a dark writhing serpent slithering over the land. With the deluge — land, river and sky had merged and looking at the lightning bolts ripping apart the night above the conurbation it seemed that the sky would come crashing down.

The typhoon had bypassed the city but the rain lashed mercilessly upon streets and the freshly harvested cornfields, pouring over chrome and glass, beating the roof of their car with the ferocity of a destroyer, doing a *tandava* dance. The hum of the diesel engine filtered into the cabin, a low somnolent drone, the chant of a robot follower of a future religion.

The skyscrapers gave way to apartment blocks and older residences and finally the tail of service stations, garages and workshops till they had left the city behind and joined the expressway. They had driven for little more than an hour when the woman turned towards him, 'I contacted you because they need help.'

'You do have style. I have to give you that.'

She watched him driving, a flickering unsure look on her face.

'That fox business at the cafe, how did you hit upon that?'

'Please excuse me but I cannot explain everything. When we arrive, you will know.'

Where had he seen her, Kar tried to remember? She did look familiar. Ah! The woman with the travellers! Kim had shown him her grainy security camera photos on his mobile. Of course!

How could he miss the resemblance? Those intense eyes and the smart hair cut. How could he? Surely he was losing his touch. But he would feign ignorance. If he played his cards carefully he might be able to help the lost people. He would wait till she took him there. So he concentrated on the road and after a while said, 'Sorry, I didn't get your name. Is it Kim?'

'Park,' she said in a faraway voice and kept staring at the rain-washed road.

'My name is Kar, I guess you know that already?'

She nodded without saying a word. He looked through the corner of his eyes and saw how she was staring into the distance.

'What are you thinking?' detective Kar asked as the SUV gobbled up the kilometres of metalled highway.

'The weather's ugly.'

'I realised that,' Kar said.

'The sky will fall tonight.'

'Looks like it,' Kar responded telegraphically.

'They say it ushers in the end,' the woman beside her said.

'I wouldn't doubt that, Miss Park,' Kar said and in a moment of distraction he steered the car too hard to avoid a roadworks sign and rammed against the median.

The wheels hit concrete screaming furiously as Kar tried in vain to control the car. Vehicles behind them skidded, ramming those in front, brakes squealed as drivers pushed down brake pedals. Engines died, sputtering in protest. Then it was only the sound of the rain, falling in torrents on the motionless traffic lined up for miles along the expressway.

While the airbags had failed to deploy the seatbelts had held on. The struggle for control between man and machine had continued for some more time. He had tried cutting the engine while jamming the brakes but the big car had begun to climb the median, lurching violently from side to side. His head had bumped against the glass but still he hadn't let his hands go off the wheel. Then suddenly the wheels caught. The car shuddered and came to a halt.

The rain was falling noiselessly on the other side of the windscreen. He checked to make sure she was not hurt. He shifted gears trying to reverse the car but it would not budge. Finally he gave up, wringing his hands.

Luckily the doors hadn't jammed. Kar managed to extricate his rucksack and a sling bag from the boot. They carefully crossed the road through the downpour, lit up by the angry headlamps of cars and trucks. As the two of them were getting soaked to the skin in the chilling rain, waiting on the roadside, under Kar's flimsy umbrella, in the middle of absolutely nowhere, the woman said, 'Next time, I will drive.'

He felt like laughing out loud though he knew all his plans to reach the travellers that night were screwed for good.

'Does your head hurt?' she asked.
'No. Just a bump.'
'Would you mind if we change plans?'
'Not as long as I can find the travellers.'
'Yes, we will go there, but we have to take a different route. A trek up from the other side of the mountains. We should be able to make it by the time the sun is up.'
'You are quite amazing,' Kar said.
She suggested they walk up to the crossroads and try to wave down a bus. But walking wasn't easy in the driving rain. They

could hardly see anything ahead of them and these roads were not meant for pedestrians. Still they managed somehow, sharing the umbrella.

A bus arrived in a while.

It was full of dozing passengers and a surly man at the wheel who wouldn't let them board. She managed to convince him and luckily there were empty seats at the back. 'We will arrive in an hour,' she said.

Kar had hung his jacket from the back of the seat and was regretting the fact that he hadn't stashed a soju in his rucksack. He was shivering and hoping he would not come down with a fever. She handed him a bottle of *nokcha*. Where did she get that from? She was only carrying a small handbag. 'Drink it, you will feel better.'

'What about you?' Kar asked.

'I don't need it,' she said.

On the way, they stopped outside the bus station of a sleepy little town. Most of the passengers got off there. As they pulled out of the last stop of the town she said, 'I can't be with you throughout this. I have to attend to something. So watch everything carefully when we arrive there.'

What does she mean, Kar wondered, as he kept staring through the windows at the typhoon-lashed land.

It was three in the morning when their bus pulled up at a deserted station up in the mountains. Last stop. There was no motorable road beyond this point. The driver alighted and disappeared into a log cabin which looked like a rest room for the night.

Kar was dead tired. He laboured to adjust his rucksack which weighed down like a ton of bricks. It would be difficult to trek with this load. The rain had let up and now it was a drizzle emptying out on the mountains through which a path snaked its way up into the darkness. He looked around and couldn't see her.

He peered into the darkness ahead and noticed a movement. She had already walked up and was standing at the top of the path gesturing him to follow. He took a deep breath, patted his rucksack and began trudging up the slope.

She flitted ahead like a sprite. Neither the typhoon nor the accident had daunted her a bit and she was bursting with energy as she led the way through the forest. It was pitch-dark along the trail and rain water was cascading down the slopes and streaming across the path, making it a treacherous ascent. She walked too fast, her flashlight was dead and the bump on his head had begun to throb.

The darkness of the rain-soaked woods was of many dimensions. Here it was primeval, dense like the blackest dream. It wrapped around him like a blanket that would choke him off if he didn't keep moving, following the scrunch of her boots on the small rocks. It was an unsettling, wave after wave of pitch-black harmony, coming at him from every side, sailing through his body as if he was transparent to black noise.

After a while, it was tattered and mist like, punctuated by a crepuscular light that the forest radiated as the world slept. It was as if the trees were awake and someone had placed little tea lamps along the trail. Perhaps it was the moss on the gnarled tree trunks that glowed for some reason or it was the light of their eyes reflected by the night. Possibly it was the glow of stardust, a faint sidereal light, a hint that they were all children of the stars.

Soon they heard the roar of water. It was to their left but they couldn't see the stream through the walls of trees and darkness. The forest smelt of rotting mulch, aspirating under their boots, like exhausted hikers heading out for the last stretch of a tortuous climb. In a while, the trail began to narrow and the giant trees stood closer almost blocking their way.

The sound of water sluicing down a mountain stream became clearer and suddenly Kar realised he was falling. He had missed a step. Hundreds of metres down into the gorge through which the stream was carrying away the spoils of the night.

A slap on his wrist and then something ice cold wound tightly around it. A vice-like grip. Strong as tempered steel.

Her eyes flashed. She was standing on the edge of the ravine. But he was safe on this side, lying prone near the foot of a pine tree. His heart thumped madly. 'They only save you once,' she said. 'We cannot wait here any more. We have to keep moving.'

Kar was still numb from the shock. He didn't dare move. Had his skull smashed against the rocks below and he was dreaming that he was still alive? The stream thundered away hundreds of feet below and for a while all the universe was that sound of rushing water.

'How?'

She looked at him calmly, her eyes shining through the darkness. 'They are around here everywhere. That is why you are alive. But you get only one chance,' she made to go.

He was leaning against the tree trunk trying to collect his energies when he realised his rucksack was gone. He must have lost it in the ravine. 'What do you mean?'

'They are all around us. Koreans, Americans, French, Chinese, they died fighting in these hills. The snow was thick in the mountain passes those days and artillery shells cracked in the sub-zero temperatures. Their fingers fell off chewed by frostbite as mortars whistled above their heads. They killed each other on St Valentine's day, they died in tunnels and valleys, on tank turrets and inside foxholes. When they couldn't kill each other with guns they charged at the enemy with bayonets, ripping out their guts. If you are alone passing through this way, you can still hear the bugles that the Chinese blew as they went to battle. A Frenchman might walk up to you from the gorge and ask for Gauloises.

'Blood flowers bloomed on the pristine snow and the cries of the wounded reverberated through these mountain passes drowning out the whistling wind. They have been kind to you today but we won't be lucky a second time. We have to push on. Take a little rest then keep following this track. It will lead you to the tourists. I have to move along. I will see you in a few hours,' she had started to walk and her words trailed off as she vanished around a bend in the track.

The darkness was thick as ever. Kar closed his eyes leaning against the trunk of the pine tree. He stretched his legs and took a few deep breaths. He felt strangely lightheaded as he stood up with effort. His legs were shaking and he took some time to steady himself before continuing along the track, following the footsteps of Miss Park.

It was getting light. The forest had begun to transform. It was changing slowly. The rocks were whispering among themselves. Leaves rustled and hidden creatures scurried through the undergrowth as a chorus of birdcall broke out from the treetops. A faint blush was spreading over the soft line of hills, silhouetting the pine and fir trees along the track.

The light grew clearer, row after row of green hills appeared through the mist. The trail was slushy, littered with leaves and branches. And the stream was never too far, he could always hear the sound of water filtering through the trees. The light grew brighter, hurting his eyes. Kim must have checked at the hotel and would be surprised to find him gone.

Gradually the trail all but disappeared and he had to make his way thrashing through trees. Presently he reached a hill meadow circled by giant trees. Pine, silver birch and maple but they didn't look like the trees he had seen before. Each was a giant towering high up in the sky.

He ambled through the meadow for a while. It skirted the hill, guarded by the lines of tall trees. Then he spotted a gingko tree. It looked like a hermit with a shock of windblown hair. Its branches were swaying in the wind. He was tempted to collect his gingko leaves now. It would save him a lot of money.

But he continued walking along the green bed of grass. After a while he found a decaying log and stopped to catch his breath. He looked around again. At the procession of giant evergreens guarding this hill. He pinched himself, wondering how he was still alive.

The grass was a fiery green. He caressed it with his hands. The stalks were cold from the night rain and looking closer he noticed little pink flowers peeping out of the wet earth. Somehow they reminded him of the red blooms of blood on the icy mountain pass that Miss Park had mentioned.

As he kept looking at the little flowers, he was enveloped by a pleasant perfume. The flowers were growing bigger, the stalks grew taller, the petals spread out wide, the scent was thicker now, stronger.

He was remembering a garden at his school, it was tended well and was bursting with colours in all seasons. Next to the garden was the playground, where among other things they had physical training classes.

A vine crept out of the earth twining itself slowly around the log. Little yellow flowers bloomed on the vine stalk as it slowly covered the tree trunk, enfolding it in soft shiny greenness. Gradually the gnarled trunk transformed into a green bed of dew-drenched leaves and flowers, where he could sleep for ever.

A shadow fell across the log. He looked up and saw a man wearing a straw hat, standing in the distance. He kept looking and slowly the figure of the man changed into a giant mushroom — pearl white. He rubbed his eyes. The mushroom had sprouted from the foot of a tree trunk whose canopy touched the cottony clouds flitting across the towering blue sky of autumn.

The vine was twining around his feet now. The tendrils tickled him through his denims, as his legs were slowly covered by the vine and its bright yellow flowers. He kept sitting there waiting for the forest to cover him completely till he became one and indistinguishable from the trees and the hills so squirrels could come and play here while songbirds wove their melodies.

Something in the distance caught his eye. A flash of colour. Flowers. The trail leading up to the meadow had turned into a riot of colours. The blush had spread across the hillside, enveloping the trail and covering the slopes. The purple, pink and white blossoms were swaying in the wind. Cosmos! But the flowers were bigger than the full moon on a clear night. He heard joyous cries of children.

Kar reclined on the log, perching himself on an elbow and watched as two little girls came flitting through the cosmos fields, singing in ecstasy. They took in the flowers with their dewy eyes, caressed the blossoms, lingered and drank in their beauty. Then they continued towards the meadow. A wave of joy washed over him as he watched the kids flitting among the blooms like butterflies.

The children came and stood where the giant mushroom had sprouted. They kept staring at the pearl white stalk, a bemused look on their faces. In a while they saw him resting on the vine entwined tree trunk. He stood up to greet them but they did not return his greeting.

Instead, one of the two held out her little hand, offering him a grey scarf.

'Thank you,' he said. 'Is it yours?'

The little girl shook her head and pointed back in the direction from where they had arrived.

Kar was surprised to receive the scarf but he took it. It was light like air. He wrapped the scarf around his neck tucking in the ends in his shirt. His head swam a little and he sat down on the tree trunk. The cloth was soft and warm. It wrapped him like fire, driving away the fatigue weighing him down over the endless night.

The girl who gave him the scarf sat on his left. The other girl offered him some apples. He took these too but returned one back. She wouldn't take it. Kar kept the apples in his jacket pocket.

The other girl was on his right. They kept gazing at the flowers in the distance. Kar cleared his throat to attract their attention but they seemed not to notice him any more.

'Hello,' he said.

No response.

The girls kept sitting on the log watching the cosmos blooms.

Kar peered through the trees on the other side of the meadow. Far below were log cabins and a mountain stream flowing through a valley. From this height the cabins looked like little playhouses of children, surrounded by farmland and vegetable patches. Along the stream and in the terraces on the hillside were buff coloured plots of land. The fresh harvest of paddy had been stored away in grain silos and the empty plots looked like beds of yellow dust.

The travellers must be somewhere down there in that settlement, hiding away from the world in those log huts by the brook. Miss Park had said they were almost there. This must be the place. He remembered what Kim had told him about hidden valleys on the first day. What was he to do now?

The sun was already high up in the sky when he was ready to begin his descent. He had kept his jacket below his head to rest and now he took it and tied the sleeves around his waist. The giant mushroom stood still, the cosmos swayed merrily in the breeze and there was no one around.

A shiver went down his spine as he took the first tentative steps down the hillside. Here he was at last nearing a resolution. Despite many years as a private eye he still felt this quickening of his pulse when things began falling in place. The path was steep with loose rocks and wet from last night's rain. He made his way down cautiously, measuring each step.

A little way below, the lushness of the higher slopes began to go dull and the trees were again of ordinary height. Gradually the thick undergrowth gave way to a yellow weedy grass, the colour of the skin of a dead man whose blood has been drawn from the body. Kar kept negotiating the switchbacks cautiously, tapping a stick to announce his presence. He didn't want to surprise wild animals.

He stopped halfway down to rest his legs. The view into the valley was clearer now and he could see smoke curling from chimneys. This was the day of the big feast but there was hardly any movement in the settlement below. As he peered down the edge of the hill an ice cold wind rose from the valley whistling through the trees. Then he saw the small planes far on the other side of the fields. They looked like a squadron of delta wing aircraft at the foot of the distant hills.

But they were not aircrafts really, were they? No, not of any kind he could recognise. Observing for a little while longer he noticed the little planes, painted a dull yellow, were moving along the grass. Haphazardly in different directions and then again they came to a stop. He wished he had binoculars. Could it be a flock of giant mountain birds come to feed on the fresh harvest? He couldn't say. He had to reach the settlement before the sun went down behind the hills.

Kar resumed his descent. The dull yellow weed seemed to have taken over the mountains. Wherever he looked the carpet, like dead skin, covered the floor of the forest sometimes growing right over the path down which he went. The pine and birch stood faithlessly amidst this sea of other worldly vegetation but something seemed to have drawn their sap. The trees looked weak, shrivelled and febrile unlike the green canopied giants he had seen earlier.

After a while the forest stream came into view and the big water wheel. The grass at the edge of the water was green but up here in the mountains and all around him the yellow weed had claimed dominion. A resounding gong shook the forest and Kar looked up but could hardly see anything above him. There were more gongs and the sound of drums and bugles echoed all around him but he could not guess their source.

The trail was now covered with scree. He carefully negotiated his way, reaching a wide ledge that overlooked the valley about a hundred feet above it. He thought he would rest for a bit. Then the wind changed and the stench hit him.

He instinctively covered his face and looked around. There was nothing here. He crossed over to the other side of the track. Boulders at the foot of a row of pine trees and on a bare patch of earth, was a corpse. Maggots crawled over the body of a wizened old man, parts of the torso covered by leaves. He had a shock of white hair that the rain had plastered to his face. He was wearing loose trousers and a shirt which had been unbuttoned down to the waist. How long had he been dead? Kar wondered as he approached the body.

He winced seeing the face. Recognising it despite the fact that it had changed considerably from the photo he had seen. A part of the head, from the ear to the right jaw, had been bitten off. Must have been a wild animal. He looked around. What had happened to Mr Saha? Where were the others? Why did Tara have to die?

He stood there for a few minutes wondering what he should do. He was far from any help and his phone had also died on him. Perhaps the best course was to go down to the settlement. The answers to all questions should be somewhere down there and perhaps the others were there too. But where had Miss Park vanished after leading him this far?

He decided to resume his descent into the valley. The trail became wider joining another till it met the stream. The grass was green on the waterside but the weed he had seen on the way was beginning to overrun the banks, sticking out their rugged stalks through patches of dead grass.

There was a flimsy wooden bridge across the water. He crossed it cautiously, looking ahead, watching his tracks. But if anyone was still around, they didn't make their presence felt.

He tentatively advanced a few more steps in the direction of the settlement. The shrivelled trees were aflame with the colours of autumn. A thin mist swirled around their canopies and it looked like someone had lit fires in the air.

Kar wound the scarf tightly around his neck as he strode down the path that went to the row of log cabins. The air had the stale odour of a burial chamber. As he walked along the desolate track, with not a soul in sight, he got a creepy feeling. It was as if he was walking into a dungeon, a closed subterranean chamber where no living person had set foot before.

He passed by the remnants of a wood fire. Half-burnt logs, a pile of paper cups in a bin and empty soju bottles. He stopped to have a look at those signs of gaiety, but the ravaged land didn't yield, refusing to transmit any of its lost joys. Deliberately, he touched the snub-nosed barrel of the Makarov stuck inside his belt as he skirted the rows of cabbages near the cabins. It made him feel better.

There was a large stack of onggi jars where the path took a sharp turn at one end of the rows of dwelling places. The roofs of the cabins had squash vines covered by dust and the windows were all tightly shut. It looked like they hadn't been opened for a while. Then he heard something and stopped.

The sound of shuffling feet. An old man with Korean features appeared down the path along the line of houses, dragging his feet. Kar crouched low sheltering himself behind one of the brown earthenware jars. The man approached slowly, stopping every few seconds to catch his breath. Kar watched his slow laborious walk from his hiding place. The man came closer and now Kar could see his face clearly. It was ravaged by age and his unkempt white hair was tousled with dirt. He was staring straight ahead as he walked but those were unseeing eyes. Has he gone blind, flashed through his mind.

As he considered his next course of action, two more men emerged from one of the cabins, walking laboriously, like the one before them. They were all dressed in loose fitting white shirts and trousers. One of them wore a straw hat. They were walking towards him. As he kept watching, from his refuge, more men and women, Koreans and the Indians, emerged from the log cabins. Walking slowly, their steps unsure, their backs bent with the burden of age.

The children came right after. Little rag dolls, toddling down the path. Their cheeks sunken, their hair dishevelled as if they had survived a storm. Their hand-woven sweaters were all worn the wrong way.

He recognised Harvinder Singh walking towards him. The strapping Sikh businessman, now reduced to a bundle of bones with an unkempt beard, clattering on with a walking stick, almost out of breath. Some of them had paper plates in their hands. The plates were laden with fruits and savouries. Oranges and apples, bananas and pears, chestnuts and moon cakes. Some of these rolled off the plates from their shaky hands.

Again the drums boomed through the valley. It was followed by the beats of a *kwangwari* and the clang of brass gongs. But it was an eerie spiritless sound which did not stir the trees nor rend the mist which was now hanging low.

More and more of them appeared. All old and feeble, doubled over with age. Dragging their feet, some leaning against trees to catch their breath, before hobbling on towards the stream. As he watched this procession of the decrepit, the music grew harsh and piercing. It was now like the wailing of a banshee hiding in the caves up on those hills. Then it sounded like the cries of the soldiers who had perished, fighting for this land. Kar sneaked back to the far end of the row of onggi jars as they passed with their offerings of fruits and fish, meat and cakes of rice.

The mist hung still. The trees were like stone. And Miss Park who came last was accompanied by another young woman. Both of them were wearing blue-and-white hanboks and they walked side by side without talking. He noticed how they walked in step, their hands swinging in rhythm as if in a secretly choreographed dance. Faster than those ahead of them. And watching them Kar realised, they were spitting images of each other. From the bangs of jet black hair, the same oval face and finely bowed lips, there was nothing to distinguish one from the other.

Captain Old
and
the Living Dead
of
Darkland

7

The flashlight didn't reveal what he was looking for. Captain Old tried to staunch the flow of blood from his fingers with the hem of his sweatshirt. He spat on his palms and continued to move ahead, pushing through the last few metres to the mouth of the vent. The flaps to control airflow had fallen off over the years so he could peep straight into the platform.

But there were no lights there. The platform was deserted. The intelligence he had received was completely wrong. The leaders of Red Dawn were supposed to assemble their followers down below. He had assumed they would deliver their speeches from the stairs while the audience stood on the platforms and the tracks. It would be relatively easy for him to pick one off with the MSG99 while hiding inside the air shaft. But now he would have to leave the sniper rifle behind. It would only slow him down and at close range his sidearm would be more useful.

The tracks went below him, rusted rails which were now walking paths for going from one station to the other. Diesel exhaust lingered in the air and he could hear the hum of a generator. There was a faint light coming from the top of the stairs at the far end. He pricked his ears to listen for other sounds. Not a sigh or inhaled breath. He patted his sidearm and eased himself down slowly. His feet touched hard ground. This was the shoulder of the platform extending into the tunnel.

A savage kick to his kidney. He half turned to parry the next hit when a ham-fisted blow landed straight on his face. Straight out of the darkness. He tumbled and fell. Four men moved in from the shadows.

They came from behind him and tied up his hands with nylon cords that cut deep into his flesh. Another kick to his solar plexus. Old groaned in pain and rolled over, hoping they would finish him off quickly.

They searched him carefully and took his handgun. One of them pulled him up by the collar of his sweatshirt while another held a chopper to his throat, 'Protector dog, huh?'

How could he explain that he was just another hungry man. He mumbled his story, which he knew wouldn't cut ice, 'I sneaked in to steal the cables. My local barterman prizes these and ...' Another blow landed on his face.

The guards frogmarched him along an extension of the platform in the direction of stairs on the far side. Two in front, two others following. One of them pressed the barrel of an automatic to his back while another held a flashlight. A couple of eardies ahead, he saw the corpses.

Hanging by their neck from piano strings, tied to the roof of the tunnel were three men and a woman. The corpses were bloated and maggots circled over the gaping eyes. The rats had been at work — fingers and ears were missing. They were all fairly advanced in age. They must have been hanged sometime back, he thought, when one of the men behind him shouted, 'Keep marching motherfucker! Don't worry, you will join them soon.'

A rusty iron gate with 'NO SPITTING' signs led them into the long platform. Two scruffy-looking youngsters, old army rifles slung against their shoulders, stood at attention near the gate as they marched him along the length of the platform.

As they approached the other end he could hear voices. The clamour of hundreds of voices, floating down the stairs. He could hear the cries of children, cursing and occasional laughter. The gathering was up there. They had all arrived walking from the far reaches of the subterranean city, the last shelter for the migrants, the homeless and the decrepit who had nowhere to go. He had been totally misled by the faulty intelligence — the meeting will be held in the main concourse. And now the guerrillas had taken him prisoner. They led him up the stairs towards the glimmer of light and voices.

The ticketing hall was buzzing with activity. Armed men in tattered black uniforms with red stars sewn on their chests roamed about keeping a watch. The automatic ticket barriers and railings, that separated the ticketing hall from the area leading to the platforms and other entry points, were being used as clotheslines by the hundreds of families who had taken refuge in this metro station. Many of them had come from villages. The poor of the city were also there as were those who had been abandoned by their families.

Rope cots and torn beddings were lined around the walls. Cot owners had placed these closer to the ticket booths. Many more beddings were lined in the long walkways leading to the southern exits of the station. Those who hadn't been able to place their beddings along the wall had rolled them out randomly over every inch of space. Old men slept beside those who had just died and seemed to be asleep. Women stirred black pots of broth on brushwood fires that had coated the ceiling in a thick layer of soot and a pall of wood smoke hung low over the concourse. People were coughing violently and a couple of battery-operated electric fans went on whirring in vain trying to clear the air.

Men sat in groups engrossed in card games, growing old as they played the hands they had been dealt. As he watched, players died, the fan of cards frozen in their calloused fingers. The others didn't take notice till they decided they would not allow them any more time to show their hand. A circle of petromax lamps hung near the middle of the hall throwing greenish-white light to the farthest corners of the approach halls. The makeshift stage and the area near the stairs were lit by battery-operated emergency lamps, drenching the armed guerrillas who stood there in ghostly pools of fluorescence.

Volunteers and armed guerrillas wove their way through the wasteland of beddings and kitchen utensils, families and iron trunks, shouting, 'Over there, over there!' A large group had already begun to assemble in the long hallways connecting the north and south exits, spilling into the ticketing hall, trampling beds and Barbie dolls, like an army of the blind, waiting for a leader.

They led Captain Old to the area in front of the ticket booths where a makeshift stage had been erected using wood planks and a rope cot. Huge banners of Red Dawn fashioned out of gunny bags hung from the ceiling. Posters and graffiti covered the walls.

Some of these posters denounced the corrupt Darkland administration, others declared various kinds of action programmes. *Down with the corrupt DAA!* one screamed in red ink. *Support Red Dawn for a Golden Future!* another chimed in. *Direct Democracy for Prosperity! No Borders, No Nations! One Solution: Revolution! Give it Back to the People!* The words screamed from the walls, shrill in red and black.

From one of the ticket counters a few volunteers were distributing medicines and safeoil. A long queue snaked through the concourse winding back and forth on itself like the bellows of an accordion. A single volunteer went weaving right and left, distributing revolutionary literature.

When the queue finally dispersed and the people gathered around the stage for the speeches to begin, they pushed him into the ticket room and locked the door from outside.

The ticket room with the glass booths had been converted into a toilet. It was dark inside and the piss fumes almost knocked him out. He breathed slowly taking in a little of the poisonous odour till his smell receptors went numb and his lungs could get precious oxygen. He moved up towards the iron stand pipe at the corner and tried in vain to turn the tap. The rat bites had been burning with pain and with some water he could have washed the wounds. But with his hands tied he could hardly turn the stopcock. Giving up after a few minutes he walked up and peered through a ticket window.

Two men were sitting in plastic chairs on top of the cot-stage. One of them was a young bearded man with glasses. He was wearing a *panjabi* full of creases and dirty pyjamas and was deep in discussion with the other man. This man was tall and thin and his skin was wrinkled from age. He was wearing a bush shirt and brown trousers and his face was hidden behind a mask. It looked like an iron mask or one of shiny black velvet.

A semblance of order had descended on the gathering. Men and women had left their work and games and were sitting on the floor facing the cot-stage. How many were there? At least five hundred, but it's so hard to count in the semi-darkness. They held their bottles of safeoil close to their chests while in the other hand were the little booklets of revolutionary literature. Some of the dead still held their cards, leaning against the graffiti-splattered walls, watching with their dead eyes, waiting for the meeting to get over.

Meanwhile their partners had joined the audience. A mike boomed calling everyone to attention. 'Comrades, we are about to begin. But before I introduce our speaker, I have to present before you another proof that the dictatorial regime run by Kak and his corrupt henchmen had been trying their best to extinguish our people's movement which like wildfire has begun to lick at their fat rumps. Look carefully,' and two powerful emergency lamps were shone into the ticket room converted to toilet, lighting up Captain Old in a corner, 'today the corrupt protector force, under orders from the highest level, sent this assassin to target our beloved Comrade Ashish. Do you need any more proofs, comrades? The dictator Kak and his henchmen are surely scared by our resolve to break their black hands and wrench power for the people ...' As the young man spoke, the masked man in the chair turned and took a good look at Old.

The speaker rushed through recent history criticising policies that had unleashed the disasters. 'Now the corrupt leadership of our land in collusion with their Cleanland masters are hastening in the end. If we don't overthrow them today and make amends swiftly then no one will survive. There is only one way to pull us out of this morass and that is to destroy this corrupt structure by attacking the pillars of its strength.' This was the crux of his speech. Captain Old in the ticket room and the hundreds lined on the floor listened quietly, sweating, choking in the stuffy air of the underground.

The man wearing the mask rose to speak. He was once again introduced as Comrade Ashish. Strangely his adenoidal voice sounded familiar to Old. Where had he heard it before? It was shrill but powerful and the smoky concourse, luminous in petromax glow, echoed with his speech, sending it down the platforms and through the dark tunnels to far-off places where others stood listening.

He went straight into attack mode, detailing the failures and the corruption of the authorities. He also blamed Cleanland powers for being in league with the dictator, as they are profiting from the status quo. He believed an antidote for the disease existed but sinister powers are holding it back. 'Our patience has run out. Now is the time to strike back. In cities and towns, villages and suburbs people have taken a decision to take their destiny in their own hands. We cannot let our future be wasted in the hands of the dictator and his henchmen. Power must be returned to the people and direct democracy has to be established. But before that we have to attack the dictatorship and those within and outside our borders who keep it afloat. We need your help, comrades, to make this possible. You are the rightful owners of the machines that produce our cloth, the brick kilns, the forests and the land. Let it begin tonight my friends. We are with you and if we stick together then they cannot hold out for long. Let us go out into the streets tonight and demolish the symbols of the wicked administration, let us snatch the batons and the guns of the protectors. We have been putting up resistance for years but the time has now come to deal the final blow ...'

Just as he uttered these words a very old man in the crowd had a heart attack and died. Those sitting nearby shifted position but there was hardly any place to accommodate the dead among the packed crowds. He slouched forward on the back of a young man listening rapt to the rousing speech. And then the hall came alive with machine gun fire.

A hail of bullets rained down on the armed volunteers from the stairs that went up to the nearest exit. Old heard it too. Since the masked man rose to speak, he had been trying desperately to free himself of his restraints. He had managed to pull out the piece of Kevlar cord he had hidden under the label of his jeans and was rubbing it on the rope used to tie his hand. But it was difficult with his hands tied and the wounds oozing blood.

The Red Dawn volunteers returned fire. The masked man finished his speech quickly and shouted orders to the armed volunteers. The gunfight raged near the exits. People screamed and ran like headless chickens as the petromax lamps were shot down. Torchlight danced in the sudden darkness lit up by the muzzle flash of guns. Bullets whizzed through the halls as the volunteers took defensive positions firing at gates, which had been booby-trapped. And a stray bullet hit Old.

People scampered for cover as the staccato sound of machine gun fire came closer from the stairwell that went up to the entry point, where the headless king rode his stone horse. The volunteers returned fire, holding their position. Meanwhile the crowd rushed towards the southern exits, others scurried down the steps to the tunnels which provided a safer escape route. Smoke had engulfed the concourse but for the time being the armed guerrillas had repulsed the advance on the nearest entry point.

A phalanx of kravas and bonesteels were working their way down one of the southern entry points and so the action had shifted there. A giant flash from one of their impulse guns lit up the station and shrill cries followed. The guerrillas rushed in numbers to the southern points, guns blazing like mad.

Captain Old had fallen to the ground. Blood was flowing freely from the bullet wound on his shoulder. Did the chief protector use him as a bait and diversion while planning to attack this assembly and get the leaders? He couldn't think clearly any more. His whole body was an angry mass of pain. He was experiencing chills and he passed out a number of times, coming to a little while later each time.

Now he could still hear the chatter of automatic fire but they seemed to be far from where he was. He knew he wouldn't get out of this alive. Screams echoed through the halls as he lay under the ticket counter and closed his eyes.

He waited for them to come and shoot the door open, greeting him with a hail of lead. But why were they taking so long? At one point he realised that he could not hear the machine gun bursts any more. Only the sounds of isolated small arms fire came from far away and then that too died. The hall was suddenly quiet. Only the moans of the dying and the injured punctuated the silence.

He tried to get up but failed. He thought he heard footsteps coming in his direction. Metal-tipped boots. There was a noise near the door but he couldn't turn around to look. A key was turned, there was a click and the door swung open slowly. He couldn't see clearly in the darkness till the man came and stood above him.

'Get up!' That voice! The masked comrade. He had a machine gun slung across his shoulder. Where had he heard that voice before?

He stood up with some effort hoping this would be fast. But Comrade Ashish didn't fire. Instead he swung him around and swiftly cut the remaining threads of nylon rope tying his hands. Old waited, not sure what was coming next.

'We have beat them back. They are out on the streets. We are fighting them at every crossroad. Thank you for the tip. Our fighters were prepared. Hope the guards didn't hurt you too much — they were under my instructions to avoid unnecessary force.'

Old shook his head slowly while cursing the guards silently.

'I will let you go,' the masked man said, 'if not for anything else then for old time's sake. Go and fight the good fight of the people,' and with these words he quickly turned around and marched out of the ticket room. Gun at the ready. Then he was gone.

8

Captain Old floated in and out of consciousness as he lay there in the empty ticket room of the underground station. He was completely drained. The poison from the rat bite was spreading through his veins. He was experiencing chills. The gunshot wound was bleeding steadily. He dragged himself to a corner and turned the tap of the standpipe to wash his wounds. Not a drop.

They must have cut the supply. He collapsed on the floor again, wincing in pain.

He saw the Keun Sunim watching him through the glass window of a ticket booth. But as he tried to focus, he vanished. His consciousness flickered. Sometimes he was aware of his surroundings but mostly he was floating away. Back to those mountains, decades ago. He was known by a different name then. Time was repeating itself, looping his memories one more time.

It was the day he had arrived at the retreat, a few months after the group had disappeared, and found the settlement full of geriatrics. The lost tourists and the Koreans. The day of the autumn festival. Chuseok — the time for thanking nature for her bounties. An occasion for the giving of gifts and offerings to the departed, a time for feasting. He had hidden behind the onggi jars, watching the old men and women trooping out of the camp. They were followed by the twins in hanboks. One of them had walked up to him. He assumed it was Miss Park, she had led him through the forest. But he couldn't be sure, the two of them were indistinguishable.

'What's happening here?' he had asked her.
'Do you know any of them?' she had asked.
'What has happened to them? I have seen their photographs. Now they look hundred years old! And just in these two months!'
'Wish I had known.'
'What do you mean? How did they end up here?'
'We will tell you what we know. But we thought you could help us?'
'I can take them home. That's all I can do.'

The two women exchanged a glance and then turned to look at him. 'I wish that was possible,' one of them said.

Kar sighed. He knew what they meant. It would require a superhuman feat to get them out of here. Did he make a mistake by coming here on his own? Perhaps it was time to call for help. Thinking about the events of the last evening, the car accident, about Miss Park guiding him through the forest, left his mind in a daze. What ever has happened to these people was way beyond his comprehension. He was just another private eye. He could read bent minds, he knew how to survive the mean streets and he used to believe, he had always fought for the good. But what was he to do now?

'Tell me when you began to notice the change?' he asked.

'It's difficult to be exact. But we have been noticing certain signs even before the tourists arrived. Forgetfulness for one. People seemed to be getting confused about their daily routines. Someone who made the hanji paper began turning up at the kitchen instead, another didn't remember when he had arrived. In a few weeks, everyone was looking different. Their skin turned pale, their memories dripped away like water from a faulty tap.'

'Other than the tourists who are the people living here? When did they arrive?'

'The Keun Sunim knows all the answers. This is a very old settlement. It may have been around for hundreds of years. Many of the Koreans here are from the other Korea.'

'You mean the North?' Kar remembered something but kept it to himself.

'Yes,' she looked at him strangely, 'they are those who came to this country for a new life. But they faced adjustment issues.'

'So they ended up here and are now suddenly ravaged by old age ...' Kar was thinking fast. Kim had told him about defectors who had gone missing. Could they have all ended up here looking for a quieter existence, away from the pressures of life in a new country. Then what? Were these people poisoned with some secret biological agent that has hastened their decline? Why did the NIS pick him up despite the fact that he had met Kim the night before. Could he trust the twins?

She saw something in his face. 'We should meet Keun Sunim. He knows more than we do. We have to go up in the forest. You have found the tourists and also seen our people. You must have noticed how the forest down here has changed, the shrivelled trees, the yellow weed, the rice pests that look like giant birds of prey. Tell the monk what you can do. We trust you.'

Kar took some time weighing his options. The scarf the children had given him must have been a gift from the monk, he told himself. It was still wrapped around his neck. Why did the scarf matter? He took the soft cloth between his fingers feeling the weave. He should meet him before doing anything drastic. 'Okay, let's go,' he said.

They walked along the path towards the stream. The old men and women had assembled in small groups. Kar watched them from a distance. He wanted to speak with them. He could hardly match the photographs he had seen with the wizened old faces milling around the water. Harvinder was lying on the yellow grass, scratching his sores. Three old men sat on their haunches on a wooden pavilion by the water, talking. They were sharing barley tea from a copper kettle, their walking sticks leaning against a shrivelled gingko tree. Some Korean women were peeling persimmons nearby with their calloused fingers while others arranged fruits and rice cakes on paper plates laying it out on a spotless white cloth.

A woman with uncombed platinum hair was sitting by the mounds of the dead where the people of the mountains had buried their ancestors. Folds of wrinkled skin hung from her jaw. She peered at them as they passed quietly. Two old ladies came shuffling with food and offerings for the departed. They set the wooden bowls and plates of fruits and sweets neatly near the burial mounds. Soon they would light the candles as the sun vanished behind the rows of hills. The mountain stream gurgled by softly.

Kar wanted to speak to his old comrade Bose but he was nowhere to be found. Someone said he was in his room, too sick to talk with anyone.

'Don't bother them now,' Miss Park whispered. 'If they offer you the food you can't refuse. It may not be safe for you.'

Kar thought about it and continued towards the hill. His options were running out fast but for now he will do as she advised. He will hear out the monk.

They began to climb the hill, leaving the valley behind them, with its bare farmland, the gurgling stream and the old people sitting on its banks, thanking nature for her gifts.

It got chilly as the sun dropped behind the hills. Kar zipped up his jacket as they made their way up the twisting trail. They had reached the area with the giant trees, and the forest was full of whispers of hidden life. Far below in the valley, that was being devoured by the treacherous mists, they could see the faint flickers of candlelight.

He couldn't keep up with the twins. They seemed to glide above the earth and the forest made way for them pulling back the branches and sweeping away the undergrowth to show the path that seemed to have opened up just for them to pass through.

Though it was dark now he could see the trail. The white silk of the hanbok of one of the women shone faintly in the darkness as if it was dabbed with luminous paint. And however dark it grew, the hanbok continued to glow with its own light. The light showed him the way but he could not see the other woman any more. Had she fallen back?

In an hour they reached a clearing, high up in the mountain. It looked like the meadow of the morning but he could not be sure. The majestic pines stood on all sides, their canopies lit by the light of a red moon that had crept up silently from behind the hills. A little frame house stood there all by itself. Moonlight was flooding the meadow and he saw another smaller house near the trees, with a candle burning outside its door.

'Where are we?' he asked.

'We have arrived,' the woman in the luminous white-and-blue hanbok spoke softly. 'The Keun Sunim will be here anytime. He is inside the temple. Meanwhile we can sit. Will you like some tea?'

Kar said yes.

She disappeared into the house leaving him all by himself.

He heard soft footsteps and turned. It was the other woman. Her breath fell heavy. 'Sorry I cannot walk fast like my sister,' she said.

'Sister?'

'She is Jia. We are twins. My name is Jiyoo Park but you can call me Jiyoo.'

Kar looked puzzled. Was this the woman who had led him all the way to the mountains from Seoul or was she the one who had gone inside the house?

Her dark eyes were quiet. 'We got in touch with you because the monk said you have come to help. But it may already be too late,' Jiyoo said.

The door of the house opened and her sister asked them to come and sit inside. Kar took off his shoes and pushed through the paper door followed by Jiyoo. It was warm inside.

A sparsely furnished room with a clean wooden floor and scrolls on the walls. A tea lamp was throwing soft shadows all around. In one corner was a shelf with books and a metal sculpture of the pensive Mireuk — the Buddha of the future — with downcast eyes, the fingers of his right hand gently touching his cheek. Kar was studying the image of Maitreya when she brought a pot of tea and cups placing them on a low table.

The three of them sat around it. Everyone was quiet as she let the tea settle then poured it into small cups. The tea was refreshing, Kar felt the fatigue leaving his body. His thoughts fell into familiar patterns and questions began to crowd back. The woman poured him some more tea and filled their own cups.

'I don't know whether both of you know my name.'

They looked at each other and nodded. 'We do, Sir.'

'That's a good way to start but first I would like to know where is my assistant. Chaitanya?'

'He is fine at his home right now,' one of them replied.

'Huh?'

'We were desperate to get you here so we made up a story.'

'But I saw him in that funny room with the two — what were they — farmers?'

'It's too difficult to explain what you have seen but you can take my word for it — he is just fine. Once you are back in the city you call him and he will tell you he is okay.'

Kar didn't understand but he decided to let it pass for the moment, 'Now where is your monk? He seems to have gone into hiding. When I came trudging up this way, he was nowhere but he did send two lovely messengers who kept smiling. No words. But they gave me this scarf and I kind of like it,' he held up the piece of cloth. It shone in the mellow light as if it was woven with diamond strings.

They looked at each other. 'The Keun Sunim trusts you so he sent you the gift. He will be here shortly,' one of them said.

'I came here to find the lost tourists. The travel agency and their near and dear ones appointed me for this job. I am a private detective. The foreign office, police and security agencies of our countries have been puzzling over their disappearance for months. You were very kind to provide a lead and guide me,' he looked at them, one from the other, 'but from then on things have happened which need to be explained. Can you clear the mystery please? I would have enjoyed it if I wasn't four thousand kilometres from home sitting on a mountain top having tea with mystics. That's what you are, aren't you? Now tell me how did they end up here in the first place and what has happened to them now. I have to send reports to my clients and get these people home.' He was himself surprised at this sudden burst of anger but he didn't apologise. He had to do his work, however complicated the circumstances.

The woman who had brought the tea spoke first. 'It is a long story and I do not have much time. Because it is Chuseok, I came here to see my sister but it's not easy for me. I love to be where father and mother are. Where the rain trickles through the branches of the larch trees, playing a gentle music while we sleep. Like my sister, there are others here whom I knew, when I was with them. I remember them and want to see their faces. I feel I am responsible for much of what is happening here,' her dark eyes flickered or maybe it was just the tea light weaving patterns across her face. 'I will tell you what I know for if I don't, I will never be at peace. Please listen carefully.'

'I am all ears.'

She began right from the time the authorities of the North began to suspect their family after they had sent their father to a prison camp. She told him everything, slowly, without missing a detail. The first escape attempt and being pushed back by the Chinese police. Then being sent to prison with her sister and mother and how she was offered a chance to free her family. How she was sent to England. About Tanmoy Sen. Right till the time she and the scientist Eugene fled from Novingdon with the SuperRice samples and were flown in the old Russian plane to Pyongyang. The long interrogation by the Bowibu agent Mansik, Song from military security, and Kang. The brutality with which it ended when they came to know that she had passed on some of the spliced paddy to her sister who had managed to escape that same night.

Her sister listened quietly as she went on narrating her story while evening dissolved into night. Sometimes Kar could hear the beats of a wood drum outside. He looked around but the monk was still not there. He thought what the people at the settlement below would be doing now. Would they have strength to walk back to their huts after the feast? Will there be a few strong enough to help the others to their cabins. In a few days, who would be cooking for them? Will they die old, diseased and hungry, far from home?

In between, her sister went into the next room and came back with plates of fruits, yagwa and chestnuts. They ate silently.

The beats of the *beopgo* stopped and after a while he heard someone walking outside. A little while later he thought he heard the laughter of children from the forest.

He raised an eyebrow but the sisters were too absorbed in their story. Jia was speaking softly now and he had to lean over to hear her. She hadn't touched the food and something on her face made the detective uncomfortable. Though she was sitting right across the low table, he felt her voice was coming from far.

'I still remember the day they killed both of us,' she said. Kar thought he had heard her wrong but the faraway voice was like an invisible curtain which he could no more lift with his questions. 'They said we had given false statements about our assignments in England, passed on samples to a defector and that there were several discrepancies in our versions.

'But neither I nor Comrade Eugene had reckoned that the samples we brought back with us could be formulas for aging and death. The Indian professor tricked us or perhaps it is the evil that runs this world that manipulated us all. Did the professor make a mistake? What had we brought back with us?' Her shoulders drooped and her voice faltered. She turned to look at her sister. Tears were streaming down their eyes.

'What had gone wrong? Do you mean the spliced paddy had some defect and is somehow responsible for what is happening to the settlers down in the valley? But how did it end up here? Was that paddy planted in the valley below?'

His words hung in the air. He couldn't finish his sentence for something was happening in the room. A sudden gust of wind had sneaked in through the door, blowing out the lamp. He sensed movement in front of him but forgot to draw his gun. He heard a short gasp followed by a rustle of clothing. Kar jumped up, his heart thumping furiously. He had drawn the gun at the last moment when a matchstick flared as Jiyoo relit the tea lamp.

She looked at him strangely and then at the gun but she made no move. There was only the two of them in the room now. Wisps of yellow smoke were rising from the flame of the paper lantern. As they kept looking, the wisps bundled together and floated towards the window. Slowly disappearing through a crack in the paper screen.

Her voice was heard from outside, 'I have to go now. Back to where father and mother are waiting for me.' And now it was the wind speaking to them, 'The larch trees there out in the forest will fan away the pain from our bodies. Though we lie in unmarked graves, the red azaleas will bloom in spring telling friend and stranger where we rest. For the land always speaks the truth and this soil of Korea is pure and it will let us sleep in peace.'

9

The slopes are white under a low sky, propped up by the icy spears of the evergreens. The pines, their branches bending under the weight of fresh snow draw her into the darkness. Her breath freezes as she zigzags down the track, through the tunnel of trees. 'Never run in a straight line, then the dogs will come after you,' the guard had advised. There is a weak moon in the sky, which like a dead man's face, watches over the path through the forest. She had memorised the hand-drawn map with the escape route given by the prison guard but in the barren snowy waste, it was impossible to know if she was headed that way.

A few minutes earlier the guard had weighed down the electrified razor wire with a concrete slab they had hefted from a construction site inside the prison camp. The gap was just enough for the two of them to wriggle out. She had gone first. But in the hurry and because it was dark, her forearms had brushed against the barbed wire and angry blue sparks had licked her skin, singeing the flesh and tearing out some tissue. A stifled cry had escaped her lips.

The track weaved its way downhill. She went in her tattered shoes, slipping sometimes on the packed snow. She hit her head against a stiff white branch and stopped. Her head was reeling. She felt her pockets for the tubes her sister had passed on earlier. They were still there. What was inside them she didn't know yet. 'Never let pain or fear get the better of you. That will make you weak and then you are dead,' she remembered the prison guard whispering to her repeatedly when they had begun to plan the escape.

She summoned her energies and started again, like hunted game seeking shelter in the forest of the night. The security alarms went off, ringing madly as powerful searchlights began to sweep across the wooded hillside — lighted sabres slashing through the snow-drenched landscape.

The dreaded Bowibu guards were coming for them. They could hear their shouts. Shrill whistles pierced the silence of the trees and the barking of guard dogs followed. Shots rang out. A bullet whizzed past her digging deep into the trunk of an evergreen.

It was no use running ahead. The Bowibu were shining powerful torches that tore through the darkness. They would be discovered any moment now. If they tried a desperate dash down the slope, they would be sitting ducks to their bullets. The friendly guard signalled her to get into the woods and crouch behind a tree. They went down the side of the track going deeper among the snow-covered trees. But not much further. The slope was too steep here and if they tried to run they would tumble down into the swift-flowing river.

Too late. The fierce guard dogs had picked up their scent and came barking down the slope as flashlights scanned the woods. Then the dogs were upon them biting and scratching, ready to tear them apart. She was trying helplessly to protect herself with her bare hands.

She woke up in a cold sweat and sat up shivering in bed. The dormitory was dark but there was some light coming in through a window. It was four in the morning. She had hardly slept when the nightmare had returned. In the first few weeks at the House of Unity, it recurred every night.

She got out of bed, went and washed her face. Even though they were safe at this South Korean settlement centre for defectors, she was always on the edge. The years at the prison camp haunted her waking hours, she found it difficult to trust anyone. She had left her family behind. What would they do to her mother and father when they found out she had escaped with a prison guard? She dreaded to imagine their fate or that of her sister who had vanished from the camp about two years ago and had returned the day she had escaped. The little packets of paddy her sister had given her were still with her, safe. She kept them close to her always as those bore the last memories of Jia.

After wriggling out through the gap in the fence and burning herself on the electrified perimeter wire, she and the guard had kept running through the darkness. They had to get as far from the prison camp as possible but cold and exhaustion had slowed them down. Luckily the part of the prison camp where she had been kept was not as strictly guarded as the zone of absolute control where she guessed her father had been taken. That she and the guard had escaped was not noticed immediately and there were no hungry dogs yet on their trail. That night they had found a little sheltered ledge on the hillside and could rest there till daybreak.

When the green hills around them began bobbing up through the mist, they made their way down the slope finding themselves on a path through the fields. Walking through the plain open land was risky as they could be spotted from far but luckily this was not harvest season and there was no one around for miles.

They followed the dirt track for hours till they approached a metalled road going east. Careful to hide whenever a pedestrian came along, they trudged along the road quietly, keeping a wary eye for anything moving. They walked for miles. The guard had some rice cakes which they ate when hungry.

After a few hours they saw some men bent under loaded A-frames trudging along. Nobody asked them questions, which was good. In that time, when food was hard to find, speaking was a waste of precious energy. So they walked silently like other travellers and small traders making their way to the town nearby.

They hovered in the shadows of the little town for hours looking for food. The prison guard had some money and that helped them buy rice cakes and shrivelled apples damaged by frost.

Jiyoo and the guard bought their way to a rail station which was in another city where they bribed a guard to get on a freight train heading north. Without travel permits and IDs, this was the only way they could travel. There were others in the freight wagons, thin haggard men with sunken cheeks and tired eyes, people looking for work, small traders and those who didn't want to talk. At least they were not alone but travelling in a freight car with a bunch of hungry, jobless men in the middle of a harsh winter was another challenge.

The prison guard had proved to be an angel. Cruel as he was inside the camp, he had taken complete responsibility to ensure the safest possible passage for both of them. 'There would be hungry men inside that train. Traders and travellers like us. Maybe some who like us will try to cross over and never come back. Do not talk with anyone and wear this cap to keep your face covered as much as possible,' he had handed her an old army cap with a visor he had picked during his foray to buy the apples. 'It will protect you from the cold and perhaps keep the men away.'

The train meandered through the countryside, stopping at towns and goods yards unloading odd-looking machines, under the cover of night, that someone said were planetarium projectors made by a Japanese company. In the dim-lit railway yards the giant machines looked like twin-headed aliens standing on stick legs observing the icy waste. 'They are planning star shows in every city,' a trader commented peeping out of the freight car as more of the Japanese machines were unloaded in stations where the lights had been turned off because of shortage of electricity.

Jiyoo hung about in the shadows, avoiding the gazes, her head down, her back straining against the cold metal of the box car. They changed trains twice, each time slipping into a freight car, and after four long days of back-breaking travel and hiding away from authorities, they rolled into Musan on a timber-carrying freight train at the break of dawn.

The Tumen river was a little distance from this town. But there were check posts and border guards and it would be safer to cross it under the cover of darkness. So they hung about in backstreets and mingled with travellers near the railway station. Her companion the prison guard had a few dollars with which he bought them a meal of goat meat and packs of cigarettes.

The crossing was comparatively easy, a few packets of foreign cigarettes had softened up the border guards. The river had frozen over and they stepped gingerly on the ice sheet, walking across slowly in the darkness. She was nervous, for she was crossing this river for the second time and no one could be sure what lay in wait for them on the other side.

'Don't worry. Even if it breaks this river is not deep. You won't drown in it,' her companion had whispered.

'I know. This is my second attempt,' she had said.

But still they had to evade the Chinese police on the other side. The memory of being captured and pushed back by the Chinese still haunted her. She was extra cautious, waiting for a long time on the other bank to make sure no Chinese guards were around.

The prison guard knew a Korean-Chinese family on the other side who would put them up. It was dangerous but she didn't know any other way to survive the harsh winter and make their way to freedom in the South.

The Joseonjok family that gave them shelter was kind but Jiyoo was still nervous. She helped them with the work at home while always watching her back. When someone came to visit the house she would leave through another door and hide in the forest. Meanwhile the prison guard helped the family in their business.

At dinner on the very first night they gave her a warm bowl of chicken and rice and some cabbage. She took a mouthful of the sticky rice, savouring its texture. She bit into a chunk of the meat remembering its flavour from long ago. The electric shock from the fence had scarred her permanently. When she would meet Ujaan later and he would see the pink marks on her forearms for the first time, she would just say, 'It was something nasty that happened to me.'

But that would be much later. Now Jiyoo and the guard were planning the final leg that will take them across the endless country spread out before them to the land of what they were taught was the arch-enemy.

The country they would have to cross was too big. Perhaps they would have to travel through many countries. Many stellar systems, and galaxies one different from the other in degrees of humanity or lack of it. Perhaps they would find friends or end up in the hands of traffickers or border guards. The road to freedom was more circuitous and convoluted than the labyrinthine infinity of the night sky which the planetarium projectors they had seen on the train could replicate with ease.

It wouldn't be easy for them, this journey to freedom. They had to beg and scrounge their way through China, evading police, waiting tables in cities thousands of miles apart. The Mandarin she had learned at school helped. It opened more doors, created that modicum of trust which helped them along.

The prison guard had taken advantage of her while at the camp but he had proved to be a kind-hearted man once they had escaped. He would go without food sometimes so that she could eat the little they had left. She still remembered his big face, his cropped hair and toothy smile. But he hadn't made it. He was not lucky like her.

After a few months of working illegally in big and small Chinese cities, doing odd jobs, seeking shelter from kind people in churches who gave them food and money, they had met an elderly Joseonjok in Beijing who could be trusted.

He knew that they didn't have the money to pay a broker to travel across China and then through Laos into Thailand, where after months of processing they could perhaps catch a plane to the South.

'Forget it,' he said. 'The broker will be hounding you for payment and they are no angels. Why don't you seek help from the embassy?' He was a priest in an underground church in the backstreets of Beijing and he had helped them with food and money.

'You think they can help us?' she had asked.

'Of course they can and they do, though less frequently these days. You have a strong case and because your companion was a prison guard, the embassy might be more interested to help. But be careful when you go in. The Chinese police will be waiting outside to stop you and if you are caught you might be sent back.'

She had thanked him and asked if he knew where in the city the embassy was. Of course he knew. 'Try to make a dash for it. You know, you might have to scale the gates to get inside,' he said and his kind eyes wrinkled with sadness as he looked at her. 'I could have helped but alas now the Chinese police know me and will stop us if I tried to get you inside.'

They had done several recces of the South Korean embassy, watching the habits and change in shifts of the police outside, and finally made a dash for it, as the priest had advised. The police had pounced on them but she was up the gates and on the other side before they could stop her. But her companion's foot got stuck in the iron grill. She still remembered the fear in his eyes as the policemen in green uniforms grabbed his legs and got him down and into a waiting car.

Freedom! She had done it. The embassy had given her everything — clothes, food and shelter. And after several weeks, the Chinese had allowed her to leave. The elderly Joseonjok had arranged a loan for her ticket which she could pay back slowly. Her ticket to freedom.

The red brick building of Hanawon or House of Unity, among the green hills of South Korea, had been her home for months. She tried her best to pick up the skills for a new life, in a new country. It took time for she found it difficult to focus. But she didn't make friends there, the fear of being sent back haunted her waking hours. She still couldn't trust anyone. She was plagued by irrational fears and found it difficult to talk with strangers. Even if they were caring strangers like the psychiatrist Youngchul at Hanawon or the lady who gave her lessons on the computer. And the nightmares didn't leave Jiyoo till long afterwards, till she would meet the Keun Sunim, the monk of White Cloud mountain.

After leaving the House of Unity, she worked for a few months at a convenience store. It took time. 'My strong northern accent made me stand out and I had to struggle for months to adapt to the new manner of speaking,' she would tell Ujaan later. She slowly learnt to use the foreign words that had seeped into the language of this country. But the sheer variety of goods on the shelves, the plethora of choices, gave her a headache and she would sometimes stare dumb-faced at customers when they asked for her help to find something: Islay malts, chocolate truffle, bramble liqueur, kiwi fruits, thousand island dressing.

Someone suggested this PC bang in Seoul. She thought it might be easier for her there. So she switched jobs. Trying hard to build her new life. She was lonely in the city, 'People are too aloof in this country and it takes time to make friends,' she told Ujaan the first day at the settlement, when he had asked her why she liked to be in the mountains. 'Everyone is running and making a decent life is becoming difficult. Young people have begun to call it *Hell Joseon*. But still I am glad I could leave my country.'

She worked late shifts, sometimes all through the night, returning in the morning to her apartment provided by the government. She slept little, crying in her bed, thinking of her family. The cold noodles in Seoul never tasted as good as the one her omma cooked on winter nights. What had happened to Jia, will she ever see her again?

Perhaps if she could save enough money after repaying the loan for her ticket, she could help her family back in the North. She remembered Jimin not knowing what had happened to her. Could she find a broker to help her family defect, someone like Jimin perhaps? But she was not sure. Their capture by the Chinese police, the first time they had tried to defect, was raw in her memory. There should be someone in this country who can help. She had saved quite a bit from the stipend given by the government but she would need much more to buy freedom for her family. She would loan money if it came to that. But freedom had lost some of its lustre by the time she joined the PC Bang in Seoul.

It was around this time that she had begun hiking in the mountains. At first she went on short trips with groups walking for a few hours, having lunch in the shade with gurgling streams flowing by. The mountains reminded her of home where it was more beautiful and wild. Here in the South, even walking paths deep inside the mountains were signposted. But she loved the fresh mountain air and kept coming back alone. This was when she had met the monk.

Walking alone along a mountain trail, she had met him outside a Buddhist temple, frequented by tourists and locals alike. Little children in yellow and green school uniform were playing on the grass around him and he was watching them sitting on a rock. He exuded peace. She went and sat beside him. They had begun to talk.

'You have been suffering for long,' he had told her. She was surprised and also a little scared, because he seemed to know who she was. But the monk's words had been kind and he had invited her to the little settlement in the hidden valley of White Cloud mountain.

The people at the settlement were friendly and she had returned in a few weeks and then again. The monk would sit and talk with her about the old temple high up on the brow of the hill, the soldiers who discovered the valley, how people came here and stayed back, about life in the mountains.

She began to visit more often and help the people at the retreat. She brought little gifts for the monk from the city. A warm shawl, small wooden images of the Buddha, a hanji lantern with a mantra scrawled over it. She gave him the tubes of rice seeds she had received from her sister.

Ssal — it was an enigmatic word. The Korean word for paddy before it is cooked, when it turned into *bap* — pearly white, warm, sticky to the touch. It sounded sweetest in her language and now it was growing in the little terraces on the hillside. They sowed it every year and this time they had planted the seeds she had gifted, alongside the original paddy crop. Beneath the blue skies of autumn, the little terraces had burst into joyous colour and it looked like the hills had dressed up in green and gold, like a princess from a far away land. They tended the crop with care and soon the settlers in their straw hats would come lugging their wooden backpacks, silvery scythes in hand, ready for a rich harvest. In a few days, the little settlement will come alive with song and dance, as the kwangwari set the beat, joined by the music of gongs and the hourglass drum.

Gradually the pall of sadness had lifted. She was again connecting with life. The work at the PC bang did not seem as dull and dreary as it did before. In the city she began to go out, talk with people outside work, sit in a dessert cafe enjoying a bingsu all by herself. Then winter had arrived and for weeks the settlement was covered in a blanket of snow. Winter was harsh for the settlers, the firewood was never enough to keep them warm. She thought she would ask the monk to get modern heating run with solar power but before she could do that she knew what the monk would say. 'People have lived like this for thousands of years.' She wouldn't argue with the Keun Sunim.

The snow had begun to melt in the mountains and Seoul was also springing back to life with all the programmed energy of an automaton. People were beginning to hang out in the streets and parks as the sun smiled after a harsh winter. The giant display boards were crackling with energy in the crisp night air. The parks were coming alive with a riot of cherry blossoms. Jiyoo still didn't have friends but she didn't mind. Soon she would meet Ujaan and the tourists.

10

Bat wings flicker in the moon's last watch,
The ancient trees are still,
Waiting for dawn that comes within an hour.
So through my still heart flicker thoughts of you,
But I shall wait perhaps a thousand years!

—Yi Soong-in. (14th century)

Detective Kar had listened quietly while Jiyoo completed the story of her escape. But he had failed the tourists. And the

Scourge that followed was of course much bigger than him or anyone by the time it was noticed.

It had turned frosty and the chill had gripped them both. After a while the door had opened and a shaft of moonlight caressed the wooden floor. The monk had appeared at the doorway. He was wearing a grey robe.

They stood up and bowed. He bowed back and asked them to sit down. He sat with them at the low table. In the yellow light of the hanji lantern, Kar noticed the pain in his eyes. They looked like sinking paper boats struggling against a boundless tide.

The night stretched endlessly as the three sat in silence. Then Kar asked Jiyoo about her visits to White Cloud mountain and about the paddy she had brought with her. 'When was this paddy harvested?'

She said she visited often, whenever the PC Bang allowed her a break. She taught the children reading, writing and maths. She helped in the kitchen, chopping onions, preparing rice. And one day, she had handed to the monk the paddy that Jia had given her. The seeds were sown and the saplings transplanted to the terraced plots on the hillside. And wherever they were planted, the crop burst out in a shimmer of burnished gold in a matter of weeks. Everyone was surprised how quickly the new paddy had matured. They were very happy. The settlers had thanked her over and over again for those magic seeds. Last year's grain was still being used, so they hadn't touched this newly harvested paddy till months had passed. Till around the time she had arrived with the Indian travellers.

Kar interrupted her at this point. 'You said the fresh harvest was not used till the time the tourists had arrived?'

She nodded slowly. Yes, it was around then that the old stocks of grain ran out. Maybe a little earlier.

'So the poison is in that paddy from the British laboratory. My god! Instead of health the spliced paddy was pumping death and decay into their system. And I am sure the same has happened with the samples your sister delivered to her bosses in the North. Genes are unpredictable and who knows what else had gone into those artificially created seeds. We have to destroy all stocks.'

'I will get that done. But it might already be too late. Have you seen how the grass looks down there, the weed in the valley o the giant pests that are attacking the trees?' the monk said.

The realisation dawned on him slowly. The area has been contaminated by the deadly splice and maybe it was already too late. Whatever genes the paddy carried may have jumped species, who knew how far it had travelled already?

This was not the first time she got visitors here, Jiyoo had said. There were some from the North who had come to this country and found it difficult to go with the fast-paced life. 'They fell out of the race. For them it was from the devil to the deep sea. I told them of this quiet place, hidden from the world.'

They arrived with her and never went back. The other settlers were mostly from this country, those who stumbled upon it and gained the monk's trust, people who had been living here for decades.

'But I couldn't figure it out that the rice may have caused this great harm. We thought it has to be something to do with the Indians. But now it seems obvious,' she blinked helplessly.

Kar wished he would have some assurance to offer but nothing occurred to him.

She told Kar about meeting Ujaan that first night at the dessert cafe. Their little fight and then bumping into him again the next night. Quite by accident. She spoke haltingly, a little shy about sharing this. How she had begun to feel differently for this soft-spoken man. Though the monk had never approved bringing complete foreigners, she had got the group of tourists to visit the settlement, thinking they will enjoy the experience. The monk always said, 'Too many people will spell the end of our experiment.'

But it was mostly because of Ujaan that she had invited the vacationers to White Cloud mountain. 'I wanted him to be here with me, among these old hills.' She folded her hands on her lap and fell quiet.

Kar looked at the monk and then at her, 'I think I know who you are speaking about. But I don't think I saw him today at the retreat nor could I find my old comrade, Bose. I heard Bose is very sick, hope this young man is all right. Maybe I couldn't recognise him because he has changed like the others?'

She blinked hearing 'comrade'. She looked at the monk as if asking him something and Kar noticed her dark eyes quiver. The light of her heart shone through that look. The monk nodded.

'He is here with us,' she said softly. 'Come.'

She stood up and opened the door to the connecting room. The light from the paper lantern tiptoed into the next room and there he was. Sleeping on a futon, a blanket pulled up to his chin. His face was turned towards their room. Fresh and rested, sleeping the deep sleep of the content.

Jiyoo went inside and put her hand on his head and stroked his hair gently. Kar stepped back from the doorway and came and sat down on the floor. The monk was still sitting.

Jiyoo returned, closing the door softly. She sat on the floor with them.

The monk spoke first. 'I think he will be all right o if he wants to go home, we will send him his way,' he looked at the detective, 'but what if he doesn't want to leave?'

'Is there a reason for that? Doesn't he want to see his son?' Kar asked.

'Sadly most of them who lived down in the valley have been suffering from runaway amnesia. But this gentleman has fared better. I don't know why. She,' he turned to look at Jiyoo, 'would know. She has been taking care of him o somehow he has not been touched by this terrible illness. He is strong. His faculties are fine o his memory is improving.'

'Then he should be able to return with me,' Kar suggested.

'I will not stop you. You can ask him when he wakes up,' the monk said.

He did ask him once before he left but Ujaan was noncommittal. He said he would return when he wanted. Now he was fine.

Kar could not say he agreed with it himself but he didn't want to push this any further. He had some responsibility towards his clients but he wouldn't involve himself in a situation which was miles beyond his ken as a P.I. If this man was happy staying back he would let him be. Though he knew something about crime and how passion can drive someone to it, he had little experience with love and what it can do to people. He had wasted most of his growing years in the party and then he had been chasing bent minds. He knew the smell of blood but was out of depth in the presence of great ardour.

'I am with you, Miss Park,' he said.

Her face was grave, perhaps she was worrying Kar would convince Ujaan to leave. 'I promise not to allow any harm come his way,' she said. 'When I met him he was suffering. That's why he came to this country. He came here with the others. Like everyone who lived in the valley he began to go downhill too. But I took care of him. Keun Sunim was kind to let him stay in this house and share his food.'

'I trust your confidence,' Kar said.

'I hope your sister will find peace someday,' the monk said.

'What happened to the professor who created this poison seed? Did your sister tell you anything?' Kar asked.

'Unless he was wicked, which he was not, I have a feeling he wouldn't have forgiven himself for his mistakes,' the monk said.

Kar remembered it then. About the death of an Indian scientist in England, it was in the news a year or two ago. He was found in a laboratory — apparently a suicide. But the news had been sketchy and riddled with contradictions, sure sign of a cover up. Gradually it had slipped away from public memory. He would have to hunt down the details.

'The scientist is dead,' he told them. 'Now I remember — a geneticist working in southern England. It was in the news. I will check the name but I am sure it was him. But did he really kill himself or something else happened to him? Perhaps he found out too late that he had created another Frankenstein's monster? By then the spliced paddy was already out of his laboratory, with your sister.'

Jiyoo covered her face. Her shoulders drooped. He felt sorry for reminding her of her sister's role in this.

A shadow pulled over the Keun Sunim's face. 'It's meaningless to blame anybody,' the monk said firmly, 'her sister was trying to help her parents get out of prison. She had no option. Besides she believed this discovery would feed thousands of the hungry in the North. How could she or anyone know that the paddy was actually poison?'

'It's a freak incident.'

'Like a black swan appearing suddenly after a flock of white,' the monk said. Both of them looked at his face.

'But is there no way to help these people? Perhaps a doctor would know?' Kar asked.

'The temple outside is very old. It has been around for hundreds of years, nobody knows how many. In time people forgot that it existed o the forest hid it well from prying eyes. Then I came here and built a hut for myself to meditate. It was in the days of the war. Gunfire boomed in the hills all around but no soldier ventured this way, not till the last days of the battle. Some infantrymen found the valley. They came from the direction of the river, through the pine forest. They were wounded o exhausted and I nursed them, o I took care of them. A few of them stayed back. They built homes o the forest provided whatever they needed. Then a few more settlers arrived. When they fall sick, they take care of each other.

'But this time it was like an epidemic. They began to fall sick one after the other. O their memories just vanished like water on a hot summer's day. First I thought it might be some illness from the outside world. There is a doctor with us in the retreat but he said this was simply beyond him. Things began to get worse over the last few months, since the time the tourists arrived. I thought perhaps you would know something, some illness that people in your country had encountered before. At least you could make arrangements to take them home.'

'I have heard nothing like this before. I had seen a movie where a man was aging fast because of a rare genetic defect but that was a singular incident, they don't age *en masse*. Now I am certain it is the paddy that did it. I will tell the Koreans what we think happened and perhaps they can get help fast.' But he was not sure even then. Something told him this could spiral out of control. The wind can bear a lot of sadness.

'You can but the news will bring hordes of officers and scientists to this retreat o they will all be exposed to the danger. The poison has begun to spread. This earth has soaked up a lot of blood and it is this blood boiling under our feet. We are sharing the weight of past suffering, we cannot escape bearing the burden of our misdeeds. Still it will be good to try,' the monk said.

Kar had done as he had said. After returning to his hotel he had called officer Kim and told him everything. Kim was furious that he didn't take them into confidence but then he seemed to relent. 'Perhaps, in your position, I would have done the same,' the NIS officer told him, after calming down. 'I will take my boss and the police team into confidence. We can't make a big noise about it and will go in a small team. I hope the damage will be contained within that area. We have to inform our northern counterparts also. We can't let this happen to our worst enemies.'

'Don't touch the food,' Kar had said.

The special emergency services team accompanied by security officers that arrived the next day didn't find it difficult to find the valley with the colony of old people. There was no tiger guarding the track nor did the forest create illusions to lead them astray. In fact, it cleared the way for them. They crossed the stream and entered the valley, rushing to the burning silos of paddy. The officers watched from a distance.

The yellow weed that had covered the little valley seemed to have grown taller overnight. Seasoned officers stared speechless looking at the shrivelled trees swaying their diseased branches in the wind. They were surprised how they had known nothing about this place. But they didn't let the media know anything and the international cover-up that followed was one of the biggest that the world would ever see.

Jiyoo had guided Kar back through the forest and down to the other side of the mountain. They bowed, shook hands and Kar looked at her for one last time and wondered if he would meet someone brave like her ever again. He didn't feel tired on the way back, though he had not slept a wink for two nights. He had the monk's scarf, it gave him strength.

The bus to Seoul went slowly, negotiating miles of tailbacks. The storm had severely disrupted traffic. It had begun to drizzle again as the Kobus coach finally rolled through the fringes of the Seoul conurbation.

He had been thinking of the twins throughout the journey into Seoul.

In his long career as private investigator, Kar had realised that greed and jealousy were the root of most crimes. But what had happened in those mountains and before that in the laboratory of that mad genius, he would never meet, these he couldn't connect with greed, jealousy or desire.

'It is not possible to save everybody,' the monk had told Kar when he was preparing to leave that morning. He had been thinking about his clients back home. What could he tell them? This case had grown bigger than he could have ever bargained for. His feet were swollen and he was struggling to put on his Lee Cooper boots sitting on a stone outside the temple. The monk had asked him to wrap the scarf around his neck because it would be cold in the morning. He had done as he had been told. Walking the last stretch downhill and onto the flat plains of Gyeonggi-do, still lush and green under the morning rays of a watery sun, he had reflected upon those last words of the monk. He had thought he would ask Miss Park what the monk had meant but had forgotten.

11

And then the storms had become fierce, raging on for weeks together, pouring down atmospheric rivers on acres of fertile land while elsewhere the scorched earth killed crops, leaving millions hungry. Just as the weather became more unpredictable, the SuperRice Scourge began to devastate a continent, defeating every effort to destroy it by burning crops, deploying doomsday seed stocks and rice gene banks.

The wicked genes proved smarter than their masters. Hidden in the florets of SuperRice they flew overland, pollinating pristine paddy fields with its time-shortening payload. Concealed inside the golden grain, it secreted into holds of cargo vessels landing up in defenceless nations where it slowly revealed its vicious powers. Buried deep inside cells of bacteria they migrated from plant to plant, species to species.

'Unprecedented situation' and 'All out efforts' were the two expressions that had become the stock-in-trade for politicians, but in the fog of the weather events and the cover-up efforts, the effects of the deadly Scourge went unnoticed or were misinterpreted till it was too late. Meanwhile, wherever the seeds travelled, they slowly unleashed their life-shortening powers. The cruel genes jumped species affecting other cereals as more and more food sources became affected.

Fear ruled the population as the hidden enemy poured through borders, sweeping across countries, and while all this was happening the superstorms had also begun to unleash their fury. Those who still had fragments of their memories intact remembered how revered heath organisations and scientific academies gave out one confusing statement after another — 'The symptoms have been traced to a new type of retrovirus found in sheep ... avoid sneezing sheep' the WHO said while another agency put out the theory, 'Stress related to weather events and a spurt in opportunistic infections has laid the foundation for this collective delusion of ageing ...'

Meanwhile the situation deteriorated. A threshold had been crossed and it was difficult to rein in the combined fury of the Scourge and the punishing weather events. Finally the shortage of food, the burden of disease, and the millions of migrants pouring across borders had precipitated the war.

Today there are not enough healthy people left in Darkland, which cuts a wide swath across the continent. Mines have closed and power stations have gone into dead sleep. Nuclear power which had been touted as a solution, in the early part of the century, has gone out of favour after the accidents and flooding in east Asia. The pool of skilled men have dwindled and kravas, bonesteels and karmics were being mobilised everywhere. But their numbers are never enough.

Captain Old slipped in and out of consciousness as thoughts from years ago filtered through the fog of his tired brain. And still he had remained young while the others had withered away. He didn't even have to pay the gerontology cess. No doubt they loved to call him Captain Old. His friend Abul was long dead and his assistant had vanished without trace. He didn't know about Jiyoo or that young Indian banker she fell in love with. Perhaps they too had been saved. Love always finds a way to look after its own. But where could they be now?

Sometimes he still lamented the fact that his hair was all but gone. If he survived, he would have to seek hair transplant sooner than later, but it went against his ideals.

He had lost the monk's scarf which he had carried with him all these years. He had tied it over his face before entering the sewers but lost it while fighting off the rats. Those beasts had taken Keun Sunim's gift away.

His upper torso was throbbing. Waves of pain radiated through his nerves. Perhaps the rat bite had poisoned his blood. He was convulsed by spasms as he made another effort to walk.

The hall was semi-dark. The petromax lamps and battery-operated lights had been destroyed in the gunfight. A fire was raging inside the station master's room where the homeless settlers had hoarded safeoil. He leaned against the wall, breathing heavily. Exerting his will against his wasted body he managed to drag himself up to the door. He pressed his weight against it and the door swung open. He stepped into the hall and looked around, trying to fix his bearings.

Small fires were burning everywhere, licking the leftovers of the tunnel dwellers. Bodies lay strewn in pools of blood and spent bullet shells lay scattered on the floor. The walls were pockmarked with bullets and all the belongings of the people who had taken shelter there lay scattered on the floor. The fire at the station master's office crackled angrily, shooting red tongues through the half-closed door. He could still hear small arms fire but it was coming from far.

The stairway down to the platform should be right ahead so he began to drag himself in that direction. Something snared his feet and he tripped, crashing on the floor.

Krava-4 clutched his ankle with a steel grip and he fell on her. She was alive, the blue neon eyes studying him with a look that was not born of hate or mistrust or anything that bloodbabies are capable of. There was a big hole in the middle of her head.

'I think I am dying,' the krava told him.

Old just said, 'You will be all right.'

'Your wound is dripping blood,' Krava-4 said.

'I have to get home to wash it.'

But she was still holding his ankle in a steel grip.

'Do you know what they do to us when we die?'

Old didn't know and he regretted that he had never tried to find out. Perhaps Henry David would know. He seemed to be the sort of man who knew such things. 'I have no idea. It's the same as what they do to us, I believe,' he said.

'Do you think I might turn into a ghost if I die?'

He realised her grip had begun to slip. Her words slurred.

I have never heard of that, he was about to say, but something came to his mind and he said, 'Well if you wish, no one can stop you.'

'That's a relief,' she said and let him go. Her hands slipped off and the genes from the deep sea that had lit up those eyes in a blue glow, for the brief stretch of her youth, decided to switch off the lights.

He lay on the floor for a few minutes conserving his energies, listening to her heartbeat grow faint till it stopped. He closed her unseeing eyes with his shaking hand. He pulled himself up and headed for the steps going down to the tunnels. He went slowly, careful to make sure he didn't step on anyone else while stopping every few seconds to fill his lungs. He reached the stairs leading down to the platforms. Taking a few steps down he noticed the dark platforms bathed in a red halo. The platform pillars stood still like thoughts of all the dead of the world frozen in time.

As he limped down, one step at a time, the red halo changed to yellow and he could see the platform clearer now. The tracks were gleaming in the yellow light.

So he had died. He had heard that the only light that the dead can recognise is a shade of yellow and so he slowly descended, knowing full well that the end has come and now it was just the last sparks of the tired brain shooting off some fireworks. Now he is on the platform, walking towards the other end where the air duct is. Then he notices the source of the light. It looks round and it glows at the mouth of the tunnel where the tracks disappear. The signals. The old signalling system of the underground has come to life. Someone has pulled a switch somewhere and the rusty controls have whirred into action. He wouldn't mind if a train arrives from the past and takes him away now. To a safe place. To a time when nobody cared and everyone did what they liked.

12

The skirmishes that broke out between the guerrilla forces of Red Dawn and the protectors, spread like wildfire, sweeping across the barren wastes of Darkland. In the city, pitched battles continued between the well-armed protector force, reinforced by bonesteels and kravas and the ragtag army of anarchists. The sound of gunfire and the cries of the wounded echoed across streets and avenues as the old and the wasted shivered in fear behind closed doors, hugging each other, sharing the all forgiving warmth of blood.

Death became so common that people forgot to notice. They stepped around the dying and the wounded, groaning on the pavements of avenue 1, begging for a drop of water to quench their souls. Scattered across Weed Park, mowed down by machine gun fire, the dead lay blood soaked, staring glassy-eyed at the sky and it seemed the flame trees had shed their leaves before it was time.

In the Square of the Martyrs, the morning saw corpses from both sides, rotting under the sun. The protectors were often ambushed by small troops of Red Dawn fighters, armed with firebombs and stolen weapons, while they systematically cleaned apartment blocks, offices and clubs where they suspected the enemy to have established bases. There were few to claim the dead. Vultures patrolled the skies while the rotting cadavers spread disease, finishing off those who were not yet old enough to perish.

Henry David barricaded himself in the detective's flat and began spending nights in vigil. He ate little, stealing when he was hungry, like Captain Old used to do. The next-door neighbour, who was never there, still had a stock of potatoes to last him a week. He had discovered strawberry jam hidden at the back of a cupboard and two sealed packets of Tibetan wheat flour and had taken one of those.

Tanmoy's diaries, which he had lately discovered and which he intended to show the detective, were with him in a waterproof case hidden in a secret compartment of his violin case. He remembered how he had chanced upon these quite by accident, not very long ago.

When Tanmoy had let out his room to the Korean woman, he had left some of his papers and personal effects with him. Henry had kept it all in storage at Aberbourne and had forgotten about their existence completely. Only recently he had chanced upon the stacks of leather-bound diaries in the sealed box left by the scientist. He had started turning the pages and what he came across had intrigued him. The memories of his scientist friend had come flooding back and with it the desire to know what had really happened.

Not sure what he should do, Henry had contacted a London private eye called Anna Halsey, who sometimes dropped by at Greg's Oaks to stay with a friend. She had managed to dig up records of the investigation, even dipping into some classified information, where an Indian private investigator's name had popped up. Anna told him that the Indian P.I. was in Korea investigating a case, when the first signs of the Scourge were detected. 'He might be able to make sense of what this scientist,

Tanmoy Sen, had scribbled in those black books before he decided to mummify himself in a freezer. As you know, it all started from that lab,' Anna said. She did not know more but she could put him in touch with the Indian detective if he wished.

Now sitting in Captain Old's flat, Henry took out one by one all the diaries filled with Tanmoy Sen's slanting script. He read the diaries through the night, all through the next day, and then again the next night between bursts of restive slumber.

There was much he could not understand. Gene delivery, protoplast incubation and virus vectors, chemical pathways, the magic of CRISPR-Cas tools, quickly scribbled ideas, his appreciation of innovations made by colleagues working elsewhere and then this: 'Sometimes they are Red Admirals with their bright orange on black wings flapping about wantonly in my frontal lobe, or else they were swallowtails flitting from cerebellum to hippocampus or even a clutch of glowing spliced hesperiadae blushing playfully between my ears ...'

The talk of the butterflies — the lyrical passages about winged beauties, the flapping wings hovering inside his head. What was it all about? Could these be coded formulas for an antidote? He hoped his host would be able to throw some light.

He remembered the long conversations he used to have with the scientist at Greg's Oaks. He admired the man's passion and understood why he had ignored his warnings. But then, what went wrong? Perhaps nobody can be blamed, he told himself. We are born of the earth and the earth moulds us into what we become. Children of stars, the faintest starlight sparks our passion. The sky seeds our minds with dreams of the endless possibilities of our imagination. Water nurtures us, flowing through our lives, joining discordant streams in the incessant waves of harmony. But in this timeless concert of the earth, stars, water and sky sometimes a strange bird comes flying. A bird no one had seen before.

The diaries were meticulously kept. Every page mentioning briefly where his work was going. There were advances and setbacks and reports about his discussions with colleagues. 'Today had a long chat with Eugene. He had some ideas from his project which we might as well test out in ours.' A few pages later — grocery lists and plans to watch a play in the weekend. He was reading a lot in those final years. Books written for children, fantasies and that biography of Watt. The James Watt biography had been his Bible. He carried it with him to the university and read it in breaks from work. He must have read that book a hundred times.

Henry was amused to find what he had to say about their long talks at the camp. 'I am quite taken by the music teacher but he is living in another age. There is no real connection between his world and mine.' Yet he makes plans to visit him and on his return writes, 'This gentleman knows.'

He had pushed on with SuperRice driven by a single-minded determination. 'If what we are doing here succeeds, then we will have eliminated hunger from this world,' his diary said. For a few days he goes into depression reading Aldous Huxley but bounces back soon as positive results begin to emerge. 'Here we have been prospecting for gold. With these tools, we will cut deep into the rock of ignorance, striking at the veins of shiny metal. Life on earth will never be the same again.'

There was a staccato burst from the street below. Henry closed the pocketbook and walked up to the window in the back room. He peeped through the wooden slats of the French window and saw a phalanx of heavily armed protectors, closing in towards their building, taking cover behind the carcasses of junked automobiles. Snipers hidden on rooftops were taking aim, firing back at them, but in the falling light of evening, the bullets missed their mark. The protectors returned with bursts of automatic fire. At the windows of other houses along the street, he thought he could see the frail shadows of old men and women watching the scene below — bathed in the cold crepuscular light of advancing dusk. A sniper's body hit by a bullet came crashing down the roof, landing with a soft thud on the street. His head had burst open.

A powerful trumpet blared as a small elephabus making a detour was caught in the crossfire. The bus had stopped. The pair of elephants refused to budge. Eyes dilated with fear, they raised their trunks, letting out ear-splitting blasts. The passengers cowered, their heads pressed against their knees as bullets flew like the angry mosquitoes of evening, determined to feast on the blood of the living. Today a Cleanland radio station had been reporting that a truce was being worked out between both sides. The masked man had agreed to a meeting with certain preconditions. Henry David hoped things would take a turn for the better. Perhaps the detective would return soon.

He went back calmly to the front room. Making a small pile of the leather-bound diaries, he hid them carefully in the secret compartment of his violin case. If there was an antidote hidden in those pages, it has to be protected. He stowed the case in the steel almirah where there were old files and a bunch of film magazines from long ago. Jamming a sofa against the door, he stepped back into the kitchen. He was hungry. He could make flatbreads and he had the strawberry jam. But the drinking water had almost run out. It was getting dark. It wouldn't be possible to venture out for water tonight. Tomorrow he will go out to fetch some from the community standpipe. By then, he hoped, Captain Old would also return.

In lieu of a Glossary

Though it is generally held that following the disaster and after the War of the Great Basins broke out, all kinds of intellectual activities had ceased in this part of the world, this is not completely true. As had always happened throughout the tortuous course of history, in these times of utter darkness too, the light has been kept burning. A few of us, however meagre may our numbers be, still shine a light at our windows. And for you who will come afterwards, if there is to be any afterwards to come to, we have made the best effort to keep records. This is just a fragment of our endeavour. Below is a page of entries from the extensive archives of our times preserved in the People's Library and some private collections. We hope it will help you recreate a world from the darkness of a time that was never on our side.

Anniversary Day Parade of the Extinct: Reproductive physiologists and geneticists have brought back to life animals that have become extinct, using preserved cells. Many of these resurrected animals would die within hours of birth, but a few have survived in captivity. Among these resurrected species are the Royal Bengal tiger, Sumatran elephant, Amur leopard, the dromedary, Indian eagle-owl and others. On every birthday of the SUPREME GUIDE, which is celebrated as Anniversary Day throughout Darkland, these resurrected species are put on display and paraded before dignitaries and visitors from other lands.

Ash Barricades: The border separating Darkland from Cleanland, named so because of the early practice of using flyash bricks as well as ash from destroyed settlements and burnt vegetation to mark out the new territories, following the War of the Great Basins.

bartermen: As the money economy of Darkland is in shambles bartering of goods and services is common. Bartermen are individuals who facilitate this barter economy.
bloodbaby: Colloquial for people who are not genetically engineered or spliced.
bonesteel: Genetically modified human males created in Cleanland for war-fighting and disaster scenarios. They have a robust immune system, superhuman endurance powers as well as special skin cells engineered from the genes of volcanic archaeons that can withstand extreme temperatures.

Cleanland: The disastrous events created large numbers of refugees all over the world. These massive displacements and the competition for scarce resources sparked regional wars in Asia, ultimately leading to the War of the Great Basins. Most of Asia and large parts of Europe finally ended up under the control of two contesting powers. The two territories, with numerous enclaves, are respectively called Cleanland and Darkland. Cleanlanders have largely escaped, or in some areas, have been more successful in mitigating, the effects of the disastrous events because of geographical and other reasons. Inhabitants known as Cleanlanders. Also see *Darkland* below.
cleanweed: A type of cannabis originally grown in Japan (before most of the country went under the sea) which doesn't have any adverse health impacts beyond intoxication.

Darkland: See *Cleanland*. The capital of Darkland is the city of Calcutta though very few use that name any more. The ruling powers have stripped places, streets, neighbourhoods of their proper names, replacing these with numbers and generic names, so that people don't emotionally associate with these. There are no good maps of Cleanland and Darkland as territories shift continuously and more landmasses end up under the sea. If a map had been drawn, it would look like a moth-eaten canvas with gaping holes down its middle (and smaller ones elsewhere) depicting Darkland. What is more or less certain is that most of Europe, parts of central Asia, pockets in the sub-Himalayan India, northern China and Philippines are part of Cleanland. Inhabitants known as Darklanders.

dishbaby: See *bloodbaby*. Colloquial (derogatory) for genetically modified (spliced) humans. Bonesteels and kravas are dishbabies.

eardy: A unit for measuring distance.

elephabus: A form of public transport in Darkland where two or three elephants are yoked together and a canopied seating and standing area fixed atop their backs. Can carry a dozen to twenty people. Elephabuses are driven by hardy desert tribesmen.

freshface: Someone unaffected by disease and decrepitude.

holopro: A holographic projection system for watching movies.

Incident R9117 of Yangtze basin: An incident among many others where armed kravas, on being provoked by a racial slur, massacred a whole community of migrants.

karmic: Genetically modified humans created in Cleanland who can work for months without sleep.

krava: Genetically modified human females created in Cleanland for war-fighting and disaster scenarios. They have a robust immune system, superhuman endurance powers as well as special skin cells engineered from the genes of volcanic archaeons that can withstand extreme temperatures.

lab-ham: Synthetic pork grown in vitro.

memory pill: A pill which helps fight memory loss.

safeoil: Cooking oil sourced from Cleanland which is thought to have no adverse health impacts.

solar amnesia board: Electronic boards put up to help people remember common words and their meanings. Runs on solar power.

sonmi: Genetically modified humans earlier employed by the Darkland authority.

soul ticket: A badge with the image of the SUPREME GUIDE which every citizen of Darkland must wear. The badge, unique for each citizen, has a machine-readable interface which brings up and validates biometric and background information.

splices: Splices or spliced individuals or organisms are genetically modified life forms. Bonesteels are splices. More appropriately, you splice something *with* something e.g. a tomato spliced with a fish gene.

War of the Great Basins: The disastrous events coupled with the effects of climate change created large numbers of refugees all over the world. These massive displacements and the competition for scarce resources sparked regional wars in Asia, ultimately leading to the War of the Great Basins. See *Cleanland* and *Darkland*.

Year of Light (YL): Used to label years in the Darkland calendar which starts counting from the year of birth of the SUPREME GUIDE, labelled YL 1. The SUPREME GUIDE was born many years before the creation of Darkland.

youngblood: Blood of infants, which is believed to temporarily reverse the symptoms of aging.

Acknowledgements

The writing of this book benefitted from a number of international fellowships and residency awards. These are the British Council administered Charles Wallace Creative Writing Fellowship hosted by the University of Chichester, UK, a Hawthornden Castle Fellowship, Scotland, and a Korean Arts Council (ARKO)-InKo grant for travelling to Korea and working at Toji Cultural Centre. I am indebted to Richard Alford of Charles Wallace India Trust, the fellowship administrators of Hawthornden Castle Trust and grant administrators and hosts at ARKO, InKo and Toji for creating the opportunity for me to write this work of speculative fiction. While the original plots for sections of this novel, which went into my grant applications, have evolved in the final published work, this in no way diminishes my indebtedness to those who were prepared to nurture my fledgling ideas.

An excerpt from this novel appeared in *Caesurae* journal for which I would like to thank the Editor, Jayita Sengupta. The Bengali novelist Ramkumar Mukhopadhyay and poet and translator, A.J. Thomas have always been supportive of my adventures in writing. My journey is signposted by their guidance.

Noted academic and author Sanjukta Dasgupta, novelist Alison Macleod, author Arshia Sattar, writer colleagues Anu Kumar, Saikat Majumdar and Lopa Ghosh, playwright Stephen Mollett, Chunsik Kim, Mark Floyer and many other friends and colleagues in India, South Korea, Russia and United Kingdom through their support, enthusiasm, feedback, research inputs and inspiration, helped me embark on and complete this journey. I will be ever grateful for their kindness.

I first heard the story of Iain Noble and the Israeli hiker, which appears in the section 'Magic Seeds', from the writer Neal Ascherson whose brilliant conversation filled up many sherry-soaked evenings at Hawthornden castle. My introduction to genetics research and GM food happened in my early activist days but my knowledge was greatly enriched through long conversations with my geneticist friend Priyadarshi Basu. He filled me in with the science but I must clear him of any charges of having a hand in the plot. The poem by Yi Soong-in in the final section is from the book *The Orchid Door: Ancient Korean Poems*, translated into English by Joan S. Grigsby. The research about North Korea benefitted from fiction, defector accounts and other sources like Andrei Lankov's *The Real North Korea*, while the scene introducing the monk is partially influenced by a Korean fairy tale.

My biggest support has always been my wife Anuradha, my parents, my sister and my Calcutta buddies. I wouldn't speculate how this book would have turned out without them around.

Author Bio

Rajat Chaudhuri is the author of three books, *Hotel Calcutta*, *Amber Dusk* and a collection of stories in Bengali titled *Calculus*. He has won a Charles Wallace Creative Writing Fellowship, UK, a Hawthornden Castle Fellowship, Scotland, a Korean Arts Council-InKo Residency in South Korea, and a Sangam House residency, for his writing. His reviews and other writing have appeared in *Outlook* magazine, *American Book Review*, *Asian Review of Books*, *Scroll*, *Indian Literature*, *The Telegraph*, *The Statesman*, *Eclectica* and elsewhere.

Before turning to writing full-time, Chaudhuri has been a climate change advocate at the United Nations (New York) and a contributor to the *United Nations Human Development Report*. Trained in Economics, he has worked for international rights advocacy groups and for a Japanese consular mission in his home town, Calcutta. He is the editor of *The Best Asian Speculative Fiction*, a book of short stories by Asian writers.